BORN IN A
HOUSE OF GLASS

BORN
IN A
HOUSE
OF
GLASS

CHINENYE EMEZIE

DUNDURN
PRESS

Publisher: Meghan Macdonald | Acquiring editors: Julia Kim & Kwame Scott Fraser
Cover designer: Laura Boyle | Cover image: house: Allison Saeng/Unsplash; woman: sheherwithyaar/shutterstock (modified by Laura Boyle)

Library and Archives Canada Cataloguing in Publication

Title: Born in a house of glass / Chinenye Emezie.
Other titles: Glass house
Names: Emezie, Chinenye, author.
Description: Previously published under title: Glass house. Cape Town, South Africa:
  Penguin Books, 2021.
Identifiers: Canadiana (print) 20230576400 | Canadiana (ebook) 20230576419 | ISBN
  9781459754249 (softcover) | ISBN 9781459754256 (PDF) | ISBN 9781459754263 (EPUB)
Subjects: LCGFT: Novels.
Classification: LCC PR9387.9.E38 G53 2024 | DDC 823/.92—dc23

We acknowledge the support of the Canada Council for the Arts and the Ontario Arts Council for our publishing program. We also acknowledge the financial support of the Government of Ontario, through the Ontario Book Publishing Tax Credit and Ontario Creates, and the Government of Canada.

Care has been taken to trace the ownership of copyright material used in this book. The author and the publisher welcome any information enabling them to rectify any references or credits in subsequent editions.

The publisher is not responsible for websites or their content unless they are owned by the publisher.

Printed and bound in Canada.

Dundurn Press
1382 Queen Street East
Toronto, Ontario, Canada M4L 1C9
dundurn.com, @dundurnpress

For my dear sweet mother,
Mrs. Gladys Nwakaego Okonkwo,
July 1944 – November 2017,
for giving me wings to reach for the stars

PART I

PART I

One

Let me tell you a story. It's about a war. This war is not the type fought with guns and machetes. It is a family type. A silent war. The type fought in the heart. It began long before I was formed. At birth, I was named Udonwa — the peaceful child. Maybe they wanted me to bring about peace, the peace that would end the war, but who knows what goes on in the minds of adults, especially Mama and Papa. All I know is that I was the intelligent favourite daughter of my warring family. The one who, according to Papa, was most likely to become a doctor.

I cannot say exactly when it started, but I know the cracks of this war became visible one fateful day in the rainy season, while Mama was busy washing clothes outside in the rain. Mama liked to wash clothes every time it poured. She said it was the best time to do it. What she failed to mention, though, was that the torrential rain on her body would often lead to a bout of fever, aches, and pains.

Mama was the invisible pillar of our home while Papa was a man of many facets, a huge man whose hands were nearly as big as the wobbly wooden table in the centre of our near-bare sitting room. Papa was the son of a retired headmaster, a preacher by profession, and a disciplinarian by trade. Sometimes, looking at him, I wondered what Mama had been thinking when she married him, for they were as different as our blazing African sun and the snow in those European countries my school teacher, Mrs. Nwaka, told us about. But I loved them, for they were both storytellers — the one thing they had in common. I loved to sit at their feet and listen to their tales by moonlight. Papa's stories were the usual folklore full of drama and unnecessary suspense that often made me bite my nails. His favourite story was that of the old woman of a remote village in the forest who sent her granddaughter to fetch water at the stream at midnight, and, unknown to her, men from the spirit world joined her on the journey. Mama's folktales were often parables, which, more than just telling a story, aimed to impart wisdom to her listeners.

On that fateful day, my elder sister Nneora and I were sitting at Papa's feet, where we always listened intently to his nightmarish stories. Stories he told to scare us into obedience. My elder brother Lincoln listened absentmindedly a foot away from where we sat; he wasn't in the least interested in whatever Papa was saying. He knew Papa for whom he thought he was and wasn't buying any of his niceties.

The day before, Lincoln had told Nneora and me: "Listen, Udo and Nne, one day I'll deal with this man."

"Shh ... Mama will hear you," Nneora had said to him.

He'd shrugged. "Let her hear. I meant every word I said. Next time he touches Mama, I'll skin him alive."

"But isn't Papa doing that because he loves Mama?" I'd said.

"What nonsense are you saying, Udonwa — that a man beats his wife to prove his love? What sort of love is that? Anyway, what do you know; you're too young to understand."

"Who says I'm too young? I —"

"That's okay, both of you," Nneora had cut us short. "Let Mama and Papa handle their lives; it's none of our business."

"I won't give up until —"

His sentence had been left incomplete, as Mama had walked in and we had promptly dispersed.

Now, he looked as if he wanted to murder someone, and there were no guesses as to who his target was. Lincoln's eyes darted left and right as he circled his feet.

"Stop it, Linc, you're making me nervous," I said when I couldn't handle his fidgeting any longer. He responded by giving me a piercing stare. He was like that, always boiling with unnecessary fury. Justified or unwarranted, he would find ways to intimidate Nneora and me. Lincoln thought he was the commanding officer of our home, but he was not near being even second-in-command. My eldest brother Jefferson, who lived at the seminary, was a more likeable person. He was kind, gentle, and very mature for his age. He treated Nneora and me like his age mates and not subordinates.

"The men of the spirit world walked steadily behind Adaoma, the granddaughter of Nkwocha, the old witch of Akuma village, and each time she turned around to see who it was, she saw nothing until —"

"Mtcheeew … I hate this story! It's more boring than bore-dom!" Lincoln hissed as he cut Papa off mid-sentence, convincing me more than ever of his stupidity.

Papa took one look at him and within seconds the room became filled with the smoke from the fire in his eyes. Nneora and I backed away on our bottoms — we knew what it meant and what would follow. When I reached the door, I got up and hid behind the ragged curtain Mama told us she'd bought a week before Nneora's birth. In the family portrait on the sitting room wall, the curtain was one of beauty and neat, straight lines. Now, I pulled it across my face to hide my small frame, but the useless piece of cloth responded to my effort by ripping. Nneora found her way to the door leading to Mama and Papa's room, but she knew better than to open it, for we weren't allowed in there day or night.

Papa's face resembled a raging furnace. He took the whip from behind Grandpa's okwa nzu — a clay pot filled with white ash, a symbol of his Ozo chieftaincy — and in one swift move lashed out at Lincoln's back. He lashed at him three or four more times before Nneora started crying, screaming as loudly as she could for Mama and Grandpa to come. But the heavy downpour of rain, accompanied by the continuous splatter on the upside-down pots Nneora and I had washed earlier, muted her screams. The palm trees in our compound whooshed and prostrated in the strong wind. The noise in the sitting room and the one the ground-worshipping trees were making almost burst my tiny eardrums. I placed my palms on each ear, my eyes shut tight. As fast as the chaos had begun, it gave way to an uneasy silence. The type Papa often told us in his stories preceded the crossing over of spirits into the land of the dead.

When it became too uncomfortable, I opened one eye and looked around. The quietness of the sitting room was as heavy as the clay earthenware in our mud-hut kitchen. I let out my long-held breath but sucked it in again when I saw the shadowy figure on the floor. I blinked open my other eye to get a clearer view and clapped my hands over my mouth at the sight before me. Nneora's screaming jolted me from my shocked state and I turned to her, trying to speak to her with my eyes. With two swift steps, Papa stepped over Lincoln's comatose body to where she stood. With one hand, he lifted his whip above his head to render a lash but was stopped by a bony hand.

"What do you think you're doing? What have these children done to you that made you unleash your wrath on them so?"

"Nnam, stay out of this."

"No, I won't. These are my grandchildren and I will not let you kill them because you can't control your temper."

"Me, can't control my temper? Nnam, I'm warning you to stay out of this, otherwise —"

"Otherwise what? Do you think I'm one of your children, eh, Leonard? Listen, I may be old and wrinkled, but I am still your father. You are my only son, Leonard, my only child … and your ugly behaviour towards your family is a disgrace."

Papa turned to Grandpa, his entire body now burning like his face and his eyes smarting as if sprinkled with hot pepper. In that peppery glazed state, and drowning in yet-unleashed emotions, Papa pushed Grandpa out of his way.

"Grandpa!" I screamed as he fell to the ground. I rushed over to him as Mama came running into the room. Nneora collapsed on the floor, her hands cracking as she did. Mama dropped the basin of washed clothes she had been carrying, and it made a loud thud as it landed, spewing its contents onto the sandy floor. She ignored it and rushed over to Lincoln, who was now stirring and coughing. Across from her was Nneora's slumped body and Mama jumped over to her, pulling her hands to jerk her awake.

"Hurry, Udonwa! Get me water *fast!*"

The heavy rain outside had given way to a drizzle and I jumped to the authoritative yet fear-ridden voice, returning with a bowl of water. Nneora coughed as Mama sprinkled the water before she finally opened her eyes. Mama held her up and placed her on a chair. She turned around to Papa, who was now sitting with his knees knocking against each other, his weapon still in one hand even as his gigantic frame filled up the chair. Next to him was a large tumbler containing his favourite lager filled to the brim. He occasionally took a sip of his drink and when he put down the glass, he ran his hand across his half-bald head. His fiery eyes were now gradually changing to their normal colour, turning his face back to that of the Papa I loved.

Mama looked like she was going to say something, but changed her mind. She walked out of the room with Lincoln and Nneora hanging their hands on each of her shoulders. She did not utter a word. I pulled Grandpa from the floor into a sitting position and ran outside to fetch his walking stick, a stick he only used when his legs were sore. Mama returned a few moments later to help me lift him to his feet. Together, Grandpa and Mama gave Papa a short, hard look. Papa was now reading a church journal, unperturbed by the incident that had just taken place.

Things never returned to the way they had been after that night. Mama stopped telling stories and during the night she slept in the bedroom I shared with Nneora. As for Grandpa, his legs became increasingly sore and, not long after, he lost his use of them.

Now, at dinner time, instead of us sitting together, Mama would send me to the sitting room with Papa's food where he'd eat alone. I'd often sit and watch him eat, many times wracking my eleven-year-old brain about what could be going on in his mind.

Two

The obi — a single-room mud house where Papa grew up before he built our current house — was in the centre of our compound. Only Grandpa lived there, although he preferred to sit outside to read Papa's church journals. Grandpa had been educated by the British missionaries who had come to Iruama. He told us that these missionaries had tried to convert everyone to their religion but he had stood firm because nothing was wrong with the religion of his forefathers. But for someone who did not like the Christian religion, Grandpa read a lot of church journals. Once, when I asked him about this contradiction, he replied that the church secretary spoke and wrote impeccable English like himself and therefore was worth reading.

Grandpa loved English as much as he did Igbo. And he spoke it with much vigour and colour too, making him sometimes incomprehensible. When some villagers sought his ideas on issues, more often than not, he'd reel off his ideas in English, not caring if they understood him, before breaking into one Igbo proverb after the other in the form of advice. Where Mama and Papa told stories, Grandpa told proverbs. His most commonly used proverb was "Ewu si na ndi nwere ike amaghi ano." After I had asked Nneora and Lincoln what the proverb meant for the umpteenth time, Lincoln finally provided a translation for me: "The goat said that those who have buttocks do not know how to sit." And in true Lincoln style, he patted his bottom several times for emphasis when he said this, leaving Nneora doubled over in laughter. But I did not find it funny. How could I, when I did not understand what it meant. Neither did Nneora and Lincoln, nor did any of us know why it was Grandpa's favourite saying.

But more than cooking his words in the palm oil of adages, Grandpa loved to take snuff. He would take it after every meal or snack. When we had guests visiting, he'd bring out a small round tin containing the snuff, and tap the top with his thumb before offering some to them. He would then deposit the brown tobacco powder deep into his nostrils, his eyes instantly watering, followed by a marathon of sneezes. Next would be a brief pause, after which he would pat his head in a quick successive motion. Not yet done, he would give each nostril another thumb-full, before, finally, he would give his head a good shake, inhale, clear his throat and smile. It was always a fascinating routine to observe. But Papa would make fun of him, saying Grandpa had gone from being a noble headmaster to an ordinary old man who did nothing but sit and take snuff all day. And Grandpa would say to Papa that he was a two-faced man who lived in a glass house and should know better than to hurl stones at people.

. . .

As I made my way towards the obi, I heard voices. They were talking in hushed tones, almost like whispers, and I couldn't pick out what they were saying. So I tried to listen but remembered Mama saying it was rude to listen to other people's conversation — that if they wanted you to know what they were talking about, they would tell you. With that in mind, I stood outside and called out instead so that the voices would know someone was approaching.

At once, my eldest sister, Adaora, and Mama emerged. Another man was standing close by but Grandpa was nowhere in sight.

"Sister Ada," I said, running to hug her. She wrapped her hands around me and held on tight. "When did you arrive, Sister, and why didn't you ask for me?" I pouted my displeasure at her.

"But I did ask for you, Udom. I was just telling Mama now that I must come and see you."

I continued pouting, folding my arms across my chest and shaking my shoulders from left to right in further protest.

"Okay, when next I come home, I'll ask for you first, eh? I'll come straight to the house and find you. Are you happy now?"

"Yes, Sister, I'm happy. So what did you buy for me?"

"I knew you'd ask that next," she said, laughing. Hers was a hearty rare laugh that always warmed my heart. And there was something about Sister Adaora's eyes, something that made her more beautiful when she smiled yet also made her look sad.

Mama just stood and watched us. She always did that. If it had been someone else visiting, she would have sent me away on an errand or asked me to read my books, but not with Sister Adaora. She would want us to talk and catch up on lost time. Today, though, she looked unhappy as she stood watching.

"Mama, are you all right?"

"Mama is fine, Udom. She's just tired," Sister Adaora said, but I knew it was a feeble attempt to cover for Mama and I wasn't about to let it go, so I pulled my sulking face again.

"You know you can't hide anything from Udonwa, Ada. Have you forgotten how bright she is?"

"Okay, Mama, you can tell her."

"Tell me what?"

When none of them was forthcoming with an answer, I looked behind them at the man who had been standing there, stiff like a statue, not uttering a word. Their eyes followed my gaze before Sister Adaora said: "Okay, okay, I'm getting married, Udom, and that man standing over there is my fiancé. His name is Ikemefuna."

I looked at the man who was still standing as though he was a soldier with orders to stand to attention. He glanced at me and smiled before returning to his former state. I tried to smile back but my face wouldn't comply. I wasn't certain I liked him.

My face must have revealed my thoughts because Sister Adaora said: "Don't worry, Udom, when you get to know him you'll like him."

I nodded and followed as they began walking away from Grandpa's obi. But if Sister Adaora was getting married, what were she and Mama whispering about earlier? And why did Mama have the same sad look she always had for days after

Papa had displayed his anger? Who knew — perhaps marriage
was no longer a happy thing?

. . .

"Ah, this is the best news I've heard in a long time!" Grandpa
was smiling as he spoke. He was sitting outside in the yard with
Mama, Mazi Okoli, Sister Adaora, and her fiancé, Ikemefuna.
I sat a foot away from Mama. Grandpa had sent me to call
Papa, who had said he would join them when he was finished
compiling some of his old sermons. But that wasn't what I had
seen him doing. Rather, he had been focused on a newspaper's
headline about students of the University of Lagos. The students were reportedly planning to riot due to a proposed hike
in transport fares, swearing to barricade roads if the hike went
ahead. But it was not clear what Papa's concern was with a big
city like Lagos.

"Though it is normal practice for the suitor to come with
his relatives for the introduction, I'm glad you are here at all."
Grandpa was looking at Ikemefuna, who was rubbing his
hands together like a schoolboy being reprimanded for being
naughty. He had the same look on his face that Anayo, the boy
in my class with a head shaped like a mango, had when Mrs.
Nwaka caught him trying to take a peek under the new girl
Obiageli's skirt in class. But I could see that, unlike Anayo's
eyes that day, Ikemefuna's were trying to smile.

"Yes, our father is right. In our Igbo culture, a suitor must
go along with one or two or even more of his kinsmen to his intended in-laws' place. I am very surprised that you came alone.
This is not the right way to do it, young man," Mazi Okoli
clarified in Igbo, trying to sound more important than he was.

This was the same man who would drink until he forgot the way to his own house. His two wives and son would often have to come to the road leading from Akunesiobike, the palm-wine seller's house, to pick him up in a state of drunken stupor. I wondered what our good old tradition said about such men.

"Em, my fathers, thank you all. You have all spoken well. Yes, I know our tradition and I am familiar with our people's ways and customs. This trip is not an official introduction but rather a casual visit to meet the family of my bride-to-be. And yes, I may have already asked her to marry me, but that's because we both live in the city and I had to make sure she wanted to marry me too."

"Eh, it's all right, my son. You have done well by coming to see us. You can come with your kinsmen on your next trip. I'm a very happy old man now that my first grandchild will follow in the footsteps of her mother and all the mothers of this family."

Sister Adaora kept smiling like a new bride as Grandpa shared one funny anecdote after the other about her childhood. She now had a sparkle in her eyes, her former look of despair lifted and forgotten. Even Mama was displaying her full set of teeth like she always did whenever a visitor came to our house.

At last, Papa emerged from the house. His brownish-white singlet was covering a stomach the size of my pregnant teacher Mrs. Nwaka's just before she had stopped coming to school. His pair of trousers, though brown, had a clean appearance to them but hung too loosely. Lincoln often teased that Papa resembled an amoeba — a shapeless thing. Papa's newspaper was still in his hand as he joined the others. When he got closer, Ikemefuna stood up to greet him and Papa extended a hand of welcome to him, still holding the newspaper.

Grandpa cleared his throat. "Eh, Leonard, my son, we've been waiting for you for a while now. This young man here is Adaora's suitor. He has already asked her and she has agreed to be his wife. What is left for us to do now is to invite his family over for the official introduction, imego, and the igba mmanya, and he can take our daughter with him. The bride price ceremony and the traditional wedding, that's all."

"I see," Papa said, glancing towards Adaora for the first time.

She did not return the look but rather kept her gaze on the floor while circling her foot on the ground. Adaora had never been close to Papa. I'd never seen them alone together, either talking or playing like Papa and I often did. In fact, none of Papa's children was as close to him as I was, but Sister Adaora was his least favourite. While he would engage in bouts of shouting at the rest of us, he would ignore Sister Adaora like she was invisible. He was never interested if she passed her exams or not. He would berate everyone for going astray, but ignore her like he didn't care what would become of her. So I wasn't surprised this was his only response to Grandpa's introduction of Ikemefuna. I also wasn't surprised Sister Adaora had agreed to marry Ikemefuna without seeking Papa's consent first. It was obvious she was only here because custom demanded it. I suspected Papa's coldness towards her was the reason she'd left home as soon as she could and had never returned, even after she had graduated from the nursing school. Staring at her now, her eyes told me only one thing: she would rather be anywhere but here.

Mama rubbed her hands on her knees, which were covered in a faded print wrapper, before folding her hands tightly under her bosom. "Papa Adaora, the traditional marriage will be held here, but Ada and Ikemefuna have requested to hold their wedding in Awka where he lives. It's the only thing I will add at this stage." From the look on her face, it was clear she too couldn't wait for the meeting to end so they could all disperse.

"I see."

"What do you keep seeing, eh, Leonard? Your daughter is here with her future husband to ask for your permission to marry and all you can say is 'I see.' What is there to see about this? Don't you have any reasonable input to his request?" Mazi Okoli barked at Papa.

Whenever something irritated Mazi, no matter how insignificant, he would bark and threaten to grind the thing or person into a fine powder. I would often wonder if he meant it or if he was just "making mouth," as his wives would say. His irritation with Papa's monosyllabic response to Sister Adaora's engagement was understandable, but what was strange was his constant shouting at Papa since the start of the meeting. Maybe his brain had indeed been damaged by the river of palm wine he consumed. Otherwise, how could he have forgotten so soon how Papa had broken his bicycle the last time he had shouted at him, and had threatened to do the same to his scrawny neck?

"What other input do you expect from me? Hasn't it all been said?"

"Hian, Kenechukwu ..."

"Mazi Okoli, it is enough. When the cricket is tired of flying, it will fall to the frog. Leave Leonard, my son. When he is tired of running from his responsibilities, he will come and face them; they'll wait for him. Let him keep burning bridges — I won't even ask him to stop. But a day is coming when he'll realize that he's burnt off a crucial part that leads to his desired destination." Grandpa paused and cleared his throat before continuing. "Em, our in-law, it is well. We have heard your request and it's accepted. Come with your people when you can. The words in my mouth are finished. I need to retire to my room. I'm no longer a young man who sits and talks till the moon disappears into the night."

Everyone echoed: "Thank you, sir."

Papa got up and headed back to the house and I went to obi to fetch Grandpa's wooden crutches. Since the last incident with Papa, the only way Grandpa could move around was with the aid of his wooden legs, as he called them. As I helped him position the bulky sticks underneath his arms, from the corner of my eye I noticed Sister Adaora staring in Papa's direction long after he'd left, an unshed tear on her eyelid. She reached up her forefinger and wiped it off, denying it the pleasure of rolling down her cheek.

Three

Since the day Nneora and Lincoln had left home for the boarding house at Iruobi Community School, Mama had become overly protective of me. Gone was my liberty to sit at Papa's feet to listen to his stories. When I asked her the reason for this, she replied that stories were best listened to in a group. But when I asked her to join us, she replied by saying that her days of listening to what came out of Papa's mouth were long over before my birth. Yet I knew she had listened to his sermons every Sunday morning in church until he had retired from the clergy — another impromptu action by Papa which I could not understand. I had imagined Papa would die a practising reverend. I imagined he would literally have to be carried off on a stretcher from the pulpit where he would collapse while delivering a sermon on a sunny Sunday morning.

I soon became a lonely child, living in a house that once had housed the voices of storytellers and noises of painful cries. Grandpa was the only adult I was allowed free access to, and the obi was the only place I had the liberty to explore at will. Every day after school, I would race through my homework to visit Grandpa. On this particular day, he was sitting and staring at something visible only to him. As I moved closer, I saw that his gaze was fixed on a fading photograph of a smiling woman.

"Grandpa, is that Grandma?"

My voice must have startled him, because he spun around. "I don't know ... Who knows?"

I gave him a look that questioned his reply but did not say anything. I had no desire to be confused any further in the process of getting clarity.

"You know, this was one of the first photographs taken in this village. The photographer, Mazi Ezike, had been living in the mission house with the white men. One of them taught him how to use the tripod camera ... I remember that day like yesterday. It was like an ofala festival, only it was a white man's type of ofala. Iruama was the envy of all the neighbouring villages because not one of them had a photographer or owned a camera."

"Grandpa, I asked if that was Grandma and you said 'I don't know.' What do you mean by that? How can you not know if that is my grandmother or not? And what do you mean by 'who knows'?"

"You ask too many questions, Udonwa. Now go and finish your homework."

"It is all finished, Grandpa."

"Then go and help your mother in the kitchen to prepare supper. You are the only one here to help her now."

As I began to stand up, he changed his mind and asked me to sit back down. "You know," he said, "Leonard, my son, your father, was not always like this. I don't know where he learned this behaviour of torturing his own family, of being ... who he is. It is just sad."

"I understand, Grandpa. Sometimes Papa can't control his temper, but at other times he is nice." I said it as fast as I could because I wasn't sure he even wanted me to respond. He had a distant look in his eyes and spoke as if he wanted to bare his soul. So I kept quiet and listened instead.

"Look at how he behaved when Adaora announced she was getting married. What he did is nothing short of an abomination ..." As soon as he had begun, he stopped. "I won't have this discussion with you. This discussion is not one to have with a child. Go and help your mother in the kitchen."

I got up without saying another word to him. The photograph with the unknown woman in it, and his failure to speak in proverbs for the first time ever, led me to a definite conclusion: the war going on in the hearts of the members of my family had invaded their minds.

• • •

Papa had refused to attend Adaora's wedding. He said the country had been badly affected by the low supply of fuel, and the cost of travelling to Awka would be higher than his budget. Yet he had packed up his things that same weekend and headed to Lagos for Synod, a yearly gathering of the Anglican clergy.

Since her wedding, Adaora had stopped speaking to Papa. Not that he seemed to mind. And Sister Adaora, for her part, carried on like she didn't care if he minded or not, and no one could blame her. How could your own father not attend your wedding, without a valid reason like being ill or hospitalised, but with one as flimsy as scarcity of fuel? Not to mention that Awka was barely an hour's drive away compared to the several hours it took to get to Lagos. When I pointed out this disparity to Papa, he'd said the church had paid for his journey. Since then, Sister Adaora would enter the house and walk past Papa without acknowledging his presence. It was as if she just realized she had no father. Whatever Papa was to Sister Adaora, he was no longer her father.

Today was my fourteenth birthday and exactly two years and two months since Sister Adaora's wedding. Each time she came to the house, I would expect to see a protruding stomach. After all, Mrs. Nwaka's stomach had grown within a few months of her being married, and in less than a year of that, she had given birth. So I didn't understand why Sister Adaora's case was different.

The birthday songs cut into my thoughts as Jefferson, Nneora, and Lincoln sang and clapped. Mama said this would be a special birthday for me. I didn't know what she meant because all my birthdays had been special. She always made my favourite meal of jollof rice prepared with palm oil and a seasoning of ground crayfish just the way I liked it, and then topped it off with fist-sized chunks of fried goat meat.

Although I had never celebrated with a cake, today Sister Adaora said she had one made especially for me.

"My first birthday cake! Thank you, Sister," I said, as I realized what Mama had meant earlier.

"Is it only Sister who's congratulating you? You better say thank you to all of us too," Lincoln said.

I rolled my eyes at him. Going away to boarding school at the start of his senior secondary year had not only strengthened Lincoln's meanness, but had made him more annoying too. And now that he was in his first year at university, he was even worse. Nneora was in her final year of secondary school and would be off to university when the new school-year session began. Each holiday, she would regale us with stories of Lincoln bullying the children in junior classes at their secondary school. One time, Lincoln had ordered a boy to wash his underwear in the middle of the night. The boy had developed a fever and had to go home. On his return to school, his parents had accompanied him and insisted that Lincoln's parents be brought to face them. Lincoln had lied that Papa was away on mission duty to another town and that Mama was too sick to travel.

Today, I just rolled angry eyes at Lincoln one more time and decided that I would not say what was on my mind — something that would make Papa wipe that smirk off his face.

"Today is a lovely day. Iruama is such a beautiful town. Look at all the trees and fruits and the dirt roads. I miss it," Sister Adaora said, smiling.

"I'm sure Awka has enough trees, and fruits and dirt roads too," said Lincoln with a wry smile.

"I know, they do … but Iruama's are different." Adaora laughed.

"Ah, Sister, I can understand your missing the udala tree and the guava trees, but the dirt road? Why do you miss this … this … dust?" Nneora asked, disgust on her face. Ever since she had begun her final year of secondary school, she would engage in casual chatter with unnecessary seriousness.

"Jokes aside, Sister Adaora's favourite thing in the world back then was to draw in dirt," said Jefferson with a chuckle. "Ah, you people don't know her at all." Pointing to the tree behind the obi, he continued: "She liked to sit under that udala tree where the dust is high up to the waist, holding a book in one hand and the other playing with the heap of sand. She'd be at it until it got dark." We all laughed along with Jefferson.

"I may have been young then, but I'm certain I saw her scoop a handful into her mouth once. Sister was a dirty child," said Lincoln.

Horrified, I spun towards Sister Adaora. "Chineke! Lincoln, don't speak to Sister like that."

But Sister Adaora laughed it off, clutching her stomach. "Eh, you people will not kill me. Lincoln is right, though. I did love dirt as a child, maybe a bit too much! That dusty place under the udala tree was my place of solace and comfort. It was the one place I could find peace in this house."

We all knew what she meant but none of us dared say it. Jefferson had mentioned in the past that when they were younger, Papa used to beat Sister Adaora so hard that one day he'd knocked out her two front teeth. Jefferson had gone to save her and had been whipped so hard, he'd run away. Mama was not home at the time and no one could help them. Mazi Okoli's last wife, Mama Ekene, had come looking for Mama to borrow ogiri for her pot of soup, and had been their saviour that day. But the locust bean was abandoned when she'd seen Adaora's condition. A knocked-out tooth lay in a corner of the room, useless to Adaora's bleeding mouth, while a second tooth was so badly damaged it resembled finely crushed chalk. Sister Adaora's only consolation was that they were milk teeth;

otherwise right now her mouth would look like a free-flowing expressway.

"Okay, enough of the dirt talk; today is all about Udonwa. Udom, I have a gift for you." Sister Adaora brought out a bulky wrapped parcel from her handbag and placed it on my lap.

"What is it?" asked Lincoln, as annoying as ever.

"Wait for her to open it! Can't you see the box is big and heavy?" said Nneora.

I unwrapped the box; inside were seven stacked books. They were all foreign books written by foreign people and I was certain they contained foreign stories. I wondered if the story of the long-haired princess was one of them.

"These were donated to the children's ward of the hospital where I work by a visiting couple from America. Every year this couple, who are originally from Awka, return to do what they can for their home town. You won't believe, they donated almost a truckload of books to some hospitals and the library in Awka! According to them, it's the way they do it abroad — reading books to sick children in hospitals makes them not miss home. But I think it also helps them to heal faster. Many schools received a donation of books too."

"Schools in Awka use foreign books to study?" Nneora asked. "We had none of those in our syllabus in community primary. Even now, we only read *Macbeth*, *David Copperfield*, and *Oliver Twist* in senior class and never in forms one to three."

"I'm sure it's just a few private schools in cities that include these books in their syllabus," said Jefferson.

"Just as well, because I know I wouldn't have wanted to read about some stupid princess living in a stupid castle somewhere in a stupid country. What's wrong with the tortoise and the hare storybook or *Chike and the River*?" Lincoln said, wrinkling his nose at the books.

Folktales were my favourite stories too, but I wasn't about to let Lincoln know I agreed with him.

"Nothing's wrong with them; those are good books and so are these. Books help a child's mind develop, whether they are folktales or fairy tales," said Sister Adaora. Turning to me, she added: "Don't you like them, Udom? I thought you enjoyed reading these stories, or are you too big for them now?"

"Of course not, Sister. I still enjoy reading them. Don't mind Lincoln. Mrs. Nwaka allowed me to read one during breaktime the other day. Her niece in America bought it for her child. Thank you, Sister," I added, perusing the books. They felt smooth and smelled like freshly cut firewood stored in a yam barn.

We continued chatting, and Nneora had just opened one of the books, when we heard footsteps. Collectively, we knew whom they belonged to. Papa walked in before any of us could exhale, and Nneora started coughing, her eyes watering and turning red at once.

Jefferson stood up to greet him. "Good afternoon, sir."

Papa responded in his usual way of silence and putting his head up, lowering it and blinking once. Lincoln was the next to offer his greeting, but he remained seated. Nneora was still coughing. Sister Adaora simply ignored him. When he called my name, I went over to where Papa stood by the door holding a plastic bag.

He handed the bag to me. "This is for you."

The silence in the room was so unnerving, I was certain if I listened hard I would hear everyone's breathing, including mine. Inside the bag was the most beautiful dress I had ever seen. A light pink dress spotted with tiny rose petals. Nneora could not stop coughing and looked as though she might pass out. When she finally stopped, her face showed a mix of different kinds of fear.

My attention returned to the dress. It had bold pink-and-white ribbons tied into a bow on both shoulders. The lower part of the dress was pleated in the same colours and outline as the bows. A knee-length pair of white socks and black patent shoes were also in the bag. Squealing, I wrapped my arms around Papa's waist and he patted my back, then swung out of the room like he hadn't been there.

Mama walked in with a tray containing the jollof rice and fried goat meat accompanied by bowls of water to wash our hands. Oblivious to the tension in the room, she asked Nneora to bring bottles of cold drinks from the cooler in Grandpa's room in the obi. Mama had stopped keeping the cold drinks in the small old fridge in her and Papa's room the day Lincoln had broken one bottle. Actually, the bottle had slipped from his hand as he'd taken it from the fridge and Papa had nearly sent him to join our ancestors. The cane had descended on Lincoln's back before he'd realized what had hit him, and after beating him until his back had broken the cane, Papa was heaving at him to lick up the spilt contents of the Coke off the floor. Lincoln, as expected, had stubbornly refused. Fearing the worst, Nneora and I had run to the bedroom and locked the door. Peeping through the keyhole, we had seen Papa launch at Lincoln again, threatening to take the cost of the broken bottle from his school pocket money. Hearing he might return to school with less money, which would be sheer torture for him, Lincoln had given in to Papa's orders with tears streaming down his face. Humiliated and distraught, he had just begun to whimper when Mama had walked in and, without a word, picked him up from the floor. By this time, Lincoln's tongue had been cut by an invisible piece of the broken bottle and was bleeding slightly. Mama had taken him away and returned with the cooler box, packing the remaining drinks into it before putting it in Grandpa's room. Even though Lincoln had not completed Papa's order, Papa did not carry out his threat either.

Papa did not toy with our education. When his salary arrived from the mission house, he would head straight to our school and pay the fees. It did not matter whether we were on holiday or if the fees were due or not. Sometimes, he would mistakenly overpay and the headmaster would return the excess to our home in an envelope. All the school teachers and headmaster admired Papa for that. He could fume and rant about anything, but when it concerned our education he backtracked. It was one of the reasons I loved him.

Now, Nneora returned with the bottles of drinks and we started eating and chatting again, the incident with Papa forgotten.

Then Sister Adaora announced: "I'm taking Udom to live with me in Awka."

Four

Awka welcomed me into her arms like a mother would her long-lost child. The compound where Sister Adaora lived with her husband was smaller than ours but less dusty. In fact, the cemented floor was the first thing I noticed. The yard contained many trees like ours too, but after walking round it a few days later, I was disappointed to see there was no udala tree.

The one-storey building which served as the official quarters for teachers of the nearby State Institute, where Uncle Ikemefuna taught, contained four flats in total, with two upstairs. A central pair of staircases in the middle running across each other led to the upper flats. The backyard housed two pairs of taps and several clotheslines that served the occupants of the flats. We lived in the flat on the right facing the main gate. The sitting room contained a television on a small wooden stool at the front of the room, a small bookcase in the corner against the wall separating the hallway from the sitting room, a wooden set of chairs with thick covered cushions, and a table in the centre. Unlike ours in Iruama, the centre table's four legs appeared sturdy and straight. There were two bedrooms, a kitchen, and a joint bathroom and toilet, which completed the interior of the flat.

Although the decision to take me to Awka had been as impromptu as it was shocking, I approved of it the moment I stepped into Sister Adaora's house. Our home in Iruama had not been the same since Mama had stopped me from listening to Papa's stories and Grandpa had become weaker and weaker. Also, with Mama getting busier with the Iruama Women's League, I practically had no one to talk to.

Nneora was writing her final examinations and wouldn't be coming home for a long time. Jefferson had returned to the seminary, and Lincoln was back at university. My family had become like a colony of ants where everyone was busy building one thing or the other. In the new school year, Nneora would join Lincoln at the University of Nigeria to study microbiology, while Lincoln was studying towards a BSc in business management. Although Medicine had been her first choice, Papa had given Nneora explicit warnings that, if she applied for it, she would have to pay her fees herself. Everyone knew Nneora would make an excellent doctor — everyone but Papa, who, for reasons best known to himself, insisted I was the only doctor he wanted in the family. Yet it wasn't difficult to imagine that, on the day Mama would see Nneora off to Eke Iruama motor park to board a bus to Enugu, she would not look like someone being denied her right to choose her own career path. If anything, I was certain Nneora would be delighted to be going very far away from home.

. . .

Uncle Ikemefuna, who had been away for a three-month educa-
tors' board training course in Abakaliki when I arrived in Awka,
would finally be returning home. Very early in the morning,
and appearing a bit agitated, Sister Adaora had instructed me to
wash all his dirty clothes and iron them, which I did in addition
to my daily chores of filling up the big basins in the kitchen
and bathroom with water, and scrubbing the floors of the whole
house. Sister Adaora's only chore was to cook. I was sprawled
on the floor in front of the bookcase, choosing a book to read,
when Uncle Ikemefuna walked in. With just a look at his face,
I knew I would never feel welcome in my sister's house as long
as he was around. He looked at me from head to toe as I sprung
to my feet to greet him and marched into the bedroom without
acknowledging my greeting. Lincoln also did this sometimes,
but I understood it as nothing more than sibling rivalry and,
well, Lincoln being who he was. I couldn't understand Uncle
Ikemefuna's unexpected hostility towards me.

Lying in bed that night, I tried to reconcile this Ikemefuna
with the quiet man who had come to the house a little over two
years ago to ask for Sister Adaora's hand in marriage. I tried to
remember without success what I had said or done to offend
him. Unable to come up with any reason, I concluded that
perhaps Sister Adaora hadn't informed him of my arrival. But
then again, I was his wife's sister and not a stranger.

In the morning I was awoken with a loud thud which made
me jolt straight up. I glanced in the direction of the clock on
the wall and it read four-thirty. Wiping my eyes, I made to lie
back on the bed, but a louder bellowing of my name sprung
me to my feet instead. I opened the door to Uncle Ikemefuna

standing there with just a towel around his waist; he was holding some clothes in the curve of his elbow.

I rubbed my eyes, looking away from him. "Good morning, sir."

"C'mon, take these clothes and iron them fast-fast, and
when you're done fill up a bucket of water for me to bathe.
And hurry up with it!" he barked, ignoring my greeting and
throwing the clothes at my face.

"Yes, sir." I gathered the clearly ironed clothes into my hands.

When I was finished re-ironing his clothes, I went to inform
him and found him standing in front of the bathroom mirror
shaving. I was heading back to my room when he stopped me
with another bark.

"Where do you think you are going? C'mon, go and put
the kettle on for me, osiso, and make me tea. I'm sure you can
make tea? And by tea, I mean teabag, not Ovaltine. And I don't
want it in any village style, so make sure the water boils to the
highest degree."

"I can make tea, sir," I said, swallowing hard. I made to
turn around when he stopped me.

"Don't forget to polish my shoes."

I walked past Sister Adaora standing at the door to their
bedroom. Her eyes were hiding unspoken words.

· · ·

The days and weeks that followed were no different from that day,
but instead of waking up to loud banging on the door and the
barking of my name, I would wait for Uncle Ikemefuna in the sitting room ahead of time. Today, he was returning to Abakaliki for
another conference and I had just concluded the normal routine.

"Uncle, I'm finished," I said to him. I was standing in front of the locked bathroom door, holding his pair of polished shoes.

"What lunch did you pack?" he asked from behind the door, where I imagined his face scrunched up at me the way you would look at someone whom you wanted to disappear.

"I made fried eggs and bread the way you like it, sir."

On his insistence, I described how I took three eggs from the crate and whisked them, then cut one bulb of onion into three pieces and thinly sliced two small tomatoes, before adding half a cube of Maggi. The first time I had made fried eggs for him I did not ask him how he wanted them, and had prepared them like Mama would. Uncle Ikemefuna had thanked me for my efforts by delivering two hard knocks to my head, which would become a normal occurrence.

As the days went by, the head knocking and barking had graduated to hot slaps across the face, the first time being the weekend after his return.

Uncle Ikemefuna travelled to Abakaliki every fortnight and spent an equal amount of time there. The weekends he travelled were the happiest, not only for myself but for Sister Adaora too, if only for the end to the constant commotion coming from their bedroom on a nightly basis.

Last night had been exceptionally bad. Their rising voices, the sharp sound of what seemed to be a series of slaps landing on someone's body, followed by whimpering kept me up all night. I had lain frozen on my bed, helpless, listening to my sister sob like a child.

I was lost in thought in front of the cupboard, thinking about the night before, when Uncle Ikemefuna walked into the kitchen barking.

"Aren't you finished? I thought you said you were finished! Don't you know it's a long drive to Abakaliki, eh? C'mon, will you hurry up with that."

Shaking, I hurriedly packed his lunch. "I'm sorry, Uncle, I'm almost done."

"What! You dare talk back to me?"

A slap landed on my face with such force that I staggered backwards, trying to catch my balance between the floor and the kitchen cupboards. Bent over, I held on to the cupboards, fighting off stinging tears while he collected his lunch bag and walked out of the kitchen. He pushed past Sister Adaora, who was standing at the door mute and clutching her right cheek. She returned to their bedroom where she stayed until the sound of his car was nothing but a miserable whisper.

Later, when I was sitting in bed with my hands folded in my lap, Sister Adaora tapped on the door and entered with two tablets of Panadol.

"Take this — it will make you feel better." She put her hand on my shoulder but avoided my eyes as she handed me the tablets. "Udom, please don't worry too much about Ikemefuna … He's just angry I haven't fallen pregnant yet. I promise you, when the baby arrives, you'll see how he'll loosen up and be more welcoming."

Even though I wanted so much to believe her, her words were little comfort. Awka became the place I learned how to cry. I would wake up with my pillow soaked every morning, the tears from the pain in my body from doing too much housework and from being beaten without reason. But, more than anything, they were tears for prayers for Sister Adaora's baby to come so the pain in my heart would stop.

Five

The streets of Awka were busier and noisier than the roads in Iruama and less dusty too. My school was situated in the same compound as the hospital where Sister Adaora worked, so we left home together.

I had just said goodbye to Sister Adaora and was walking towards the school gate when a voice stopped me. I turned around and saw a face I recognized from class.

"Hello, my name is Ifenna," he said. I repeated the name in my head, pondering its meaning — it was a little presumptuous but undeniably beautiful.

"I like your name," I said before I could stop myself.

"No stress. Join the queue. So you're new, right? I'm also new, sort of. I returned from the US two years back. My father said something about my needing to learn the ways of our people."

I stared at him. "Do you know what it means?"

"What?"

"Your name. Do you know the meaning of your name?"

"Yeah, I suppose. Something about light ... God ... Whatever."

"The light of God. Well, literally, Ifenna means 'Light of the Father,' but the 'Father' in this sense is God."

"I heard you the first time though. And you, I hear the teacher explain your name all the time in Igbo class. I don't see the big deal about Igbo names or any other native ones. Really, I don't see the problem in naming my kids English or foreign names."

"My two brothers bear foreign names. The eldest is Jefferson, and the other one is Lincoln. Jefferson is training to be a priest and Lincoln is studying business management at the univer—"

"For real? I was expecting something like Mark, John, or even Vincent. Why did your father give your brothers such fancy names?"

"Jefferson and Lincoln are not fancy names, but names of former American presidents. You know that, don't you?" His face looked like I had just spoken French so I added: "As in Thomas Jefferson and Abraham Lincoln?"

"Of course I knew that." He shrugged. I knew what he was doing; Lincoln did that all the time when I corrected him. I had come to realize it was all an act, a defence mechanism for people who knew nothing but would never admit it.

"But they are still fancy names for a couple of village kids."

"Well, you may be right —"

"Oh, I see! Now I get it. Your dad is smart; I like him. He named his two sons after presidents so they could be one when they grow up, right?"

"I suppose you're ri—"

"But, instead, your brothers gave him the middle finger by going way off his plans. One will end up behind a desk in some boring office, and the other, a priest, a fucking priest."

"How fucked up is that!" he sniggered.

And with that, he walked away, and I resolved never to speak to him again, beautiful name or not.

. . .

Eighteen months into living with Sister Adaora, like her, I forgot what it meant to be happy. Uncle Ikemefuna now hardly returned home, and when he did, he stayed no longer than a weekend before going away again. Sister Adaora had stopped talking as often as she used to, and would lock herself in her bedroom for hours. Increasingly, she was waking with puffy eyes that appeared as though they hadn't been closed or rested for a year. They were huge and full of stories I knew I would be the last to hear, if I ever did.

I began to miss Mama and wished my nightly dreams would transport me to Iruama.

The night before Jefferson came to visit for the first time since I'd arrived in Awka, I was going to the bathroom when I saw something on the sofa in the sitting room. On closer inspection, I realized it was Sister Adaora sleeping with her thighs curled up to her chest, her arms wound around her body. It was disheartening to find that even in her sleep she looked troubled.

The next morning, though, Sister Adaora advised me to put a smile on my face, just like she had told me when Mama had come to visit a few months before. This advice was unnecessary, as I would have been happy even if she had said a monkey or an antelope was visiting. I was tired of the faces in Awka.

During Mama's visit, she'd refused to lift her embargo on telling stories, even though I'd begged and begged. She insisted on her old stance, before adding: "Udonwa, you're in secondary school now; folktales are for little primary school children." And I'd agreed with her, not only because I noticed how tired she always was, but also that telling stories must remind her of that ugly incident when Papa had almost killed two of her children. Two things stood out for me during Mama's visits: all the strands of hair on her head were grey, more from worry than age; and I realized how alike Mama and Sister Adaora were. They both possessed the ability to pretend all was well when it was clear even to a bat that things were falling apart.

Jefferson's visit was also troubling, but for different reasons. He and I were in the sitting room gazing into each other's eyes, playing the game to see who would blink first. Minutes into the gazing, our eyes would get misty and tears would roll down our cheeks. When I was much younger, and before he went to live at the seminary, Jefferson and I would do this almost every day. I won most of the time. When we tired of each other's eyes, we would gaze at the stars; Iruama was never short of the sky diamonds. One star-gazing night, Jefferson had said he'd seen a shooting star. But I wasn't sure I believed him. Mrs. Nwaka had said such occurrences only happened in fairy-tale lands, and Iruama was far from being a land so magical that a star would shoot across its sky.

During today's game, I noticed Jefferson's eyes looked different because they appeared dark and dim. Gone was the twinkle, the ability to find magic in the sky. My gaze, despite the rules of the game, followed the movement of his hands. They were slimmer and unusually smooth. His hair shone from being smeared with what appeared to be too much Vaseline. His lips were also coated with the same petroleum jelly, highlighting the small hollow above the centre of his upper lip. It made the gap in the upper row of his teeth seem wider when he smiled. And his shoes were so overly polished they shone like new. His socks were white, whiter than the whitest white. I couldn't take my eyes off him.

"What are you staring at?" he asked. "You've lost!"

"I'm looking at you. You look different."

"Don't be silly, Udonwa. I'm almost a priest. Of course I will look different."

"Your eyes ... They appear too dark. Like there's something other than your pupils in them."

"You are something else, Udo, you know that?" He laughed, but even that was strange.

"I know your eyes, Brother. I've gazed into them for a long time to know what I'm talking about ..."

"You ask too many questions and you make too many assumptions. One of these days, this curiosity of yours will get you into trouble."

I continued staring at him, unconvinced by his excuses.

"Okay, Udonwa, if you must know, there's nothing wrong with me or my eyes, okay. It's because I burn the midnight oil more frequently these days. I have to study really hard to be the best priest I can be. Bringing solace and comfort to people, and administering to their needs effectively — that's what a priest practises to be. And if you're talking about my clothes and shoes, they are new. Happy now?"

"If you say so, Brother ..."

"I know so, Udonwa."

Sister Adaora walked in at the same time Jefferson got up to adjust a cushion on the sofa. These days, not only did Sister Adaora's physical wellbeing raise eyebrows but her mental state was concerning too. She would often give blank stares and had gone from slim to thin, and I wasn't the only one who had noticed this. Mama had mentioned this to Sister Adaora more than once and would call often after her last visit, asking if she ate well. And on each occasion, Sister Adaora had replied that we were imagining things.

She sat down slowly, staring at Jefferson, whose gaze was fixed on a book on demons and angels. He pretended not to notice her stare, but I knew him; his brain was as sharp as his eyes.

"Have you told her?" Sister Adaora sighed deeply.

My eyes darted to Jefferson. "Has he told me what?"

"Yes, em ... em ... Udo, actually, this is not just a casual visit." He paused, then continued: "Something has happened and that's why I'm here."

"Tell me what? What happened, Brother Jefferson? Is everybody at home all right? Is Papa all right?" As the questions came flooding out, I knew without being told that it was terrible news. And even when he quietly told me what had happened, I still could not believe it. I did not want to believe it. My heart ached and my body longed to be in Iruama.

Six

Grandpa had died because there had been no one to help him position his wooden legs underneath his arms. He had tried to do it himself and they had slipped out. He'd fallen and hit his head on the desk in his hut and collapsed, right in front of the photograph of my late grandmother. Mama had found him in that state when she had returned in the evening from the women's meeting and was taking his supper to him. She said there had been blood trailing from the sides of the photograph of Nwamgboli Afomma. Looking around the room now and remembering the photograph, I couldn't help but recollect the striking resemblance between my grandmother and Papa, which made me more curious about Grandpa's reply to my question that day a few years earlier.

Growing up, my grandmother's name had been taboo in our house. Mama had mentioned once that, even though she'd never met her, Mama's own mother had told her things about her mother-in-law, things only choice words could describe — words that children are not supposed to hear or repeat. On the wall in the living room where all the photographs of the family hung, Nwamgboli Afomma's was missing. I grew up not only thinking Papa no longer had a mother but that he'd never had one. It was as if a concerted effort had been made to obliterate her memory from existence. But one thing I knew was that Grandpa had loved her. Otherwise, why was he tracing the outline of her photograph while staring intently at it that day?

Being in his room now brought back memories of times spent with him. My eyes welled up as I remembered our encounter on my first visit home after I'd left for Awka. After dropping off my things at home and greeting Papa, I had gone straight to Grandpa's obi. He wasn't there, so I'd waited. About twenty minutes later, Mazi Okoli's wife Mama Ekene had helped him in. His face had beamed into a sunshine smile when he had seen me. "Udo, my daughter, nwajiudo welu bia uwa — the child who came to the world with peace." He had then recounted the story of my birth, something I had heard a million times before — how I was the calm after the chaos. "Do you know you were the first baby I know of who came into the world without a sound, not pim. At a child's birth, we are meant to hear the mother's laughter and the cry of the baby, but it was not so with you. You were as quiet as Amokwe cemetery."

"Hei, Grandpa, I can see you're in a very jolly mood tonight, eh … Mama said you were not even there when I was born," I had teased as I helped him settle on the flat mattress.

"So, what difference does it make? Even though I wasn't there in the flesh, I was in spirit. And why wouldn't I be in a jolly mood when my granddaughter is here looking like a big woman? When you left you were this small," he'd said, lowering his hand below his hips.

I wondered if he had been thinking about me when he'd fallen. I wondered if he had reunited with Nwamgboli Afomma.

• • •

We all stood around Grandpa's corpse in the open casket as the reverend read out the last recitations before blessing Grandpa's spirit. Grandpa was dressed in his full Ozo regalia — the Igbo tribal isiagu-print top over a pair of loose-fitting trousers. On his head was a feathered red hat, and his wrists and ankles were adorned with red-and-white beaded bracelets. Placed next to his right hand was his white cowhide akupe — a handheld fan that doubled as a greeting tool for his group, bearing in bold brown letters his full title, Ichie Onye Nkuzi of Iruama. To complete the look, placed next to his left hand was an elephant tusk. He looked regal and at rest.

Earlier, Grandpa's revered group members had arrived to pay their respects and Papa and Mazi Okoli had engaged them in a barrage of insults.

"These idol worshippers have come with their carved gods to pour libation on our father. The dead does not drink water, not to talk of hot drink," Mazi Okoli had said.

But the Red Cap titled chiefs made up of seven of their leading men had ignored him. The Ozo traditional practice had always fascinated me. Members were recognized by their red caps with an eagle feather affixed on the side, hence the eponymous English translation. Membership was not usually guaranteed, as only a select few of the community were allowed to join, notably the noblemen of the community. With the advent of Christianity, however, the Ozo had become regarded as a cult and many of its members were viewed as worshippers of the non-living God. But Grandpa had insisted that it was not so, and that continuing to worship the creator through our ancestors' traditional ways was a means of preserving our Igbo culture. I remembered asking Grandpa on one occasion why there was an okwa nzu, a small clay bowl containing burnt wood ash and salt, in a corner of the sitting room in the obi, and he'd replied that it was for offering prayers to Chukwu Abiama and for decorative purposes, but that it had no fetish significance like Papa had told us.

Papa had wanted a Christian burial ceremony for Grandpa but the Red Cap chiefs had vehemently refused. There had been a series of meetings to discuss their disapproval, as Grandpa had been a distinguished member who once had held the prestigious position of the Ikenga, or lead Nze. Papa's argument had been that, although his father had never attended church, he was not a pagan either. But both sides could not come to an agreement and, in the end, Grandpa was buried in the manner he would have wanted — a mix of Papa's Christian beliefs and the ordinances of our ancestors. Papa's colleagues, however, had chosen to preside over the service of songs only and wouldn't be returning for the interment tomorrow.

Everything else continued as planned, except for when the Catholic priests arrived, their immaculate white soutanes in sharp contrast to the Anglican bishop and reverends' red and purple robes. Jefferson led their procession into the compound and Mama was on her feet the moment she saw them, bowing, greeting, and welcoming. Papa sat at the table with the rest of the umunna, and when the procession arrived at the table to greet him and his kinsmen, he looked away like he hadn't seen them. Mazi Okoli extended a hand of welcome to them and led them to their seats. For the rest of the day, I caught Papa frequently stealing glances at Jefferson, with Jefferson pretending not to notice. Papa's face looked like that of a lion who had received news of his newborn cub but when he arrived to see his offspring, he'd beheld a goat instead.

"Chukwu Abiama, please accept the soul of your son into your rest."

"Isee."

"Let his path shine through from there to light up our path here on earth."

"Isee."

It was the second day of the funeral ceremony for Grandpa and the head of the Red Cap chiefs was pouring libations of liquor around the surface of the floor above the grave as he offered prayers. He started out by pouring some of the drink into his mouth, and gurgled before spitting it out in splashes all around the open grave. Very early in the morning, the chiefs had arrived at our home, and had gone into the obi where Grandpa was lying in state, shutting the door behind them. What they did in there and how they did it was sacred to them and must remain a secret to the rest of us non-members. After the prayers, the head of the Red Cap chiefs brought out seven bitter kola nuts from his pocket and shared them among the seven men. They all chewed and spat out the nuts in unison. Then the gyrating and the dancing commenced. They danced in circles, swirling around the coffin and spitting out the kola nuts while another member dressed in a singlet and wrapper with a woollen multi-coloured cap played a traditional tune on the flute. Children and women were not allowed within close proximity of them until they were finished. Papa was sitting under the canopy with a few of the umunna, pretending not to be watching, while Mama and the women in the family were in the backyard attending to the hired women cooking the food. Jefferson was looking regal in his white soutane and also watched the proceedings from afar, while I stood with Nneora on our veranda watching with keen interest. We moved closer to the graveside when we were informed they had completed their burial rites and were ready to lower Grandpa to the ground. I gave his lifeless body a final look just before the casket was closed and noticed he had been stripped of all his accompanying Ozo regalia save for a single white beaded bracelet around his left ankle. As he was lowered, I mouthed "Jee nke oma" for the last time, and allowed the tears to flow. I stole a glance at Papa, who, although appearing angry at the traditional burial, now seemed to be holding back tears. Jefferson and Nneora held on to each other as she sobbed silently, while Mama, Sister Adaora, Mama Ekene, Mazi Okoli, his other wife, and the rest of the family looked on with sad faces.

• • •

Lincoln couldn't make it to Grandpa's funeral because he was writing his final exams. It was hard to believe he would soon graduate from university. I hadn't seen him since the last time I'd visited Iruama, and even then he'd been almost as tall as the palm trees in our compound, bearing a lighter than usual complexion and growing a beard in addition to his moustache. Nneora had mentioned always seeing him on campus with a certain girl, and rumour had it they were living together in the girl's room off campus. At the time, I hadn't shown interest due to the troubles at Sister Adaora's house, but now I was itching to hear every detail. I couldn't wait to see the girl who thought Lincoln was worthy of five seconds of her time. But, if Mama could marry Papa, then I suppose anything was possible. While I was smiling painfully at this thought, Nneora found me.

"This one, you are smiling as if you're not sure you want it on your face."

"Nne ..." I said, smiling more broadly, and wrapping my arms around her. It felt so good to hold someone again after such a long time.

"Is everyone gone?" Nneora asked.

Her fingers ran up and down the new curtain's fabric as if she was missing the old tattered one we'd grown up with. My mind drifted to that unfortunate story night and how the useless piece of cloth had ripped apart when I'd tried using it to shield myself, exposing me to even more danger. I remembered staring at it afterwards and wishing I could yank it off the knocked-in nails on the wall. But with just one look from Mama, I had let it be. She had insisted the curtain might be old but still served its purpose of keeping out unwanted sunlight and letting in a cool breeze. An explanation I had struggled to believe. I thought it was because we had no replacement for it at the time so she had rather held on to the tattered curtain than let it go. It was the same thing she did with everything else too.

"The curtain is beautiful," said Nneora. "Mama said Mama Ekene came one day and started taking measurements, that she wanted to fix up the place."

"Oh really? I thought the whole place was redecorated for
Grandpa's funeral."

"Which funeral? Udonwa, biko, start paying attention, inu?
These curtains have been here for a year now. I thought you
said you've been visiting home? I'm sure the next thing you'll
say is that you didn't notice the new kitchen fixtures, utensils,
and terrazzo flooring too?" Each question was accompanied by
a look of incredulity. She rolled her eyes and gave me a funny
stare when my face revealed what she wasn't expecting to hear.
"Okay, did you at least see the new furniture in Mama and
Papa's room? The old rusted four-poster bed is gone. There's a
new wooden bed there now."

Sighing, I replied: "Nneora, I'm sorry, okay, but each time
I came home I would run straight to Grandpa's. I didn't have
time to notice anything else. Besides, we are not allowed in
Mama and Papa's room — you know that."

"Typical. You notice what you want to notice and see only
what you want to see."

Was she right by saying I saw only what I wanted to see?
She and Lincoln had always accused me of seeing Papa through
rose-tinted glasses — that I was selective of what I saw when
it came to him — implying that I only saw his good side and
not his bad. But I wasn't sure if that was true or not. I admit I
happened to be the only person in my family who saw any good
in Papa, but I also knew his bad side. I knew it was not okay
for a man to beat his wife and children like Papa used to do.
Even though I had no recollection of Papa ever beating Mama,
which everyone attributed to the fact that I had been too young
to remember. But I knew he shouted at her. And I also knew
that I did not like the way he looked at her. A look that was
no different from the way Uncle Ikemefuna looked at Sister

Adaora. But even though I had no memory of Papa's physical violence towards Mama, I was fully aware of his harsh treatment of the rest of the family. Lincoln and Nneora were the only ones I'd ever seen him beat, but more especially Lincoln, and that was because he was a boneheaded creature who gave everyone a headache. If I were Papa, I would also beat him. Perhaps that's what Nneora meant by: "You only see what you want to see."

"Everyone is gone, Udo. It's all over," said Nneora, changing the subject. "The last group of umunna just left. Iruama loved Grandpa and that should console us."

Nneora's words cut into my thoughts and I realized how much I had missed her. How I missed us sitting under the udala tree and talking for hours until the stars disappeared into the sky. How, even though she was my elder sister, I would sometimes place her head on my lap and pat her softly until she fell asleep. But now university had turned her into a fierce young woman who sometimes appeared angry with everyone, including herself. I suppose I would be angry too if I were studying to become something I didn't want to be. I walked to where she stood by the window and locked her smallest finger in mine. Together, we stared out of the window.

I smiled at her. "Grandpa might not have been rich, but he was noble. He was a very honest man who remained true to his beliefs and principles until the end."

Tightening our fingers together, she sighed before responding: "I'm just glad everything went according to how Grandpa would have wanted it ... Except for when Mazi almost ripped the robe of one priest, insisting he must call Papa by his Igbo name and not Leonard. And Papa just sat there and did nothing."

Kenechukwu was Papa's Igbo name; it meant "Thank God." According to Grandpa, as much as it had pained him, he had had to stop calling Papa that name because, after Papa's birth, every other family in Iruama had decided to name their first sons Kenechukwu. Grandpa had said it had got to a point that people couldn't tell which Papa Kenechukwu was being referred to at certain times. Knowing Grandpa, I could only imagine his frustration at being confused with an ote nkwu Papa Kenechukwu, or an ogbu akwu Papa Kenechukwu, since he considered the professions of palm-wine tapper and palm fruit farmer far lower than his noble profession of the headmaster of a British primary school. But Mama called Papa neither of his two names because, according to her, there was nothing about Papa for which to thank God. She said that Leonard was even worse because the name spelled and sounded like leopard. "That animal that cannot change his spots!" she had jeered. She said she feared calling him that, because just like the animal, he wouldn't be able to change into a better person even if he wanted to, adding that people tended to answer to and live by the names they were called. So she chose to call him Papa Adaora instead.

In the end, the name written in bold letters after Grandpa's Ozo title, Ichie Onye Nkuzi, as was customary as the surviving son of the deceased on the printed obituary posters, was Leonard. Just like Grandpa would have wanted. Mama's first cousin, Papa Chinadimma, and half-brother, Uncle Onwura, were her only relatives who attended the funeral. Her parents were long dead but even when we were still little and her mother had still been alive, Mama's mother had never visited us. Mama's younger and only sister, Aunty Nene, lived in Lagos and her two brothers, one older and the other younger, lived in Aba and Onitsha respectively. Mama had been ostracised by her family when she'd married Papa — a decision they'd made because they abhorred Papa's behaviour. I once heard that her father had taken one look at Papa as a suitor for his daughter and bluntly uttered the famous words: "No, you won't marry my daughter; you will kill her." Even an Ozo-titled chief like Grandpa couldn't help dissuade Mama's father from his dislike of Papa. Mama had fallen on the ground weeping and only after she'd revealed to her mother that she was pregnant did they allow the wedding ceremony to take place. But there had been no traditional marriage ceremony because Mama's father had convinced his kinsmen that Papa had brought shame to their family by impregnating their daughter and would not be given the pleasure of marrying her in their compound. Papa had just been conferred a reverend at the time, so it hadn't been difficult to convince the bishop to wed them. And in the absence of any member of her family, Mama had married Papa. A marriage her family still referred to as nefarious.

"I'm off to Enugu first thing tomorrow morning," Nneora said in a low voice, cutting into my thoughts. "We may not see each other again before I leave. You should come to Enugu some time to visit. Just let me know when ahead of time so I can arrange everything."

I nodded and smiled.

Seven

The morning after everyone returned to their respective homes and places of study, Papa called me to the sitting room for a meeting to discuss my future. Sister Adaora had instructed I board a taxi back to Awka, as she had only been given two days off from the hospital and couldn't stay for any extra days. There had been no mention of Uncle Ikemefuna coming to pick me up because he had stopped visiting our home after their wedding. He said Papa had treated him and his family like rubbish. When Uncle Ikemefuna would complain about it, Mama would remind him of the Igbo adage, "Ogo bu chi onye," which translated to "One's in-law is one's god," but it yielded nothing. His father and some elders of his family had attended Grandpa's funeral because they said

Grandpa had treated them with the respect they deserved during Sister Adaora's marriage ceremonies; otherwise, they had no business with Iruama. And they'd proven their point by avoiding Papa throughout the burial ceremony. I couldn't help wondering that, knowing how badly Papa led our home, perhaps they were scared he would teach Uncle Ikemefuna his ways of running his own family and Sister Adaora would end up miserable like Mama. If only they knew there wasn't much difference between the two men.

Our sitting room had undergone extensive changes. Mama Ekene had simply outdone herself, I thought as I tried to take it all in. I hadn't noticed it before now, or any of the other changes in the house. Mama said Mama Ekene had arrived early one morning and, after a short discussion with Papa, had gone to the faraway Onitsha market and bought the materials for the curtain and padded cushions for the chair. Even the old centre table had been replaced with a glass-topped one. The curtain's edges were finely sewn with a red thread running across it all the way down the drapes. Its bright-coloured sunflower pattern ran throughout the entire fabric with two black dots atop the flowers like bees feeding on nectar. The padded cushions were made from the same fabric but with white backing. I supposed the floral material had run out and they had had to improvise. From where I was sitting, I noticed the glass top on the wooden centre table had several smudges of glass cup bottoms printed on it like a decoration. I made a mental note to clean it before leaving. The windows appeared dust-free and were wide open to let in as much air as possible. Even the air in the room smelled different. I was so engrossed in the new look of our sitting room, I didn't notice Papa come in until he coughed and cleared his throat.

"Good evening, Papa." I stood up to give him a hug.

He smiled, revealing lines across his forehead that looked as if an angry cat had been playing with its claws on his face. There was also extra flesh hanging from underneath his eyes, extra saggy flesh. He started talking before I could ask if he was okay.

"You are still going to be a doctor, right?"

I looked at him and my face must have said much more than my mouth because he knew exactly what I was thinking.

"I'm sure you're wondering where this question is coming from, but with all the changes happening in this family for some time now, I need to know I still have a child who respects and obeys me."

I nodded.

Papa kept rubbing his right eye as he spoke. I wanted to tell him to stop — that his rubbing would make the eye puffier and saggier than it already was. But I couldn't. I just stared at him. I was eleven again, trying to understand what was going on in his mind, trying to figure out if there was a way I could help him.

"Promise me you'll study to become a doctor and make sure you're the best doctor Iruama has ever seen."

"I promise, Papa."

"So is Awka treating you well?"

He had stopped rubbing his eye and was reaching for a newspaper, his glasses positioned right on the edge of his nose. I waited for him to sit up before answering him. I had wanted him to talk about Grandpa, to talk about Jefferson, to talk about Mama, even Mazi Okoli and his craziness. I expected him to talk about the Church and the bishop, and why he had had to retire so early if he was so bored with life. But what I didn't expect him to talk about was Awka because there was no Awka talk without the mention of Sister Adaora. I was shocked he cared about what happened to her and how we lived in Awka. But before I could answer, he flipped through several pages of the newspaper and carried on as though he had forgotten he had asked me a question.

"You are almost through with secondary school now. Before you know it, you'll be off to university."

I tried to smile. I knew I wanted to, but my brain told my face not to respond and I just stared blankly at him instead. Did I know who my father was? Who he really was? I wondered as he continued to speak.

"I hope that man is treating you well. I hope he realizes you're not his maid?"

So he knows? I stared intently at his half-hidden face, only looking away when he put the paper down. I knew Mama was not aware of the situation in Awka. Sister Adaora would rather drink acid and pluck out her eyes than speak to anyone about what happened in her house. I looked up at him again, to see if he was just guessing; perhaps this was a mind game to figure out how I would react. If he had asked me about this three years ago, when I had just started living with Sister Adaora, I certainly would have told him everything. Just like I would do when we were little and Lincoln was mean to me and I wanted him to be punished. But then again, would I have? Uncle Ikemefuna was Sister Adaora's husband and anything Papa did to him would affect her too … I shook my head. Maybe I wouldn't have. And the many times I'd told on Lincoln, it had served him right. Papa would have found out, anyway.

"So does he treat you well? Are you happy living with your sister?"

"Yes, Papa, I'm happy living there. Don't I look well?" I said, trying to smile.

"I didn't say you don't look well. And those are two different things, not so? Someone can look well and still be unhappy."

He was making more sense than he realized in light of my experience in Awka.

"You're right, Papa."

"You know you can always talk to me about anything. If you're tired of living there, you can always come back here. This is your home. It's just that when your mother and sister conspire to do something, trying to oppose them is like trying to stop a deer from running to a stream of water. The whispers of two women plotting are more powerful than the voices of ten shouting men."

Papa never spoke in riddles, nor illustrated his words in parables; he had always been a blunt-mouthed fellow. Something we all knew Lincoln got from him. But, unlike Lincoln, he spoke less. Grandpa used to say he would have preferred having a talkative, harmless son than one who spoke with his fists. Papa was what people would refer to as an action man. Perhaps it was Papa's way of dealing with Grandpa's death, by trying to sound like him. To say something Grandpa would have said, only that Grandpa would have spoken in Igbo.

"When is your sister expecting you?" he asked, interrupting my thoughts.

"She said she will go somewhere straight after work so that will be around late afternoon. She's on the early morning shift this week."

"Good, then you can accompany me to Nnewisouth."

"Ah, Papa, Nnewisouth kwa, what special event is happening there today?"

I laughed as I remembered the last time I had accompanied him there. I had been ten at the time. He'd said a friend of his was having a grand ceremony for his wife's birthday and he wanted me to go with him. We had had to pass through Akunesiobike, the palm-wine seller's shop in Afor Oheke, to buy a keg of palm wine, which we'd delivered to his friend. Nnewisouth was a beauty to behold. The array of mansions lined up on the streets we passed through before getting to Chief Aforjulu's house was the sort available only in big cities. I remembered Papa saying: "There are no poor men in this town," that everyone was rich or had a family member who was too rich. And that some were so rich, they did not even know how rich they were. At the time I had pondered that statement, wondering how anyone could not know the status of their wealth, or how wealthy they were. Probably, they had given a lot away and had lost count, and their giving brought back huge fortunes to them. Wasn't it written in the Bible: "Give, and it shall be given unto you; good measure, pressed down, and shaken together, and running over, shall men give into your bosom." That was what I understood by what Papa had said. But when we had arrived in Nnewisouth that day, I had realized Papa could have saved his breath telling me how rich the people of the town were, how illustrious their sons were, how many of them had their children studying overseas even from primary-school level, for wealth and affluence were all the eyes could see.

"Nothing special is happening in Nnewisouth today," said Papa. "But I'm bored and want to visit my friend Chief Iweka Aforjulu's house. He just returned from America last night, and Reverend Pius will also be there. I thought you'd like to come — I noticed you liked the place the last time we were there."

"Yes, Papa. Are those swings still there? I know I'm now a big girl, but I don't think anyone is too big to go on those swings in Chief Aforjulu's compound … I mean, they are gigantic; I wouldn't be surprised if that swing was built for both children and adults!"

"But of course. Iweka left the swing in his compound even though his children were at school overseas. They are now grown, but I'm almost certain the swings are still there."

"Ah, Papa, if that's the case, what are we waiting for? Let's go now!"

"Where are you people going to?"

Mama's face was covered in sweat, the rippling type that settles around one's face if one has been in a very hot place for too long. Our kitchen might have undergone significant changes, but some things never changed, such as cooking Papa's food on a firewood burner. This was non-negotiable because, according to Papa, the aroma of a meal cooked on a firewood burner was much better than that of food prepared using a kerosene stove. And everyone agreed. In fact, every meal was tastier when prepared on firewood. But the tedious task of putting on the fire, fanning the flames to burn faster, and the smoke that invaded every part of the body, especially the eyes, not to mention the several hours it took to wash off ash stains from pots afterwards, surely meant it was wiser to switch to a gas cooker. Not for Papa, though. When one of Mazi Okoli's twins, Ekene, bought one for his parents from South Africa, Papa had refused to eat any of the food cooked on it. He'd said his favourite ora soup for the first time tasted like sand mixture. Lincoln had remarked at the time that Papa would never provide Mama with anything that would make life easier for her. At the time I thought he was exaggerating about how cooking with a gas burner would make one's life easier, until I started living in Awka and realized how correct he was.

"Udonwa and I are going to Nnewisouth. I need to see Iweka for an urgent matter."

Mama stared at both of us, then, looking at me straight in the eyes, said: "What time did Adaora say you should come back?"

"Ah ah, Mama, I want to spend some time with Papa, biko; it's been too long. I miss him, you know." I was laughing gently now, but Mama didn't see the amusement in what I had just said. All I could see were her eyes darting from me to Papa. After a long pause, she finally agreed.

"Okay, you can go. But I'll be at Mazi's house to call your sister every half-hour to find out if you've arrived in Awka."

"Don't bother, Mama. Sister won't be back till around four p.m. She's visiting Pastor Humphrey after work. Hian, Mama, it's only ten o'clock now. I'll be back before Sister comes home."

Papa's brows lifted when I mentioned the pastor's name. Was he actually interested in Adaora's comings and goings? But if he was, he didn't ask in the twenty minutes it took to get to Nnewisouth.

. . .

The gate of Chief Iweka Aforjulu's compound was constructed between the mouth of a lion in an apparent yawn. The mane of the beast was carved with precision, like the rest of the body of the animal, with every strand moulded onto the enclosed surrounding. Several sharpened fang-like teeth hung from the open mouth. The lion's head was even positioned to the right, as though it were posing for the sculptor. It would have been beautiful if not for the piercing eyes primed to resemble those of a real lion — an angry and hungry one. I dragged my eyes away from the clay king of the jungle and peeked between the wrought-iron bars of the gate to catch a glimpse of the swing in the backyard. But it was too far and the space between the iron bars too narrow. A guard soon appeared to open the gate, and we drove in. I couldn't help feeling like we were driving through the insides of a lion.

"Reverend Leonard Kenechukwu Ilechukwu!" Chief Aforjulu hailed Papa from the balcony on the second floor of the three-storey mansion. Papa mumbled something back, but I didn't stay to hear, running instead to where I remembered the swings were in a mini playground. I had just settled my bottom on the flat metal of the swing when I saw a shadow appear from inside the house. As the figure got closer, I realized it looked familiar.

"Ifenna ..." I half-said, half-exclaimed, looking at him with a mixture of suspicion and curiosity. "What are you doing here?"

"What do you mean, what am I doing in my own house?"

"You're Chief Aforjulu's son?"

He nodded, a cheeky grin on his face.

"I didn't know that ..."

He looked at me as if to say, *And how were you supposed to know* ... But he said nothing and took a seat on the four-seat swing.

"What are you doing in my house?"

"Eh —"

"I said, what are you doing in my house? You still under-stand English, don't you?"

If I had had any doubts he was really Ifenna, that question had cleared it up. The boy was nothing but rude.

"I came with my father, Reverend Ilechukwu," I said, trying to remain calm.

"I don't know him. Is he an old friend of my father's?"

I shifted in my seat, about to answer Ifenna, when the hem of my dress caught between the bars of the seat and the handle of the swing. Ifenna kept talking, but I wasn't listening anymore, pulling at my dress to free it. Worse, Ifenna did not notice my struggle and, if he did, he offered no help. Fearing my dress would tear, leaving a gaping hole exposing my thigh and rear, I asked for his help.

"What do you mean, your dress is stuck? Didn't you know that would happen? This is an old swing, you know. It's just been repainted to freshen it up —"

"Look, I don't need a lecture on the swing's birth; I just asked for your help to remove my stuck —"

"This swing does not like dresses. You should only sit on it with long pants or jeans shorts or tight skirts."

I stared at him in disbelief. Lincoln was definitely an angel compared to this boy. How could anyone see someone struggling and proceed with a lecture instead of a helping hand? I was desperate: I couldn't get off the swing, and I couldn't move on it. Either action would tear the dress. I was sitting there, mute in my discomfort and unsure what to do next, when another man appeared.

"I'll help you," said a voice that belonged to an older version of Ifenna. "Excuse my brother's manners, or lack thereof. I'm Chinua."

As he spoke, he began pulling my dress carefully from between the swing's seat and handle.

"I hope that smile is for me?" my new acquaintance said, taking an empty seat beside me. I looked down to find my dress was free from its imprisonment.

"Em, sorry," I said, blushing. I hadn't realized I'd been smiling. "I was just marvelling at the beauty of your name. The way it sounds. Tell me, is it the same as Chinua Achebe's, the full name, I mean?"

"Oh, you mean 'Chinualumogu'? I suppose, in a way, yes. But mine is actually 'Chinanulumogu.'"

"Oh, I get it. One is a plea — *God, fight for me*. And the other, a statement of fact — *God fights for me*. I like yours better. But why aren't you called Chinanu for short then, instead of Chinua? I think that sounds more appropriate for your name, don't you think?"

"It's a long story," he said and positioned his full weight on the swing.

"That's the name of my late sister, his twin. She drowned as a baby. Her name was Chinanu. *God hears*. It'd be inappropriate to call him that now, don't you think?" Ifenna said.

I'd forgotten Ifenna was still with us.

"Oh, I'm so sorry. I didn't know," I said, giving Chinua a quick glance and catching his smile.

"How could you have? It's okay. I never knew her, though. We were still babies. Now, enough of sorrowful talk. Let's talk about you. Where are you from?"

"Iruama, but I live with my sister and her husband in Awka."

"So that's where you guys met," said Chinua, turning to look at Ifenna. "We live in America — Seattle — but Ifenna lives with my grandma in Awka. You see, he had trouble being normal, so he was sent back home to Nigeria."

I laughed, then asked: "As punishment, or what?"

"That, and for him to learn his lesson too."

"Did it work? I mean, has he learned his lesson?" I was now pretending that Ifenna wasn't even there — and for all I cared he wasn't. He was too much like Lincoln and I couldn't stand it.

"In a way, he has, although he would never admit it. But we all know he's quite different from the naughty chap he used to be. Trust me."

"He must have been very, *very* naughty then. Because he's still —"

"A piece of work? I know. Most of the time he's an asshole. But he's a good kid. How old are you?" The question caught me off guard, and I took a while to gather my senses before providing an answer.

"Seventeen. I turn eighteen early next year."

"You're almost an adult, then."

"How do you mean?"

Chinua grinned. "Every time I say something, you reply with a question."

"Really?"

"See, you're doing it again."

"What did I ... Oh, okay. That's another question. I'm sorry."

"Don't be. I like it. One of my professors always says that people who ask a lot of questions do so because they want to know more. In other words, they are smart — smart people always want to know more."

I looked down and smiled, then asked: "So what university do you go to?"

"The University of Lagos. I prefer it here to the United States."

"I've never been to Lagos. Actually, I've never been outside of Anambra State."

"Whoa, that's a first. Lagos is far but not very far — it's like a quarter of a day's journey if you travel by road. I'm sure

you'll get there if you really want to. So, you'll be starting your
WAEC exams soon ... Have you thought of where you would
like to study?"

Until that moment, I'd never really given it much thought.
But his question made me realize I needed to start thinking
about it. I'd allowed Papa decide my degree for me, and Nneora
and Lincoln had assumed that the best place for me to go to
would be the same university as them. Nobody had ever asked
me what I wanted. It was a foregone conclusion that Udonwa
Ilechukwu would study medicine at the University of Nigeria.
Not until now did it occur to me that I could make another
choice. I knew Papa wouldn't mind because he had never re-
stricted us to a particular school. All he was interested in was the
course we studied, or rather, the course he wanted us to study.

"I haven't really thought about it," I said to him, still deep
in thought.

"Then you should start thinking. The time to decide is
around the corner."

• • •

And that's exactly what I did. On the way home, as Papa drove
quietly, I was also in my own world of silence. I wanted to see
another part of the country. And if I were to live in Lagos, I
wouldn't be with total strangers. Aunt Nene, Mama's sister,
lived there with her family, and I'd spoken with her the few
times I had accompanied Mama to Iruama community centre to call her on the telephone. Her two daughters were both
grown up and one lived in America, the other in Europe. The
last I'd heard, she lived alone with her husband, who was a
lawyer, and a son who was about three years younger than me.

I walked into Sister Adaora's sitting room that evening to find Uncle Ikemefuna watching TV, like a normal person would, only that in his case he was as normal as sunlight at midnight. Sister Adaora had stopped sleeping in their bedroom for a while now, sleeping on the sofa in the sitting room instead, curled up like a giant baby. On the last occasion I had woken her and asked her to sleep in my bed with me, she'd said my bed was too small for two people, so I had asked to switch places with her, but she'd still refused. It took living with my eldest sister to know she enjoyed suffering and took pride in it, as though it were a trophy she had won.

Eight

A month later, Sister Adaora and I were in the sitting
room when she repeated Chinua's question. I couldn't
believe my luck. I'd been meaning to tell her of my decision to
attend UNILAG after Chinua had made me start thinking of
my school of choice.

"Sister, I've decided to go to UNILAG."

She sat straight up on the sofa, staring into space without
saying a word.

Finally, she spoke: "Who put you up to this idea?"

"No one, Sister ... I just want to be far from home, that's all.
Iruama and Awka are all I know; I want to experience other places."

"In that case, after your exams, you can go to Aunt Nene's
house and experience Lagos and then come right back. You

don't know anyone or anywhere in Lagos. Lagos is too big for you, Udom. Lagos swallows people up."

I frowned at her. I did not understand what she was talking about, since I could count on one finger the number of times she had been to Lagos.

"Sister, Lagos is not in another country; it's just a few hundred miles away. If you're worried about how I will cope, please stop, because I know the way back home. I'll come right back and transfer to UNEC in a worst-case scenario."

She looked at me and sighed. "Okay ..."

"Okay? You no longer object?"

"No, I still object, but I trust Aunt Nene to take good care of you and look out for your welfare. So, good luck with your exams."

I flung myself on her, planting mini kisses on her face as she tried without success to contain her laughter.

Mama, on the other hand, when she was informed, took the next available transport to Awka, refusing to leave if I did not change my mind. She said a seventeen-year-old was still too young to understand anything about the outside world, especially a big city like Lagos, forgetting that I would be eighteen-and-a-half by the time I left for Lagos. But my mind was made up and I couldn't be dissuaded. I had entered the University of Lagos as both my first and second choice on the university-entrance form.

On the day my admission letter arrived, I took early morning transport to Iruama to inform Papa. He was in his bedroom when I arrived and refused to come out, even after Mama and I made enough noise to wake the entire of Iruama.

"Is Papa all right?" I asked.

"He hasn't been well for some time now," Mama said, and continued with arranging the cushions on the new sofas. I could tell she was enjoying the new decor of the house, maybe a little too much. She had also learned how to crochet and she was busy making head and arm placements for the sofas and armchairs. Indeed, she did not look the least interested in anything else. I sighed and sat in an armchair, running my hand across one of the completed arm placements.

"Nice, eh? Mama Nkiru came back from omugwo in London and taught everyone at the mission centre. You won't believe what we have learned. It is true what my mother used to say: 'A learned skill is superior to magic tricks.' Everybody in this world, especially women, must learn a skill. If it will not help you personally, in the long run, it'll help you help someone else. If you see Mama Nkiru, eh, you'll not recognize her, Udo."

"Mama, what's wrong with Papa?" I couldn't believe she was going on about Mama Nkiru when she'd just informed me that Papa had been sick for some time.

She continued with her crocheting, before saying: "He came back from Nnewisouth the other day complaining of a headache and chills. I don't know what is wrong with him. If he had allowed Nneora to study medicine like she wanted, I would have sent for her to have a look at him."

"Hian, but Mama, even if Nne were studying medicine, it would still be too early for her to do anything now. Studying and practising are two different things, Mama — it takes years to qualify as a doctor."

"Ooh, I have heard you, Udonwa. But your father brought whatever is wrong with him on himself."

"What do you mean?"

"We are in the rainy season and you know how it rains profusely here, sometimes for days. Well, some time last week, on one of the days when the rains took a break, your father decided that he must go out, even though he said his head was banging as if Nwakaibeya the carpenter were knocking his hammer on it. He insisted on going to see the bishop. And it was very cold that morning. That day, the wind was blowing all the dust from the entire east of the Niger right into this compound, but still, your father insisted on going. So was I surprised when he came back sick? What do you think that type of weather would do to a man of his age?"

Mama did not look up from her crochet work once while speaking; she kept on passing the thread to the curved mouth of the steel crotchet hook. My eyes followed the movements of her fingers and how they worked around the two materials as she spoke. Finally, I sighed and glanced towards Papa's bedroom, not sure if I should go in there.

"May I see him?"

She looked at me for a few seconds before replying. "You can go. But knock first and please keep the door open. I want to hear what he has to say."

Papa was lying on the edge of the bed with his hands clasped between his inner thighs. The old bed was gone, like Nneora had said. The room completely different from what I remembered it used to look like. Everything smelled new and fresh. He was snoring gently, unaware I was standing over him. I had never fully entered Papa and Mama's room before now. Papa had always said it was his most private space and children were not allowed to invade that space. But not Lincoln. Once when we were still little, Papa had gone to the mission house for a ministers' meeting and left his bunch of keys behind. Mama had also gone to the ministers' wives meeting. Lincoln had opened the door, entered the room, and sat on the bed. I remembered the fear that had swum through my mind that day. How Lincoln had later teased me that the look of horror on my face appeared as though I had seen all the ghosts of the dead buried in Amokwe cemetery. Not satisfied with just bouncing his bottom on the bed, Lincoln had leaned further to the other side of the bed, opening and closing the drawers and cupboard door of the bedside table. Through it all, Nneora had kept shouting that he would be dead if Papa found him. But Lincoln, as always, had not listened to her. I remembered standing in between the hallway and the open door, unable to move my feet an inch towards the bedroom. When Nneora couldn't bear it anymore, she had marched in there and threatened to lock Lincoln in if he didn't get up from the bed at once. He'd finally obliged, and Nneora had then straightened the creased bedspread and reorganized the pomade and combs and church journals on the cupboards and tables just as they'd been before Lincoln's transgression. I remembered Papa coming home late that day, the only reason he probably had not noticed that his personal space had been invaded by intruders — his children.

Papa stirred and smiled when he saw me. He tried to get up, and I rushed to his side to help him into a seated position.

"Mama said you were not feeling too well ..."

"Ah, who said? You've forgotten that the Lord's servant does not fall sick. When did you arrive, my child?"

"Not too long ago."

There was no chair in the room, so I remained standing. The thought of sitting on the edge of the bed, in the same position as Lincoln had sat so many years ago, just didn't feel right. Even though Papa was there in the room with me, it still felt like an invasion.

"Won't you sit down?" he asked as if reading my thoughts.

I positioned myself on the edge of the bed. It was the most uncomfortable thing I had ever done, and I was certain my face showed it.

"You know, my child, you're the only one in this family who cares for me. No one else seems to care if I live or die."

I turned to look at him when he said the word "die," wondering how he could talk about death when he wasn't even as old as Okongwu Akunafia, whom everyone in Iruama knew to be as old as the world, yet still farmed and continued to take more wives, each new one younger than the last.

"Papa, please don't talk like that. Nothing will happen to you. And Mama is here to take care of you."

He sighed and got up from the bed, opened his cupboard and took out a shirt, which I noticed was new. When he turned, my gaze was drawn to the brand-new watch on his wrist. He put on his shirt, and sat next to me, grinning, looking anything but sick. No wonder Mama wasn't too worried.

"You don't look too sick now you're out of bed. I think you just needed to rest. But you should be careful about going out in this cold rainy weather, Papa."

"You mean I don't look too sick now that you're here," he said, smiling, and I smiled back. "The moment I turned and saw you standing there, the fever left me, fiam."

"Ah, Papa, so I'm now the Holy Spirit who heals with his presence?"

"Ah, who knows what God was thinking when he made you. You know, your mother and I were finished with having children when you arrived ... I didn't think it was still possible. That is why Nnam named you Udonwa. And, true to your name, you've been nothing but a source of peace."

"Not according to Lincoln," I said.

"So why are you here? Because I know your mother didn't send for you. If Ekene and his mother, Akudo, hadn't come to visit, she wouldn't have told them I was sick. In fact, I lay in this bed for two nights unable to sleep before I insisted that your mother get me Panadol."

As I listened to Papa, I heard what he was saying as well as what he wasn't saying. The swift manner in which he'd changed the topic when I'd mentioned Lincoln was one thing I heard him not saying. Papa and Lincoln had the weirdest father-and-son relationship I had ever seen. They had no respect for each other. Papa hated Lincoln and Lincoln hated Papa twice as much, if not *much* more. He had often said he loathed Papa and couldn't wait for him to die. I had hit him so hard that day, it had taken the combined effort of Nneora and Jefferson to get me off him. No matter what Papa had done to Lincoln or who he thought Papa was, nothing gave Lincoln the right to wish Papa dead. But although I could understand why Lincoln disliked Papa, I couldn't understand why Papa did not like Lincoln. He was his son, after all. Jefferson, on the other hand, played it safe with Papa. The only sin I knew he'd committed against Papa was joining the Catholic seminary to become a priest when his own father was an Anglican reverend. It was the one thing Papa never spoke about. And I knew it had not only severed Papa's relationship with Jefferson, but was also what had put the nail in the coffin of Mama and his marriage. As I grew older, I noticed that Mama had stopped caring for Papa. And she couldn't care what anyone thought, felt, or said about it.

"So Ekene is around?"

"Yes. He said he's home to begin work on his building. That small boy, barely older than Lincoln, yet he's already about to become a landlord."

I couldn't help wondering if that was the reason Papa didn't look happy when he saw his own children, especially his sons. Perhaps he felt his own children were less accomplished compared to Mazi Okoli's. Papa was very fond of Ekene and his twin sister, Ebube. Every Christmas, when we were much younger, Papa had always given them Christmas presents, which he would personally hand over to them. Sometimes the presents were new clothes and shoes, just like Papa bought for us, and sometimes he would give them biscuits, sweets, and fruits. Mama had never complained or interfered when Papa had done these things; after all, they were his cousin's children. Although they were the only cousin's children for whom he seemed to care.

"I'll go to see Ekene before I leave. It's been a long time since I saw him."

"I'm sure he'll be very happy to see you."

I cleared my throat before saying: "Okay, sir, erm, Papa, I'm here to tell you I've gained admission to the University of Lagos. I will be leaving in two weeks' time."

He looked at me and said nothing. So I waited for the weight of what I had said to sink in. Even though I didn't think he would be too worried about my going, I was certain he would worry about my leaving so soon — a decision I'd made the moment the letter had arrived, even though Sister Adaora had said it was too hasty. But I saw no reason for waiting any longer. Lagos was beckoning and pulling me to herself so hard, I couldn't resist. Among other things, I couldn't wait to get as far away as I could from Uncle Ikemefuna.

"The University of Lagos is fine. Bishop Onuora's last son is schooling there. Also, my friend Chief Iweka Aforjulu's son is there. I think he's in his final year."

I pretended not to know he was talking about Chinua because a simple mention of his name was all it would take for him to cancel everything.

"So your mother does not mind?"

"At first she did, but I was able to convince her. Even Sister Adaora was opposed to the idea."

He looked away, staring through the open window, then leaned forwards and brought out a wad of notes from the cupboard. After counting out some, he put them in an envelope.

"Take this, for now — I'll be sending the rest of your school and accommodation fees in due course."

I opened the envelope and gasped at the amount of money I saw in there. I wanted to ask him from where he'd got so much money but I knew that would be considered impolite.

"Thank you, Papa," I said, touching his knee, smiling.

"Take care of yourself, Udonwa," he said and covered my hand with his, before adding, "and please come home often to see me."

PART II

Nine

On the day I arrived in Lagos, the bus driver made two stops before we arrived at our final destination, a motor park in a town called Alafia. Through the bus window, I saw a sea of people moving around, relaxed but with purpose. I had never seen so many people at the same time, or even thought it was possible, not even during Iruama's annual ofala festival. It felt as if there were thousands of people in a space three times too small for them. Like a dozen tankers of water being poured into an already overflowing dam, I couldn't help feeling that my arrival only made it worse.

Lagos is mostly an island, and its shortage of land space had resulted in the overcrowding of people and buildings. It was clear right away that every space would be shared with the next person. One of my course mates would later tell the story about her next-door neighbour whose bedroom windows were so close to hers that she had heard him make loud farts numerous times, had heard his snoring as he slept each night, and had even heard him and his partner moaning in their frequent throes of ecstasy.

Aunt Nene lived in the Sabo area of Lagos, which was not very far from my campus. This made her insist I attend lectures from her home to save costs on hostel accommodation. I agreed, even though I knew Papa would not approve. But after a month, I found shared off-campus accommodation closer to my school. Aunt Nene allowed me to leave on the condition that I spent every other weekend at her house.

Oyingbo Market was one of the many open markets in Lagos and where Aunt Nene did her monthly household shopping. In my second month in Lagos, I accompanied her and her house help, Ngozika, to the market. From the entrance gates, we were bombarded by hawkers who were not asking but insisting we buy their wares by shoving them in our faces. As for the stall owners, a simple glance in their direction was considered an immediate interest in what they were selling. All I heard around me were shouts of "Aunty, come and buy now! Look this side, fresh tomatoes re o, straight from the farm!" ... "My epo is not mixed with ororo, o; this one is fresh palm oil!" ... "Aunty, fine Aunty, buy from me today now!" — and on and on it continued from one stall to the next. It did not matter if you were interested in buying their wares or not. It did not matter that you were merely looking around because your eyes could only stay focused in one direction for so long; you had to buy because they had to make a living. This was so unlike Iruama, where buyers already knew what they wanted to buy and headed straight to the stall which they knew stocked the item they wanted to purchase. Even at Awka's busiest market, that was the case. To be fair, there was far more on offer at Oyingbo Market, but I still felt the aggression of the "I-must-make-sales-today-or-I-will-die" system of trading was too uncomfortable to ignore. I would discover later that there was a certain group of people who did not seem to care about this assertion as much as others.

At this market, and I supposed for others around Lagos, the haggling that went on between customers and traders was another strange phenomenon. Where Mama would haggle with almost every seller in Iruama in the good-spirited faith of getting a bargain, in Lagos markets, I discovered that traders, of whom ninety-nine percent were women of Yoruba origin, could decide not to sell to you if they felt you were haggling their ware too low. Some traders would resort to raining abuse on shoppers whom they accused of trying to steal from them by trying to make them sell their wares below cost price.

As we made our way through the market, I assessed all the items we'd bought. Not only did we require assistance from two of the young baggage carriers lurking around in the market, but our arms were filled with various items, because Aunt Nene's monthly shopping was done as if in preparation for a feast. It was a spending that was highly unnecessary, especially seeing that the only people at her home were her and her husband, my cousin Kosisonna, Ngozika, and, after I moved out, a fortnightly visit from me.

The butchers and meat sellers occupied the stalls behind the market where they displayed their meat on tables soaked in the dried blood of the slaughtered animals. Your nose, eyes, and ears would be assaulted when you neared their tables. And the foulness would linger for days. No other smell can compare to a smell that feels as though a giant bloated cow farted into your open mouth and left fragments of its rotten offal behind.

A puddle of putrid water in a rain-induced pothole was right next to almost all the stalls, making it impossible for any right-thinking person to shop without holding their breath. I imagined that the only reason people exhaled was that they needed to breathe.

I continued to hold my breath intermittently as we walked from stall to stall until we were stopped in our tracks when we heard shouts of "Ole, ole, ole!" Thief, thief, thief!

I kept looking around expecting to see someone running or being chased as I'd been told happened when you heard the word "ole" in quick succession. I was starting to feel dizzy from swivelling my head in different directions to find the thief, when I realized no one was running because no one was being chased. Rather, a woman the size of a sumo wrestler was screaming at a customer, who was screaming back. They were raining such abuse on each other, taking it in turns to shout, "Thief," that it took a while to figure out who was who. Some people had gathered and were trying to pacify the big woman, who was the more vocal of the two.

"Stupid useless woman! Old witch!" said the big woman in Yoruba as Aunt Nene, Ngozika, myself, and other onlookers stared. "You want to reap where you did not sow. Why don't you come and take all my goods for free? Thief!"

"You are the one who is a thief — who would sell that worthless thing for one hundred naira? Useless mad woman!"

"Ashewo huuu … shio!" the big woman ululated at the other woman, who had already moved on to the other side of the market.

"This is what we see in this Lagos," said Aunt Nene as the crowd dispersed.

Ngozika's giggling did not decrease my shock as I continued to look back in disbelief.

"Aren't they worried about chasing serious customers away if they keep treating people like this?" I said.

"It doesn't bother them. Women like that big woman are not your regular poor market trader. The ones who behave this way are usually the big businesswomen who have two or more stalls in this market and elsewhere. Didn't you hear her being referred to as 'alhaja'? That title does not come cheap — at most it involves a pilgrimage to Mecca, among other expenses. These are big businesswomen; on a non-market day or during their Muslim holidays, you wouldn't recognize them. They will dress up in the most expensive lace in town, deck themselves out from head to toe in the costliest gold jewellery. And the next thing, you'll see them in cars jetting off to owambe."

I nodded to all that Aunt Nene said, but I was still confounded by this strange new world.

. . .

Aunt Nene's house was one of only six houses on a street called Dalley Close. The house wasn't the most beautiful on the street in terms of structure, but it was the only one with two buildings in the same compound. Behind the duplex where Aunt Nene lived with her family was a two-storey building with four flats in the front and back which Aunt Nene and Uncle Patrick let out. I had never seen a yellow exterior to a house before now. The interior also showed off Aunt Nene's eccentric taste.

Aunt Nene's husband, Uncle Patrick, was a customs officer before he'd become a lawyer, and then he'd stopped practising law altogether. Between the two professions and years
of service, he had been able to amass enough wealth to erect
these two buildings in a big city like Lagos. In addition,
Aunt Nene owned two shops in Yaba's Tejuosho Market not
very far from her house. She had two salesgirls in each shop,
but would still go to the shops first thing every morning.
What Aunt Nene lacked in interior decor taste, she had in
fashion and style. I used to think in the first few weeks after
I'd arrived in Lagos that she was a mobile advertisement for
her business, as she had and wore almost all the clothes she
sold at her shop. Whenever her friend Aunty Rozito came
to the house, they would both go through different materials until they decided on one in which to attend another
owambe party. These parties, I soon understood, made up
the fabric of Lagos and its residents, with a party occurring
every other Saturday.

My first time at the market was one of those Saturdays.
Driving into the compound, we sighted Aunty Rozito and another lady all dressed up and sitting on the veranda waiting.
The excess of gold jewellery and beaded necklaces they were
wearing looked just about enough to pay for my school fees till
graduation.

I greeted the two women before dropping the heavy bags
of foodstuff on the floor next to the door as Aunt Rozito held
onto my hand. Ngozika and Aunt Nene had gone past me into
the house with the rest of the items.

"Ah, Udonwa, I didn't know you were around. How is
school?"

"Fine, Aunty."

"Joo, who is this beauty?" said the other woman, while a smiling Aunty Rozito still held on to my hand, preventing me from going into the house.

"Ah, Risi, this is Nene's sister's daughter Udonwa. She's studying Medicine at UNILAG."

"Ehn, ehn ... Where has she been hiding her? And am I the only one seeing what I'm seeing?" the lady said.

"What are you seeing?" said Aunt Nene, laughing as she came out to the veranda to join us.

"Her beauty, of course. Do you know, for a minute I thought I was looking at Mammy Water," the lady, Risi, said, her mouth wide open.

"God forbid," Aunt Nene said, snapping her fingers over her head in disgust. "My niece is not a mermaid, please; she's just beautiful like the rest of her sisters. Wait till you see Adaora and Nneora — beauty started and finished in their bodies."

"Thank you, o, Risi. I was also screaming like a mad person the first time I saw her. Such beauty is very rare indeed. Can you see her skin? So supple, kai!" said Aunty Rozito, running her fingers up and down my hand.

I stood there giggling like a schoolgirl, unable to move past them because they were blocking the entrance to the house.

"If only Jafaru, my son, were of age, o hei. So this is how I'll miss such a beautiful daughter-in-law," Risi said in mock lament, exposing three gold-capped teeth in her upper jaw.

"You're talking of small Jafaru, how I wish Okey, my young-er brother in America, would visit home like normal people do. At least he won't have to worry too much about choosing a wife. Abi, Nene, my friend?" Aunty Rozito said, smiling.

"Enough of the harassment, ladies. We have to leave early before Sunny starts to perform, o. I promised myself I would relax and have fun today," Aunt Nene said and stood up to go and change into one of her flashy outfits.

The two ladies got up to make room, finally moving their frames away from the passage in order for me to gain entry.

As we walked into the house, Aunt Nene turned to me and said: "I'll be back before your uncle returns. You can rest before lunch is ready. I told Ngozika to make your favourite, jollof rice."

Later, as they all walked to the car, I watched from my bedroom window as their heavy attire dragged behind them.

Ten

D r. Wilcox was concluding his lecture for the week when I walked into Introduction to Chemistry 101 that morning. Thankfully, his back was turned to the class and he hadn't seen me walk in. As one of the meanest lecturers in the college of medicine, Dr. Wilcox did not think twice about failing any student absent from his lectures. But Fridays, when his classes were held, were always difficult to attend because of the weekend spirit already in the air, and for me it meant running off immediately to Aunt Nene's house to eat proper home-cooked meals after days of food from the school canteen. Food that I suspected was possibly prepared in an unsanitary environment because of how often it upset my stomach.

Facing the class, he began reading what he had written on the board as he closed the textbook in his hand. He positioned his glasses firmly on his face before putting his hands into his pockets as he paced the lecture hall, peering into notebooks from desk to desk.

"Studying the chemistry of diseases in humans and in animals involves the development of new drugs, and this in turn involves chemical analysis and synthesis of new compounds. The chemistry of the disease, as well as how the drug affects the human body, must be studied because a drug may work well in animals, but not in humans. This should be your take-away from this course, if you get nothing else. The future of healthcare depends largely on chemistry."

With that last statement, he walked back to his desk in front of the class, gathered up his belongings and left. One after the other, students exited the lecture hall, their voices getting louder as we all scampered outside. Many of the students were rushing off to their hostels to get ready for the weekend; some were headed to the nightclubs, some to parties, and some had planned a weekend getaway with their lovers, while a small number were actually heading home to be with their families, and I was part of the last group.

• • •

A week before our final exams of my first year were due to start, they were cancelled indefinitely. The body in charge of the academic staff of Nigerian universities went on strike, as the lecturers had not received their salaries in six months. Not getting paid was a normal occurrence for Nigerian civil-service workers. It was baffling how any worker was expected

to feed their families and take care of many other responsibilities without receiving their due salaries. Apparently, the last
strike action had been called off after months of deliberations
with the government. But this time around the government
had refused to meet with the association heads on the grounds
that their demands were becoming too greedy. So, in order to
register their displeasure, the lecturers had embarked on an
indefinite strike. This was frustrating, as writing these particular examinations would signify the end of my first year as
a medical student.

I had informed Aunt Nene I thought it best to go to Enugu
to spend time with Nneora during the break, but she had refused and insisted I should rather help her out in the shop
because she suspected one of the salesgirls of stealing. Nneora,
Aunt Nene said, could come stay here with me instead.

Lincoln had been posted to Lagos for the mandatory youth
service year, which he had just completed. He was now staying
with a friend in Ajao Estate, but had arrived this morning to
talk to Aunt Nene and Uncle Patrick. When he had called
to inform me he was coming, I knew his girlfriend, Anuli,
couldn't resist tagging along. There was something about Anuli
that screamed desperate in the ugliest way.

I was just coming down the stairs of Aunt Nene's house to
greet Lincoln when I heard Aunt Nene's and Uncle Patrick's
voices rising.

"How can you say that, Patrick? Eh, Patrick, how can you
say that? Since Lincoln came here and started that job at Ojees,
he's been influencing this boy. He no longer wants to study
engineering but now wants to be a musician. A musician,
Patricki!"

"All I'm saying is, let him follow his heart. His dreams."

"Yes, and that is engineering. Have you forgotten how he liked to fix things as a little boy? Besides, don't pretend you don't know that many musicians are drug addicts."

"C'mon now, Nene, you're being ridiculous. Not all musicians use drugs and you know it. Please stop with your insinuations."

"So you're saying that Kosisonna was born to be a musician, eh, Patrick? A musician?"

"Look, Nene, I'm not saying that, nor am I saying he can't be an engineer. But he has a passion which is singing. Have you heard that boy sing? Have you heard him play the guitar?" said Uncle Patrick. "Take me, for example: I became a customs officer out of necessity, but I always knew I was born to practise law. Leave this boy to pursue his dreams; times are changing, and at a fast rate."

I had just reached the entrance to the sitting room when Lincoln interjected: "Aunt Nene, Uncle is right, you know. Kosisonna performed at the club the other day and, I tell you, it was awesome. He got a standing ovation from everyone. Especially when he gave that rendition of 'Love Like a River.'"

I greeted my brother and his girlfriend before taking a seat on the couch opposite them.

"I thought you'd never come downstairs," said Lincoln, as charming as ever.

"I was downstairs already, just in the dining room."

"You know Anuli, right?" he said, without looking at her.

"Yes, we met the last time."

"You look beautiful as always, Udonwa," said Anuli, slipping her arm underneath Lincoln's, which he promptly retracted. Her lips were coated in shimmering red lipstick, and lined with what appeared to be black eye-liner. Her mouth looked as if it were about to burst open as she chomped and blew bubbles with her chewing gum.

"Thanks," I muttered before turning to Aunt Nene, who was frowning in disgust.

"Not only love like a river, it will soon turn into a river for real and drown you all ... mtchew," Aunt Nene said in Igbo, in response to Lincoln's earlier statement, making me burst out laughing. It wasn't just what she had said but the manner in which she had said it. Soon everyone was laughing, including Aunt Nene herself. Aunt Nene was often serious, except with her friends, but today she laughed and laughed. Rather than talk about our family, especially her sister, my mother, Aunt Nene preferred talking about her shops, the money she had or hadn't made that week, or who she suspected was stealing from her. It was a relief to see her lighter side around her family.

"Please, Mom, I'll earn my biggest pay from this upcoming gig. Let me do that one if you don't want me singing forever, please, Mom," said Kosisonna, looking endearingly at Aunt Nene.

Just like that, Aunt Nene was serious again. And, without another word, she got up and left the sitting room. I followed her into the kitchen.

"You can at least let him try, Aunty. Let him get tired of it, or even fail. If you continue like this, he'll think it's a big deal and keep defying you. He'll never want to stop."

The notion of what I was saying was strange, yet I was beginning to understand the logic behind it: teenage boys always seemed to defy their parents. At least that's what I'd gleaned from Lincoln, who did it all the time. In fact, he was still doing it. If Papa said to Lincoln, "Take a right turn," Lincoln would turn left before heading straight. He hated being told what to do, especially by Papa. But while Papa hated being defied by Lincoln, Anuli saw Lincoln's defiance as a sign of his unending love. As far as she was concerned, the sun rose and set in Lincoln's eyes. I could not understand if Anuli's infatuation was because he trimmed his beard into thin sideburns which accentuated his tight jawline, or because his light complexion appeared to beam every day. It couldn't be Lincoln's personality. He now looked exactly as Mama would often call him: "omuma asa aru" — the one who has no need to bathe.

When Aunt Nene had calmed down, we went back to the sitting room. Lincoln was in the middle of telling Uncle Patrick about what he had been doing since he'd finished his mandatory service.

"I've been looking for a job, as you all know. I tried to get posts in reputable organizations like banks and oil companies, but nothing has seemed to be forthcoming. Every day, I would go from one organization and government entity, but none was able to offer me anything. In the end, I found myself as a DJ in Ojees Nite Club, a place I used to hang out in."

Anuli shook her head as she wiped invisible tears from her eyes.

Lincoln continued: "Ojees is the same place I've been taking Kosisonna and where they are about to sign us on permanently. The club management stressed we have to be a team, otherwise the deal won't go through because they want both a DJ and a singer. They really liked Kosisonna's last performance."

Lincoln had clearly been hoping that, hearing this, Aunt Nene would understand his plight and how much he needed Kosisonna to sing at the club. But Aunt Nene just sat and listened without response.

The first time I'd heard my cousin sing, I had been in the shower trying to sing as well, and I'd thought it was my voice that was sounding so good. The next day, while making lunch in the kitchen, I heard the voice singing again, this time accompanied by a guitar, and only then did I realize to whom it belonged. Ngozika had squealed that I hadn't heard anything yet, that Kosisonna was the best little Black thing since Michael Jackson and I should wait until he sang one of MJ's songs to me. Without any persuasion, he gave a rendition of "Man in the Mirror" that gave me goosebumps.

Now, Aunt Nene took a deep breath and said: "Okay, but it's only because of Lincoln, that's all. He needs that job."

I wrapped my arms around her. "Thank you, Aunty." Despite my frustration with Lincoln, I wanted him to succeed.

Kosisonna screamed in delight at the good news. Anuli joined him, screaming louder than him and longer than necessary. It took a stern look from Lincoln to make her realize she appeared like someone dancing to music that was no longer playing.

Eleven

Nneora arrived a week after Lincoln, and from the moment she walked into my room with her luggage, I noticed something different about her.

"Nne!" I squealed and ran into her arms.

"That's enough, Udonwa," said Nneora after we'd held each other for a while. "You'd think I was returning from a long trip abroad."

"Well, it feels like it. And I'm sorry about not coming to Enugu again. Aunty would not allow me," I said and sat on the bed beside her.

"That's fine. Lagos is bubblier than Enugu, anyway. It's even worse now with the strike; the place is like a ghost town. Anyway, on to more important news." It took much begging from me before Nneora eventually said: "Okay, okay, I'll tell you. Don't eye me to death, biko. Papa now has a brand-new Mercedes-Benz. Guess who gave it to him?"

"Who?"

"I said you should guess, not ask me."

"Okay, I know. It's from the mission office. They are thanking him for all his years of hard work and service."

"It's not only the mission house; it's the Archbishop of Canterbury himself!" She pulled a face at me before saying: "Biko, the car was a gift from Ekene!"

"Ekene, Mazi Okoli's son?"

"How many other Ekenes do you know?"

"Our cousin Ekene bought a car for Papa? Wonders shall never end."

"It's not a small wonder, o — both the act and the car."

She got up to begin unpacking her clothes and putting them in the wardrobe. And I couldn't help noticing that there were several white overalls and medical equipment in her luggage.

"Is that a stethoscope?" I asked her.

"Yes," she said, and carried on unpacking as though it were the most natural thing in the world for a microbiology student to have a stethoscope in her bag.

"Am I right in what I'm thinking, Nneora, or do you now check for the heartbeat and pulse of micro-organisms?"

"*Doctor* Udonwa, you are one funny girl. How will I know what you're thinking if you don't say it? Am I now a mind reader?"

"Okay. Nneora Ilechukwu, are you studying medicine?"

"Yes, Udonwa Ilechukwu, I'm studying medicine."

The manner with which she said this, as if this news would not change our lives — her life — forever, was too much for me to bear.

"If Papa finds out, you're dead."

"Who will tell him. You? Besides, I don't think he can do anything."

"How on earth did you manage to change your course to medicine? Didn't you —"

"Udonwa, must you always ask questions, eh? Anyway, if you must know, I changed after my first year. I couldn't put it off any longer. I went to a medical students' conference with Nnamdi and I knew it was time. He's always said how I would make a great doctor ... Actually, he said I will be the best doctor ever — after him, that is. But anyway, there and then at the conference I made up my mind and made the necessary arrangements. The rest, as they say, is history. No one knows except Lincoln and Aunt Nene. Aunt Nene said if Papa finds out and refuses to keep paying my fees that she will gladly take over. I had no idea she hated him that much, Udo — you need to hear some of the things she said about him. I almost felt sorry for Papa," she said, laughing.

"And you couldn't tell me?"

She did not say a word but rather gave me a look that suggested that she could not trust me not to let slip to Papa, and I couldn't help wondering if she was right. But if I were to do that, it would have been out of concern for her and not for anything else. And only Lincoln and Aunt Nene knew about it, which meant that Mama's only sister was more involved in our lives than we were able to admit. Trust her to be a part of anything that went against Papa's wishes. When we were younger, Aunt Nene had been the only one from Mama's family who had been bold enough to challenge Papa and tell him off to his face. On her only visit to our house, Papa had called her a mad woman who controlled her husband. Aunt Nene had stormed out after swearing never to set foot in our house again, and, true to her word, she hadn't. When Mama wanted to speak to her, she would go to Iruama Community Centre and use their telephone to call her, and sometimes Aunt Nene would send her money. But Mama had been too busy caring for her family to worry about what her siblings thought of her husband. A husband she herself did not think much of but would never admit out loud. Sister Adaora had been the first out of all of us to visit Aunt Nene and her family in Lagos, but by then Sister Adaora was already almost finished nursing college and I now suspect it had been Aunt Nene who had put her up to leaving home early like she had.

"Did you see Anuli outside when you were coming in?"

"How could I miss her? With that bright red lipstick she has on those fat lips of hers. Of course I saw her, chomping gum as usual."

"She's here every day since Lincoln arrived. I don't think I like her very much."

"You are still thinking? Me, I know I don't like her. But you need to hear how UNEC boys crawl around her like ants to a heap of sugar. That thing she has between her legs must be original Eke Iruama honey."

Even though I didn't want to laugh, I couldn't help myself.

"Eh, but the boys themselves who are following her around like you say — aren't they also guilty of the same thing? Why should only she be referred to as loose? What of Lincoln — shouldn't he also be branded a womanizer? After all, it takes two to tango."

"It's like you've not learned anything yet at your university. So you don't know it's a man's world? That when a man sleeps around, he's a stud, but when a woman does the same thing, she's a slut?"

"That's not fair."

"Welcome to the world, Udonwa. This world is not a fair place, especially Nigeria."

"Hmm, na wah. Come to think of it, do you know he has slept with her in this house before? Last weekend, when Aunt Nene and Uncle Patrick travelled to Port Harcourt. That night I couldn't sleep. The noise they were making, Chineke! Anuli is so stupid, sleeping with a man who clearly has no regard for her."

"Like I said, Udonwa, Lincoln is a man. If a woman decides to be a kezaya, a *distributor*, do you think any right-thinking man will refuse to *collect*?"

"But Aunt Nene and Uncle Patrick knew they were going to spend the night here. They didn't even try to tell Anuli to go back home to her house. The whole thing is embarrassing. Papa would never have allowed such a thing."

"Papa is a hypocrite."

"Nneora!"

"Yes, you heard me right. He is, and a big one for that matter. Please don't get me started, Udonwa. I just arrived and I need to rest."

"I still think Uncle Patrick is too liberal-minded for his own good — allowing his wife's nephew to bring a girl into his house. Can he swear that he did not know what they would do under his own roof in his absence? It does not speak well of a responsible Igbo man."

"You like to talk nonsense, Udonwa. So you don't know Lincoln is old enough to get married, eh kwa? Or don't you think Uncle Patrick understands Lincoln because he must have done the same thing at his age? Look, Udo, we know you're a virgin, but please stop carrying on as if the rest of the world were the devil. Lincoln is just being a man."

Within seconds of thinking about Nneora's statement, the logic behind her reasoning became clear to me. I needed no further elaboration, and neither did she provide any because she could tell that I already knew what the answer was. So I settled for the specifics of the *how*, and not the *if*.

"So how long have you been having sex? Wasn't it painful?" I said softly.

"How long, I can't remember. Was it painful? Yes, but only the first time, and just for a brief second. Afterwards, it was as if nothing had happened. It was beautiful, Udo. Still is. Nnamdi knows what he's doing," she concluded in Igbo.

I gave her a look that said she must be another person in my sister's body. But then again, since she'd arrived, I had already established that fact. With her back turned to me, I looked her over and noticed her thighs were balanced on her waist like two yam tubers, strong and firm. Her hips were protruding on both sides and appeared as though, if touched, they would wobble like two mushy mangoes. Yes, she hadn't been living on food alone. Something else had been feeding those hips.

"Biko, wipe that look of disgust from your face. Sex is a natural part of human life. Humans need sex to survive," Nneora sneered as she put away the last of her belongings into the wardrobe.

"Sex is for married people. Marriages need sex to thrive, Nneora."

"And how has that helped Mama and Papa, or were they not having sex? Why didn't their marriage thrive? Biko, I see nothing remotely wrong with sex before marriage except for the Bible saying it is. And why it says so baffles me because it's the most beautiful thing ever. That merging of two bodies into one ... ooh."

"God have mercy," I said, staring at her with my eyes and mouth wide open.

"Amen. And on all of us, including you," she retorted and walked out of the room.

If I were not also at university, I would have said it was the university life that had got to Nneora. But I knew that people chose their own path to follow. Some were on a high-speed train to God knows where while others were taking their time. Sex, as far as I was concerned, was the last thing I would engage in as a young, unmarried woman. I'd already seen first hand what it did to the minds of young girls who weren't prepared for its addictive effects.

Twelve

Chinua and I started dating after he returned from America. When I arrived at UNILAG for the first time, I had expected to see him, but on going to his department, I had been informed he was one of the final-year engineering students chosen for an exchange program to a university in America for eighteen months. Even though I'd been disappointed, I knew if he wanted to hear from me he would find a way. And he did. One evening, after a late class study session, I had marched straight to the canteen with hunger pangs threatening to rip my stomach open. Frustrated to find their meals had run out, I was contemplating where to go next to find some food when I found Chinua standing under one of the many canopies outside the canteen chatting with a group of guys. Looking as confident as ever with his hands in his pockets, he had walked over the moment he saw me, smiling widely. On noticing that the plastic bag in my hand was holding an empty bowl, he offered to buy me dinner at a restaurant off-campus. And eating out was pretty much what we'd been doing since then.

"Come in. You said you'd be here by six. It's past eight already," I said, frowning. Chinua was a habitual latecomer. When I realized this, I had been shocked by it. I had told him he acted like an American most of the time but when it concerned keeping to time he was a typical African who thought being late was fashionable.

"I know. I was caught up in the office. Today was one of those hectic days."

"Excuses, excuses," I said, rolling my eyes at him.

"Are we going to go through the same phase of sulking for the rest of the evening again because I arrived late?"

"You are over two hours late today, Chinua. You know I'm not an evening person. I'm likely to fall asleep in the restaurant."

"Then let's stay in … But I know you'll reject the idea too."

I gave him a look, before saying: "Okay, fine. Just give me a few minutes to get ready."

After months of the strike action, it had finally been called off for us to write our exams before commencing second year. This was almost my third year in Lagos, but I was still at the start of my second year at the university. At this rate, I would graduate in my thirties if the strikes continued in this manner.

University education in Nigeria was laughable, but people like Chinua had it good. He'd told me if he hadn't been picked for the exchange program, he would have transferred to another school in America to finish his studies, but as fate would have it, he'd been chosen for the program. And just when the program was ending, the strike was called off. Afterwards, he'd received a job offer in the States, which he'd turned down because he'd sensed something was waiting for him back home. He liked to think I was made for him. Except when I refused to give in to his request of sharing his bed.

"I wonder when we'll have a normal relationship like a normal couple. And I know the next thing you'll say is: 'A relationship is not all about s–e–x.' Damn, you can't even say the word without spelling it. It's not a bad word, you know ..."

I could hear him all the way from the bedroom where I was getting ready but pretended not to by not replying. Chinua had been trying to get me to sleep with him for a while now, saying he'd waited long enough. The only thing left for him to do was to give me an ultimatum about leaving me if I didn't give in. And I hadn't figured out how I would react if that situation presented itself.

I shared my off-campus flat with two other women, Nifemi and Amara. But I might as well be the only person living there because they were hardly ever home. If Nifemi wasn't with her boyfriend, Tunde, she was with one of her rich alhaji and chief lovers, who paid for her expensive lifestyle. Amara, on the other hand, was a divorced mother of three and the eldest of the three of us. She had got married at her family's insistence when she was nineteen because they were in desperate need of a helping hand to alleviate their suffering. She said they were so poor that the family everyone knew to be the poorest in their face-me-I-face-you compound once referred to them as "that poor family in room thirty-five." After she got married, her husband had begun to shower her with beatings and abuse instead of the wealth he'd promised her and her family. To make matters worse, he had banned her family from visiting. Even Amara's mother had not been allowed to come for the mandatory omugwo: a time where a new mother is cared for, usually by her own mother, with the necessary childcare and help required during her period of confinement. She said she had to care for her infant child all by herself. Since she couldn't seek help from her own family, Amara had decided to seek assistance from his. But, according to her, that had spelled the end of her already-shaky marriage. So, after seven and a half years of wasting her life away, as she put it, with three children, Amara began to look for ways of escape. Her family was on her side, seeing that their saviour had turned out to be their destroyer. Apparently, on the day she left, she had taken a bag filled with her children's clothing and food to last a few days and nothing else. There was no way she could have managed to carry anything else, anyway. With her children safe with her mother in the village, she had got a university-entrance examination form and prayed to God that, for the sake of her three young children, he should help her pass if it was the last thing he did for her. Although it was baffling what she got up to in the name of studying; she was doing anything but studying. Amara had repeated one year already and was carrying over so many courses, it was uncertain she would pass this year. And on the many occasions I had broached the subject with her, she had replied that her studies wouldn't provide the money for her to take care of her hungry children.

As for Nifemi, her family background should have meant she had no business dating men for money. Her rich investment-banker father provided everything for her, but she was one of those spoiled children who had been so shielded from the real world that when she had finally got a taste of it, she had gone berserk from the sheer amount of freedom she had. She had been dating Tunde since secondary school, but as he lived outside Lagos, he had no idea of her double life.

Both Amara and Nifemi were shocked by my relationship with Chinua, telling me they'd yet to see a man as besotted by and dedicated to a woman as he was. They never failed to remind me that most men would have dumped me within a few weeks of sexual rejection.

"I'm ready," I said, heading towards the front door.

He looked at me and got up quickly, whistling. Standing with me at the door, he took my waist in his hands and planted a kiss on my mouth. As he made to part my lips, I pursed them. With his eyes closed, he took a deep breath, his breathing uneven and slow.

"I don't know how much longer I can take this, Udom. This is too much for one person."

"Chinua, please, I can't do this. You know I'm not ready yet ... And I'm —"

I was still talking when he took me in his arms and began to kiss me. His tongue slid in and out of my mouth and he was soon licking my neck, face, and ears. He was like a hungry lion and I a sacrificial little lamb. His fingers were working the buttons of my blouse by the time I caught my breath. His shirt was already tossed to the couch, and he wasted no time reaching into his pocket for his wallet. My heart skipped when I saw him pull out a condom, prompting my mind to return to full gear. I shoved him off so fast he fell backwards.

"What do you think you're doing?"

"I ... thought ... I ..." he stammered, staring at me with eyes covered in layers of passion.

"Will you put that thing away right now? Is something wrong with your head?" I barked at him in Igbo.

"But … But … I thought … Never mind. I'll put it away. Dammit, Udom, lighten up. You're too uptight. Jesus Christ! It's just a condom."

"Don't use your stupid American slang on me. And don't you ever pull that stunt with me again."

He put the condom back in his wallet. "I said I was sorry, okay?"

"No, you didn't."

"Okay, Udom, I'm sorry."

I looked down and saw that his jeans were pulled tight by a throbbing penis.

"You have to leave right now."

"I've said sorry, now. I'm not going anywhere," he said, heading straight to the bathroom. When he emerged a few minutes later, cleaned up and normal again, he picked up his car keys from the table and headed towards the door. "All right, Udom, it's fine. I'll go. Whenever you're ready, I'll be waiting."

Just like Sister Adaora, Chinua called me Udom instead of Udo or Udonwa like everyone else did. He said it gave him a certain sense of calm — that I was *his*. Especially since Udom means "my peace."

"You don't have to go," I said and sighed. "There's a new restaurant in town, next to the Olympiad. I thought we should try it out."

He wiped his forehead and shook his head. "Okay."

When we got to his car, he walked around to the front passenger side and opened the door for me as always, as though nothing unpleasant had transpired between us earlier. We drove in silence for a few minutes before he said: "Let's hit

Higgles afterwards — I promised Tobe and Franklin we'll meet up there." His hands were tapping the steering wheel as he manoeuvred along the bumpy roads.

"Please, not again, Chinua. You'll have to disappoint them tonight."

His eyes shot straight at me. "And why would I do that?"

"Have you forgotten so soon what happened the last time we went? I've had enough for today, please."

"I thought I already promised there wouldn't be any repeat of that? Jeez, Udom."

I looked away and tried to concentrate on the road ahead while stealing glances at him. Chinua's nose, like his brother Ifenna's, was the type people refer to as an "oyibo nose" — pointed and pert. But his smile made his mouth the most beautiful part of his body and he seemed to know this. Today, he had on a white shirt, one of the three I'd given him for his birthday. I liked the way it popped against his chocolate skin, which was now shimmering, his sleeves rolled to the elbow like always. Chinua took care of his skin like a woman. He used a specific cocoa-butter lotion and had another cream for his head called Sportin' Waves, which made him smell like freshly baked bread with butter and jam. And he wore the most delicious aftershave, scented with burnt lemon zest. I would say to him he smelled like what I imagine a white man's breakfast would smell like, and he would look at me, smiling through an immaculate set of teeth, and peer down my face until I felt weak at the knees. Yet the thought of giving myself to him scared me to the point that I would completely shut off.

Nneora told me I was taking him for granted, and that soon he'd find someone who appreciated him. But my question remained: why should sex be the only way to show appreciation to my boyfriend? Surely, buying gifts and providing moral support still counted for something in a relationship? I loved being with Chinua and enjoyed spending time with him, but there was no telling what he was capable of after a night out at the club.

"Fine, if you insist, we won't go to the club," he said with a deep sigh. "But I need to do something fun with you. Eating just won't cut it."

"We could go to the museum?"

"The museum! Please tell me you're joking. Are you the most boring woman or what? What on earth do you want us to go to a museum for?"

"You know Lagos is an interesting place where you'll find enough women willing to relieve you from the bondage of boredom I've placed you in," I said, and turned my head to stare out the window.

"You don't have to be like that, Udom, I was —"

"You started it."

The last time we'd gone to the club, he had met up with Tobe and Franklin, friends from school days, and had had too much to drink — something I knew wouldn't have happened if we hadn't gone there. I still couldn't pinpoint if it was the blaring music, the shimmering disco lights, his friends, or a combination of all three. Chinua usually didn't drink, except on special occasions, of which birthdays did not even count. Although, when he did, he preferred brandy to beers. Later, when he'd dropped me off at my flat, he'd followed me to the door instead of leaving. I had just unlocked the door and made to say goodnight to him when he'd held the door back and ushered himself in and, just like earlier this evening, he hadn't been able to keep his hands to himself. It was safe to say that nightclubbing made him frisky and I had had enough of that for one day.

• • •

Sisi Calabar was the newest restaurant close to campus and, according to Nifemi and Amara, it beat the rest. The interior was basic, if not almost bare, but it appeared clean and tidy.

"I'm starving," said Chinua, scanning the menu as a waitress walked up to take our orders.

Chinua ordered the rice and fresh catfish pepper soup, while I went for my usual jollof rice.

I stared at him and picked up the menu again.

"I know you're wondering about my order," said Chinua when the waitress left. "It's a special Calabar delicacy. I ate it once on my work trip down there. I pray theirs is as scrumptious."

As he spoke, all I could think about was Papa's face wrinkling at what he would refer to as the audacity of messing up a whole fresh fish on rice. We Igbos only ate fresh fish with watery yam pottage.

"I'll pass, thanks. Rice and pepper soup? Never heard of it before."

"You'll never know unless you try it."

"I'm good with my jollof rice, thank you."

The waitress soon arrived with our meals and Chinua immediately dug in. As we ate, he kept repeating how delicious and delicately boiled the fish was.

"Are you sure it's not because you're hungry that it's making you sing about food like this?"

"No, Udom, this broth is way better than the one I ate in Calabar. This is something else. Wow."

After the meal, we were planning our next outing, but he couldn't contain his excitement and called for the waitress.

"She did nothing special, Chinua, she just served us food," I said to him, knowing exactly what he was about to do.

But my words fell on deaf ears, as Chinua brought out his wallet and, after paying for our meal, handed several notes to the waitress, who almost fainted from shock.

"This is for you for the delicious meal and for the excellent service. Keep it up," he said, grinning.

"Thank you so much, sir. Thank you, ma. God bless you, sir." She carried on genuflecting and repeating her greetings as we left the restaurant.

That was, without a doubt, the biggest tip that waitress had ever received. Although I'd told Chinua several times that, unlike in America, tips in Nigerian restaurants weren't necessary, he chose to ignore me. But, as we drove out of the restaurant parking lot, I stole a glimpse at his face, my mind still ringing with the waitress's million "thank you"s and "God bless you"s, and my heart swelled with admiration for my boyfriend's generous heart.

. . .

We arrived at the Nigerian National Museum in Onikan, straight from the restaurant. The first time I'd gone to the museum, on Kosisonna's birthday in my first year in Lagos, I hadn't expected to have fun, but I did.

However, it was saddening that there was almost no record of the Nigerian Civil War in the museum, and many others around the country, as I later got to know, with the War Museum in Umuahia serving as the official reminder and final resting place of the artefacts of the brutal Biafran War. When I'd brought up the subject with Uncle Patrick on that first visit, trying to figure out the reason behind it, he'd replied that he'd never thought about it before and it would be a good thing for all Nigerians and not just south-easterners to visit the war museum. This was a crucial point, because it appeared that many south-easterners who had children growing up outside of their parents' place of birth knew nothing about the war. A perfect example was Kosisonna. Aunt Nene was of the opinion that talking about the war was like reopening old sores, that the past was best left where it was. I vehemently disagreed with her reasoning. Why shouldn't a child be furnished with details about a war that had nearly wiped out his ancestry? To children like Kosisonna, who had grown up in Lagos, the Civil War had not happened because none of the books in his school syllabus had any record of it. In Lagos and virtually everywhere else outside of the south-east, it was as if Nigeria's history had been mainly peaceful, other than the slave trade.

Kosisonna told me that, from his primary school days, he had learned about the slave trade, and had visited the Badagry slave trade historical town with his school, even going to the house where Bishop Crowther had lived when he'd translated the English Bible into Yoruba. Indeed, children in Lagos had been taught everything except the crucial Biafran War. A war Nigeria had engaged in with eyes wide open but had chosen to obliterate from living memory.

General Murtala Mohammed's bullet-ridden car always fascinated me whenever I visited the national museum, and I would often imagine Papa being in his fancy new car and driving past, while Lincoln opened fire on him, until Papa collapsed with his head against the steering wheel. Tonight, with Chinua beside me, I was again staring at the bullet-ridden car so hard, Chinua put his arm around me and asked what I was thinking. When I told him, he didn't say a word but gave me a look I wasn't sure he would ever explain.

"Let's get out of here. This place gives me the creeps," he said and turned me away from the car.

Seeing the car again, and thinking about how the general had died, filled my head with thoughts about Papa. Why had Ekene bought such an expensive car for him? The last time I had visited home, I had been chatting with Mama after Papa had left for his early morning drive, a daily occurrence. When I'd asked Mama where Papa always went so early, she'd replied that he'd been doing that since the day the car had arrived. That he was either with the bishop or all over Iruama boasting that his nephew from abroad had bought him a car while his own children had abandoned him. Mazi Okoli also had the same V-boot Mercedes-Benz but his was maroon, while Papa's was white. According to Mama, Ekene had chosen the contrasting colours on purpose, saying that white signified the purity of heaven, which Papa, as a reverend, represented. "Between the two of them, Iruama is on fire. No one can drink water and put their cups down anymore because of the two Nwaokoli-Ilechukwu kinsmen," Mama had lamented.

As Chinua drove us out of Onikan, I had a deep sense that something was wrong with Papa. And it had something to do with that unnecessary car my cousin Ekene had bought for him.

Thirteen

"The major problem I have with holier-than-thou Christians is not that they are boring, or that they think they are God's personal assistant. Not even because they think they are the only true worshippers while every other person serves the devil …"

Nifemi was hitting out at Christians again, one of her favourite things to do; in fact, it was a hobby of which she never tired, although she maintained she was just stating the facts.

"Are you going to make your point, or will we have to endure line after line of reasons without arriving at any concrete conclusion? Udo, are you listening to this girl?" said Amara, concentrating on painting her toenails.

I wanted to stay out of it, so I continued with the novel in my hand. It was one of those stereotypical romance novels, with the knight in shining armour chasing after a distressed lady-in-waiting. A few pages in, I could already predict it would end with the filthy-rich, golden-haired, bronze-skinned, six-foot Lothario breaking down the damsel's metaphorical walls. The type of novels Lincoln had once claimed were written by bored pretentious writers who made up equally pretentious stories. I sighed but continued reading — anything was better than listening to Nifemi whine about Christians and all they were doing wrong. The last time the topic had come up, it hadn't gone well when I'd disagreed with her. For someone whose investment-banker father served as a deacon in a church, I found her attack on Christians bizarre.

"You see, eh, Nife, my friend, I know you don't like holier-than-thou Christians, or whatever you call them, but please make your point now, ahn ahn," Amara said as she carried on painting red dots over the sparkly-gold polish on her toenails. It was the most ghastly combination ever, but I kept my mouth shut. The last time she'd asked for my opinion on another dreadful combination, I'd just escaped with my head still attached to my neck.

"Okay o, since you people will not let me exhaust my list of why I do not like them, I'll limit it to the main point," Nifemi said, gulping the glass of juice in her hand.

"Exactly, and hurry up with it. The party is starting as we speak," Amara said and got up, carting her load of many colours to her bedroom before returning.

Every night for the past week, there'd been one party after the other happening in town, and Amara had insisted she wouldn't miss any of them. Nifemi also had her line of parties queued up and, between them, I wondered who was influencing whom. To say they were birds of a feather was to state the obvious — Nifemi, with her striding height and tar-like skin tone, and Amara, with hers resembling something dyed by the sun, with a stout length. They contrasted with and complemented each other perfectly. On campus, some of my classmates had expressed disapproval of our living arrangement, referring to Nifemi and Amara as wild, saying they couldn't understand what I had in common with them. But I did not have to be like them to share a home. We stayed out of one another's way most of the time because they were hardly around. And, more than anything, they provided the support I needed when I worried about being by myself. Apart from inviting me occasionally to their endless parties, invitations I'd always politely declined, I had never been cajoled into doing anything I didn't approve of. Even Nifemi knew to smoke only in the bathroom, and we'd insisted she take the master bedroom with the ensuite bathroom due to her habit. A habit no one on campus except the three of us knew she had.

"You know, for a deacon's daughter, you're something. You amaze me with your ideologies," I blurted out and immediately regretted it, for it seemed to spur Nifemi on even more.

"And you know you're one of those HTT folks right? Pastor's daughter, or what did you say your father was?"

"Nifemi, please be nice. Not in this flat, abeg, please," Amara tried to mollify her as Nifemi came to stand within a hair's breadth of my face, wagging her forefinger at me.

"But she started it. Did I mention her name?" said Nifemi, returning to her former position.

"All right, go on, it's okay," said Amara.

But I had heard enough, and I saw her action as my cue to leave. I picked up my book and went into my bedroom. Even from there, though, I could still hear her voice as she continued with her stupid ideologies and insinuations.

"You see what you've done?" said Amara.

"Mtchew, so what? Let her go, please. That girl's own is too much, abeg. Why won't I speak my mind about what I'm feeling, ehn? Is she the only pastor's kid in town?"

"So are you going to make that point, or should I go and get ready? I will not miss that party because of your nonsense today, I swear."

"Okay, fine. All these yeye *rubbish* HTT people have no idea what they are missing, that's all."

"Is that what you've been trying to say all night? Na wa for you, o."

"It's not just that. Think about it this way, seriously speaking now. Those folks think they are normal while the rest of us are the abnormal ones. But if I know one thing, it's that Christianity is not about stifling passions and living a fake life. I think it's all about choosing to do and live right. I mean, I'm not harming or hurting anyone."

I just shook my head. I knew without seeing their faces that Amara would agree wholeheartedly with Nifemi, even though she knew Nifemi was talking nonsense.

"You're right, you know. But try telling that to some people and they'll skin you alive. I mean, my ex-husband was the epitome of a Bible-reading Christian. He would read the thing through the night into the next morning, yet whatever he read had no impact on his life. At least, it had none on our marriage. That man made domestic abuse look like something children played on a playground."

"My point exactly, same with my father. Mister almighty deacon, yet I know he has a mistress whom he caters for like a wife. What am I even saying, much better than his own wife. Look eh, Amara, as far as I'm concerned, the whole Christian commission is about people going into the world and preaching the good news and not what the Christians of today are doing. Tell me, what is good about hell? Yet that's all we hear. If you do this, you'll go to hell. Hell awaits you if you don't do that. It's all about hell, more hell, and its coming punishment. No one is preaching about the goodness of God anymore, only his ability to punish."

"Kai, you're fired up this evening. I'm sure whoever it is you're speaking to has heard your point loud and clear. Oya, make we dey go — e don do. Go and get ready, o — let's go."

"I mean, think about it now, why shouldn't I wear trousers, eh? I've searched from beginning to end of the Bible, yet I can't for the life of me find where it is written that women should not wear trousers. Who made trousers exclusive clothing for men — God? Did Jesus and his disciples even wear trousers? You know, our forefathers used to walk around stark naked. So what are they even saying? Mtchew."

I chuckled when I heard the last part. At the same time, Amara burst out laughing.

"You know what, these days preaching has lost its spark — that's why the race for soul winning is being lost," Nifemi continued. "It's being done all wrong. Trying to scare people into believing won't yield good results. Instead of using scare tactics of the fire and brimstone of hell, and telling women not to perm their hair, or wear flashy jewellery, or paint their nails ... or all of that nonsense, rather tell them about the goodness of God and the beauty of heaven."

"That's true, you know. I can't remember the last time I heard anyone talk about how beautiful heaven is," I heard Amara say. "But I can tell you about the severity of the fiery furnaces of hell, plus the sizes of the demons and what they will do to folks who end up there. Hmm, Nife, my friend, you've made a good point."

"Yet it has deterred no one! Sometimes I think these preachers are just preaching for preaching's sake. They don't really want people to be saved. They just want it to be on record that they've done their part in getting the so-called heavenly rewards, that's all."

Amara started to laugh again as I heard Nifemi head towards her bedroom to get ready for yet another party with one of their sugar-daddy boyfriends.

"Udonwa, we are going," Amara shouted from the door as they left. "We'll get some souvenirs for you. See you when we see you."

I shook my head at the thought that, in a matter of hours, Nifemi's purported insight would be wasted on the bed of a strange man. For someone who claimed not to be hurting anyone, you would think she'd know that hurting someone did not imply physical harm alone, but included sleeping with another woman's husband.

I got up when I heard the door slam shut and went to the kitchen to make my dinner. The oil was starting to sizzle in the pot when the phone rang. The landlord had installed one in all his flats as a way of ensuring the rent was higher than other surrounding apartments. And I complained about it every time the bill arrived. We hardly ever used the thing, but it was a condition for our lease, so we had no choice. On a day like this, though, when I heard Aunt Nene's voice on the other end of the line, I appreciated the phone, for what it's worth.

"Udo, your mom is in town," I heard her say, imagining a smile curled on her face. "She wanted to speak to you, but I told her to rest. It was a long journey. When will you come to see her? Or do you want her to come over?"

"No, Aunty, I'll come. I'll be there first thing in the morning."

• • •

The exterior of Aunt Nene's home had been repainted in a duller yet no better colour. The two-storey building behind the main house now wore the former shocking yellow of the duplex. At least the buildings were neat and shone with perfection. Aunt Nene and Uncle Patrick seemed to be the only landlords in Dalley Close who appreciated their homes, not just as places of abode but as structures of investment.

No one was in the living room when I walked in, and the door had been left ajar, as usual, to let in air — the little air the fiery Lagos weather would give, that is. Beads of sweat dotted my face with some bubbling away onto my exposed shoulders. I reached for my handkerchief in my handbag and realized I had none. Chinua would have dipped his hand into his pocket and brought out a spare. He always carried more than two on any occasion and would always complain that heat was the only thing that would make him consider moving to America permanently. But whenever the thought crossed his mind, he would remember me and forget the idea. A smile crept across my face at the thought, and I dropped my bag to see Mama staring at me from the bottom of the staircase.

"Mama ..."

"I knew I smelled you from upstairs," she said in Igbo.

"You smelled me kwa, Mama. Hian, do I have such a strong smell?"

"Are you asking? Those cushions in the parlour at home still smell of you since the last time you visited. Even after washing them three times. This perfume must be original, o."

I knew she wanted me to talk about Chinua again, but I looked away. The last time I was home, that was all we had talked about. She hadn't been too happy when I'd mentioned he was Chief Aforjulu's first son, but she'd kept her reasons to herself. And I hadn't probed further, imagining it must be because he was Papa's best friend. Chinua had bought the perfume for me, along with other items. They were designer accessories, he'd told me, as if I could tell the difference between them and what was available in downtown Yaba's Tejuosho Market. Even Amara had screamed in delight when she saw the Calvin Klein belt and stiletto shoes by another designer. A complete waste of his money, I had told them. I'd always preferred my feet firmly on the ground and those pin heels did not afford me that pleasure. Fortunately, Chinua had never asked me why I hadn't worn them or any of the other items he'd bought.

"You look well, Mama. How's Papa, and everyone at home?" I asked, changing the subject. And she took the hint.

"He's fine; we are all fine. Except for that big machine of his."

"Machine kwa, you mean his car?"

"Is that thing a car? His former one, yes, that's a car. This one. Mba o. That thing can kill. Do you know Mazi had an accident in his own car the other day? And your father was in the car with him."

My mind ran to the general's car again and my fear about Papa that day, months ago now.

"Is Papa all right? When did the accident happen?"

"About a month ago. Your father is fine — he keeps saying you and Ekene saved him, that on different occasions, you have both instructed him never to enter a car without putting on that belt."

"You mean fastening his seat belt?" I'd learned that from Ekene. Apparently, it was a requirement in South Africa where he lived.

"You see, Mazi should learn to listen to his son. The fool was not wearing the belt, o. And your father was reminding him as they drove out. I heard him tell him, over and over, but Mazi refused to listen. He was discharged last week from the hospital, but the car is still at the mechanic," she said, releasing a deep sigh.

"Hian," I said and looked at Mama as she relaxed onto the sofa and wiped her face with the edge of her wrapper. She looked tired, her eyes ringed with lack of sleep.

"Are you all right, Mama? I mean, you look well, only that you seem a bit —"

"I am fine, Udo. It was a long journey and I didn't get much sleep —"

"You didn't get much sleep after dozing off the moment you arrived?" Aunt Nene interjected from the dining room where she was setting the table with Ngozika.

"Aunty, good afternoon, I didn't know you were around."

"You know I'm always around on Thursday mornings; it's the market environmental clean-up day."

"Oh, yes," I said, remembering the day I'd rushed early to the market to get some urgent materials for a class project only to find the gates locked. On enquiry, I had been informed that all markets were closed for cleaning on Thursday mornings until noon. I was yet to figure out the purpose of the exercise, though, for mere hours after the clean-up, the dirt would pile up again.

"It looks like something is bothering Mama, Aunty."

"You were right about her, Obianuju," Aunt Nene said to Mama. "She is too intelligent. You can't hide anything from her."

"Her mind is too sharp," Mama said.

"You're right, Udonwa, your mother has something on her mind. There's something bothering her," Aunt Nene said.

"It must be very serious for her to come all the way to Lagos," I said, turning to Mama.

My voice was calm but my heart was pounding. I already suspected something was wrong for her to come without prior warning. I'd spoken to Nneora two nights ago and she had not mentioned it.

"Mama, what's wrong? Are you sure Papa is all right like you said? If anything is wrong with him, you know you can tell me. I can take —"

"It's not your father, Udonwa. It's Jefferson."

Fourteen

"What do you mean by 'It's Jefferson'? What is wrong with Bro Jefferson, Mama?"

"Udonwa, your mother is still trying to come to terms with the news herself. It's not been easy on her. Please calm down."

"But, Aunty, I would calm down if I knew what both of you were talking about, eh. Is Brother Jefferson dead? Is that it — is that what you can't tell me?"

"I wish it were that simple, Udo. I wish it were as simple as death, o. At least I would know how to shape my mouth to cry. But with this one, I don't know how to begin. I don't even know where to start. Where did I go wrong in this life, eh, God? Why are you bent on punishing me like this? Why?"

"Obianuju biko, biko ozugo. Please, it's all right," Aunt Nene said as she came to sit beside me and took my hands in hers. We both sat and watched Mama, waiting for her to stop crying. But it looked like she wouldn't stop, as though she would carry on crying forever.

"Aunt Nene, please tell me what is going on. Is Bro Jefferson dead? Did something terrible happen to him?" My chest ached, my hands shaking as I stared at her.

"No, he's not dead, Udo. But yes, something terrible has happened — both to him and someone else."

I looked at Mama, then at Aunt Nene, and back at Mama again. They were both not making sense, Mama with tears streaming down her face and Aunt Nene talking in riddles.

"What on earth could have happened to Jefferson that would be worse than his dying? Whatever it is, as long as he's not dead, I will be okay with it," I said to Aunt Nene.

She took a deep breath and released it before she finally proffered an answer. I pulled my head back, concluding I had heard wrong, certain Aunt Nene had made a mistake and mixed up her words and the wrong things had come out. But she repeated the words again, as though she could hear my thoughts.

"What do you mean, Bro Jefferson raped someone? Raped who? Where did he see a woman? He's a priest now, Aunty. He can't rape anyone," I said, looking in Mama's direction for support. But she had covered her face with her hands and was sobbing louder than before.

"They said it's one of the altar boys, Udo. He raped an altar boy. Or at least that's what they told your mother."

"Oh my God. This is not happening. Bro Jefferson did what! How can … How can … Aunty, Bro Jefferson is too gentle … too calm and caring and loving to do anything like that … No, it's not possible, Aunty. Mama …"

I had jolted to my feet on hearing the news and was pacing up and down the sitting room looking for something to hold on to. From the walls, to the now slightly open door, the ceiling perhaps — anything at all to provide me with the support I desperately needed, but the lifeless things just stared back.

"Udonwa, we are all shocked by the news. I haven't even begun to assess it yet. Maybe when I do, I will start recovering from the shock. But right now it is too much. Just too much …" said Aunt Nene, sighing.

"You people must be joking," I said, raising my voice. "Yes, this is a joke, a cruel one that must stop right now, this minute!"

In the distance, I could hear Aunt Nene call Ngozika, saying I was out of control, before I realized I was writhing on the floor. They pulled me on to the couch, and I sat there trying to control my breath as I sobbed.

I hadn't seen Jefferson in a long time, maybe over a year. But I knew he was all right, or so I'd thought. I should have known something was wrong when I tried visiting him and he said he was travelling again. He'd been travelling for as long as I could remember, which made it difficult for anyone to get hold of him. When I had brought up the subject with Nneora, she'd insisted I worried too much about Jefferson, that Lincoln was also living far away in South Africa and I had never bothered to ask how he was doing. I knew he must have told her that, perhaps referencing the unwritten understanding in our family that Lincoln was Nneora's brother while Jefferson was mine.

The last time I had visited Jefferson, I was told he was in the chaplaincy praying when I arrived and had to wait. When he returned and saw me, he wasn't too excited I was there, and it had worried me that he would feel that way. He had looked good and very clean, like always, but because of the mood he was in, I could not bring myself to ask him why his hair was always shiny from being covered with too much pomade. He was also wearing burnt lemon zest aftershave like Chinua. An observation I again kept to myself, unlike in the past. He then apologized, saying that he should be happy I'd come all the way from Lagos to Onitsha to visit him rather than being irritated with me. But the visit had been strange, especially when Father Simmons, the French priest who was visiting from Europe, came to tell Jefferson he was waiting for him in the car so they could head home. I didn't think anything of it at the time but, thinking about it now, Father Simmons had looked too feminine for a man. His fingernails were long and well manicured, as if he were returning from the beauty salon. His hair was long, falling over his ears. And he had been carrying an overnight bag that I'd later realized was Bro Jefferson's. The bags were gifts from Ekene to Papa and Mama; Mama must have given hers to Jefferson.

"How can God let this happen, eh? Since I heard the news, I've been thinking maybe I'm dreaming, that I will wake up and find that it's a terrible dream, like the type induced by iba — you know, the *feverish* dream. But it's not a dream. Jefferson nwam has destroyed my life. My own *child* has killed me with his bare hands!"

I looked at Mama and wondered when this issue had become about her. For all we knew, it could be a rumour; nothing was certain yet. No matter how my head tried to spin it, to make it more suitable for grasping, it remained inconceivable. I just couldn't grasp the thought of Jefferson hurting anyone, much less an altar boy.

...

"Are you going to tell me what is troubling you, or are we play-ing the guessing game?"

I was sitting across the hallway from the open kitchen door staring at the empty space above the kitchen sink, ignoring Chinua. He had been sitting in his car, waiting for me outside my flat, when I arrived. He often told me that if our relation-ship were normal, he would have his own keys to the apartment so he could let himself in. He said he was getting embarrassed with having to wait outside in his car while my neighbours peeked at him through their windows.

Spent from crying, Mama was quiet when I left Aunt Nene's house. I needed to be in my own space to process my thoughts. Aunt Nene had promised to take care of Mama, in-sisting she would not let her go back to Iruama until she was mentally fit. I had left Aunt Nene's house without many of the answers I needed because I had not asked the questions that would provide them. I wanted to ask if Papa knew, and I want-ed to ask what had become of Jefferson's priesthood in the wake of the allegations. I still considered him innocent of the claims until I could look into his eyes to confirm the news.

And discussing it all with Chinua was the last thing on my mind.

"Do you have anything to eat? I'm starving," said Chinua, heading into the kitchen.

"There's chicken stew in the freezer. You can boil rice." I returned my gaze to the freshly painted kitchen wall.

"Is everything all right?" he said, opening the freezer and putting a pot on the stove. "Okay, forget I asked that because it's pretty obvious. Did something happen at home, or is it one of those wicked lecturers? I hope they are not troubling you? Maybe it's time to inform some of the cult guys I used to know. Or maybe even send one or two MOBILE POLICEMEN to scare them. By the way, this place smells of kerosene, or is it pai—"

"Chinua, stop bothering me, biko. You talk too much sometimes, ahn ahn! It's no one. Please leave me alone. Can't you see I don't want to talk?"

"Okay. I can see your mood is beyond bad today. I'll just put the rice on to boil and stay out of your way. Do you want some?"

"What?"

"Some rice. Do you want some? I need to know how much to boil."

"You remember my brother Jefferson?" Once the words left my mouth, I knew I couldn't take them back. But Chinua seemed so preoccupied with feeding his stomach, I wondered if he'd heard me.

"Where's the lid for this pot? I can't seem to find it anywhere …" I stared at him. "Oh, sorry, you were saying … Yes, yes, your brother. Isn't he the priest? I give up. I can't find this lid. The rice will just have to boil without it."

"He raped someone. They said my brother raped someone in his church. One of the altar boys."

Just then, the pot lid fell from the top of the cupboard and hit the floor clanging. I wasn't sure if it was the raucous noise that brought on the look of fright on Chinua's face or because of what I had just said. But it could have been a combination of both because he picked up the cover and placed it in the sink, deciding to leave the pot uncovered. He walked quietly to where I was seated and held me, and with tears streaming down my face I explained to him what Mama had come to inform us. He listened as I poured out my heart, my head against his chest. The sound of his beating heart soothed me, and it was in that moment that I realized how much I loved him, even though I had never admitted it to him or myself until now.

"I'm so sorry about your brother, Udom ... I wish there was something I could do to help."

"You can," I said and lifted my head to look at him. He was looking at me, running his fingers through my braids gently, purposefully, untangling the braids one tiny strand after the other. It felt so good looking at him, just having him there. "Please come with me to Onitsha. I need to go visit him."

"Oh ... Udom ..." He sighed. "I wish I could ..."

"Why not? You could take time off work. It's not like you have anyone you report to. Just call the national director and tell him a story, any story. I'm sure he'll buy it. Please, Chinua —"

"Oh ... gosh ... I don't know how to say this, Udom ... This is even harder than I imagined." He dropped his head between his hands.

"What do you mean?"

He tried to pull me towards his chest again but I held myself back. I wanted him to say whatever he had to say to my face. I wanted to see his face when he said it.

"I'm going away, Udom. I'm leaving town. Actually, I'm leaving the country." He paused again, and let out another sigh. "A position for a chief engineer came up and the head office in Seattle recommended I take up the post."

I tried to remain calm. "For how long? How many weeks will you be away?"

"You see, that's the thing. The main project will take about eighteen months and then an additional three months for completion of the corporate admin process with all the regions involved. So, in total, I'll be gone for twenty-one months … But, I'll be right back — I promise you. You could visit … You —"

"Is this a joke? You'll be gone for two years! Chinua, two whole years … Oh my God!"

"Not exactly, it's still three months short, but —"

"And what difference does that make, Chinua?"

"Please, Udom, stop screaming. Please try to understand. That's what I came to inform you. I didn't know something bigger had happened. I wish I could cancel the whole arrangement, but it's already signed. Both the agreement terms and the contract —"

"And what it would mean for your career obviously …"

"What?"

"You're heading up this position because it would spell an instant leap for your career."

"Maybe … But that's not the point, Udom. That's not why I took the offer, besides not being given an option. But if I had known about your brother earlier, I would have opted out. I would have recommended someone else. I know several of my colleagues are willing to take the post."

"No, Chinua. It's all right. I'm just being silly. Of course you should go. I won't stop you from trying to advance in your career. That would be selfish of me."

"Udom, look —"

"I said it's okay, Chinua. You can go to America. I'll be fine. I've always been fine. I can take care of myself," I said through a plastic smile so painful it hurt the corners of my mouth.

He nodded and got up to head back to the kitchen. Obviously, there was nothing more for him to say. Nothing he had to say would mean anything anyway. It wouldn't make him stay.

Fifteen

Sister Adaora was laughing so loudly when I opened the door, I wasn't sure whether or not to join her. In one swift move she dropped her bag and stretched out her arms towards me and I walked into them, placing my head on her chest. She rubbed her hand up and down my back, as if she could tell it was what I needed in that moment — a reassuring touch from a loved one.

Chinua had left six weeks ago. On the day he was leaving, he had come to the flat to say goodbye, but I'd refused to see him, my tears soaking my pillow while Amara and Nifemi nearly knocked their knuckles off on my door.

"Udonwa, please come and talk to him now. He's almost in tears," Nifemi had said, shocking me with her caring attitude.

"Udonwa, what do you want this young man to do? How can you let him travel out of the country like this without seeing you, it's somehow, now," Amara had screamed in Igbo. But I wouldn't budge. I knew I could not face him.

Chinua had then come around to the back of the flat to tap on my bedroom window, but as soon as I saw him standing there, I quickly went to pull the curtains together, still sobbing.

"Udom, please, let me see you, just your face, please ..." I heard him say from behind the curtains. After a few minutes of silence on both sides, from where I was sitting on the floor between my bed and the wardrobe, I saw something fall into the room and land on my bed, but I did not attempt to touch it. It was only the next morning that I picked up the note to read it.

> *Udom, my love,*
> *I'm sorry we have to part this way and I'm even*
> *sorrier for having to leave at such short notice.*
> *Please find it in your heart to forgive me. I'll be*
> *back before you know it, I promise. Please don't*
> *worry too much about Jefferson; I'm sure there's*
> *been a huge mistake somewhere. I'll call you*
> *often, and if it becomes unbearable for either of*
> *us, we can make arrangements for you to visit.*
> *Take good care of yourself for you and for me,*
> *and I promise to do the same.*
> *Your forever love,*
> *Chinua*

Since then, each day had been a struggle. A struggle to get out of bed, a struggle to study, to sleep, and sometimes even to breathe. According to Nifemi, a zombie had nothing on me in the moping department. And, for the first time, I saw reason in her words.

Sister Adaora and I must have stood holding on to each other for what seemed like forever, because Amara eventually came to the open door and picked up Sister Adaora's bag while admonishing me for my rudeness.

"I'm sorry, Sister. I should have let you come in first."

"You should have, leaving her standing outside like that. Please come in," Amara said and led her in.

With my hand clasped in hers, Sister Adaora walked in. I couldn't help staring at her outfit. She'd never been one for fashion, but today Sister Adaora's appearance took my breath away. Her red leggings and matching red flowing blouse reminded me of the beautiful rose Chinua had given me last Valentine's Day. It had been one of the embarrassing times when I had forgotten to get him a gift. He had smiled and said he understood, and we had carried on as usual. But, thinking about it now, it made me question if I hadn't taken him for granted like everyone said. Amara had given me the strangest look the last time I'd asked her if there was something more I could do for Chinua, before stating emphatically that I should "fuck him and get it over with." According to her, apparently, Chinua and I were both displaying classic signs of sexual frustration. I had replied that Chinua perhaps was, but certainly not me. I needed to have had sex at least once to be frustrated by not having had it again.

"Your flat looks nice and simple. I like it," Sister Adaora said and sat down on the single sofa in our sitting room.

I had not realized how sparsely furnished the flat was until Chinua had pointed out that it reminded him of one of those empty art galleries in New York or Paris that needed one's brain to be zig-zagged to appreciate the weird-looking paintings. A bland, colourless space, he had called it.

In our defence, my flatmates and I kept our possessions in our individual bedrooms because that's where we spent most of our time. But apart from a radio and bedside alarm clock, I had nothing of particular value. I had disapproved when Chinua had insisted on buying me a television set and VCD player, as they were nothing but distractions for any medical student. Nifemi, on the other hand, in addition to a VCD player, had a fairly large television set, a stereo system, a mini-bar fridge, and a soft luscious carpet covering the entire floor of the room.

"Your flatmate is nice," Sister Adaora said, glancing towards Amara.

Amara smiled in response as she continued to brush her hair and adjust her mini gown in front of the full-length mirror next to the entrance. As usual, another party was happening tonight and she wouldn't miss it for anything.

"The other one is out. She's the crazy one," I said and laughed, and Amara joined in.

Sister Adaora looked so robust, I couldn't help wondering if she had finally fallen pregnant. It was now almost seven years since she'd got married. But I chose not to ask her in the event that wasn't the case. I wouldn't want to spoil her jolly mood.

"Sit down — there's something I want us to discuss," Sister Adaora said with a certain seriousness that took me back to years before. It was the day she had wanted to have the very important puberty talk which Mama had somehow forgotten was her duty to do. I still remembered the day so vividly. Sister Adaora had been fidgeting, anxiety written all over her face. "You see," she had begun, "when a little girl starts to grow, her body experiences changes …" I'd smiled patiently as she had continued until I'd gently informed her that Nneora had beaten her to it. "Oh," had been her curt reply as her face had deflated, a sign that I knew so well to mean that she would have preferred to be the person who revealed the all-important talk of life to me. "You know, you're very lucky, Udom — you have two elder sisters who help guide you in everything. I had no one. When I was growing up all I had were two naughty brothers," she had added with a smile. I had wanted to remind her that she had Mama, but I understood what she meant. Mama was too preoccupied with our church's women's ministry when Sister Adaora was growing up. And now we were all grown, Mama was too busy stressing about being worried about all of us that she had no time worrying about anyone in particular.

"So what is it, Sister? You always ask me to sit down for a discussion when you have something important to talk about."

"You know me too well. Anyway, I wanted to inform you I'm going to apply for my master's degree."

"Sister, that's awesome news! Now you'll get that matron position you've always wanted."

"What matron position? There's nothing like that in my plans anymore. I'll be applying for the senior administrator — that's the post I've been eyeing for a while now."

"Eh! Sister, I'm very happy for you. If anyone deserves this, it's you. You've worked so hard all these years."

"I know, and it'll happen. I feel it in here," she said, tapping the side of her head before patting her chest. Her face became more serious when she said: "Nneora said Chinua is away. When is he coming back?"

I knew she couldn't resist asking me about Chinua and it was just a matter of time before she did. I got up and went to stand by the window. Desperate for some fresh air, I pulled back the curtain and the brick wall of the next building stared right back at me.

Sighing, I picked up a booklet to fan myself across the face as I replied: "I don't know."

The building housing my flat and the one next to it belonged to the same family. Many of the old properties in the mainland of Lagos were owned that way, passed down from generation to generation. Many of the landlords, and mine was no different, seemed to be more interested in taking in the profits than upgrading the lodgings of their tenants. As a result, these properties were left in a deplorable state, and still the rent went up every year.

With the two buildings so close to each other, it meant the only time we enjoyed any form of breeze was when the fans in the flat were switched on — that is, if there was no power outage. It's as if the country's electricity provider hired children to play with the power controls by switching them on and off at intervals. And depending on how carried away they became with their playing, these buffoons at the power authority would forget to switch the controls back on for days, sometimes weeks.

I continued to fan myself as Sister Adaora wiped her sweating face with a handkerchief that smelled of flowery perfume. Just like the airlessness of the flat, talking about Chinua was nothing but hopeless. The ensuing silence must have spoken volumes, as Sister Adaora did not probe further.

Sixteen

Sister Adaora's visit lasted two weeks — fourteen days I wished would not end. I went to stay at Aunt Nene's, where Sister Adaora was staying, towards the end of her visit, so that we could have enough time and space to relax and talk about things I did not want my nosy flatmates to hear.

Aunt Nene had left me some of her clothes in the bedroom she insisted was mine, but out of fear I still packed a small overnight bag filled with my own clothes whenever I visited. I had had a nightmare once in which I had been wearing some of Aunt Nene's clothes and had bumped right into Papa as I stepped outside the front door.

My bedroom in Aunt Nene's house had originally belonged to her eldest daughter, Muna. Muna was the same age as Jefferson, and her younger sister, Bialibe, was close to Lincoln's age, with Lincoln born just a few days before Bialibe. Aunt Nene would speak with her daughters occasionally over the telephone, and most times they would ask to speak to Kosisonna. Never had they asked to speak with me, though. From that, I concluded that they probably did not know I was even in Lagos. The last time we had all seen one another was when we were all still very young.

Our first meeting with our cousins hadn't been a pleasant one. Nneora could hardly hide her disgust with them, while I had chosen to be diplomatic about the whole thing by not speaking much to either of them, although it didn't take much effort on my part because they both did a good job of avoiding everyone by choosing to speak only to Lincoln and Sister Adaora. Lincoln would say afterwards that Bialibe's head was full of boy stories and that Aunt Nene was sending her away because she was a handful. I remembered pondering the logic behind Aunt Nene's reasons for sending her daughters out of the country to America because, to me, it seemed that was akin to throwing them into a pit full of boys. But Aunt Nene was nothing like her elder sister, who only did the opposite of what she felt. Aunt Nene, unlike Mama, felt free to do whatever she wanted and however she saw fit, a character trait I firmly believe Nneora had inherited from her, especially since Nneora was named after her. Aunt Nene had changed her name from Nneora to Nene, saying that her Yoruba friends were murdering the name by pronouncing it "Nora," a name she said she detested because it was the name of the principal of the all-girls Catholic school she and Mama had attended as children. Both she and Mama had often described Mother Nora as an old witch. Lincoln would later remark, though, that Aunt

Nene had changed her name because it sounded more modern than her real name.

As free as she was, though, Aunt Nene had her depressed days. Days when she would sit at the dining table, a bottle of spirits and a half-drunk glass next to the bottle, with her staring at something only she could see. Many times when I'd seen her in that mood, the telephone was always by her side and I knew the mood had something to do with either Muna or Bialibe, especially Bialibe.

When I arrived at Aunt Nene's, I could see today was one of those days.

"Aunty, is everything all right?" I asked, dropping my mini travel bag on the floor next to me as I sat down.

Aunt Nene responded by wiping her eyes with the edge of her wrapper and continued staring into space, but only after she had taken a sip of her drink.

I tried to reconcile the Aunt Nene before me with the woman who during the early years on a rare visit to our house in Iruama had butted heads with Papa. I recollected now with a shiver her voice that day as it had rained abusive words on the man she referred to as "the worst husband on earth." Papa had raised his hand to smack her, but Mama had stopped him by reminding him that their entire hometown of Ameke would gather at our house in an instant and he would be history. Aunt Nene was as fierce as they came then, and I often could still see that side of her, especially when she wanted to do something and Uncle Patrick raised an objection. Seeing her crying for the first time was as shocking as it was unreal.

"Did you receive a phone call, Aunty? Is it Bialibe? Please, Aunty, tell me."

Again she stared at me and opened her bottle and poured another drink. I wanted her to stop and talk without getting drunk, so I was glad when I noticed that she had poured the last drink and the bottle was now empty.

"Munachi has killed me. This child has exposed my legs outside my compound, o. Hei, so this is how my life journey will end!" she lamented in Igbo.

Aunt Nene was not making sense by mentioning Muna instead of Bialibe. As for what she said, from what I understood about mothers, I knew she was not talking about her own life in particular; it was a pattern common with mothers. Everything about a child's life was by extension that of the mother, something I was all too aware of since Mama was the chief of that.

"What did Muna do, Aunty? What happened to her? Is she sick or something?"

Aunt Nene did not respond, so I held her hand in mine and rubbed it like Chinua would do whenever I was sad. I was still rubbing the back of her palm when Sister Adaora came downstairs.

"Udom, you're here. When did you arrive?"

"Not too long ago." I stood up and with a hushed tone beckoned to Sister Adaora to follow me into the kitchen. Aunt Nene was now slouched on the table with her head resting on her curved arm.

"What's wrong with Aunty? I've never seen her like this before," I whispered.

"Stop whispering. She can't hear us, not in her present condition."

"But, Sister, what could have happened that would make Aunty like this? This is not the strong Aunt Nene we all know."

I peered back at my aunt through the doorway. She was now snoring gently.

"I know, Udom, it's unbelievable indeed. It's Muna, o. Munachi of all people. She got pregnant ... She was pregnant ... "

"What! But ... Wait, Sister, what do you mean by she *was* pregnant?"

"You'll need a seat. In fact, we both need to sit down. Come, let's go upstairs."

The climb upstairs felt unusually long. For the first time, I really noticed the banisters — steel with glass holdings that concealed the figures of anyone on the stairs if looking from downstairs and vice versa. The terrazzo stone slabs of the stairs shone brighter than ever, all their ingrained pebbles appearing particularly vivid.

I sat next to Sister Adaora on the only chair in the bedroom and couldn't help the feeling of knots tying and twisting the insides of my stomach.

"Muna got pregnant by her boyfriend," Sister Adaora began. "But apparently this was not her first. Do you remember how she and Bialibe left Nigeria abruptly years ago?"

I nodded, although I had no recollection of how abrupt it was. What I knew was that they had left earlier than Aunt Nene had told Mama they would because Mama had called one day to speak to her nieces and was told they were already gone. But I wanted Sister Adaora to get on with it, so nodding was the quickest way to get her to do that.

"She was pregnant then, too."

"Ahn ahn, Sister, she was very young then, ah. She must have been sixteen or something then?"

"Exactly. Their cook at the time got her pregnant."

"Hei! What sort of nonsense is this now? What was Aunt Nene doing when all of this was happening?"

"Aunty Nene travelled at the time with them and, when they arrived in America, the first thing they did was to abort the pregnancy," Sister Adaora continued, ignoring my last question. But then again, after hearing what she'd just said, I understood why she was not shocked about Aunt Nene and her capabilities as a mother.

"Abortion?"

"Yes, Udom, abortion. Munachi had an abortion at sixteen."

"So what happened this time around? Why did you say she *was* pregnant? Or did she have another abortion?" I clasped my hand over my mouth as the realization hit me before she replied.

"Unfortunately, yes. She said she was dating someone and —"

"Wait, did you speak to Muna?"

"Yes. I've been speaking to her. It's part of my reason for coming. She begged me to come speak to Aunt Nene and Uncle Patrick to forgive her and let her come home."

"Why won't they let her come home? Aunt Nene has always complained about her daughters not visiting home enough. I thought she would be overjoyed that one of them wanted to visit. Or is there more to the story?"

"Yes, Udom, otherwise Aunt Nene wouldn't be in the state she's in."

I sighed and braced myself as she continued.

"The guy she was dating is married ... I know, I was shocked too," she quickly added, responding to my widened eyes. "Muna swears she had no idea. The painful part is that, although she was already six months gone by the time she found out, she still went ahead and had an abortion, and in the process she lost her womb." She paused and sighed before saying very slowly: "And they were twins."

I jolted to my feet. "Chineke! Twins ... Oh my God. Who aborts a six-month pregnancy? Twins, for that matter!"

"Shh ... We don't want Ngozika to know about this. And promise me you won't tell anyone. Not Nneora, not Jefferson, not Mama ..." It was now her turn to whisper.

"I promise, Sister. You know you can trust me. God have mercy, this is ... This is ..."

I couldn't stop the quakes threatening to rupture my insides, quakes that came as a result of the suppressed emotions surrounding Jefferson's rape allegation, Chinua's unexpected travel, and now this news about Muna.

The news would keep me awake many nights, wondering how Sister Adaora must feel about our unmarried cousin aborting her third child while she had prayed for so many years to birth just one.

• • •

The night before she left, Sister Adaora and I were relaxing in the bedroom eating groundnuts and garden eggs.

"Is Uncle Ikemefuna in town or is he on one of his seminars again?" I asked, unable to stop myself any longer from finding out what he was up to.

Throughout our discussions at my flat, not once had Sister Adaora mentioned Uncle Ikemefuna. Although she rarely spoke about him to anyone unless asked, with me, she was always free to talk about him because I knew him better than most people. But as much as I wanted to hear about him, she must have guessed it wasn't out of concern. So when she did not mention him at all, I took it as a cue she likewise did not want to talk about him.

She pretended not to hear me and continued blowing the chaff off the groundnut. I knew I should have bought the de-chaffed type but she had insisted that the groundnuts with their skin on were more flavourful and nutritious. A hundred grains of groundnut later, and I realized after she responded that I should have kept my mouth shut.

"He left."

"What do you mean, he left?" I asked, staring at her. Uncle Ikemefuna's constant travels in the years I'd lived with them had ensured I'd spent a good part of my time trying to figure out if he actually worked in Awka at all. But, within seconds of his return, I would secretly wish he would leave again when he would announce his presence in more unpalatable ways than one.

"He left, o, Udom. He said he needed a break, that the house was too stifling. Can you imagine that? Stifling?"

I could totally imagine what she meant and I could also imagine how Uncle Ikemefuna would say it, with his lips shaped like two pumped rubber tires as he yet again broke my sister's heart.

"How can a house with only two people living in it be described as stifling? What is stifling about that house, with just me and him and our furniture? Maybe he was referring to me, who knows? Anyway, this time around I did not stop him. Let him go. Ike agwugom sef — I am tired."

As shocked as I was to hear her last sentence, I understood her stance. I was also tired of Uncle Ikemefuna even though I didn't live in the same house as him anymore.

"You know he's been seeing someone else for a while now? I think they're already living together. It's possible they even have a family by now."

My shoulders slumped when I heard her say those words, her face mere inches away from mine.

"Sister, you shouldn't worry yourself about that, or Uncle Ikemefuna for that matter. You said he's gone. Let him go."

"Exactly, Udom, let him go, o. I won't waste another grain of thought on that man."

The appearance of the person sitting opposite me might have been that of my sister, but what I couldn't figure out was who she'd become. The moment she'd walked into my flat in that outfit, her newly developed high-pitched voice, not to mention the laughter that accompanied almost every statement, and everything else unfolding at the moment, all spoke to someone other than the Sister Adaora I had known all my life. And all because Uncle Ikemefuna had left? If this was what his leaving had done to her, may he go far, *far* away and keep going.

With the room wrapped in silence, Aunt Nene's gentle tap on the door was all the reminder we needed to fall asleep for Sister Adaora to wake early to catch the first bus to Awka. A reminder that more than deflated my already-dampened mood. Without another word, I watched as Sister Adaora slipped under the covers of the bed and dozed off as soon as her head hit the pillow, her soft snores soon filling the room.

• • •

The next day was reminiscent of the day Chinua had left. Although Sister Adaora was going only a few hundred miles away, the emptiness that came with separation resurfaced, this time bringing with it a few revelations. My love for my eldest sister had grown exponentially, which I attributed to the years I'd lived with her, from seeing her at her most vulnerable, wanting to protect her from Uncle Ikemefuna, to the helplessness of being unable to do anything about the one thing she needed most — a child. And my love for Chinua was affirmed as the kind of love that occurred just for the sake of love. It was hinged on nothing.

"Will Jefferson be found guilty?" I asked Sister Adaora as we stood watching the bus conductor load her luggage into the boot of the bus conveying her and fifteen other passengers to Awka. Aunt Nene had opted to wait in her car across the road from the motor park.

"I wish I knew, Udom. I really don't know."

"Won't you go to see him? You live closest to him … If not for my exams, I would have gone."

"I have tried to make arrangements, but I was told not to bother. No one has seen him yet, so stop worrying. The parish priest, the bishop and all those people over there have refused him contact with the outside world, until they complete their own investigations."

"But Mama said she went to see him …"

"She went, but that does not translate to her seeing him … You know what, Udom, I really don't want to talk about Jefferson, or Ikemefuna, or Papa, or any of those men. Or any man at all. I just want to be happy."

I looked away from Sister Adaora, trying to take in what she'd just said. Her grouping of Papa, Jefferson, and Uncle Ikemefuna as one did not make sense to me. I knew Papa could not be termed as one of the best fathers there was, but he was still a better man than Uncle Ikemefuna and both of them did not come close to Jefferson. Jefferson was of a different breed; he was incapable of hurting a fly, no matter what anyone else thought or believed.

"Sister, I know you don't want to talk about men, but Jefferson is our brother, and the good one. We cannot allow him to be punished for an offence he knows nothing about."

"If you say so, Udom, but what can we do? What can anyone do other than wait? So, let's just wait it out, okay?" She sighed before continuing: "I'll be back when Munachi arrives. Hopefully everything will have calmed down by then, and Aunty Nene and Uncle Patrick will be on speaking terms again. Apparently, he has been shouting at Aunt Nene that it's all her fault how Muna's life turned out. Uncle Patrick has to return home from wherever he went to cool off, as Sister Adaora mentioned he had said before storming off from the house, and face his family. Leaving home in anger like he did is not the best way to handle a situation."

Aunt Nene was still waiting patiently when I returned to her car, her latest gift to herself — a brand-new mint-coloured 505 Evolution with tinted windows. The past few days she had said little, only mumbling a reply when greeted. She had not been to her shops and Ngozika was now doubling as a housemaid and occasional salesgirl supervising the assistants in both shops. Aunt Nene's face was free of the heavy makeup that used to adorn it, while all her artificial nails had been removed. And Ngozika had told me that all the drinks in the bar had been poured down the drain.

As soon as I was seated in the car, Aunt Nene turned on the ignition. "Patrick is coming back tomorrow and Muna will be back next week Sunday."

Even though we had not talked about Muna, it was obvious she knew Sister Adaora had told me everything.

"But Sister said she will be back when Muna arrives. If Muna is coming back so soon, shouldn't she have waited instead?"

"I did not tell her that Muna called last night to confirm. Adaora has her own problems."

At those words, all I could do was stare ahead out the windscreen, lost in my own thoughts. Indeed, Aunt Nene, like everyone else, believed that Sister Adaora had many problems all due to her childless state. I wanted to tell Aunt Nene that she had changed. I wanted to inform her that Sister Adaora did not care any more about people more than she should. But somehow I knew she would not understand, so I did not respond. Nobody would understand the new look I'd seen on Sister Adaora's face. A look that had not been affected by all the recent bad news in our family.

"Let her deal with her own problems," Aunt Nene said again, sounding more cryptic than she intended, perhaps.

It seemed Sister Adaora had told her about Uncle Ikemefuna's leaving, which was not much of a problem, seeing how happy it made her. But realizing now how strongly Aunt Nene felt about it, I had to respect that by not trying to change her mind about not informing Sister Adaora of Muna's trip back home next week.

As far as I was concerned, Uncle Ikemefuna's departure paled in comparison to Muna's situation. For as hard as I tried to blot out the image of those aborted twins, they kept flashing across my mind like two miniature clones of Muna. I could only imagine what mental torture Aunt Nene had to endure.

Seventeen

I ruama had been on my mind for a long time and I couldn't resist the urge to visit anymore. Its serene atmosphere — the shades of fruits and luscious leafy trees lining spacious compounds; the clean fresh air that filled every breath and greeted my face whenever I arrived; the priceless feeling of my footfall on its dusty roads — was in sharp contrast to the airless hustle and bustle of Lagos. The unhurried manner in which small-town people conducted their daily affairs was a freedom ignorant critics mistook for laziness. I would pick living in Iruama over anywhere a million times over. The only downside, which was the main characteristic of many villages like Iruama, was that everyone knew everyone's business.

And so, passing through Eke Iruama, I knew it was only a matter of time before the whole village was aware of my arrival. Nwakaibeya the carpenter was hammering away at a stool when I passed by his shed. He boldly displayed his company name on a makeshift signboard, Nwakaibeya and Sons Worldwide Enterprise, above his workshop, but his furniture was anything but world class. Doubling as his showroom, the little corner beside the shed had on display several finished lopsided wooden stools and centre tables (which Chinua had insisted should be called coffee tables, and to which I had replied that in Nigeria these tables were used to serve everything but coffee because, as far as I was aware, Nigerians did not even drink coffee). Whatever the correct name, a table is not of much use if it can't serve its purpose of holding up items, much like the old one, which Nwakaibeya had built, in our sitting room. I remembered defending him back then, that he must have hurriedly put the table together a few days before Christmas that year because I could see no other logical explanation for the table's wobbly legs. I couldn't stop wondering how he could have missed the uneven legs. "This is my Christmas gift for the noble reverend," he had said with pride to Nneora and me as we'd received it on Papa's behalf that day.

"Good evening, sir," I greeted him, stopping to examine some of the wood carvings on display.

"Ah, Udonwa nno, the good Reverend Ilechukwu's daughter, welcome home. How is everyone in Lagos?" he said in Igbo, flashing his gunk-coated yellow teeth.

"They are all fine, thank you, sir," I said and smiled back, dropping the unidentifiable carved object before I continued walking home.

The gate to our compound, as always, was wide open. Leaning against the fence on the inside of the compound was a new gate, reeking of fresh paint. The gate appeared to be much taller than our current fence, and I wondered what Papa planned to do with it.

Papa's car was in its parking spot, so I knew he was home. There was another much bigger and older Mercedes parked further down from his. An empty tiny flag holder was visible on the bonnet of the car and a small sticker next to it read "Biafra." Perhaps the sticker was a replacement for the former Biafran flag, which, for obvious reasons, could no longer be displayed. As I walked to the backyard, a fresh breeze blew tiny speckles of dust across my face, and memories from my childhood days of playing in the yard surged through my mind.

Our old obi was gone. Mama said it had to go to make space for her workshop. Apparently, Papa would have preferred for it to be turned into a garage for his Mercedes, but Mama had been adamant on rebuilding it to be used for her weekly meetings with the women of Iruama community forum where she doubled as the chairwoman and project coordinator. It was as if her strength only increased as she got older. Mama had mentored many of the women in Iruama and even the neighbouring Iruobi community, many of whom had started their own workshops. The last time we had spoken, Mama had informed me that Mrs. Umeh had wanted to take over from her, but the women had insisted that Mama was the only mentor they wanted. They had said Mrs. Umeh's tutoring was on a lower level than Mama's training approach. But I think the real reason was that the women preferred coming to our house as an excuse to be with Mama and hear her stories. When Mama stopped telling folktales, she had started telling real-life stories.

She always had news from her friend who had returned from omugwo in London — the same friend who had taught her needlework, how to crochet, and every single craft she knew.

During Nneora's last visit, she said she'd watched as Mama spent hours making what Mama was adamant was a duvet but ended up looking like a rug that should be placed on the floor rather than a bed. According to Nneora, Mama said abada wrappers were now too ordinary to cover her at night, and that she needed something more elegant to grace her bed, so she had started making duvets. Nneora said she had taken one duvet back with her to Enugu but had locked it up in her travel box after just one night of use because of the excessive sweating she had to endure. Still, Mama couldn't be convinced that not everything from abroad was appropriate for use in Nigeria. Appropriate uses aside, Mama's handcrafts were of a professional standard, and Mama easily could have had her own craftwork store.

Nearing the back door, I heard two voices that broke into laughter when I appeared.

"The greatest doctor of Iruama! Welcome home, my darling daughter!" Papa hailed my name like he usually did while opening a bottle of beer.

"Good morning, Papa, good morning, sir," I said, bending over to greet Papa and Chief Aforjulu.

"Welcome, my child. How was your trip? I hope the driver was not one of those crazy drivers of today who speed like mad dogs?" Chief Aforjulu said, staring at me. A medium-sized keg of palm wine and a glass cup stood on the table between him and Papa. When he spoke, the table shook and the glass cup nearly fell over.

"I trust Udonwa, Iweka," said Papa. "She's too smart to enter the vehicle of a madman. Once she sees what the driver looks like, ehn, she can tell if he is a good driver like her father or not."

Chief Aforjulu kept his gaze on me while Papa was speaking, and when I turned to him, we locked eyes before he looked away, sipping his glass of palm wine. Papa as a reverend was wise not to consume alcoholic beverages in public, but at home, he would polish off three bottles of beer in one sitting. It was one of the reasons why Mama disliked Chief Aforjulu. She insisted it was he who had taught Papa how to drink alcohol, and that when she had first met Papa, he had not even known what a beer bottle looked like. Fact or not, all I knew now was that Papa loved to drink.

When we were younger and after he had finished preparing for his Sunday sermons, Papa would pour a bottle of lager into a brown tumbler to give the impression of drinking Ovaltine or some other hot beverage. But when Nneora and Lincoln would go back to their boarding schools, Papa, perhaps thinking he had no one else to hide it from, would drink from a bottle without fear or shame. This would make Mama roll her eyes repeatedly but she wouldn't utter a word to him. In private, though, she would lament that Papa had gone from bad to worse and was nothing but a drunkard reverend, his stomach protruding like a pregnant belly.

In the last few years, however, Mama had found her voice.

"Will it kill you to drink ordinary Coke and Fanta, eh, Papa Adaora!" she had barked at him the last time I was home.

"So that my body will be pumped full of sugar?" he had replied while swigging his beer. I had never seen Mama so fired up like she had been that day; it had left me wondering how different our home would have been if Mama had been that way when we were growing up.

"Is Mama inside?" I asked Papa before making my way towards the front door.

"I don't know where she is. If she's not in the bedroom, then she's with her women liberation group," he said, burping as he dropped his half-drunk bottle on the table.

"Women liberation group, kwa? Papa, you mean her community women's forum … it's not even the Anambra Women's League!"

"What's the difference? That's the only thing she has time for these days."

I knew there was no use arguing with him. As I made my way inside the house, I overheard Chief Aforjulu asking Papa if I was the same one and Papa replied in the affirmative before adding that I was the reason he was still living.

"She's such a beautiful young woman. Well, all your daughters are beautiful …"

"Yes, they are."

He was starting to narrate how I had saved his life when I'd come home one time and found him almost unconscious from fever when I entered the main house.

Through the wide windows of the sitting room, I could see the uncompleted mansion my cousin Ekene was building. The old fence adjoining ours in the backyard had been torn down to make room for the double-storey edifice. Staring at the magnificent home, I remembered Papa mentioning Ekene's promise to him to rebuild our house too, and his reply to Ekene that he must not worry; if Papa's own sons could not build anything new in their own father's compound, then we all deserved to live in it the way it was, he'd said.

I was still staring when Mama walked in.

"Kamsikwa — I thought I heard your voice."

"Chineke, Mama, what is going on here? It's like every time I come home, something new is happening."

"Oh, you mean Ekene's house? Our old gate is going soon. You must have seen the new one outside?"

"It's huge. I was wondering what it was for …"

"The boy is on a mission. His mother said that when he's through with these projects in Iruama, he will start work on his hotel projects in Enugu, Awka, and Lagos."

"Ehn ehn, biko, what is he doing in South Africa?"

"Amam — how would I know? It's you young ones I should be asking. Ask Lincoln, I'm sure he knows."

"I already did, Mama, but he said he does not know because they don't live in the same city. Lincoln lives in Johannesburg, but he said Ekene lives in another city called Durban or something like that … Nekwa building, plus hotel — is this still the same Ekene, our Ekene?"

"The very same one, o. My dear, let's leave those things for now. Tell me, how was your trip?"

"It was fine, Mama," I said, slumping on the sofa. "I saw Papa and Chief Aforjulu outside and when I asked Papa where you were, he said you were with your women liberation group," I said, laughing.

"Please, leave that old fool. He and that man he calls a friend who does nothing but lead him astray. Okwa, they are still outside drinking?"

I stared at Mama as she spoke. She sat opposite me, fanning herself with a hand-held fan woven with plastic thread. The fan had a small cane stuck in the middle that served as the handle. I didn't need anyone to tell me she had made it herself. She was wearing a short skirt I'd seen before. The skirt appeared one size bigger than her size as it fell a little below her knees. From the fit of her blouse I could tell she had made it herself but the skirt was without doubt from Aunt Nene.

In the last few years since we had all left home, and Mama had started spending more time with Aunt Nene, she had found her voice. These days, not only did Mama challenge Papa, but would often refer to him in the choicest of degrading words. Perhaps the ugly words had been lying dormant within her all these years, waiting for the right time. After all, Grandpa used to say, *One does not learn how to use one's left hand in old age.* And, at the rate at which she spewed them, it appeared as though she was on a mission to clear the backlog of years of silence.

"Lincoln called me yesterday. He said he wants you to visit South Africa, but you've been giving him excuses?"

"I will visit when I can, Mama. Now is not a good time."

"Hmm, why did I have the feeling you'd jump at the idea of travelling outside Nigeria? Anyway, I hope it's not because of …" She left her last word hanging but I knew she wanted to say "Chinua."

"It's not because of anybody, Mama. And no, I've not heard from Chinua."

I stole a quick look at her face when I realized that her concern about Chinua indicated a bigger issue.

"Mama, what is troubling you?"

"Everything is fine, my dear. Now, tell me how is Lagos and school life in general?"

When Mama was asked a question she didn't want to give an answer to, she would promptly change the subject to the person she's talking to. But I was not having any of that today.

"Mama, are you sure everything is all right? You ask about Chinua, and the next thing you get this troubled look on your face and you tell me it's nothing?"

"Udonwa, biko rapum — let me be, please. Your father and that friend of his are both a law unto themselves and … In fact, I don't have to tell you anything about him — you'll find out soon enough."

"Ogini, Mama? What is it?"

"Okay, do you know your father has not slept in this house for two days? He only just returned because you called last night to inform us you were arriving today. Since this morning they've been sitting out there doing nothing but drink."

"That's unlike Papa," I said quietly. "I know he loves to go out, but he has never slept outside this home except when he travels out of town. Mama, maybe he told you where he was going but you were not paying attention."

She glared at me before saying: "Your father slept over at Aforjulu's house in Nnewisouth."

"And why would Papa do that?"

"Oh oh, why don't you go and ask him — he's right outside. Besides that, Aforjulu himself has been coming here a lot."

"That's strange," I said, a little irritated, but thankfully Mama did not catch on, otherwise that would have encouraged her even more. "But Chief Aforjulu never used to visit here before … I wonder what has changed?"

When I was little and Papa would always visit Nnewisouth to see his old friend, I often wondered why Chief Aforjulu never reciprocated. So one day I asked him the reason for this and that was when he took me along with him to Nnewisouth for the first time. According to him, a visit to his friend's house was all the answer I needed to my question. He was right.

"Look, Udonwa, your father and Aforjulu are birds of a feather; as long as they flock together it does not matter to them where they are."

I remembered Mama would frown each time Papa mentioned he was visiting Nnewisouth. A frown so deep that nothing could wipe it off and it would remain on her face hours
after Papa's car was heard driving down our dusty road.

"Anyway, it's a good thing he's been coming around often,
otherwise I wouldn't have heard some of the things I've been
hearing about his family," she added.

Eighteen

Mama didn't mention Chinua's name but it was all I heard her not saying. Our relationship must have played a huge part in his father now being able to frequent our home regardless of what she said. Mama, I suspect, had begun to grow a soft spot for Chinua ever since she saw a photograph of him in my purse.

Right after Chinua and I had first started dating and Nneora had informed her, Mama had called to warn me to be very careful. That in itself was a surprise because Mama had never before bothered with her daughters' relationships or even acknowledged we had one. If she knew Nneora had a boyfriend, she never mentioned it. It was a common practice among my parents' generation. Not acknowledging their children's relationships, especially those of daughters, was a way of ignoring the fact that they could be having sex. They just couldn't handle the possibility of that reality. The boys, on the other hand, got it easy. Mama would often tease Lincoln about his many girlfriends and go as far as asking him which one he would be bringing home. Although we all knew she was joking about the bringing home part, this was a privilege not extended to the girls.

"So you say you've not heard from him?" she asked.

"No, Mama, I have not." I knew she was referring to Chinua. "But he is fine. I saw a former colleague of his and he mentioned something to that effect."

"I know he is too. He is all his father talks about when he comes here. Chinua this, Chinua that. He also mentions the other one … I can't remember his name right now."

"Ifenna? Chinua has just one other brother, Ifenna. He's nothing like Chinua, though. We went to school together in Awka."

"I know."

"Excuse me?"

"Adaora told me …"

"You people must talk about me a lot if Sister Adaora told you about Ifenna."

"It's nothing important. But, if going by what Chief Aforjulu says about him, that boy is not good news at all."

"Neither is Lincoln …"

I had no intention of supporting Ifenna because Mama was spot on about him; I'd only switched to Lincoln as an effort to change the subject.

Mama responded by giving me a sharp stare and got up to go to the kitchen.

Our house had been undergoing constant renovations for a while now. The kitchen was now located inside the house in Sister Adaora's former room. I still remembered the old kitchen and how I used to sit on a stool to help Mama prepare ofe ora for Papa. I would pluck the leafy vegetables off their stems and set them aside; then Mama would place the peppers and ogiri and crayfish into a mortar and hand me a short pestle to pound the ingredients into a rough paste. I'd sit back and watch the dish bubbling away until Mama would take it down from the three-legged cast-iron firewood burner. It seemed not too long ago but felt like ages at the same time. For years, Sister Adaora's old bedroom had been used as a storeroom after she'd moved out. Initially, Mama wouldn't let anyone go in there because it was packed full of her old abadas in aluminium tinker boxes. The room had also served as storage for her coolers and old items from yesteryear, and then was used for her knitting, crocheting, and baking materials, before becoming the new kitchen.

"Em, Mama," I said, following her into the kitchen, "earlier you said you've been hearing things about Chief Aforjulu?"

"I thought you'd never ask. Hmm, I've heard a lot of things about that man. Not that I'm shocked, though. I've always known there's something very sinister about him."

"Something like what, Mama? You don't even know him that well."

"That man has too much money for one person. Not that you'll understand what I mean ..."

"Ma-aa-ma!"

"Okay, this same rumour has been going around for years, but I never really paid much attention to it ... I heard from very reliable sources that all the children that Ifeyinwa Aforjulu lost were because of diabolic ritual purposes. Their deaths were not natural."

"Mama! Where did you hear that?"

"Like I said, it's been going around for years, but I did not want to pursue it. Why do you think I was always against his friendship with your father? But now with you being involved with his son, I couldn't ignore it anymore and —"

"But, Mama, do you know this for sure, or are you just reporting a baseless rumour? You know how people like to gossip. Not every rich man is a ritualist, Mama. Chinua made it clear his father was a textile merchant of repute in his heyday and he owned several factories where school uniforms were manufactured for various primary and secondary schools in the country, and even neighbouring Cotonou. Surely you of all people should know that's a money spinner."

"I don't know about his business. All I know is what I heard and everybody in Nnewisouth seems to agree with me."

"Jealous people, perhaps. And I'm not defending him; all I'm saying is be careful what you say about people. What if you heard people gossiping about our family — what would you say then?"

"Well, it's very suspicious that a woman can give birth to seven children and end up burying five, including her first son as a teenager." Mama must have seen the look on my face because she continued: "Oh, you didn't know? Now you know what I'm talking about. Biko, let me go and prepare something for us to eat."

I went back to sit in the living room, Mama's words reverberating in my mind. Apart from the twin sister who Chinua had mentioned had died when they were still babies, I had not heard of anyone else dying, either as a child or later in life. To hear he had an elder brother who had died as a teenager was a shock, plus there had been four others!

Mama returned with two plates of ukwa and its accompanying salted liquid. She placed the dishes on yet another new addition to the furniture of our home — a shiny white-and-gold-coloured dining table. This table was different from the last replacement which had been practically new. While we ate, Mama explained that Papa had returned with the new furniture items from one of his many recent trips, but she had not cared to ask where exactly they had come from. I needed no one to tell me they were imported — that much was obvious.

Eating the ukwa brought back memories I would rather forget, at least for the time being. This was the first meal I had prepared for Chinua not long after we'd started dating. He had arrived that day in high spirits with a plastic bag containing the ukwa grains, saying how hungry he was. He had insisted he did not want anything from the fridge but freshly cooked ukwa. He had offered to help but I had refused and tried to replicate how Mama and Sister Adaora used to make theirs. I couldn't say it tasted like Mama's, but judging by the way he kept smacking his lips afterwards, I think it was pretty close.

"Ehn ehn, I thought I smelled the aroma of this delicious meal all the way from the yard," said Papa, entering the living room. "Obianuju, where's my food, or did you prepare for just you and Udonwa?"

"When you are ready to eat you'll be served," said Mama, barely looking at Papa.

"And why do you think I'm asking for the food now?"

"Udonwa, biko, go to the kitchen and bring his food. You'll see it on top of the cupboard."

I jumped out of my seat at her request. It was as if there were two lions living in the house now that Mama had found her voice. Mama's animal spirit seemed to have awoken from years of deep slumber. Her body language, plus the way she spoke to Papa, resembled someone ready to pounce on anything that encroached on her territory. From the kitchen, I could hear Papa talking. I could also imagine his eyes fixed on Mama and wondering what his mind was conjuring.

"Obianuju, this is our new system … Hmm … Hmm … So, I'm now expected to enter the kitchen and fetch my own food, eh kwa?"

"I thought you and your friend were going to eat only beer today. I'm surprised there's still space inside that mini mountain you call a stomach."

Papa's mouth had just opened to respond to Mama's latest verbal assault when I returned with the meal and placed the tray on the centre table, a decision I'd made because I wasn't sure which lion would survive, if at all, if they both sat at the same dining table.

. . .

Mama left for Awka very early the next morning, saying that Sister Adaora needed her urgently. I thought that perhaps Mama just wanted to get away for a while since I was at home to take care of Papa, but I too was leaving for Awka that evening. And, while having a talk with Papa later in the morning, he told me that Mama left him alone most of the time and he often had no choice but to call Mama Ekene to help him until she returned. I wanted so much to believe him, but I wasn't sure if Mama's hostility towards him had got to the point where she was willing for him to starve.

Papa was sitting on a chair on the veranda when I found him that morning. It was a relief to see him reading a newspaper, rather than drinking first thing in the morning like Mama had said he'd been doing lately. He was so engrossed in the paper that I thought not to disturb him. I had just headed for the gate leading to Mazi Okoli's house when I heard my name.

"Sir?" I turned back towards him.

"Am I invisible?"

"Sorry, Papa, I didn't realize you saw me. I thought you were focused on your reading." I walked back to where he was sitting.

He smiled and placed the newspaper on the floor, patting the stool beside him. "Come, sit next to me."

Papa's head was now almost nothing but scalp. His stomach remained the only thing that appeared not to reduce in size.

"How is medicine treating you?"

"The studies are fine, Papa. We are not yet in the clinical stages, if that's what you want to know."

"You've always been good at reading my mind. So you're not yet able to carry out an autopsy and so on?"

"If you mean dissecting a cadaver, then no, not yet."

"Just negodu egedege Ekene kwuwalu. This is indisputably the best house in the entire Iruama and its surroundings," he said, swiftly changing the topic.

I followed his eyes to where they were gazing at Ekene's ongoing construction. It was indeed worthy of what he'd called it — *a structural masquerade*. The only aspect of it that I did not like was that it was blocking the view of the udala tree with the waist-high dust that Sister Adaora said she used to sit under when she was a little girl. The way the building was spread out, at first glance it appeared as if it were located in our compound, if you were standing outside the back gate looking into the yard, something I think made

Papa's heart happy. He had always had a soft spot for Mazi Okoli's only son.

"If you want, we can go inside and have a look. I have my own keys to the house. Mazi keeps losing his bunch so Ekene decided I should have a set with me for safe keeping — the cost of replacing the keys keeps rising with each loss."

I told Papa I'd fetch them from the bedroom. When I entered the room, I was shocked to see that Mama's clothes and belongings were nowhere to be found. Mama's things used to be everywhere in their bedroom, even after she'd stopped sleeping in it. In the past, there would have been several abada wrappers, a special blouse made with georgette fabric, or a pile of ichafu somewhere on the shelf. But now there was nothing to suggest she had ever been a part of this space. It was bare of her. Even the black-and-white photograph of her and Papa when they were still courting was missing from the wall on which it had lived for years.

After going through several bunches of keys in the drawer Papa had told me to look in, I found one with a keyring of the letter *E* and a piece of red cloth tied around the key holder to differentiate it from the rest.

As I was about to close the drawer, I saw a photograph hidden underneath the keys. It was of Papa, Mama, Sister Adaora, Jefferson, and baby Lincoln sitting on Papa's lap. Mama had a beautiful bag on her lap and her hair was plaited in long tight strands intertwined with thread. This was all before Nneora and I had been born. They were all smiling at the camera. Papa's smile was the brightest and you could see why — not only was he married to the love of his life amid major opposition from her family, but she had given him three beautiful children. But then something had gone wrong and shattered whatever it was that had held it all together.

• • •

Ekene's house looked even better on the inside than it did from the exterior. A lounge at the entrance led to the first sitting room and, from that, a sunken sitting room. It appeared that all the interiors were imported, and the corner of the largest sitting room looked like a mini warehouse heaped with wrapped cartons full of bathroom and kitchen vanities as well as plumbing and tap heads. A huge chandelier was hanging from the ceiling.

"This had to be put up with the cementing of the ceiling, according to the builders, because it will be too heavy for the ceiling if done otherwise," Papa said. I nodded in agreement because I couldn't imagine how else it could have been done. Although it looked like it would take down the house with it if it ever were to fall.

After touring the ground floor of the house, we headed upstairs to the bedrooms. There were six bedrooms, all with en suite bathrooms and ceiling-to-floor wardrobes. According to Papa, another sitting room just off the first-floor landing would serve as the meeting space or prayer room for all the residents of the house.

"Ekene really outdid himself here, Papa — it's such a magnificent house."

"Yes, he did. That boy has shown signs of greatness from a very young age. When he completes this house, he will be returning with his wife and children for the grand opening."

"He has a wife and even children? I didn't know that."

"Don't worry, you are not age mates. I'm sure Nneora or Jefferson knows about them."

"Lincoln …" I muttered, stealing a quick look at Papa's face. Papa should have said Lincoln and Nneora, but his denial of

Lincoln's existence had widened as the years had progressed. With Ekene and Lincoln both closer in age, it was only natural to expect that Papa would mention Lincoln in the context of what he had said. Jumping straight to Jefferson was not only absurd but worrying. It was like he regretted siring Lincoln. My mind shifted to the old family portrait of Papa smiling with baby Lincoln on his lap.

As I left for Awka that evening, for the first time in a long while, I did not worry about Papa and how he would survive. He seemed to have found himself a new means of keeping himself happy between Chief Aforjulu and Ekene's largesse.

· · ·

As usual, the gate to Sister Adaora's block of flats was bolted in place. I slipped my hand through an opening to unhook it, smiling as I realized some things never changed in the sleepy town of Awka. Sister Adaora's front door was wide open, which I did not find strange. Awka was always humid during this time of the year, and I knew from my time living there that Sister Adaora would open the door to let whatever breeze she could into the flat. What was strange, though, was that there was no one in the sitting room. If the front door was open, Sister Adaora always insisted someone should be in the sitting room. It had undergone a bit of a makeover but not as extensively as our house in Iruama. The old bookshelf in the corner of the room had been replaced with a bigger one holding thicker books. One item that used to be conspicuous was missing — the wedding portrait of a rarely smiling Uncle Ikemefuna that used to hang on the wall next to Sister Adaora's. Hers was still hanging in place.

Hearing Sister Adaora's voice coming from her bedroom, I headed towards the door, but stopped before knocking when she said: "Mama, it's been more than seven years now. Every single prophet keeps saying the same thing, the secret must be revealed before I can conceive. I think it's about time."

"Adaora nwam, please," said Mama, "we have to still wait a bit, o. Now is not the right time. Lincoln is just settling in in South Africa and Jefferson is still going through his own issues. Nneora is my only child without impending doom over her head like a cloud. Nwam, biko, now is not the right time. Let's wait a bit, o. Let the dust with Jefferson settle first, please. You hear?"

For the first time, I couldn't stop myself from eavesdropping on Mama and Sister Adaora's conversation because what they were talking about was as intriguing as it was daunting. I wasn't sure if I'd heard what they were saying correctly. I stood transfixed behind the door leading to Sister Adaora's room. She was telling Mama something I would never want to remember. And Mama was replying and providing suggestions to something that did not make sense. There were intermittent releases of hisses and outbursts of disgust. It was as if what they were talking about was being spoken about in this manner for the first time. Like a lid had been placed on it for years and now, seemingly out of necessity, the Pandora's box had been opened.

PART III

Nineteen

Higgles had a better reputation than the rest of the nightclubs in the area. In my early days at UNILAG, long before it became a frequent hangout spot for Chinua, his friends and me, it was all Nifemi and Amara had spoken about on Friday nights. Tonight, the club was buzzing. Each person on the dance floor was trying to out-dance the person next to them. The guy dancing next to me was holding a bottle of whiskey in one hand, a cigarette dangling from the other. The woman beside him clutched a bottle of beer to her chest and would occasionally take a puff from his cigarette. From the fat wrap of the paper and its odour, I knew it was no ordinary cigarette. Combined with the sweat of the clubbers, bouncers and waitrons, there was a rather musty smell.

Not too far from the dance floor was a pair of eyes that kept meeting mine. The eyes belonged to a decent-looking man — at least he appeared more decent than most of the guys there. He turned to face the bar and, just then, something about the way his back arched struck me as familiar. I kept my gaze on him and then he turned around just in time to meet my now-full gaze. Realization hit him and I saw him take a few sips of his beer before he walked to where I was. I wanted to say something but froze. He was the last person I'd expected to see.

"Ifenna!" I choked out.

It was him all right, but a more mature-looking version. It was hard to believe that this dashing man standing before me had once been the lanky teenager who had annoyed the hell out of me back in secondary school. He looked like someone out of a men's fashion and style magazine. And he looked anything but annoying.

"Udonwa, right?" he said, grinning. "How are you? It's been years since we last saw each other."

"Absolutely. And you never kept in touch. You decided to just move on."

"Well, blame it on my dad — I was practically bundled back to the States as soon as we completed our final exams."

I was nodding while he was speaking, hoping he would mention Chinua's name. But I noticed he was trying to avoid mentioning him. My mind jolted back to Chinua's last message. He'd wanted to know why I had suddenly stopped replying to his letters and what it was that had kept me so busy that I did not want to visit. I did not want to deal with that right now so I refocused on the person standing before me.

"So let's catch up," he said. "What have you been up to all these years?"

"Nothing major ... just the usual — life, school. You know, that sort of thing ..."

"Oh, wait, you're still in school ... You must be studying medicine; you guys take the longest to graduate."

"Well, yes ... Sort of."

I wanted to change the subject and ask him when last he'd heard from his brother ... Did he know I'd been Chinua's girl-friend until twenty months ago? How could he not know? I kept wondering if they weren't on speaking terms and, if not, why; but seeing that he did not want to bring up Chinua's name, I also did not have the courage to do so.

"So, you must live around here then?"

"My flat is a few minutes' drive from here but on the other side of the bridge. And you, what do you do at the moment? I must say, I'm quite shocked to see you in Nigeria."

"Yeah, I only just returned after finishing college months ago — chasing some projects here and there, nothing major. So, you said you were 'sort of' studying medicine? Don't tell me you're bored? Isn't medicine a boring course for boring people like you?"

"It's a long story. But I'm not boring and neither is medicine."

He tilted his head back in mock shock. "Oh, yes, you were — back then at least. But not as boring as those girls who wanted to get married straight after school. I guess I'm not surprised you're pursuing a career."

"Thank you." I frowned. "I guess."

By this time, I was convinced he had not been in con-tact with Chinua in years. Who knows, perhaps those times in high school might have been the last time they spoke to each other. Otherwise how else would he not know anything about Chinua and me. Looking at him now, he appeared more serious-looking than I'd remembered him, but, other than that, nothing much had changed. His head still carried a bed of curls sponging out like someone was experimenting with them. I still found it strange that a man could have a head full of hair longer than that of a woman. I imagined Papa taking one look at Ifenna's head and jeering in Igbo that it was "the head of a madman."

"Do you want something to drink?" Ifenna asked. "I noticed you've had nothing since I got here."

"I'll have what you're having. And how do you know I've had nothing since you got here? Have you been watching me the whole time?"

"Am I in trouble? If you must know, I'm not the only one admiring the Lord's beauty that you are. Every single man here has been looking in your direction since you walked in. But I'm sure you know that already. You're breathtaking."

It must have been the way he said it because my head shot right up, my eyes locked with his, and I knew it was all I would be thinking about for the rest of the night.

Ifenna returned with our glasses of drinks before I could tell him I had changed my mind about having more. I had had at least four cans of beer before our eyes had clicked earlier but there was no stopping him now.

Our eyes met again for the umpteenth time and this time around I knew instantly that our thoughts were in sync judging by the way his eyes pored over mine and I quickly looked away. I looked back at him to find him still looking at me as though I were the only woman in the room, and realized I shouldn't have but it was too late. I don't remember how we left the club or how we got to my flat after that.

. . .

One look down and I noticed a bulge nearly tearing off his trousers. I reached out and held on to it, squeezing lightly. He let out a soft but heavy moan and grabbed my hand and led me to unzip his trousers, and then he placed my hand on his penis which felt like a rock. I was on my knees within seconds as I couldn't resist the warmth of the thing. His moan kept climbing as I worked my magic. Stopping, I took a peek up at his face and he grabbed my shoulders and pulled me up to him. Our clothes were discarded within seconds as though they were caught in a raging flame and we landed on my bed with a gentle thud.

Although I needed his guidance, I got none, and rather arched my hips forwards to let him enter me. In what seemed like a flash, a sharp pain ripped through my body that lasted only a few seconds. Two or three strokes later, I began to move to his rhythm, our moaning also in sync. His thrusts matched my pulled-in rear again and again and I moved my hips each time. I did not want it to end. I wanted him to occupy me forever. As his groans began to get stronger and deeper, my moans got deeper and louder. He grabbed onto my breasts and sucked, and I lost control. I was ascending a mountain and kept climbing until I got to the peak and let go. My body was soon convulsing to the rhythm of my descent and Ifenna's fast and deep thrusts, and within seconds he also reached his own peak and joined in the fall. I held onto him as he writhed and groaned. At that moment I knew sex wasn't just about a vagina meeting its male counterpart but a combination of everything else unimaginable.

. . .

Ifenna fell asleep immediately and like a log did not stir or move all through the night while I kept my eyes on the ceiling watching the fan twirl. Although I thought my heart would be beating faster than normal, it wasn't. I took slow deep breaths, trying to trace the night from the moment he'd approached me in the club to when we arrived at my flat. It was all a blur, and the five beers I'd had at the club hadn't helped my memory. It was a struggle trying to decipher what to and what not to think. At first, I kept my eyes on him as his chest rose and fell while he slept — the sort of look I heard a new mother gives her sleeping child to ensure the baby was still alive as it slept. But in this case, I could not determine if it was because I wanted him alive or not. Yet I was certain I wouldn't be able to resist a repeat of what had happened if it were initiated again.

When the sun's rays broke through my curtains, he began to stir.

"Are you an early bird or is it something I did that woke you up this early?" he said sleepily, smiling with a hint of unmistakable mischief. He looked totally relaxed, like what we had done was a normal occurrence, a practice he often engaged in with strangers. Only, we weren't strangers. He was Chinua's brother. "Are you okay? You look a bit distant."

"Shouldn't I be? I can't seem to process my thoughts. Last night feels like a blur."

"Well, let me help you remember. I will never forget how you clung to me and refused to let go."

The horror on my face must have stung because he provided a softer version of this account immediately.

"No, I don't mean it that way. But you pretty much held onto me the whole time we slow danced at the club," he said and sat up on the edge of the bed.

"Slow da — We danced?"

"Of course we did — don't you remember any of that? Anyway, it wasn't for long because you wanted to leave almost immediately. You practically dragged me out of there."

I sighed and relaxed my head back on the pillow. Our clothes were scattered across my bedroom, his shirt hanging on the door of the slightly open wardrobe, my blouse lying on the carpet next to my micro-miniskirt. Perhaps it was my clothing that had led to all of this; perhaps it was something more. I got up from the bed and reached for my blouse and, with the bedspread covering my lower body, hopped to the wardrobe to fetch another piece of clothing, something more decent-looking.

"Are you hungry?" I said over my shoulder. "Sorry, I usually don't eat breakfast but I can make you something to eat if you wish."

"That would be nice, thanks."

I tried not to watch as he got dressed. He left his shirt untucked over his jeans, his sleeves unrolled all the way to his wrists. Buttoning his cuffs should have been a mundane act, yet was significantly heightened to my senses because it was something his brother would never do. I left him in the bedroom to finish dressing while I headed to the kitchen to make breakfast. When he came out to the sitting room, I served him a plate of fried eggs and bread and a cup of hot cocoa, before I returned to the kitchen, where I remained while he was eating. When he was finished, he called out to me that he was leaving and I stood before him at the door, small and awkward. He did not make to hug me and I likewise did not initiate any body contact.

"Thanks again for last night. It was fun," he said, smiling.

I smiled back through the daggers cutting my insides as I unlocked the door for him to leave. Once he was out of the flat, I collapsed on the couch. What on earth did I just do?

Twenty

Mayokun was waiting outside the flat when I got home, a scene resembling the first time we met. As always, all I could think about was the sex we would be having in a short while. Since we had started dating, it was what we did during our spare time when not meeting up with his friends.

I often recalled the first time and the stupid conversation we had had afterwards.

"Thank you, Udo-n-wah."

"Thank you for what?"

"For what we just did — for letting me be your first."

I had turned my face away.

"Although I must confess, I heard you were a virgin, but I did not believe it. I mean, who can blame me? It's Lagos we are talking about here …"

"Hmm ..."

"I know, I know ... It's embarrassing and you don't have to say anything. Still, it came as a surprise to me. I couldn't believe there were still girls like you in this Lagos. I don't know how you did it, how you managed to remain fresh and untouched all this time. You're so succulent; I can't get enough of you."

From what I'd come to know, Mayokun was a typical Yoruba boy — loud, self-righteously cultured, and annoyingly ignorant about a lot of things. I'd let his words swim in my mind, while I had thought about what Chinua would have said if it were him.

"So, can I give my verdict?"

"What?" I gasped, shocked at his effrontery.

"Yes, my verdict of your performance, since it's your first time. Can I rate the whole act?"

"You really want to score me? You mean this is not a joke?" I had struggled not to show my rage.

"Joke, ke? Of course not," he had said, grinning stupidly.

"Go ahead, Mayo," I'd said, displeased beyond measure.

"So, for your first time, I'll give you eighty-five."

"Eighty-five? Is that good enough? Why not a little closer to a hundred?" I had rolled my eyes in mock intrigue, which he had stupidly mistaken for real interest.

"Eighty-five is excellent for a first timer, Udo-n-wah. You did great. But I know it will get better. In fact, you deserve more, but next time I'll score you closer to a hundred."

I had kept quiet like I knew I was supposed to after such an expository remark. It was all I could do not to explode.

Mayokun and I had started dating about two months after I'd lost my virginity to Ifenna. Although it had been many months since then, Mayo still believed he was my first. In practice, he may as well have been my first because I had bled for two days afterwards. Two days that saw him doting on me like a new mother.

The first time I met Mayo, he was standing outside the door of my flat that dreadful day I had run out of Sister Adaora's house. I had arrived in Lagos in the late afternoon and headed straight to the flat with just one thing on my mind — sleep. Instead, I had found someone standing at my front door. A stranger who somehow looked very familiar.

"I'm Mayokun, Nifemi's brother. Thank goodness you're here. I've been waiting here for ..."

My head was still swirling from my trip and I felt as though I was floating in mid-air. All I needed was to head straight to bed, and I unlocked the door so I could do just that, but as I stepped into the flat and was about to shut the door, he held onto it.

"Won't you let me in? I said I'm Nifemi's brother. My name —"

"I heard you the first time. You're looking for Nifemi. As you can see, she's not here," I said, clutching the door handle.

"Yes, I can see that. You must be her flatmate — Udo-n-wah, right? She talks about you and the other lady a lot; I can't remember her name now."

He stood by the entrance, wiping his feet on the rubber mat. I took a quick glance at him and noticed he was covered in sweat. I stepped aside from the door.

"Come in."

"My name's Mayokun, or you can call me Mayo for short." He was clutching a travel bag in his one hand, while the other kept wiping beads of sweat from his forehead. "Thank you, I've been waiting for God knows how long."

"Nifemi's room is the other one down the hall," I mumbled, turning towards the door of my bedroom. "She keeps her key under the mat sometimes. Goodnight."

I disappeared into my bedroom without waiting for a response from him and, with a deep sigh, landed on my bed. Closing my eyes, my mind drifted, straight to Awka, past Sister Adaora's front door, past her sitting room. I was standing in front of her door again, listening and wishing I had knocked or coughed or done anything to announce my presence, anything that would have ensured I did not hear them, or that what I had heard must have been a joke. I turned on my side to get into a better sleeping position but Mama was all I could see. I turned to the other side and again Sister Adaora stood there gazing silently at me. I had just one desire — to be left alone, by the whole world, not just Sister Adaora and Mama. I lay on my back, staring at the white ceiling. I tried to shut out the earlier events of the day but had ended up darting my eyes left and right. It was only after I did something to help me forget that I fell asleep.

The next day, I was awoken by a voice that sounded distant yet close at the same time.

"Udo-n-wah, open up. Open the door, please. Udo-n-wah, Udo-n-wah …"

"I'm coming." I pushed myself up slowly from the bed and crawled to the door.

"Are you okay?" the voice said.

I stared at the face of a person and it took me a while before I could recognize it, albeit faintly.

"You've not woken since last night. Do you want something to eat? I made rice and stew with some goat meat I found in the freezer."

Rice, stew, goat meat … Everything he said sounded foreign to me. Worse, I still could not figure out who he was and why he was in my flat.

"You don't remember who I am? It's Mayokun, Nifemi's brother," he said, which I considered to be the wisest thing I'd heard since I opened the door of my bedroom. "You let me in last night?" He was staring incredulously at me and only then did it click and I nodded.

"Now I remember," I said and slowly headed to the sitting room. As much as I wanted to crawl back into bed, I preferred the couch for some inexplicable reason.

"What time is it?" I asked him.

"I think it's around four-thirty."

"Four-thirty?" I looked around the room before my eyes settled outside the window. "Why is it so bright?"

"It's four-thirty in the afternoon …"

I turned and stared at him. "You mean I've been sleeping since yesterday?"

He nodded, staring at me. "When I had to go out in the morning, I called out for you to lock the front door behind me. I returned around two in the afternoon and let myself in when I realized the front door was unlocked. I figured you might be in but I wasn't sure so I knocked on your bedroom door just to confirm. Then I got worried when you didn't answer, and I knocked and knocked and kept knocking until you finally opened."

I lay my head on the soft cushion of the couch and closed my eyes again. "I'm sorry."

"I can dish up for you if you want to eat now. I hope you like goat meat? Everybody does. Well, not everybody, but most people I know do …"

"I haven't brushed my teeth yet. I need to wash my face and maybe take a bath."

"You know what, I think all of that can wait. You look very pale and I think you should eat something first before going back to bed, although I don't think it's a good idea — going back to bed, that is."

The sound of his voice and his choice of words, plus the way he kept looking at me, all spoke of concern. For a moment I was made to forget what I had heard Mama and Sister Adaora talking about. For a moment I did not wish Chinua were around to help me deal with it. He had never been of much help to me when I'd needed him anyway. Just like he hadn't been around to provide the support I'd desperately needed to deal with Jefferson's rape allegation.

"Okay." I looked up at him, smiling for the first time.

Mayokun had made a delicious stew with deep-fried goat's meat that tasted like a replica of Nifemi's, the few times she had been generous enough to cook enough for Amara and me. I ate slowly in silence while he watched the news on TV. Chinua would have been watching a documentary on science and technology or the environment while browsing for any channel airing sports. His favourite sport, basketball, was not readily available on regular Nigerian television and he would always settle for his second favourite sport, boxing, which had come as a shock to me at first.

The plate of food was not going down. I knew I was hungry but I could not bring myself to swallow anything.

"You know you are not getting up from that seat until you are done eating?"

"What?"

"I said, I will not allow you to go into your room until you finish eating every grain of rice on your plate."

I managed to put a smile on my face again. He was being very kind and he was still a total stranger.

"I spoke to Nifemi earlier. She said she will be out of town for a while. Is this the way her department always travels, or is there something I don't know?" He had no idea how much he didn't know and wouldn't like to know of what his sister got up to on campus. "I mean, the last time I was in Lagos, she was also out of town and I stayed with a friend until she returned. For some reason, she didn't want me to come here. Not that I knew this place, though, otherwise I would have found myself here regardless."

I smiled again. He seemed like a nice guy.

"You said you are Nifemi's brother, right?"

"Yes, I'm her younger brother by exactly twelve months and no more. And as you can see, I am way bigger and taller than she is."

And he was. If he hadn't mentioned it, I would have thought he was her senior by no less than three years.

"So what time are you attending classes today?"

"Huh?"

"Not that it's any of my business — I just want to be sure you're okay, that's all."

I glared at him silently and rested my back on the couch, before shutting my eyes.

"Okay, I'll take that as my cue to leave," he said, and got up, still looking me over. "I'm meeting a friend. So, I'll see you later then."

When he returned that evening, I stayed in my room. As far as I was concerned, I never wanted to leave my room again.

. . .

The next morning had been the same routine of staying put in my bedroom, but he must have got the message that I did not want to be disturbed. On the third day, however, Mayokun was back at the door knocking, and this time I had no choice but to answer.

"Hi," he said, smiling, and handed me a cup of hot cocoa.

I sighed and took the cup from him, stepping backwards into the bedroom to sit on the bed. With his hands deep in his pockets, he welcomed himself in, looking around the room. Behind the mug, I really took in his appearance for the first time. He was tall, very tall, with a dark brown complexion. The two sides of his face were faintly hollowed by a pair of dimples that deepened with each smile. It made sense why I had thought he looked familiar the first day we met; he was a male version of Nifemi.

"I'll be leaving later today and just wanted to make sure you'll be fine all by yourself since your friends aren't here yet. Or do you prefer I call your family? Clearly, you are unwell and something is seriously troubling you."

I glared at him, and then took another sip of my drink. "I'll be fine. Thanks for everything."

"I will be back in a few months' time and would love to check up on you, if that's okay?"

I nodded, and found my face softening into a smile at his kindness.

"Also, you should try and go to your classes. Aren't you supposed to be a medical student? Missing classes isn't the best, I can assure you of that."

My frown reappeared. "I said I'll be fine. Surely you can understand English?"

"I'm sorry, I didn't mean to pry — I was just looking out for you —"

"No, I'm sorry, I'm not usually like this ... I'm just not myself."

"That I can tell, although I don't know anything about you at all. Anyway, if you can't go to class, perhaps a library will suffice? Who knows, it may help with whatever it is that's bothering you. But whatever you do, please take care of yourself."

I looked up at him with a tight smile, watching as he walked out my room towards the sitting room, where I could hear him pick up his bag, open the front door, and close it behind him.

It was easy forgetting there was anything like class, which my decision from days earlier had helped ensure. For the first time in my life, I did not want to know more than I already did. Also, I wasn't ready to share my anger with anyone. I moped around for a few days after Mayokun left, and then one evening I left the flat to go to Higgles. I soon became a frequent visitor at Higgles, as I realized that drinking and dancing the night away seemed to make me forget many things I wanted forgotten. Then, on one of those fateful nights I ran into Ifenna.

By the time Mayokun returned for Nifemi's graduation ceremony and visited like he had promised, from the moment I saw him all I wanted to do was have sex with him. By then I had stopped attending classes completely, even going as far as missing my semester final exam. He had apologized for not coming sooner, maintaining that he hadn't been able to get me off his mind. I believed him.

After Nifemi graduated and moved out, Amara left too, but without completing her studies. I started looking for other accommodation and found my current flat away from town. Not too long after that, I made the decision to leave medical school, and therefore UNILAG. Mayokun was staying in a friend's place but would visit the flat every other day. Soon we were hanging out and would go everywhere together. He later introduced me to his friends, a bunch of mostly loud uncouth men who were so far removed from Chinua's friends, I didn't know what to make of them. Apart from their ill-mannered behaviour, disguised as casual banter, which often infuriated and embarrassed me, the idea of spending most of my spare time with a man other than Chinua was not something I had ever considered. But after sleeping with Ifenna, I reasoned it might be the best for everyone. How could I live with myself knowing that Chinua would someday find out? Or that I would have to see them both together at some point? The thought was so daunting that I decided to put it out of my mind completely. And the more I did not think, the more I needed to be held every night, by a man. Preferably, one who did not remind me of who I was supposed to be.

• • •

As soon as Mayo and I walked into the flat the phone rang. Nneora's calls had been going unanswered since that day I had left Awka in a hurry. I would pick up the phone and, at the sound of her voice, hang up immediately. The same thing would happen over the weeks that Sister Adaora called. But the voice on the other end today was neither of the two; it was someone who was in the same town as I was. And she had only a few words to say: "I'm on my way."

I jumped to my feet, running around the flat, trying to organize everything. "Mayo, please, you have to go right now. There's someone on her way here."

"Who?"

"You don't know her. Please go. I don't want her to see you here. My family cannot know about us, please."

"You keep telling me this, and I don't know why. For goodness sake, you are an adult, Udonwa. I'm sure your family understands that it's okay for you to have a boyfriend."

"You won't understand, Mayo …"

"Then enlighten me!"

"Mayokun, please go."

He wouldn't budge, so I mellowed a bit and tried reasoning with him. "Okay, I'm begging you. You can go to my neighbour's flat and wait until she's gone. I'm sure she won't stay long."

Mumbling, he ignored me, and tried to slot a disk into the VCD player. I lost my patience and yanked it out of his hand, pulling him off from the floor towards the door. He had just walked through my next-door neighbour's front door when Aunt Nene appeared at my front door. She wrapped me in her arms the moment she entered the flat.

"You've been very scarce, Udonwa, my dear. How are you?"

"I'm fine, Aunty. You're looking good," I said, forcing a bright smile.

"I can't say the same for you." She pulled away from me and tilted her head back to assess my appearance. "You don't look well at all, Udonwa. What have you been up to?"

"What do you mean, Aunty? Of course I look well!" I held out my dress for her to see I still weighed as much as I always had. But from the way she looked at me, I knew I had not convinced her — or myself, for that matter.

"I heard you people are on holiday and you haven't bothered to come home, twice now. Why?"

She was talking about UNILAG's medical students. By now, exams would have just started for the other mainstream courses in the university, but not for the medical students, as most were already relaxing in their parents' homes. That was no longer my problem. The same day I'd left UNILAG, I had gone straight to the school of architecture where I was referred to their evening school. I was offered the choice of starting from scratch in regular school or second year in evening school, and, without deliberating on it, I chose neither. I had heard about the Xenox Institute for Architecture and Interior Design from advertisements around campus. I knew they offered practical training while studying, so I had wasted no time in making my decision. And it had proved to be the best decision: I had interned at a firm since I had begun with them and, from the looks of things, I might get a permanent spot in this firm owned by one of the directors of the school. But I was not prepared to share any of this with my family yet. Since Papa deposited my school fees into my bank account, I still had enough funds to pay for my studies without worries.

"Udonwa, I know you very well, and if there's one thing I can swear about you, it's the fact that you don't play around with your studies, and the second, that you also do not play around with your family and holidays. So I don't understand why you've been avoiding everyone and refusing to come home often like you used to do. Did something happen?"

"Aunty, nothing happened; I just need some time to myself, that's all."

I avoided her eyes, realizing that I should have picked up Nneora's calls because there was no other person who could have put Aunt Nene up to this. She was a far more likely candidate than Sister Adaora or Mama.

"How did you know where to find me, Aunty? Who told you about this place?

"So you thought no one would find you? Udonwa, Lagos may be big but not too big for someone who knows their way around it. I only have one question: why are you hiding from your family?" She looked at me for a very long time. Then, seeing I wasn't forthcoming with an answer, she continued: "So who is the man who took away your innocence?"

"Hei, Aunty. You're embarrassing me. I'm no longer a child, haba."

"Even the way you talk, everything about you has changed," she said and sighed.

"Oh, Aunty, please. I'm still the same old Udonwa."

"Listen to yourself, your voice doesn't even sound convincing. Anyway, I know you're no longer a child, but you're still my sister's child and by extension mine. You can't hide anything from me. Maybe from everyone else, but not from me."

Too shocked to say anything, I sat motionless and speechless as she continued.

"You forget, I raised two young girls like yourself. Two girls who were already sowing wild oats at your age. And where are you hiding the young man I saw you with a moment ago?" Seeing my widened eyes she continued. "So you think I didn't see you people? I was sitting in my car for a very long time observing the area before I decided to come out. Besides, it's written all over you — with just one look I knew."

I broke down then, the words streaming out of me. Only when I stopped speaking did I realize I had told Aunt Nene about Ifenna but not Mayokun. I left him out. In fact, I left everything out except for that night with Ifenna. It was the only thing I could bring myself to talk about, as though it was announcing itself as the one thing that had led me down my current path. How could I tell her that after Ifenna I had been practically living with a man I slept with regularly? How could I tell her that every man who so much as looked my way and showed a little interest in me was a potential sexual partner if I was approached by them? How could I tell her it did not matter if the man was married or not, just like Mayokun's friend Osas, whom I suspected from the first day we met was going to ask me to sleep with him and that, when he finally did, I wouldn't resist saying yes? How could I tell her that the interest to sleep with a man could emanate from as simple a thing as staring at the flat surface of the man's trousers, imagining a bulge to be present? How could I tell her all of these things when I couldn't even say them to myself?

"Lincoln wants you to visit him in South Africa."

"I know, he's been inviting me for a while ..."

"Well, now is a good time to go. You people are on holiday. Getting away will do you good. But, more importantly, my dear Udonwa, everyone is worried about you. Worried sick, actually. We all know you are going through something serious."

The way she looked at me told me she knew what had set me off on this journey. It all began to make sense. When I ran out of Sister Adaora's house that day, I had looked back up and, for a split second, I had seen a curtain open slightly. The hand that was behind that curtain had looked very much like Mama's. I should have known she had seen me. No wonder they just kept calling and did not come physically looking for me. I supposed they had become worried after someone else must have answered the calls at the old flat, someone who must have told them she didn't know any Udonwa. I knew I was running from myself and everyone else, but I had no idea no one was pursuing me. They were all aware I had found out and decided to leave me alone, for the time being.

Aunt Nene continued talking about my proposed trip to South Africa.

"Lincoln insists you must go down immediately. You have to go and apply for your visa. I will go with you. He has already sent the money for the plane ticket."

I wanted to ask if Nneora, Jefferson, and Lincoln knew. I also wanted to ask if Papa was aware I knew. I wanted to ask — I wanted to talk about it all — but I could not open my mouth.

Twenty-one

Osas and I had started sleeping with each other before we could properly pronounce each other's full names. He was one of the senior consultants at the Xenox Institute, where I was training. I only found out he was Mayo's friend the day Mayo had come to take me out for lunch and we had bumped into him. Mayo's best friend or not, it did not stop our impending lustful quest. Before any of this happened, I had caught him a number of times giving me suggestive looks. Although I knew he was married, I had no idea how newly married he was.

I looked up at the wall clock across from my desk, worried I would be breaking the promise I had given to Mayo about coming home earlier in order to meet another of his old friends today. Not that I was particularly excited to meet any more of his legion of friends.

"Come in," I said to the person knocking. I knew who it would be — it was always the same person who visited my office when I happened to be working late. And just like the other nights, he had one thing in mind.

"Workaholic, what are you working on today? It's way past closing time, madam."

The aroma of the amala and ewedu in the plastic container in his hands greeted my nostrils as I looked up. "Just give me a moment, Osas." I was smiling in spite of myself. There was something about him that made him irresistible, and it wasn't just his looks.

"What exactly are you working on?" He came behind me to peek at my work on the desk, his freshly sprayed cologne filling the air around us. It was clear that he'd sprayed it on himself just before coming to meet me.

"This won't take long. I'm rounding up these figures for the new clients Mr. Adeneye commissioned; he insists it must be on his desk first thing in the morning."

"Oh, that can wait," he said and pulled me up from my seat.

He was wearing a black shirt and grey trousers, and his black-and-white-striped tie was hanging loosely from his neck. It took just one look at each other's faces and, with our eyes melting into each other's, I pulled him onto my desk and we were tearing at each other in seconds. It was a major miracle that my desk had not broken in two from the pounding it received from Osas and me every other day.

• • •

"Typical Nigerians, believing what they want to believe regardless if it makes absolutely no sense." Osas was talking calmly while giving me the look he'd been giving me since the first day I met him in Xenox's reception hall.

"Such as?" Mayokun said, sipping his drink.

"Such as what Ambrose is doing now. Marriages aren't meant to be celebrated only through white weddings. There are different types of marriage, each taking on a different form. Are you saying that without the white man we Africans wouldn't be getting married or that we were not doing so before the Europeans came?"

"What I've discovered is that arguments like yours are just a means of trying to justify having children before getting married," retorted Ambrose, an old schoolmate of theirs. He was a "brief man," to describe him like Lincoln would — a very short and stout fellow who was as brash as they came and, like many men of his stature, always needed a platform to announce himself. Every time we hung out, there was usually a different tall woman hanging from his arm, but today he was alone. Yet he was still insecure and making his voice the loudest in the room.

"Point of correction, had children before they wedded. I was already married — don't forget that," said Osas.

We were all in Osas's sitting-slash-dining room and his wife was in the kitchen with her maid putting some food together. I had volunteered to help out but Osas's wife had declined, insisting I was a guest.

"What proof do you have of that, other than trying to convince yourself that you were?" Ambrose said to Osas.

"What nonsense are you saying?" Osas's wife cut in as she entered the room, heading towards the dining table, in her hand a tray of peppered fried chicken covered with fresh onion rings. She was closely followed by her maid with bowls of water for everyone to wash their hands.

"There you go again, Mabel — you always say that when you don't know what else to say. It's like having a discussion with a child."

"Wait ... Wait ... Wait, stop right there. Are you calling my wife a child?" said Osas, almost leaping to his feet.

"All I'm trying to bring across to your missus here is that marriage without a wedding is no marriage."

Mabel shook her head as she dropped the tray on the table and promptly left the room. She was slightly plump but had not crossed over to the fat side yet. She had on a pair of green leggings and a big black blouse with see-through chiffon at the back. As she walked out, her bottom bounced and swung from side to side.

"If that is the case, then you've given me no choice but to support my wife. I was trying to avoid being accused of being a woman wrapper, but now I know I must. She is right. I mean, sure, all our parents had a white wedding, apart from Mayokun here, whose mom is a second wife. Nonetheless, a traditional marriage is in the same category as that of any other form of marriage, including that conducted before what the Americans call a justice of the peace, a civil marriage."

"What are you saying, Osas? That's an unintelligent argument now. If you don't know what to say, please do us all a favour and keep quiet, haba. Is it by force to talk? Must we all say something? A marriage conducted before a justice of the peace and that done before a man of God is one and the same. Ba wo? How is that even up for discussion?" Gbenga said. He had been busy eating from the platter of chicken on the table while everyone else talked.

Ambrose, seeing he had a supporter, laughed out loud and washed his hands to take his own big piece of chicken.

"You can insult me all you want, Gbenga, but you know I'm right. Marriage is marriage, period. A white wedding is not the final word on marriage ceremonies. Get that into your head."

"Well, what I know is that all of you are right." It was Wale's turn to add his voice to the discourse.

"Hun hun, Wale, you must take a stand. There is no joint support here — either you are for one or the other. Or else I'll turn into God and spew you out."

"Iro lo npa — you're a joker, Ambrose. Comparing yourself to God for that matter. Your mama no born you well. You are a bastard for saying that."

"Calm down, Wale, it was just a figure of speech. He did not mean it literally," Mayokun said with a weak smile.

"You are the one who is a bastard," said Ambrose, springing to his feet.

"Calm down now, both of you," Mayokun said again in a bid to quench the fire that was taking the route of an inferno. It was obvious he was getting irritated by his friends' attitude, like I was.

"Wo, mi o care o — I don't give a fuck. See, if the bastard wants to say nonsense, he must try his luck with someone else. Was I talking to him when I spoke? Stupid fool," Wale continued to bark, ignoring both Mayokun and Osas, who tried to pull him back down onto his seat.

"You can call me all the names available in your head today, but what I said remains. We want either/or for opinions, not a fence-sitter," said Ambrose, rolling his eyes while sucking and cracking the bones of the chicken drumstick in his hand.

"Heartless Bini imbecile!" said Wale.

"And you are nothing but a typical Yoruba man — a coward!" Ambrose retorted.

"Okay, that's enough, everyone. This is still my house." Osas got up and called out to his wife not to bring out any more food until the noise ceased.

"Ah, I'm surprised you're all talking like this, and you call yourselves professionals? O ga o. Nigeria is in trouble," said Mayokun, wiping his face.

"Big trouble," Osas echoed, then turned to Mayokun. "Mayo, your woman has been quiet for too long — doesn't she have anything to add? Maybe she should say something. Who knows, she might put a cap on this boiling pot and quench the fire."

Osas kept throwing quick smouldering glances at me, hidden with an outward smile. Since the last time we had slept together, I had tried to avoid being with him and Mayo at the same time, but he was either ignorant of this fact or deliberately ignoring it.

Mayo put his arm around me and began to speak, squeezing my shoulder and drawing me closer to him, as though he were marking his territory. "I don't think she wants to say anything — she would have if she wanted to. Besides, I won't take kindly to anyone who calls her names because she has a different opinion. Why can't we have an intellectual discussion or even argue in peace without it getting into a near fracas? The only thing stopping a few people from tearing one another apart is because we are in someone's home. If this were in public, someone's blood would have been flowing by now."

"How can we have an intellectual discussion when some of us are educated illiterates? Some passed through school, but the school did not pass through them. Some people here have

fraudulent Oluwole certificates and claim they are educated.
Let's face it, many of us here are high-school dropouts — that's
why our discussions always take this route."

"Okay, Ambrose, don't start again, please. I am trying
to quell the fire here; please don't ignite it any more," said
Mayokun.

I swallowed hard, for the umpteenth time since the discussion started, just like I'd been doing since the first day we
had hung out together. As always, I'd been made to speak up
at intervals, either to give my opinion or to proffer a solution.

"Many people were married in church but their marriages
are nothing but lies," I said, with my parents' and sister's marriages at the back of my mind. "To my understanding, getting
married in a church or the registry is for legal purposes. The
reason a marriage licence is issued after a marriage is for the
purposes of official documentation and record keeping, to recognize that a marriage has been conducted and to protect the
married partners in the case of any legal recourse. Other than
that, every marriage is considered the same — whether it was
conducted by an imam in a mosque, a rabbi in a synagogue, a
pastor or reverend in a church, a monk in a Buddhist temple,
and so forth. One is not higher than or superior to the other."

"My point exactly!" Osas slapped his palm on the table.

"And mine too," Wale added. The toothpick which he had
been using to pick pieces of stuck meat from between his teeth
was now halved and placed in the corner of his mouth.

"When exactly did you make that point? Was it when you
were busy dancing around the fence afraid of picking a side?"
said Ambrose and gulped down his bottle of beer.

For some reason, he was the only person drinking beer today while the others drank Five Alive and Just Juice. He put

the beer bottle down, burped faintly, and said, "Excuse me," as if that made any difference. No one said a word about his inexcusable behaviour because it was normal to them. I took a deep breath, swallowed what felt like pints of saliva, before I continued speaking, even though all I wanted to do was get up and run.

"In the part of Igboland I come from, the traditional bride price ceremony and wedding precede the formal white wedding, without which one is still considered unmarried or not properly married. If one wants to leave out the traditional wedding ceremony, that's fine — although it's very rare to see that happen — but the bride price ceremony is non-negotiable. After a bride price has been paid, if the couple decides for whatever reason that they do not want to hold a church wedding but rather in a court, like Osas was saying, it is still a valid marriage. If the same couple decides to wait before having a white wedding, say, after having one or two kids, fine, they are still married, and not just in the traditional sense, but truly married."

"Mayo, dis your woman na correct — don't dare let her go, o," Wale said in Yoruba, now unabashedly chewing the toothpick in his mouth.

"But … But … Wait, o … What happens in the case of a couple who has no form of formal wedding after the traditional one? What happens if they do not want to stay married anymore but want to get divorced? Will they need to go to a court to get one, since they were never married there in the first place?" said Gbenga, getting up in full view of everyone, unbuckling his belt, and pulling out his shirt before taking his seat again. For a moment, I thought I had died and gone to the Lagos version of la-la land. I had to remain calm.

"There will be no need for that. The bride price paid by the husband to the wife's family is promptly returned to him if he's no longer interested in the marriage. Even if it's the wife who is no longer interested, she would simply ask her family to return the bride price to her soon-to-be ex-husband's family. Once that is done, the marriage is over," I said and released the breath I'd been holding in.

"Interesting." Wale and Gbenga nodded in unison.

"But for anyone to suggest that someone is not married just because they have not had a white wedding or do not intend to hold one, or would prefer a court or African traditional marriage, is ludicrous," Mayo said, tightening his arm around me.

"I tell you, Mayo, it's rather unfortunate that some people think like this. For goodness sake, marriage is a commitment between two people, and in the case of our African culture, between two families as well. All this other talk is bullshit, mehn," said Osas and relaxed into his seat, staring at me with eyes so dim it was a mystery how he could see with them at all.

I excused myself and went to the balcony, from where I could hear them continue to talk.

"Wo, look, she has said it all. There's nothing more to add. You're a good daughter of your mother, Udo. Continue to make her proud. See, ehn, Mayo, I hope you heard me, o. Don't let her slip away. Mo ti so fu e — I have told you before many witnesses. She is gold," Wale said, dancing.

"Who sang this song?"

"You don't recognize that voice? This is the king himself ... KSA, Sunny ni, now," Gbenga and Osas echoed.

Ambrose stood up to join him and they continued dancing.

Mayokun joined me on the balcony and, through the open sliding door leading into the sitting room, I saw Osas out the corner of my eye, staring at us with his hand underneath his chin.

"What time is your flight tomorrow?" asked Mayo.

"Nine-thirty."

"And you still don't want me to drive you to the airport?"

"I already told you, Mayo, there's no need for that. My aunt will take me."

"Yes, you don't fail to tell me. You're not ready for me to meet your family yet."

"It's an Igbo thing; don't take it personally. We only introduce our partners if we are ready for the next stage, and you and I know we are far from that stage, so ..." Telling him this lie was easier for me than having to deal with him meeting anyone in my family. The thought alone made me so uncomfortable I wanted to shut it out forever.

"Okay, okay ... But call me first thing after you land."

I smiled the same way I had been smiling since that day in Awka. The smile was hollow at its core.

Twenty-two

There was only one word to describe Johannesburg in the mornings. Cold. I wasn't sure what I had been expecting, but to be smacked across the face with a wave of biting cold, the strongest kind ever, did not make the list. Lincoln and his wife had never mentioned it any of the times I had spoken to them in the days leading up to my trip. "You need a break from that godforsaken country," was all Lincoln had to say over and over, adding briskly, "and I'm paying for your flight, so just come over and chill out a bit."

Both Aunt Nene and Sister Adaora had called him, I gathered afterwards, and in typical Lincoln style, the deal of negotiation and refusal had been off the table; I no longer had any say in the matter. Due to our history, I had rejected many offers from Lincoln because I knew a repayment would be requested at some stage which usually would comprise what I could never afford, but he was insistent this wasn't the case when I brought it up. "Don't be silly, Udo, this trip will cost you nothing in the future. Those days are long gone. I'm a different me and you're a different you. We are adults now. C'mon, you'll love it here, I promise," he'd said.

So I had begun my earnest preparation for my visit to the City of Gold, and Aunt Nene had helped me with getting my visa. Surprisingly, that wasn't as difficult as I had expected, probably because of Lincoln's letter of invitation and supporting documents. His wife had included her signature too, and they had both attached copies of their South African identity documents. Documents that Lincoln had warned me to guard with my life, saying that if they got into the wrong hands, there was no telling the number of fraudulent activities he could be linked to (which I of course took as a joke). It was the book of life, he'd said, without which anyone in South Africa was regarded as a persona non grata or amakwerekwere.

I didn't have much to pack except for some food items Aunt Nene said Sister Adaora had sent over from Mama and a few others she had bought herself.

"When you return, you'll stay at the house for some time. I don't think it's okay for you to be alone at this time. You need family around you. It will never be the same, Udonwa. That bastard Ifenna, or whatever his name is, took away something precious from you," she had added.

Her hands were steady on the steering wheel, her mouth pursed and her head firmly on her neck, one of the few times it wasn't swinging left and right. Still, I knew she was livid. I supposed it had done Ifenna all the good in the world that he had left the country immediately after our night together, otherwise I wouldn't know what would have become of him if Aunt Nene had seen him. I hadn't told her the part where I kept returning to the club with hopes of bumping into him, although I had no idea exactly why I was hoping for that. And on one of those trips I had ended up on my back in the backseat of the barman's car.

"Aunty, I'm a grown woman; I knew what I was doing."

I wanted to be in control, to act like I had really wanted it. And I had at the time. Only when I'd realized he wasn't Chinua, that he was Chinua's brother, did the regret set in. But it was already too late either way. The good thing from the whole saga was that I did not miss being a virgin. On the contrary, I enjoyed having sex. Now I got what Nneora had been on about when she used to fill my ears with her escapades. Now I didn't squirm when the V-word was mentioned around me.

"No, Udonwa, you did not. You were drunk, and in a civilized world, what he did constitutes rape. He took advantage of the state you were in at the time; he took advantage of you. Tell me, if you were sober, really, with your normal eyes and mind, would you have given your virginity to Chinua's brother just like that?"

She had snapped her fingers when she said *just like that*, affirming how serious she was about the incident, but the snapping had brought on a repulsion of the worst kind, not with her or even with Ifenna, but with the topic. I had wanted to scream it over and over that Ifenna wasn't the only man I had been with since then. I had wanted to say it out loud that it was fun being with men. That it was no big deal. I had wanted to say it over and over and over again. But the more I thought about it, the more I could not believe it myself.

The rest of the trip to the airport had been quiet, and even when Aunt Nene had wanted to know more about my studies and training at Xenox, I had given her half-hearted replies. She had concluded by saying she knew I would make a fantastic architect. But by then I was already pretending to be asleep, shutting her and the rest of the world out.

. . .

Lincoln waved and rushed to meet me at arrivals, wrapping me in a warm embrace as we walked out of the airport. He was wearing a sweater over a checked shirt on top of a pair of jeans. As soon as the doors flung open, a wave of cold hit my face.

"It's so coooooold," I said, shivering and rubbing my palms together.

"Yes, it's usually cold in the early mornings. Come, I have a jacket for you in the car." He took the luggage trolley from me as we walked to the car park. "So how was your first time flying? Scary, fun, or both?"

"Both," I said, laughing.

"And the trip, was it smooth?"

"Only in some parts — there was a bit of turbulence at some point. Nothing too scary, though. So, where's your wife? I thought she'd be here with you," I said, looking around.

"Oh, she couldn't make it. She went to work."

"So you're a professional DJ now?"

"Madam questions! As opposed to when? I've always been a professional DJ, whatever that means. You, eh, you've not changed at all."

I smiled as I looked at him and realized that my smile no longer felt empty. At least, it was fuller than the ones I gave

Mayo and his friends. No one in my family knew about Mayo and I wanted it to remain that way. I did not want to share his story with anyone. For one, I was not even sure if there was anything like "Mayo and me" — what we had couldn't be classified as *us*. And I felt no remorse for constantly cheating on him with his friend; I didn't even mind if he found out about it. There was so much about me that I was not ready to share with anyone, not even myself.

Lincoln lived in a place called Noordwyk pronounced "Nod Vick." This was the first thing I would learn in the country about the language called Afrikaans — that, as African as its name sounded, it was not a language of the Black people of South Africa but rather a language spoken by the minority whites and mixed-race people, who, unlike their American counterparts, preferred to be referred to as coloured.

"So what language is predominantly spoken here?" I asked Lincoln as he offloaded my luggage from the boot of the car when we arrived at his home.

"Zulu, in Johannesburg and perhaps around the country. In other provinces, though, like in the Eastern Cape, for instance, the predominant language is Xhosa — and to answer your next question, yes, that is Mandela's language."

I laughed heartily when he said that. And I realized it was my first big laugh in a very long time.

Lincoln stared at me like I knew something he didn't want me to know, and for a moment we were kids again. Me, looking at him knowing exactly what he was thinking and what he was about to do next, and him, looking straight at me, daring me with his eyes to divulge what I knew about him to whomever was there, which was usually either Papa or Nneora. He looked away before I could register what the look meant.

"How did you know that was what I was going to ask? You are now a mind reader okwia?"

"I know you, Udo. I know you."

If only you knew the new me, I thought, following him inside.

A portrait of Zukiswa in a gold frame was the first thing I saw on entering the apartment. It was a small living space that made me wonder if the contractors had been challenged to build a family home in a tiny space. What could comfortably have been a spacious one-bedroom apartment had been turned into a two-bedroom duplex. The kitchen opened up on to the sitting room and there was nothing else downstairs except for the adjoining garage. The two bedrooms upstairs shared a bathroom. There was no other bathroom in the entire house save for that. We would have to wait in turns to use the bathroom every morning.

"This your house, na wa o. Why didn't they just make it a flat? This space where the staircase is located could well be a bedroom or another bathroom. They just wasted space. They did not make good use of the little available space they have at all."

"Ehn ehn, you're really studying about building and design for real. Who would have thought ... Udonwa, an architect ... But I hear what you're saying, though, don't mind the oyibo people. Everything is gradually becoming commercialized in this country and it never used to be so. Especially housing — it has become so commercialized that nobody considers the family unit anymore when they are building; it's become a money-making scheme for them. But in older towns, you'll still find houses that are more spacious than many of these new ones. Our estate is fairly new."

"My training is geared more towards interior design than all-round architecture, and yes, I can see your house is new — it looks barely lived in."

"Not because of that, though. Houses here are all usually pretty well maintained, unlike back home."

I understood his point. Chinua used to compare the houses in America with the ones in Nigeria and he would shake his head at our lack of "maintenance culture," as he called it. How we Nigerians loved to build big houses but found it hard to maintain them. Or how beautiful a house would look on the outside but once you got inside you would discover the horrible interior design and distasteful decor. I couldn't understand what he'd meant at the time, but now it made sense.

Zukiswa was adorned in Igbo attire of gorge wrapper and a lace and sequined blouse in the photograph occupying the entrance wall of the apartment. I'd seen the same attire at Aunt Nene's house. Mama had instructed it be sent down as a Christmas gift from her. She looked nice in it but whoever had tied her ichafu needed to be brought to the village square and given twelve lashes of the cane, as Grandpa would have said. Twelve, because that was the number of creases visible on the sides of the scarf; there were even visible pins on them, all twelve of them!

"She's beautiful, right?"

"Yes, she is. But her ichafu in this picture … odiegwu o!"

"You and your mouth. For the record, I tied it for her. I remembered how Mama used to tie it with office pins and I tried to replicate it."

"How does this look like any scarf you've seen on Mama's head? Hian, you are lucky I'm the one here and not Nneora — you would have heard nwi."

"By the way, how's Nne doing? I haven't heard from her in a while. She used to call almost all the time. She's the only person that tries to out call Mama. As for you, nobody ever hears from you."

"I haven't heard from Nne in a while either. She must be busy with her residency or Nnamdi."

"Or both," we both said at the same time, laughing.

"That is one stable relationship. I never envisioned Nneora to be the one who would stick to one guy for as long as she has done. Imagine, almost her whole life. If Nnamdi ever leaves her, I'm sure she'll commit suicide," said Lincoln.

I wondered what he'd say if he knew what I had been up to. If he could tell I was no longer a virgin, and that I had a boyfriend I cheated on regularly with his best friend, a married man.

"Where's your mind half the time?" I heard Lincoln ask me. "You seem to zoom in and out of thoughts."

"Oh, it was a long flight. I need to change into warmer clothes and get some sleep," I said, brushing him off.

"Of course. Don't mind me. We have three whole weeks to catch up. You can use the room on the left — that's the guest room."

• • •

Zukiswa, wearing a blue house coat, was standing in the kitchen when I came down later that evening. She looked just okay in person. Hers was the type of beauty that Nneora would refer to as "faraway beauty." The closer you got, the more the beauty appeared to fade.

"Hello, I'm Zukiswa," she said and stretched out her hand for a handshake. "You're Udonwa; I know who you are," she swiftly added, laughing at my attempt at introducing myself. "I hope you had a good rest. Are the sheets warm and comfy enough?"

"Everything is fine," I said, smiling.

She brought the food before I could add anything more. The sitting room doubled as a dining room and we all placed our meals on our laps and ate.

"May I have a glass of water, please?" I asked.

"Sure," Zukiswa said and walked across into the kitchen. I watched as she opened the tap and filled up a tall glass with water before bringing it to me. She returned my confused stare. "Don't you drink tap water? Sorry, but that's all I have. We don't have bottled water because we don't drink it."

"Is it safe to drink?" I asked, looking suspiciously at her and the clear glass of water.

"Yes, very much so," said Lincoln.

"You mean everyone drinks this water, straight from the tap? Don't you have to boil it first and then filter it?"

"Oh, that!" Zukiswa laughed. "I should have known that's what you were driving at. I'm so sorry. Lincoln had mentioned something about you guys doing that back home. No, here we don't boil our water before drinking. We drink straight from the tap."

The way she said "you guys" did not shock me as much as it would have under normal circumstances, as I was fixated on the matter of this miracle tap water. "Really?" I asked.

"Yes, of course. Don't look so shocked. Please go ahead and drink. Would you like some more? I could fill up a jar and bring it over."

I knew she wasn't being sarcastic, but it sounded like she was.

"That would be nice. Thank you," I said.

I had already gulped the first glass while she was still speaking, and then another and another. If water could be said to be tasty, then this would be the tastiest water ever. Its taste was that of purity and freshness, and it smelled of nothing, just like water should. I soon realized that drinking it evoked a feeling of being rejuvenated. A feeling I concluded had to do with healing from ailments one never even knew one had.

After the meal, Lincoln got up to put his dish in the kitchen and Zukiswa followed him. She washed and rinsed the dishes while he dried them before packing them away in the cupboard. With their backs turned to the sitting room, I watched Lincoln doing something I had never seen him do before. Washing the dishes was Nneora and my chore when we were children, which Lincoln had enjoyed watching us do and never lifted a hand to help us. But here he was, not only helping but being nice to someone other than himself. And I couldn't figure out if it was Zukiswa or the fact he was living in another country that had changed him, because standing in that kitchen was a different Lincoln from the one I'd known my whole life.

Twenty-three

Zukiswa insisted I take a bath instead of the showers I'd been having since I had arrived in Johannesburg. Lincoln agreed with her — according to him, a bath was the only way I could really warm up. I ran the bath with some bubble bath, another new thing Lincoln insisted on. He pointed out that I should take a look at the soles of his feet, insisting it was a sure sign to confirm if someone actually lived in or had visited a foreign country. "The soles of foreign returnees are always crisp and clean because they take bubble baths," he said with a straight face that should have been laughing. "So make sure you soak yourself in it every day while you're here, and when you get home, everyone will know you've crossed the border."

Just when I was about to step into the bath, the telephone began to ring. I ran downstairs, wiping my wet hands with a flap of the housecoat. "Zukiswa and Lincoln's residence," I answered.

"Hello, Udo, inukwa Zukis ... and Lincoln's blah blah blah ... biko, it's me o. Madam South —"

"Nneora ... Nne, is that you?" I clutched my stomach laughing.

"Yes, it's me. Who else did you think it was? How are you? How's South Africa? So you left without telling me?"

"It's not like that, o Nne. It's been very hectic."

"I know, I know — it's been one very busy time for all of us. I've just completed my housemanship and I'm being redeployed, but I don't know where yet."

"Wow, Nne, congrats. This is awesome news. Finally, Doctor Nneora Ilechukwu!"

"That's me!"

"Nne, I'm so happy for you. I like how your new title sounds."

"There's a lot we have to talk about ... Starting with this architecture-slash-interior-design thing you're doing — is it the best for you? Are you sure you don't want to go back to medicine?"

She said it like it was something we had discussed in the past. She did not bother to ask me why I had left medicine in the first place. She did not ask me why I had not contacted her or anyone in a long time. As she carried on talking, I could imagine that the family had all probably had a meeting and decided they would carry on as if nothing had happened until I was able to face them all.

"I'm pretty sure that ship sailed a long time ago. You are the only doctor in our family. And that's how it's going to be."

"So Chinua is history, just like that — he left and never came back?"

I knew she would bring him up. There was never a time I spoke to her that she did not bring up the subject of Chinua. But she knew as well as I did that Chinua did not want to be with me, not with the way he had gone silent. And it wasn't something I wanted to talk about.

"Are you sure he's even okay? Maybe it's time you went looking for him. Maybe reach out through his brother. You know, someone said they saw him in Lagos a while back. Who knows, he might still be in town. We could ask around, you never —"

"Enough, Nne, please. I don't want to talk about Chinua and his brother."

"Okay, is that why you want to bite my head off? Hian!"

"Please, let's leave it at that. I have a new boyfriend now. His name is Mayo, and he's been good to me." The moment the words left my mouth, I regretted saying them, but there was no going back now.

"Kick me in the teeth!" she screamed in Igbo. "Udonwa, why are you just telling me about this now? Who's he? Where's he? And when can I meet him?"

I had succeeded in not telling anyone about Mayo until this moment because it was the only way I could stop Nneora from talking about Chinua. Wanting to know things I could not tell her, things I had no answer to, because it was only after I had arrived Johannesburg that it had dawned on me that Chinua had stopped communicating with me over two years ago and been gone for almost three. So I told her about Mayo and even gave her the same lie I had fed Mayo about him being my first. I figured that since only Aunt Nene knew about Ifenna, it was best kept that way. And for the umpteenth time in recent times, I could not help wondering when my life had become such a mess.

"When I return, we'll make a plan to all meet. He's been dying to meet you too. In fact, he wants to meet everyone."

"And I'm sure he must be good looking for you to have been banging him since … hmm … Udo … Jirikwa nwayo, o kwa nwayo nwayo — take it easy with the sex o, easy does it. I should've known you're the type that will never let go once you taste that thing. And these Yoruba boys dem sabi do."

"Which Yoruba boys? No, no, Nneora, don't tell me you cheated on Nnamdi … tufiagi nwa," I said, withholding the part that I too was cheating on Mayo. I wondered what she would say if I told her about Osas and our liaisons. But, as close as we were, I could not bring myself to tell Nneora certain things, things that I preferred to take to my grave. Not for fear of being judged but just for the sake of fear. I did not like to say things I did not want to be repeated back to me. It was bad enough that the deed had been done. There was absolutely no need giving power to the words by voicing them.

"Biko rapukene ife anwa — please leave that matter. It was just once; it was never repeated. Nnamdi himself, is he committed? I've lost count the number of times he's cheated on me too."

"Are you serious? You never told me. Nnamdi cheated on you. Why?"

"How would I know and why should I care? Udo, such is life. We've been holding on to this relationship because we've come a long way and we can't throw it all away now … Otherwise, eh, please … I have to go now, chei. I've run up too much money on this call o, but I'll call you again before you return. Hope Lincoln's wife is treating you fine?"

"She seems really nice — nothing like the clingy Anuli."

"Thank goodness. Mama said she can't wait to meet her. You know she helped him get out of jail?"

"Jail? What jail? What happened?"

"You are the one who disconnected from your family and does not call anyone unless you are called. Ask him yourself — you're in his house. Udo, let me go. My money has finished on this phone call."

"Okay, Nne, we'll speak again. Take care and greet Ma—"

The line disconnected before I could complete my sentence. Nneora was one person I knew who would never change; the times when she did change, everything seemed to change along with her. How she could hold a conversation like we just had and in no time divulge all she wanted to say. Dropping the bombshells of cheating on Nnamdi, someone everyone thought was the love of her life, and then justifying it by saying he had been cheating serially on her too. Also about Lincoln going to jail. Throwing it out there as though it were a toy that I was somehow supposed to catch but missed. But, as shocking as it was to hear, it would have taken a miracle for the Lincoln I had always known not to see the inside of a South African police cell by now. If she had been sitting across the room from me, I was sure she would have forced out of me details of my night with Ifenna, my one-night encounter with the barman at Higgles, as well as how I had started sleeping with Mayo's best friend, Osas. In that moment, I felt an urge to speak to someone about what was suffocating me. A feeling that had begun that night on Osas's balcony while the arguments were going on, when all I could think about was that day in Awka. Being in Osas's home with Mayo and his friends — people I realized I did not particularly care about — had been the first time I had felt the need to deal with this. It was high time I spoke to someone about it, and not just the half-hearted type of discussion I had had with Aunt Nene.

. . .

Zukiswa was following at a close distance as we walked through the mall, doing what she referred to as window shopping. We stopped to look at the displayed clothes, home goods, and jewellery through glass walls of stores, many of which were now closed for the day as we headed to the mall exit. This was not a particularly big shopping centre, but still larger than the last one we had visited. Where Nigeria invested in residential houses to accommodate our ever-increasing population, South Africa seemed to be catering to an obvious shopping addiction of its citizens, with every neighbourhood appearing to have a shopping centre.

The sun had just disappeared but in its place was another kind of brightness. From the little I'd seen since I got here, the streets of Joburg lit up every night from an innumerable number of street lights, a shocking contrast to Lagos where, once the sun went down, darkness descended as though there had never been daytime. There were literally dozens of street lights lined up on the roads, all in working condition. Another wonder. I wrapped my arms around my upper body as we walked to where the car was parked, the piercing wind feeding on my exposed limbs.

"I'm so sorry I didn't check when we were leaving the house. I thought there was an extra in the boot. Lincoln always leaves one there."

"Pardon?"

"A jacket. It's your first time in Joburg; you mustn't leave the house without a jacket."

"It must have slipped his mind. He has a lot more important stuff on it."

"This is equally important. As a first-time visitor to Mzansi, I don't think you've been educated enough about the lifestyle of this place. And I'm so sorry we've both been too busy with work to do that. Hopefully that'll change soon. Here, take my jacket."

I took the jacket from her and tried to smile through the overpowering cold but could only manage a tight-lipped grimace, imagining that if I opened my mouth any further, it would freeze. It didn't help that the wind was dragging me backwards as we walked through the parking lot.

"How is it in winter if summer is this cold?" I said.

"Cold? This isn't cold, Sisi, it's just windy."

"You know what I mean … It is really cold. I mean, harmattan has no hold on this. Kai."

"Hayi, summer is almost gone — we're approaching autumn now, which is the start of winter. If it were serious winter, you wouldn't dare leave home without extra clothes on. I mean, you'll be decked out in warm clothing even while relaxing at home. Joburg winter fears no one. Even we locals are not spared from its fierce cold. And another thing, you wouldn't be able to speak — not like you're doing now, anyway. Your mouth, cheeks, and nose would be frozen by now."

"Really?"

"Yep," she said, laughing. "This way, the car is parked over there."

One touch of a button on the car remote and the headlamps flashed as the car doors unlocked. In the comfort of the car, the cold still permeated my body. I watched as small showers of rain began to fall, sliding down the car windows. Even with the windows wound up, the wind could still be heard, strong and steady, its sound mimicking the whistling of a giant in a mountain cave, its gush echoing back and forth. In complete

contrast, I realized, the streets of Lagos would have been swirling instead with sandy dust and litter. Litter comprising old
newspapers used to wrap the popular grilled beef suya, eaten-
and-tossed-out-of-the-window sweet wrappers, empty biscuit
wrappers, gala wrappers, empty water bottles, eaten cobs of
corn, ube seeds, mango seeds, and virtually all the seeds of
every fruit in season. I thought of how this filth would be flying
mid-air and covering static electric street poles and comatose
traffic lights. I imagined that open gutters would have filled
up and be spilling over onto the streets and roads. But here
it was just the wind and rain, the smell of which was like the
start of harmattan in Iruama, like the budding season of udala.
Relaxing against the seat, I closed my eyes and took it all in.

• • •

Lincoln was sprawled on the couch in the living room, clutching the TV remote. There were remotes for virtually everything
in this house. There were speakers hidden in compartments in
all the rooms in the tiny house, including the single bathroom.
Lincoln's desire to listen to music at all times had been the one
thing that had kept him safe from engaging with Papa in the
later years whenever he'd returned home from university.

I'd wanted to spend time alone with Lincoln since the day
I had arrived but had not been able to do so, because when he
was working, I was usually fast asleep. In the mornings after
Zukiswa left for work, he was usually home but would be asleep
throughout the day. Just when I would be getting ready to engage with him, he was off again.

Lincoln's huge frame filled up most of the couch, and he
had to get up to make space for me. He had grown so tall when

he had returned from his secondary school final exams that Mama had started referring to him as a giant. He and Jefferson towered above all of us in the house, but where Jefferson was tall and lanky, Lincoln was bulky and seemed to have started lifting weights, judging by his upper arms and chest. He still had his trademark sideburns trimmed to a perfect line, accentuating his bone structure and complexion. As children, all I had wanted to do was avoid him by all means; now here I was in his house complaining of not seeing much of him. Aunt Nene was right — visiting Lincoln was the perfect distraction I needed, if only for how close it had brought us, in a way I'd never thought possible.

"So you are not working today?"

"Nope. I'm off today. My assistant will stand in for me." He looked at me. "And what's the smile for?"

"I don't know, maybe because I'm happy to finally sit and talk with you … alone."

He was silent, and I thought he would ask me something personal and I wouldn't be able to resist telling him about my life since the day he had left for South Africa. But he instead drew me close to his side and put his arm around me, and together we watched television in silence.

"So what's this I hear about you going to jail?" I asked after a few minutes of silence.

"Who told you that? Uh, forget I asked. It can only be Nneora and her big mouth."

"Hian, Linc, so are you saying Nne did a bad thing by telling me what I'm supposed to know, or what?"

"What you are supposed to know, how? Do I know everything about you, or about her for that matter? What do I know about anybody besides what I've always known?"

"Well, if you want to know anything about your siblings, the best thing for you to do is to ask and —"

"As if you'll tell me ..."

"How do you mean? Anyway, all I'm saying is that I seem to be the only one in the family who had no idea you went to jail. What was it for? And please don't change the subject again."

"I don't want to talk about it, Udo." He tightened his arm around me instead of releasing it.

"Ehn ehn, it was that bad ..."

He pulled away to stare at me briefly and quietly returned his gaze to the TV.

"You know what I mean; please tell me what happened, biko. I have a right to know, o, especially now that I'm in your house ... I don't want wahala on my head, o."

"What wahala ... Ehen, so you are thinking I'm a criminal, right?"

I burst into laughter. "I didn't say that now, haba."

He threw a cushion at me. "But you were thinking it."

"Okay, okay, I'm sorry ... So, tell me what happened."

"It's no big deal, although at the time it was. I thought it was all over for me, that I would lose everything I'd worked for." He sighed before he continued: "Firstly, I was not in jail but in a police cell — those are two totally different things. I was arrested for drug dealing ..."

"What?" I sat up straight on the couch. "How do you mean. Linc ... Drug dealing, how?"

"You need to see your face, Udonwa. That I said I was arrested for drug dealing doesn't mean I was actually dealing in the drugs. Na wa for you, o." He hissed and increased the volume of the television.

"I'm sorry, Linc, I didn't mean it like that … It's just that the shock of … I'm sorry."

He put his arm around my shoulders once again and lowered the volume of the music channel.

"The drugs belonged to a colleague of mine at work. He wasn't even a dealer but a user. He kept them in the bathroom at the club and an off-duty policeman happened to be there that day, and had walked in on him and saw the drugs where he'd left them on the toilet. Instead of the fool owning up or denying the drugs belonged to him, he mentioned my name as the owner when interrogated."

"Kai! People are heartless. How could he do that?"

"My dear, to cut a long story short, I was arrested on the spot in the middle of a gig."

"Just like that?"

"Ah, it's like you don't know this place — the favourite words of the South African police are 'Nigerians' and 'drugs.' Nothing sets them off on a course like those two words."

"So how did you get out? Nne said it was Zukiswa that —"

"I knew it had to be Nneora … Anyway, during the court proceedings, Zukiswa mobilized a group of friends who all testified to my good behaviour and my boss also gave his testimony. In the long run, all the evidence pointed to my being innocent. In fact, let's just say the hand of God played a huge role because the judge saw reason and released me without a single charge. Mehn, there are people who deal in drugs in this country but I'm not one of them. I didn't slave away for years at university to become someone Mama can be proud of, just to throw it all away for something callous like drug dealing. Do you know what drugs do to people? Nna mehn, I'm better off using my intellect and creativity to make money."

I couldn't have been prouder of anyone as I was of him at that moment. Perhaps I'd missed something about him when we were children, something that would've revealed this side of him. I felt bad that I might have misjudged my own brother my whole life.

"So you would have been rotting in jail for something you knew nothing about?"

"I tell you, my sister, my life would have been over by now."

We allowed the silence to speak the rest of the words we did not want to voice until Zukiswa, returning from work, drove into the garage. When she walked into the house, I had a new-found admiration and love for her.

. . .

Zukiswa stood with me as we watched Lincoln offload my luggage from the car and a porter loaded the suitcases onto a trolley.

"Thank you so much for your hospitality, Zuks," I said.

Lincoln walked ahead with the porter while we both walked behind them.

"Oh, it's nothing, Udo."

Like the rest of my family, she had adopted my pet name and tried to say it like a native Igbo speaker. She was wearing her work uniform, a pair of black trousers which as always outlined her robust hips. A navy-blue T-shirt neatly tucked into the trousers revealed an unusually tiny waist, and was inscribed with the name of the company she worked at above the left breast. Although not strikingly beautiful, her smile made up for it. When she smiled, two faint dimples appeared on both cheeks. She wore her natural hair in a bun on the top of her head. Like always, she wasn't wearing lipstick but light lip-gloss. Two small earrings dotted her ears and a slim gold-plated watch completed her look. Compared to Anuli, she was a breath of fresh air.

"No, I insist, you've been most kind and the whole family will hear about it."

She smiled and hugged me tighter. "Goodbye, Sis, and have a safe flight."

When we got to the check-in counter, Lincoln wrapped me in his arms. We were in that spot for what seemed like forever before we heard the call announcing boarding for my flight. Slowly we disengaged and Lincoln wiped off two rolls of tears from my cheeks before wiping his own. He walked back to where Zukiswa was standing watching us; I could see she was trying to control herself from tearing up.

I spent most of the trip back to Lagos reminiscing about my last days spent engaging in many more honest discussions with Lincoln. He had asked me about a few personal issues, although he had avoided mentioning Chinua — and relation-ships of any sort — focusing rather on my part-time schooling and work. And just like Nneora, he'd skipped the part of what had prompted the change in career, and simply said he'd al-ways suspected I was not cut out to be a doctor but a creative instead. He'd even said that when the time came, I would help him design and build his own house. As strange and new as these discussions were, I felt they were a necessary start to the many difficult ones awaiting me and the rest of my family in the near future.

Twenty-four

Mayokun started acting strangely when I returned from South Africa and two weeks after his visit to his mother. He would walk into the flat, ignore me, and a few minutes later leave with a plastic bag stuffed with some of his personal belongings. He did this over the course of the week and nothing I said to him mattered.

Thinking that Osas had finally snitched to him, I knew it was only a matter of time before he exploded. But that assumption changed when I received Osas's invitation to his house. According to him, his wife and daughter were visiting with family in Canada so we'd be free to be together. It'd be the first time I'd be visiting his house without Mayokun and I wasn't sure of what to make of it. I told him I would think about it, in the hope Mayokun would come around and tell me what was troubling him. Days passed, though, and Mayo was still not forthcoming on the reasons for his strange behaviour. One day after work, to calm my mind, I took Osas up on his offer.

I climbed the stairs leading to Osas's apartment on the second floor of the two-storey home to find him waiting at the front door, keys dangling from his fingers, and a sheepish smile playing at the corners of his mouth. He led me straight to his bedroom. The room was painted a ghastly lemon-colour that nearly blinded my sight. But I was there for one purpose only. Ours was one of those affairs that made absolutely no sense. It was just a case of two people who enjoyed screaming obscenities at each other in the throes of passion. But on this particular day I had no intention of allowing his body on me; instead, I wanted to do the least I could do and leave as fast as I could.

He stripped naked and I was shocked to see his erection beckoning to me. He relaxed on the bed and gestured to me to join him.

"Come down from there," I said, surprising us both.

"What?"

"I said come down from there ..." I said again, with a mix of fright and boldness.

I gave him a look that suggested I would not budge, and reluctantly he dragged himself to sit on the edge of the bed. Without wasting another second, I took him in my mouth. It must have been the shock of it being the first time I had done this, or perhaps it was the force of my action, because he shook from the moment his flesh hit the insides of my mouth and my tongue circled around him, and within seconds he became limp like bread soaked in water.

He lay back on the bed while I battled my nausea. It took everything in me not to throw up all over him and his clean blue sheets. I got up, clutching my unbuttoned blouse together, and walked into the adjoining bathroom where I spat him out of me and gargled mouthwash until I could no longer taste his slimy matter. When I returned to the bedroom, I found him snoring, still lying in the position I'd left him. At that moment, staring at him — his form, his limp average-sized penis — I knew I did not want to be with him ever again. I no longer cared about the suggestive looks he'd give me which usually weakened my resolve. I no longer cared about what Mayo and the rest of their friends would say if they found out what we had been doing.

I sighed, picked up my handbag, and left his house.

I needed no one to tell me something was awfully wrong with me, Udonwa Ilechukwu, when I walked into another woman's home to sleep with her husband.

. . .

Two days later, Mayokun walked into the flat silently, refusing to accept even a glass of water. I was busy with a design proposal and wasn't really paying much attention to him. He went straight to the sitting room and watched television until he announced he was leaving. Still busy with my work, I mumbled a goodbye and didn't see or hear him leave. He returned later in the evening, in the same way he always entered my home, by letting himself in. But today I had a freshly cooked bitter leaf soup simmering and was just setting down the accompanying Semovita when he walked in. Mayokun, who would give up his legs and arms for a good meal of bitter leaf, just strolled in looking like he wasn't sure if he wanted to be there or not. Like a bad case of déjà vu, the scene was reminiscent of the times Papa and Uncle Ikemefuna would walk into their respective houses and for no reason ignore their wives, as if Mama and Sister Adaora were invisible, treating them as though they were objects not worth their attention.

I knew Mayokun wasn't anything like that, but I couldn't help feeling I might have somehow encouraged him to exhibit such hostile behaviour towards me. Perhaps I was starting to act like Mama and Sister Adaora, albeit unwittingly.

He cut into my thoughts, saying: "There's something that's been bugging me that I need to discuss with you."

I looked at him and said nothing. I knew that whatever it was must be very serious for it to take weeks for him to be okay to talk about it.

"I won't beat around the bush …"

"Did something happen at home? Is your mom okay, or is it work?"

"Is your mother really your mother, or are you the child of your sister? No, wait … Let me rephrase that. Are you the product of an incestuous affair, Udo-n-wah?"

I looked away, trying to pretend I hadn't heard what he'd said, or that perhaps for a fleeting moment I was dreaming, or that something else entirely different from what was happening was actually going on.

"Aren't you going to answer me?"

"What do you want me to say, Mayo?"

"How about the truth? Tell me the truth. Who is your birth mother? Your real mother?"

I thought about his question, asking myself who my real mother was. But I wasn't prepared to say that to him, because

I could see he was shaking his legs about, like he did when he was angry about something.

"Damn it, Udo, say something. Who the hell is your mother? I demand to know this instant." He was standing right in front of me, so close that his face was nearly merging into mine, and I could smell the strong scent of alcohol on his breath, like he had been drinking from dawn.

"You've been drinking ..."

"I swear to God, Udo-n-wah Ilechu-ku, if you try to avoid my question again by throwing one of your stupid remarks at me one more time ... I swear I won't be responsible for my actions. Who the hell is your real birth mother?"

Is that why you are huffing and puffing? I heard myself say over and over again in my head. But when I opened my mouth, something else came out.

"Can't we talk about this rationally like two adults?"

He pulled out one of the dining chairs and sat down, avoiding the couch where I was now seated, as though being in the same place in which he had made sweet love to me in the past would somehow contaminate him. I knew what his every gesture meant — his hands that curled into fists, his eyes that darted left and right before finally settling on my face.

"Yes, you're right, Mayo. I'm not my mother's child like you say. I am my sister's child. My sister was raped by my father at the age of fourteen and she fell pregnant with me and —"

"Unbelievable! What sort of disgusting thing are you talking about? Just hear how it sounds so normal in your mouth. Aren't you ashamed? That you're a product of incest ... Is that something to be proud of?"

"I don't understand what you mean, Mayokun Adegbemiwa." If he could register his rage towards me by calling me by both my first and last name, I could do the same. "Are you suggesting that somehow this is a tradition in my family, or that my sister encouraged my father to sleep with her, or that —"

"See eh, just shut up. Do you understand me? I don't want to hear any more. This is disgusting. You are disgusting. Your family is disgusting. How can a father sleep with his own child? How on earth can that be? And you're here walking around acting like you are something special."

"Oh, you mean I should crawl into a hole and remain there just because I have a sick man for a father? How is it my sister's fault she was raped by her own father? Isn't he a man like you? Is this not a clear case of misplaced anger? And how is it my fault that I'm a product of that unholy liaison? Didn't God know what was going on? Could he not have prevented my sister from falling pregnant with me? How on earth can a young woman be sexually abused, and then people like you turn around and blame the abused instead of the abuser? How on earth is it my fault that my life began the way it did, or my sister's fault that she was raped? Please tell me how that is any of our fault, because I don't get it. Answer me, Mayokun!"

"Please keep your voice down, abeg, before the whole world hears your dirty secret. Before your neighbours hear that I've been sleeping with someone who is cursed."

He moved closer to the windows and closed them one after the other, then pulled the curtains together, flattening and straightening them. "Ah, abomination! God forbid. To think I believed that because you were a virgin when we slept together, you were sweet and special. To think I was planning on proposing in the near future." He walked to the curtains in front of the sliding door and pulled those closed too. "Thank God I listened to Nifemi when she said there was something off about you, that you were too secretive. Thank God I started asking questions ... Thank goodness I listened to my mother after she told me a prophet in her church revealed there was a dark cloud hanging over your head. I'll forever be glad I listened to her advice to ask around ... To think ... To think I would have married someone who was ... who is ... This is disgusting, mehn. Ah, I'm out. I'm out, Udo. No wonder you did not want me to meet your family. No wonder! We need to end this relationship right here, right now."

"You don't have to say so twice." I walked towards the front door, before saying: "If I had known I was dealing with a wicked soul all this while, I would have ended it a long time ago myself."

He placed an open palm on his chest, glaring at me. "Me, a wicked soul?"

"You're not a good person, Mayo, and I pray for your sake a woman falls straight from the sky into your arms because that is the only way you will find an untainted woman in this world. Let me tell you something, in case you don't know: every family has secrets. Every family has one thing or another they are hiding from the rest of the world. It may not always be as *disgusting* as mine, as you put it, but there will be something. For your sake, I suggest you start looking into the sky as soon as possible for your prized possession."

That was all I could bring myself to say to him, although I wanted to say more. Since he wanted to hurt me, I wanted to hurt him right back. To think I had been starting to allow myself to feel something for him. Just when I was starting to make myself stop thinking about Chinua in a bid to try to convince myself that he, Mayo, was now *the one*. Just when I had made

up my mind to stop sleeping with Osas. Just when I was ready
to be faithful to him. Just when I was finally okay with introducing him to Nneora on her next visit. That was all gone now.

I wanted to hurt him with my hands and with my words.
I was itching to tell him about Osas, to say that he wasn't my
first because I wasn't a virgin when we met. Although I had not
told him I was one, I had not corrected him either. I wanted to
let him know I had slept with his best friend, not once but several times. But the words wouldn't leave my mouth because, as
much as I wanted to hurt him, my real anger was reserved for
Papa, Uncle Ikemefuna, Mama, and Sister Adaora, and even
Chinua.

I knew it was a good thing that someone had finally voiced
out loud the Ilechukwu family secret. I had no interest to know
who it was who had been generous enough to offer such information on a platter. If he could hear it just like that, then it
must be well known already.

He was frantically stuffing the last of his shoes into a big
plastic bag when I turned towards him and sighed. He scowled
and let out a short hiss, but before he could say another word,
I beat him to it.

"Get out of my house."

PART IV

Twenty-five

T he Gospel Centre International was one of those churches you stepped into and knew right away nothing would change, that you would remain the same. Yet I walked in there with Grandpa's words, *One does not shy away from a fight because one fears being defeated*, reverberating through my mind as the hot Lagos sun seared my skin.

After the somewhat flashy manner in which Mayo and I had broken up, I knew I had to do something, although I had no idea what until I saw a sticker on one of my neighbour's cars. Funke was one of those Christians who let you know they were one the moment you met them. A simple greeting of "Hello" was all it took for her to respond with an exaggerated "It is well, my sister," accompanied by a smile and vigorous nodding. The first day I

moved into my new flat, she was the first person who knocked
on my door and, after exchanging pleasantries, handed me a flyer
announcing a church program at the Gospel Centre, and said:
"The place where the undiluted gospel is preached." On her way
to several church services, I would see her handing out more flyers to other tenants and neighbours and even random passersby
on the street as she walked to church.

The church, located just a few houses away from my block
of flats, was one of the new-generation churches, or "mushroom
churches," as Papa preferred to call them. One of them had
sprung up in Iruobi a while back, and I would never forget
Papa's face when he sternly warned us never to be seen anywhere near it. "These churches started as a result of rebellion
against the orderliness of the orthodox form of worship; they
are worse than the Catholics who do not see anything wrong
with bowing down to carved images," he had stated. And so I
had avoided looking at their flyers.

Since moving to Lagos, attending church services hadn't
been a priority for me. It did not help matters that Aunt Nene's
family were of the Catholic faith, and even though Papa was
far away in Iruama, I always imagined him looming over me,
feeling betrayed if I walked into their church.

Now, entering the Gospel Centre, I was about to discover
why Papa would refer to them as churches headed by a bunch
of untrained men who had no reason to be called pastors. These
churches, he said, were headed by men who hadn't been called
by God; they had called themselves.

Pastor Asuquo fit the stereotype of such pastors with his well-
oiled hair and a huge gold cross always hanging from his neck. I
would later notice that he was more colourful on Sundays when
he mounted the pulpit in crisply ironed multicoloured shirts.

Today he was wearing a pair of jeans with a T-shirt announcing a church crusade from the year before. He said hello as I walked into his office, revealing a mouth that looked as though it contained an abnormal amount of teeth, and told me to sit down.

On his desk were several items with which I momentarily distracted myself. He spoke with the trademark funny mix of local and foreign accent many of his fellow new-generation pastors had acquired from God knows where. On his left wrist was a gold-plated watch and on his wedding finger a bulky silver ring which said nothing about his marital status. A family portrait was on the wall behind him but, instead of images of a man, his wife, and children, it appeared to be one of him, his parents, and siblings in black-and-white. There were five children and the youngest, a boy, sat on the lap of the woman whom I presumed was his mother. There were also several framed award certificates on the wall.

"So what brings you to the GCI?" he said, smiling, his lips revealing his abundance of teeth.

"Um, I don't know how to begin ... Someone directed me here. My name is Udonwa."

"Hello, Sister Udonwa. You are lucky to be meeting me today. It takes a minimum of a week to successfully book an appointment to see me. You must be a special child of God."

I swallowed hard and tried to take it all in, but I felt my face staring blankly back at him.

"One of my neighbours told me about the church, but I couldn't make it to the Sunday service last week."

"What's the name of the sister?"

"Funke ..." I said, pondering his conclusion about my neighbour being a woman, and whether it would have mattered significantly if it were a man who had invited me.

"Oh, Sister Funke, all right. She's a good sister of the church. So what brings you here on a counselling day? What is weighing heavy on your heart?" he said, and brought out a pen and notepad from his desk drawer.

Perhaps it was the fact that he went straight to the point, but I quickly spilled all the contents of my heart. Much more than I knew I had been harbouring. In the end, I realized I had said quite a lot. Through it all, Pastor Asuquo kept writing, looking up briefly at intervals, but did not flinch until I got to the last part.

"And then I found out my father raped my sister when she was very young and I was the product of that unholy liaison."

His eyes shot up and he said: "Sorry, but could you re-peat the last thing you just said ... I'm not sure I heard you correctly."

"I said I'm the product of incest between my father and my elder sister. My father raped my sister — or the person I thought was my sister, but who is actually my birth mother."

He dropped his pen and looked up at me, his mouth hang-ing open. "Blood of Jesus! Are you serious? I mean, are you very certain about that?"

With my eyes fixed on him, I wondered what part of me suggested I would joke about something as serious as this. I'd often been told that there was something about me, some-thing striking that no one could quite place their finger on. According to Chinua, that *something* was my innocence. But, judging by all that had happened, if he were to see me now, would he still be struck by my innocence? Perhaps, with that innocence now long gone, the *real me* that had been lurking somewhere beneath was starting to show. Perhaps the so-called innocence Chinua had seen was nothing more than a mark of how I had been produced. What if it wasn't anything else but the fact I had been conceived in incest that struck people about me? What if, all along, people could tell there was something about me because there was truly, well, *something*?

"I'm sorry, my sister, that I seem shocked by what you have just said. I've counselled many people, including maids who have been molested by their madam's husband, plus women whose husbands have slept with their own sisters. You know, many atrocities have been committed by heartless men, but forgive me if I say I've not met anyone born from an incestuous relationship before. I don't even know where to begin to counsel you."

"Me too, and I've not been able to deal with it myself since I found out about it. I realize it has consumed me in ways I did not expect." I sighed before continuing: "Pastor, I've found myself in the arms of men I do not even like. I feel like it could be linked to that, right?

"But of course, of course. Where is your family now? I mean, your mother and your father. Can they come over here?" He paused but continued to stare at me. Leaning back, he said: "To be very frank with you, Sister Udonwa, incest is an act that brings a curse, both on the perpetrator, and on its victims and products alike — in fact, its effects have been known to transcend generations. In view of that, I need to see your entire family. We have to start from the root cause, which is your father. I strongly believe it's the only way to go about the counselling. Otherwise, I'll be wasting my time and yours."

I took one good look at the man and imagined him crouching like a cockroach under Papa's overbearing and imposing stature. I imagined Papa holding him in his palm like a biscuit, twisting and crushing him until he screamed for help from the angels in heaven. He had no idea what he was asking of me.

"My family lives in the east and my siblings are scattered all around the country. My father cannot come; he does not attend Pentecostal churches."

"Oh, I see. But this is a very important issue and I can sense that your family has not dealt with it."

"Yes, they kept it a secret from me all my life ... Actually, I found out by accident."

"I can imagine."

"I believe they all know I'm now aware of it. But it seems they're carrying on as if what I found out is not devastating. I'm worried that we may never get to talk about it as a family, that they just want to carry on with their lives as always. And that's because they've always known and did nothing about it. But now that I know, I don't think it should be business as usual. Don't you think so, Pastor?"

"You're absolutely right, my sister."

"I mean, how do they expect me to deal with this on my own? How do you propose I deal with it, Pastor? My sister, who is at the centre of it all, and also my mother — how do I deal with them? They are the two people who decided to keep this secret from me. And how can I look at my father the same way again? I don't know where to begin or how to handle any of this. How do I —"

"Sister ... Sister ... Sister Udonwa, that's why I said all members of your family need to come down here for family deliverance and not just you alone. Although you are the one who has been inflicted with this demon that won't leave."

"But how? How's that so, Pastor?"

"Listen, Sister Udonwa —"

"There must be another way, since family deliverance won't be possible? Can't you recommend a series of prayers or counselling sessions for me or something? Like starting right now? Surely you can do that? Funke said you sometimes hold night vigils for special prayers — I can attend those too, if that is what I'd require to be myself again."

"My sister, of course I'll pray with you right now, but I'm afraid that's not all that is required to set you free. You will need much more than that. You see, this case is very different. Your case is a very special one. Your whole family will need special deliverance, a very serious one. This issue you are dealing with is not a small matter. It has to be dealt with both delicately and vigorously. I hope you get me?"

I nodded, although I could not understand what on earth he was talking about. Maybe if I pushed him more for prayers he might accept. Sister Funke had once told me that a series of prayers by Pastor Asuquo was all it took for whatever was wrong with anyone to disappear, that nothing extra needed to be done. She had said that sometimes, in stubborn cases, the prayers would be accompanied with several smacks on the forehead, or, as the Spirit led the pastor, the person would be healed of whatever ailment they had, spiritually or physically. She was emphatic that no additional or special rituals were required, unlike what happened in other new churches. So why was my case different?

I released a deep sigh. "Okay, I hear you, Pastor."

"Let me pray with you. Father Lord, your daughter is here with a very serious issue weighing on her heart. An issue that requires that you provide her with help that will allow her to live a normal life. Lord Jesus, please come to her aid and heal her. Heal her broken body and heal her broken spirit. Help her navigate her way through this ugly world of ours and show her your mercy. This I ask through Christ our Lord, amen."

"Amen," I echoed.

I made to stand when he motioned that I put whatever I had in my heart as the Lord led in the basket on his desk. I opened my handbag and searched for the highest denomination of naira, and placed it in the basket, and stood up.

"Tell the young man outside to come in."

Without another word, I left his office and passed on the message to the man outside. His shoes were so covered in dust, it was difficult to distinguish their original colour. He was wiping brownish sweat from his face with a dust-covered handkerchief. His white T-shirt with the inscription "NYSC" in bold green letters clung to his body, revealing a well-toned abdomen. He stood up from his seat and smiled at me.

"Hello, the name's Fortune."

"Udonwa," I said, and excused myself. I was approaching the gate when he caught up with me, panting.

"Hello again, so sorry, but I had to do that. I didn't want you to leave before I got to know you."

"Oh," I said, trying to decide if I should smile that he had run all the way to catch up with me, and what message the smile would send to him.

"So do you stay around here?" he asked, and wiped his face again with his handkerchief.

"Yes, and why do you want to know?"

"Em, I'm new in town. I just completed my youth service camp and need someone who knows the area to show me around some fun places. Since you stay around here, you should know some places where someone can have fun."

I was irritated that he had phrased this more as a statement than a question, and pushed open the gate to leave.

"So what were you doing in the church? What demonic possession do you need deliverance from?"

I spun around to face him, my brows arched, and he laughed.

"I'm sorry. It's just that, from experience, anyone who comes to see my brother for counselling usually needs deliverance from something."

"Oh!" It was now my turn to laugh, more from relief than anything else. "I see, you're the pastor's brother … I thought you looked familiar. You're the little boy in the picture in his office?"

"Yes, that's me. I'm surprised at how people always figure that out. I was ten months old, for crying out loud."

"Some faces don't seem to age at all. I could place your face almost immediately."

"So you say your name is Udonwa? That's a beautiful name."

"Thank you. And I assume you know what it means?"

"Of course. I'm very familiar with Igbo names. I live in Ikot Ekpene — Aba is just a stone's throw from my town. So where exactly do you stay?" He fell in beside me as I began walking to my flat.

I pointed to the building in the near distance and he noted he had a cousin who used to live there, but had since travelled out of the country.

"Everyone seems to be travelling out of the country these days."

"These days? Nigerians have been travelling out of Nigeria before some African countries gained their independence. We are literally everywhere."

"I know. It's just that it's become so much more common these days. Before, it used to be just the elite who could afford trips outside Nigeria but now, anyone with a bit of money can afford to do that."

When we arrived at my flat, he said: "So this is where you live …"

"And what about you? Staying with your brother?"

"No, although I was supposed to. This is a new place for him too — the new church premises, that is. It used to be somewhere else in town. He had to move from his old house to his new one here. But all of this is very far from the bank where I'll be doing my service, so I'll be going into town to stay with a friend."

His explanation provided a lot of answers to the missing links in my head about the church's appearance, the neatness of the compound, as well as the brightness of the painted walls. As for Pastor Asuquo setting up his church in an upmarket part of Lagos, that did not come as a surprise to me at all; he did not appear to be one of those preachers who did not take literally what chapter nine of First Corinthians meant when it said *those who serve at the altar partake of the offerings of the altar.*

"So where are you headed now?"

"Not sure, although I wouldn't mind going to a buka to have something to eat. I'm famished."

Perhaps it was my own hunger that made me say: "You can come to my place. That's if a plate of rice and stew will help ease your hunger."

"It will. A homeless corper can't afford to be too choosy …" He followed me into the compound. "So what do you do for a living?" he asked. "Do you work, own your own business?"

"I work for a small architectural firm."

"Nice, fancy."

"Fancy? So architects are fancy people, or is it architecture that is fancy?"

"Well, compared to what I studied, it is. Geology is the most boring course ever. And I'd rather die than dig the earth in the name of exploration. I was born to be a banker. That I'm sure of. My father thought I'd make the best engineer, so I kept applying to study engineering at university but never made the cut-off mark in JAMB. So after the third time, I settled for geology. It was the closest course to engineering on offer at the school. I couldn't stand physics, chemistry, or any of those boring science subjects. I knew from childhood I was born to be in the social sciences, but my father wouldn't hear of it. I wasted years repeatedly writing JAMB while my peers were already in university. My father thought the idea of being an engineer was nobler. Can you imagine that?"

I smiled within; he had no idea how much I could relate to his story.

"Please have a seat." I pointed to the sofa and headed straight for the kitchen.

I returned with two plates of rice and chicken, and found him sitting at the dining table going through my work articles and a copy of *Homez* magazine. He had cleaned up in the bathroom while I had been in the kitchen.

"Are you a writer?" he asked.

"No. I'm not, although I know about writing. I mean, I do write when it's needed. Not everyone who puts words together is a writer. I'm convinced that to wear the writer tag requires certain skills that I do not possess. My duty is to ensure that all the articles follow the rules of construction and design, that's all."

"Fancy," he said, repeating that irritating word again. I rolled my eyes in my mind and smiled.

We both ate in silence while he stole glances at me. I returned a few quick ones too, and noticed that, now he was cleaned up, he was strikingly handsome — much more so than his brother. Perhaps the flat waves of oily hair on Pastor

Asuquo's head, all his teeth, and his showy appearance hid his handsomeness. Fortune's head was clean shaven and his teeth count appeared normal.

It was past nine in the evening by the time we finished eating. Realizing the time, I stood up, wondering when he was planning to leave and whether he'd still find transport.

"Is it easy to get transport from here?" he asked, as if reading my thoughts, at the same time as moving to sit on the couch. "I don't know why my brother chose this part of town to move to."

"Well, in his defence, the outskirts of town is the best place to find land."

"I suppose you are right."

Relaxing his full weight on the couch, he appeared to be making himself more comfortable rather than figuring out how to leave.

"My friend lives in an estate in Ilupeju," he said, "and he warned me that the entrance gates are locked by 10 p.m. I don't think I'll make it before then, even if I leave now. Besides, I'll be disturbing the whole neighbourhood and my friend will not like that at all."

I swallowed hard. "Is there no one in the church you can call to come pick you up? Or better still, somewhere you can sleep over there?"

"Unfortunately not. My brother said he would be travelling out of town after I left. In fact, that was the reason he asked to see me. He wanted to inform me he would be away for a three-day crusade in Calabar."

I swallowed hard again. "I suppose you can sleep here then. I'll fetch you a blanket; it might rain later, judging by this gushing wind."

"Don't worry, I won't bother you at all. You won't even know there's anyone here."

. . .

I woke up in the middle of the night to a storm that was literally shaking the roof of the building. The heavy rain was starting to pour through the kitchen window by the time I got to it, and I reached for a nearby stool to stand on to close it. Fortune was sound asleep, uncovered and shirtless, when I walked past him in the sitting room. I was trying to get the second window in the kitchen to close, when I heard the curtains in the dining room flapping and some of my documents blown to the floor. I was just wondering how a grown man could sleep through all this commotion, when he walked into the kitchen. By this time, the upper part of my body was drenched from the incoming rain, with my nightgown clinging to my breasts. I turned around to find him standing behind me.

"I've closed all the other windows. Let me help you get down from there."

My slippers must have slipped on the wet chair because I fell into his arms rather than being led down gently.

"I'm sorry ..." he said, staring at me in my damp nightgown.

I knew the right thing to do was to walk past him into the bedroom, but I did not utter a word when he lifted my nightgown over my head. He cupped my left breast while caressing the right. "They're so firm and beautiful ..." he muttered under heavy breathing. Rather than slap away his hands, I released a moan and he saw that as a sign to bend down and take one breast in his mouth. I moaned at the warmth of his tongue circling my taut nipple. He lifted up his head and I guided it to the other breast, where he repeated the same motion. He carried me to the couch, and with one quick snap, he parted my legs and slipped inside me. I was screaming by this time and was thankful for the thunderous rain shielding my voice. He was not the silent type either. He was so big and firm and hard and rough and smooth at the same time. I pulled away from him gently and turned my back to him; he entered me from behind and with two more thrusts he was singing and grunting at the same time. With each thrust, my body shivered from head to toe. With one last stroke, he said my name, groaned, and relaxed like a heavy sack on my back. We both released heavy breaths one last time and slept without disengaging from each other.

Twenty-six

"Udonwa Ilechukwu?"

"Yes, who is this?"

"Don't worry about who I am, just go down to Oyegun Village in Ogun state. There's a surprise waiting for you there."

"A surprise? Wait, who are you? And why should I go to this village?"

"If you don't know where Oyegun is, it's the last town after Iba — it's not very far from the express. Your brother, the priest, is there. You'll find a surprise there. Something interesting ... That's all I can say ... Goodbye."

"Who was that?" asked Fortune when I put down the phone.

Fortune and I had continued seeing each other after that first night at my flat. He had returned the next day and the next. He was still undergoing his service year, and not gain-fully employed, so I had loaned him some funds and together we had found a small two-bedroom boys' quarters closer to his office. We had just returned from his apartment when the phone started ringing.

"I don't know. Some strange person who refused to leave their name, saying I should go to a village near Iba." I turned around and took a seat, thoughts racing.

"Go to Iba, tonight?"

"Of course not. Maybe tomorrow or the next day, I'm not sure when ... Or if I should even go."

"I can come with you if you want — it sounds exciting."

"Of course not, Fortune. C'mon, don't be silly."

"You know that was a joke, right? Don't let it stress you. Come, let me reassure you for tonight; we'll worry about to-morrow when it comes."

. . .

"Ah, is a very simpul man, our shief," said the taxi driver when I looked up from the *Homez* magazine my face was buried in. "Ah, Shief Ogungbe, our shief, is a very good man. Ah, is very umbul." He must have noticed the look of shock on my face in the rear-view mirror as we passed one mud house after the other, because he then said: "Is ouse is very fine, not like all dis dirty nyama nyama ones — ah, you'll see now."

"Oh, nice. Good for you and your people. Your people must like him a lot."

"Ah, eferybodi like im o. Even you, you will like im when you see im. Ah, is ouse is the best ouse in our small town. Ahh, feri feri fine ouse," he repeated.

"I would imagine," I said and smiled curtly, still trying to focus on the latest edition of *Homez* on my lap. With this edition's publication had come a huge increase and the much-needed promotion I'd been waiting for for over a year.

I wasn't sure what had put me off first — his accent, beginning every sentence with "ah," or his mismatch of phonics characterised by his omission of the letter "h" in every word it should begin with, or the fact that he was disturbing my reading, or his annoying proclamations of the town's paramount ruler in a tone signifying deep admiration. It was no surprise that the ruling chief's house was the best house in town — not with the level of corruption in the country. And I wasn't surprised that his people, rather than seeing the wrong in that, would praise him instead.

"E no even build it," the taxi driver said after a long silence. Silence I mistook as a sign he had finally got the hint that I did not want to be bothered by tales of an-unknown-chief-in-an-unknown-village from a talkative taxi driver with a bad case of small-town chief obsession.

I ignored him and kept my eyes on the magazine. But he was undeterred, reeling off Chief Ogungbe's one thousand and one achievements and noble deeds. The joy on his face was palpable when he announced how the chief had decided not to build his own house but had relied on the community to contribute funds. We finally arrived at the chief's house, and I was relieved to be released from the taxi driver's litany of adoration.

The yard was big, but cluttered with plants and trees hugging its walls. The moment I pushed the gate and it creaked open, I expected to see a face peep through the window. The curtain on the left side window of the bungalow was slightly open, but not enough to make the room behind it visible. A soft breeze blew in the yard, scattering leaves across the ground. There were four mango trees and three guava, one orange tree and two pawpaw. A small army of shrubs stood in a straight line beside the left wall. Closer to the front door, a scattering of bright red hibiscus smiled back at me. The floor of the veranda was covered in black pebbles. At first, I reflected on how chic it was to find such a design in a rural place like this, but then it occurred to me that the builders must have run out of cement and improvised.

Knocking on the door, I called out: "Is anyone at home?"

I was about to knock again when Jefferson opened the front gate behind me and entered the yard.

"Who am I seeing here ... Udo, is that you?"

"Who else would it be? Of course it is me now. And where are you coming from, and why is the gate left open when you are not at home?"

"Aha, it is you, all right, Little Miss Questionnaire ... I should have locked the gate, but I knew I wouldn't be long so I didn't bother. You haven't been waiting a while?"

"Only a few minutes. So you live in the chief's house, eh?"

"Who told you that? Oh, you must have met Silas."

"Who?"

"Silas, the loudmouth taxi driver. He brought you here, didn't he? He is the town gossip. Actually, gossip is his full-time job; he only transports people for fun."

"I believe so, although there's nothing funny about the money I paid him. I've never met anyone who talked so much in such a short amount of time. He was so annoying I almost cried."

"Hmm, you've not seen anything. The day he brought me here, eh ... Come, let's go inside first." He picked up my little travel bag from the front door. "This is heavy, o. What's inside — isi mmadu?" he said, laughing.

"Please, there's no human head in my bag, o, just books and magazines. I brought you some books and old copies of *Homez*, the magazine my firm publishes. You still read, don't you?"

I smiled, looking him over as we entered the house. I'd missed him so much, I felt close to tears. Stepping into the living room, I was shocked to see the interior of the house was the clone of its exterior. "Cluttered" didn't come close to describing it.

"Why is there so much stuff in here? Where did you get it all from?"

"Stuff? When did *things* become stuff? Oh, let me guess, since you went to South Africa and stayed for a maximum of ... wait ... three minutes?"

I burst out laughing. This happy and vibrant Jefferson was new to me. Apparently it was a disposition that had started when he was transferred out of Onitsha. Nneora had told me he was so chatty now, laughing unnecessarily the whole time like a little girl.

"I know what you're thinking," Jefferson said, smiling coyly.

He was looking around the room as though it had just occurred to him it was a contender for the most horrid-looking room award.

"Answer my question first, brother, please: Where did you get all this from?"

"Is that your number one concern? All right, if you must know, nothing here is mine. My friend's father had the place decorated before he arrived."

I sighed and relaxed on the single couch in the room.

"Oh, now you're happy because I said these things are not mine. You trust me too much, baby sis," he said and disappeared down the corridor, laughing.

Now all I wanted to do next was ask more questions. To find out if what the anonymous caller had said — or rather, hadn't said — was true. To find out if I was correct in what I thought I had heard.

My mind was still racing when Jefferson returned with a tray of juice and two small saucers of chin-chin.

"Oh, I didn't know we had a guest," a voice behind me said, prompting me to sit up straight on the couch.

The voice belonged to a tall dark man with a towel hanging around his neck. He was standing at the entrance to the house, his back to the living room as he took off his sneakers and socks. He was wearing shorts and a matching sweatshirt with the word "BIG" on the back. He had curly hair which was shimmering with too much hair oil. He turned towards me, using the towel to wipe his head. As he wiped, I couldn't help but notice the shape of his penis swinging from left to right in the shorts, its length mimicking the inscription on the jersey. When he walked closer towards me, I saw that his left ear was pierced.

"It's a pleasure to finally meet you. My name's Bolaji, but everyone calls me 'Big.'"

I extended my hand to him, my eyes darting from him to Jefferson and back again as I tried to slow my breathing. "You must be Udonwa. I've heard so much about you. The architect, right?"

Jefferson, who had remained quiet all through the encounter, said quickly: "Yes, she's my baby sister. Udo, meet Big, he's my —"

"I know what and who he is."

"Okay ..." Jefferson muttered, his head bowed.

Jefferson sat on the opposite couch, which seemed to swallow him as he retreated into it. Jefferson's lifestyle was obvious to me, and it worried me that he planned on carrying on with this ridiculously named fellow without detection from the town. Who exactly was this Big?

"Big is in the country for a short while before he leaves again," said Jefferson, his voice more quiet now. "He lives in California."

"Are you also a priest?" I asked.

"Excuse me?"

"I said, are you a pr—"

"I heard you right. I'm just surprised you would ask me that. This is not something one decides for oneself, you know. I've never had to hide who I am."

"That's debatable," I said, rolling my eyes as I looked away. "What of your family — what do they have to say about it, or don't you have any?"

"You sound exactly like Jeff said you would. More like a journalist than an architect," he said and placed his legs on the centre table, the only furniture in the room that made any sense.

I noticed he was trying to charm me. He had an attitude that spoke of nonchalance, as though he didn't care what anyone thought of him. Save for his strong thighs, which I reckoned he must have got from sports, everything else fit the stereotype of "homosexual." Now I felt stupid when I thought of how I had defended Jefferson to Nneora years back, when she'd suggested he might be different from other men. I had brushed off her assumptions, arguing that just because a man was effeminate, it did not make him a homosexual.

"You know what, Bro Jefferson —" I had just begun to say when Big cut me short.

"So how was the trip? I hope you found it easy to get here?"

As soon as the words left his lips, it dawned on me who had made the call. That would explain how he'd known I was coming. It would also explain Jefferson's feigned look of surprise earlier, and why the gate had been unlocked.

"So you knew I was coming, Bro Jefferson? Why did you plan to tell me this way?"

"I'm sorry, Udo," said Jefferson. "But you are the only one I felt would understand. You've always suspected I was different anyway —"

"Brother!"

"Okay, maybe I was wrong about your being sure of your suspicions. But remember when you were much younger, how you would notice certain things about me? I ... I ... Anyway, the point is ... What I'm trying to say is that I don't want to live a lie anymore. I'm tired of lying to myself."

"But you are a priest, for crying out loud, Brother Jefferson! A man of God. How do you hope to reconcile these two things? How?"

"We will cross that bridge when we get there," said Big.

"Excuse me?" I said, glaring at him.

"Big, please excuse us. I need to do this alone. Please." Jefferson turned to him, eyes pleading.

"If you say so," Big said and shrugged.

He hummed as he walked down the corridor and disappeared into one of the bedrooms. I let out a loud hiss, taking another inventory of the room before settling on a coronation ceremony photograph between a stack of books on the corner table.

"Is that what I think it is?"

He turned to where I was looking and nodded. "Yes, that's Big and his father. The Oba of Oyegun."

"Chineke! Brother Jefferson, you and the chief's son! What kind of scandal are you brewing? Please, in the name of God, this thing you are doing will surely kill Mama."

I stood up and began pacing the room. In light of all that I had just seen and heard, asking him the one question I had been dying to ask him for years now seemed necessary, almost urgent. What I was witnessing was not what I had expected from my eldest brother. Growing up, I had believed Lincoln would be the sibling who would bring shame on the family. It was all we had heard as children from the little time Papa had spoken without his fists. But here I was, staring at my favourite brother as he revealed a nightmare about who he truly believed he was. I was furious I had not put it together sooner. And I was ashamed that Mayokun might be right about my family being cursed. A family with a legion of dirty secrets like ours was a cursed one indeed.

I sighed and stopped pacing, turning around to find Jefferson with his hands on his head, tears streaming down his face. I rushed over to him, and removed his hands one after the other from his head, wiping the tears from his cheeks. "I'm sorry, Brother. I'm sorry. It's okay … It's your life to live, not mine." Tears filled my own eyes. "I might not approve of any of this, but I won't judge you either. Please don't cry."

He smiled as I took his hands in mine, staring at me through teary eyes which glowed his relief. The smile, I imagined, carried with it dreams of a brighter future and hopes of possible acceptance from the rest of the family. Looking up at him, I realized I was nothing but a hypocrite. I was no better than him in the fornication department. We were only doing it differently. Suddenly I was the one weeping while he cradled me in his arms.

I cried as I imagined the scandal this would birth. I cried as I imagined how the people of Oyegun would burn them both alive, perhaps first helping the chief's son escape before burning only Jefferson. I let out a staccato laugh at the thought and wiped my eyes. I imagined how Silas, the taxi driver, would be the chief broadcaster of the tales. Silas was not the best in his gossip trade, though, if he was unaware that these two very unlikely people were living together, like husband and wife, in one of the almighty Chief Ogungbe's houses.

. . .

Early the next morning, Big drove us to the motor park for my transport back to Lagos. Except for the music playing in the car, we were all quiet. When we got to the park, Jefferson pointed to the bus that would take me to Lagos. With my bag in his hand, we both walked silently towards it while Big remained in the car.

Before I got on the bus, I turned to Jefferson one last time and summoned the courage to ask him the one thing that had been lurking in my mind for many years now.

"Brother, please don't be offended, but I really need to know this ..."

He looked at me like he already knew what I was about to ask, as though he had been expecting someone to ask so he could provide an answer.

"That altar boy years ago, did you ...?"

"No."

Relief spread through my body as I heard the one word that I could have heard years ago if I had been bold enough to ask him. And at that very moment, I could not care less what anyone thought of him or my family.

Twenty-seven

"I think we are having too much sex."

Fortune's words caught me unawares. It was a few days after my visit to Jefferson, and we were lying on his bed, exhausted from another hot love-making session. I had gone to his house to offload a little of what had transpired in Oyegun while carefully leaving out important details. It was difficult not to tell someone else about the loud-mouthed Silas. I couldn't wait to laugh about it.

What did he mean by "we're having too much sex?" I stared at him for clarification. He sighed before he continued, and all I could think about was how I would survive listening to him explain how he was tired of sleeping with me. The room suddenly felt like the inside of a deep freeze. I got up to change the air conditioner's setting, alternating between reducing and increasing the temperature until I was satisfied with a certain number. I then turned and saw him still staring at me. Slowly, I returned to the bed and sat on the edge.

I knew that the last months had been like a blur; it had all come too quickly, and was progressing too quickly. And, like everyone I'd been with in the past, it felt like sex was all we had. Although he'd been helping out with the design of Lincoln's house, which meant we'd been spending considerable time together at Lincoln's building site, it was really only at night when we were alone together.

A few weeks before, I had tried to enquire if Pastor Asuquo suspected anything was going on between us, and Fortune had replied that it didn't matter what his brother thought of his love life. But I knew that a pastor's unmarried brother engaging in a sexual relationship with an undelivered demon-possessed sister of the church could not be classified as something that did not matter.

"Are you finished?" he said. "Is the air condition okay for you now?"

His voice snapped me back to reality. I tried to keep my head up.

"I'm sorry I startled you, but I really do mean what I said. Don't you think so too? Aren't we having too much sex?"

"I don't know what you want me to say, Fortune."

"I'm sorry, I can imagine how you feel ..."

"Oh no, you have no idea."

How could he imagine how I was feeling when once upon a time I had been a chaste young woman who took great pride in who she was; but who overnight had turned into an ever-willing sex partner for men? Unlikely men, who previously would not have got a second glance from me? How would he ever know how it felt to hear him say he had had enough of me?

"Udonwa, please ..." Fortune tried to put his arm around me but I knocked it off. Shrugging, he continued: "You are a very beautiful lady and —"

"So what's the problem then? I'm no longer beautiful?"

"It's not about that ..."

"Did you speak to your brother, Fortune? Did Pastor Asuquo say anything to you about me?"

"Of course not ... I ... Listen, all I'm saying is that there ... is —"

"Wow. You can't even deny it. It's written all over your face. Your brother told you something!"

"Please, let me finish, Udonwa. It's been too much — too much for the little time we've been together. I want to save some for —"

I couldn't wait for him to complete his sentence before bursting into laughter. "You want to save some for what? For when we are married or what? Are you listening to yourself, Fortune? I thought this was all you men wanted, someone ever ready to jump into bed with you?" I said and got up from the bed.

"Look, Udo, what I'm trying to say is, I would really like us to slow down on the sex and get to know each other more — that's all. Like, besides your work, I don't know anything else about you. I don't know any member of your family or where they are. I don't know why no one visits you. I don't know why you don't talk about anyone else but your colleagues and boss. I know practically nothing about you ... Don't read any more meaning into it than that, please."

I sighed deeply and sat back on the bed. "Okay, I've heard you."

"This is not easy for me, either. But I sense the sex is becoming something else. It's like a let-out for you. An avenue for something you don't want to deal with ... and —"

"Stop right there. You know absolutely nothing about —"

"There you go again. Any time I bring up a topic that has to do with your feelings, you flare up. Do you know what that tells me? That I'm right. It tells me there's something that's seriously bothering you, and this whole thing of you and me is just a means for you not to sort that thing out. You go visit your brother, you come back, and you tell me nothing about him or the reason for your emergency visit. You get a call from another brother and the only thing you mention is that he wants you to design a home for him. You say nothing else about him; I don't even get to know his name. It's not healthy, Udonwa. Trust me, it isn't."

"And what did you think I was doing in a pastor's office? What do people go to see pastors for?"

"So my brother was right, then? After I defended you and said it didn't matter that you were ... Look, Udonwa, you've done so much for me and the sex is so great with you but —"

Finally, he'd admitted what I had suspected all along, and it was all I needed to jump to my feet. I picked up my handbag from the floor and the condoms fell out, one after the other, along with my lipstick and the keys to my flat. My eyes did a quick sweep of the room, searching for my jeans, my bra and everything else. The urge to leave right away was nearly choking me.

"I'm sorry. I didn't mean to upset you. Please stop acting this way."

"I should stop acting this way? You mean I should react calmly to being called a sex addict? Because that's all I'm hearing. Me, Udonwa Ilechukwu, a sex addict!"

"Please, keep your voice down, Udonwa. I never said you're a sex addict. On the contrary, I know you as a smart, intelligent, and —"

"But you implied it. I'm broken, Fortune, broken. Is that what you want to know about me? You want me to confirm what your brother told you about my fa—"

"No, you are not broken, Udonwa ... I ..."

I turned sharply to face him, daring him to say anything else contrary to the way he actually felt. He sighed and sat back on the bed. And that singular act hurt me more than his earlier words. What was I expecting to hear him say? To carry on denying the obvious, that Pastor Asuquo had informed him what we had discussed in the counselling session? At least I knew now where I stood on this journey. So much for confidential information.

I knew I shouldn't trust someone who had taken fifteen minutes to get over the shock of my being born out of incestuous rape. I knew I shouldn't trust someone who had spent the best half of what was supposedly a counselling session trying to convince me my family was cursed and that I was possessed with an evil spirit. I knew I shouldn't trust anyone who could not bring any solace to my weary soul. I knew I shouldn't trust someone who had implied I could never have a normal life without having deliverance sessions carried out on me but then had failed to do anything about them. I knew I shouldn't have trusted someone who hadn't done anything to help me but was happy to take my money.

Turning to Fortune, I said: "I think it's best we break up."

He remained silent while I pushed past him to reach behind his wardrobe to pick up my bra. My eyes located my blouse beneath the fan next to the bedside mirror. From his sitting position he watched as I strapped on my bra and pulled my blouse over my head. And the whole time all I heard was what he desperately wanted to say but could not put into words.

"I'm sorry, Udonwa ... I ... I ... really do like you a lot. I'll pay you back the loan for my rent, and everything else you've spent."

I stifled an angry chuckle. "It wasn't a loan, Fortune. You can keep the money. I don't need it."

The room was quiet the rest of the time as I put on my jeans. Next I pulled out a hair band and gathered a bunch of twisted long braids that had been lying loose and covering my face into a ponytail. Satisfied, I slid one shaky foot after the other into my sandals.

I turned towards the door and left, every part of me aching with shame. I did not look back and he did not call me back either.

Outside in the corridor, I imagined him now lying on the bed, trying to push me far from his mind, and I heaved a sigh of relief for both of us.

Twenty-eight

Grandpa was standing by the door and waving at me. The window on the opposite side reflected his face and I could see he had tears in his eyes.

"Grandpa, how are you?" I ran to him with outstretched arms but he pushed his hands towards me, preventing me from getting any closer, and I stood fixed to the spot.

"Grandpa, have you seen Grandma? Is she with you?"

"No, we're not in the same place."

His eyes appeared dim and yellowish in colour, his hair aglow in cotton-wool white.

"Where is she and where are you?" I asked, confused.

"I'm sorry you had to find out the way you did. I was hoping they would tell you. It was one of my biggest fears that you'd find out the way you did," he said, ignoring my question.

I put my head down, crying. "Even you, Grandpa ... Even you knew?"

"I knew everything that happened in that house, even the things they think I didn't know."

"But why, Grandpa? Why did Papa do that to Sister Adaora? How could he hurt us all like this?"

He looked up at me and sighed. "There are so many things you do not know."

"You mean there are more secrets, Grandpa? I don't think I can take any more. I seriously do not think I can handle any more."

"Who is the young man you are carrying around in your heart?" he said, promptly changing the subject.

"What young man, Grandpa?"

"The one I'm looking at through your chest. I can see him clearly."

I looked down at my chest. "I can't see anything, Grandpa. I don't know what you're talking about," I said, my hands against my blouse as I searched for any signs to relate to his words.

"Stop looking on the outside; it's all internal, Udonwa. Keep searching within. You'll find out soon enough all you need to know."

"But, Grandpa, things are not the way they used to be. Everything has changed. I have not seen Papa for a very long time. I cannot bear the sight of him."

"And who will blame you for that? If you feel the way you do, imagine how your sister feels. How she's been feeling her whole life? Leonard is a disgrace. Just like his mother disgraced me in front of the whole of Iruama. Come, let me tell you a story."

I moved closer to him by the window and he began to speak.

"One day, I returned from the mission house after the vicar and the missionaries had asked to see me. They informed me they might require someone else who practises the Christian religion and not an African traditional worshipper like myself. That day, they made me choose between their religion and my profession."

"That's not fair, Grandpa. How could they do that to you?"

"That is the way it was back then. But that's not the story. The story is that your father was very happy about it and helped them appoint another headmaster."

"Papa betrayed you? How could he do that to you, his own father?"

Now it made perfect sense when Papa would call Grandpa names and Grandpa would refer to him as a two-faced man. Papa would retreat into his shell whenever Grandpa uttered those words. He would walk away, leaving their discussion hanging. Grandpa had been that powerful then, if only for a few minutes.

"Because of my teaching abilities, the ministers came to our house to try to convince me to choose their religion. But, after they left, I invited ndi nze na Ozo, informing them I was ready to take on the Ozo title, and that was the end of the church's request. Everybody knew that I would never be a part of the church ever again."

With no schools other than the missionary schools at the time, Grandpa had had no choice but to give up his career. It now made perfect sense when he used to tell us as children that the missionaries had brought education in one hand while holding their religion in the other. One would have to receive the latter in order to have the former.

"So which side are you on, Grandpa? You said that Grandma is not where you are … Which side are you on and which is hers?"

"Udonwa, if you must know, I have not seen Nwamgboli Afomma." He paused before continuing: "Isn't it a thing of wonder that someone whose name means 'beautiful womb' can carry and birth an evil man like Leonard?"

Yes, it was indeed ironic, and I nodded in response. In the past, I would have offered an explanation as to why Papa was the way he was or proffered a deeper, perhaps figurative meaning as to what Grandma's name might mean. But with the knowledge of who Papa really was, the term "evil" was a perfect description of him. I nodded again in agreement.

"Ah, truly … Those who have buttocks do not know how to sit. Leonard had it all, but with his own hands destroyed it all. If I had had what your father had, my life would have been much better than the way it turned out."

"But, Grandpa, I thought you were happy; I thought you lived a long and fulfilled life?"

"You will not understand, Udonwa. If Nwamgboli Afomma had been just a bit like Obianuju, your mother, everything would have been perfect. But no, it was she who started this whole thing."

"What did she do, Grandpa? Please tell me. How did she disgrace you?"

"There are no secrets anymore. Not to worry, Udonwa, you will hear it soon enough." He paused briefly, as if weighing his words. "I'm here to inform you, my daughter, that all your issues will be resolved soon. You know, a toad does not run in the daylight for nothing; if nothing is chasing it, it is definitely chasing something. You'll be well again, my daughter. But know this, you will keep chasing what it is you think you need to chase until you look within and make a heart change. Only then will the key fit and you'll be well again. Only then."

And with that, his face became nothing more than vapour on my bedroom window.

• • •

I woke up in the morning with a headache the size of Lagos, my throbbing head mimicking the noise of the city that never sleeps.

Being in Grandpa's presence growing up had brought with it a certain calm, but seeing him in my dream last night had only unnerved me. It had also taken with it the energy and desire to head to work for a final edit of the next *Homez* edition.

I sighed and looked around my bedroom, taking in its magnificence. It was the biggest room I had ever slept in and the best thing about waking up every morning alone in the past few months.

I had moved into Lincoln's house sixteen weeks ago. The house had been standing empty for a while, except for the boys' quarters, which I had to rent out, and another outside room occupied by the caretaker. Lincoln's specifications had been followed to the letter, and although the house was not as magnificent as Ekene's, it was more modern. My bedroom was located on the ground floor, much to Lincoln's disapproval, who still insisted I move upstairs to the bedroom next to the master bedroom. There were two sitting rooms on the ground floor in addition to the dining room. I had made sure to add an office with library shelves included. When the house was completed, Lincoln had invited the rest of the family to take possession of the home but no one had arrived yet.

A chandelier hung in the middle of the living room foyer cascading down and overlooking the entire living space. It had the same effect as the one in Ekene's house, with the difference being its antique style. Lincoln had been promoted from DJ to the manager of the club where he worked, and had begun saving from his salary and private gigs, waiting for an opportunity to strike. According to him, rumours had been circulating that his boss, the club owner, was planning to sell the club and was waiting for a good offer. Lincoln had seen the opportunity as a lifeline being thrown at him and had grabbed it with both hands. He had approached his boss and made him an offer to put down a cash deposit of the going price. He and Zukiswa had put their savings together, and the bank had loaned them the rest of the money.

After Lincoln had bought the club, he had renovated it, putting in a private VIP lounge on the ground floor, a Nigerian restaurant next to it, and a mini guesthouse in the outbuilding. The profits began to pour in within weeks and soon he was swimming in enough money to repay the bank loan as well as more than enough to build his own home in Lagos.

The building project had taken longer than expected after Fortune and I ended things, but the project was my saving grace as it kept me busy. I couldn't be happier that something was finally falling into place for a member of my family, albeit the most unexpected person.

I could never forget Grandpa's face and how real he'd looked in last night's dream. Trust him to withhold vital information, even in death. Why couldn't he outright tell me what Nwamgboli Afomma had done that would warrant her memory being wiped out by her own family? And why didn't he just say who it was he saw in my heart? What if the person I was supposedly carrying in my heart wasn't carrying me in theirs? Would I have to force this person to do so? What did carrying someone around in my heart even mean?

I was roused from my thoughts by loud knocking on the front door.

"Madam, e don dey knock since. But e be like say you dey sleep. So I say make I come help am knock. Abeg no vex."

"It's okay, Akpan."

Standing at the door with Akpan, who doubled as a caretaker and whose wife, Eno, would take on the position of house help when Lincoln returned, was someone I was not expecting to see.

"Mayo!"

"Hello, Udo-n-wah, can I come in?"

"Em, yes, where are … How did you find —"

"I know you have many questions … Please may I come in? I really need to talk to you."

I moved to the side of the front door to let him in. He was wearing a grey shirt over a pair of grey shiny pants. His tie, belt, and shoes matched the colour of his clothes. I would have made a funny remark back in the day but in this moment it felt inappropriate.

"How on earth did you find me after such a long time?"

"Yes, it's been long … I called Osas in Canada and he confirmed you still worked with Xenox, but directly with Mr. Adeneye running their flagship interior-design magazine."

I knew I owed him an explanation when he mentioned Osas, but I decided to focus on why he'd come looking for me as I led him past the entrance hall into the living room.

"This is a beautiful, beautiful house." He was looking around the room, gazing at the double-volume ceiling with the chandelier, taking it all in. "Wow, this is really, really lovely."

"Thank you. It's my brother's house."

"Your brother? Which one? The one you visited in South Africa?"

"Yes, it's Lincoln's house."

"You never really spoke much about your family."

"No, I didn't. Why are you here, Mayo?" I tried to look him in the eye but he avoided my gaze.

"This is simply gorgeous," he carried on, whistling. "Your brother performed wonders here."

"Yes, he did, although I did most of the design and decor myself."

"You did? Of course you did. I should have known that. I just never saw any of your completed home designs come to life."

"Now you've seen one. Can I get you something to drink? Sorry I haven't cooked yet. It's still too early."

"Too early? I see you're still a late riser. It's almost noon. Thanks, a glass of juice will be fine."

I excused myself, returning from the kitchen with a bottle of juice and a glass.

After taking a sip of juice, he said: "How are you, Udo-n-wah? Like, how are you really?"

"As you can see, I'm doing really well. I have this house all to myself. I have a fantastic job. What more can I ask for?"

"You know what I mean, Udo."

"No, I don't. I'm afraid you'll have to spell it out for me."

"Okay, but first let me start by apologizing to you about the way we parted. I'm truly sorry. I had no right to say the things I said to you."

"If I remember correctly, you said I was cursed, that my family was disgusting."

"And I'm sorry for saying that. I had no right. But please understand it was because of the shock of finding out what I did. That was my first time hearing anything like that and it shocked me terribly. I did not know how else to react. What I did was cruel but I've realized my mistakes and that's why I am here to apologize."

Other than the guilt of cheating on Mayo, I was surprised that I felt nothing more. His presence had done nothing to calm the pounding ache in my head. I rubbed my hands on my forehead and tried to keep my eyes open.

"Are you okay? You don't look too well at all ..." he said, leaning towards me.

"I woke up with a severe headache and hadn't got around to treating myself when you arrived."

"I'm sorry to hear that. Do you have any medicine? I think I saw a pharmacy down the road on my way here."

"No, that won't be necessary. I have some medicine in my bathroom cabinet. I'll get it."

"You sit down — just point me to the bathroom and I'll go get it." I looked at him. "I insist," he said, already on his feet.

"The bathroom is attached to the bedroom on the left down the corridor." I winced at the sound of my own voice.

He took one look at me and dashed off, returning with a packet of Panadol and a glass of water. As I swallowed the tablets, he began to speak again, but rather than hearing him, I heard echoes of Grandpa's voice from last night's dream. I had always known Grandpa would remain with me in spirit. And now he had come to me in a dream at a time when I was at a crossroads in my life, as though he'd been hearing my cries.

"So that's why I'm here."

"Excuse me?" I said, looking up at him.

"Did you hear a word I said?"

I shook my head. "Uh uh. I'm sorry, Mayo, today is not a good day for me at all ... I ... But I know why you are here.

You said it yourself that you came to apologize, and I've accepted your apology."

"But that's not all. I was talking about what Osas told me."

I muttered something inaudible and braced myself for what would follow.

"He said you were very special. In fact, let me use his own words, he said *you were a special human being of a different breed from the rest of us.*"

"He said that? Why would he say that?"

"Why not? All my friends knew how special you were to me."

"What else did he say? I can't believe Osas used those words to describe me …"

"You know, Osas always had a soft spot for you. You should've seen the way he defended you when I told him how we broke up. He said how you were born was not your fault. It was like he understood you better than I did. He was the one who made me see reason and encouraged me to look for you and apologize."

"Hmm."

"*Hmm?* Is that all you have to say?"

"I'm short of words, Mayo. I mean … that's very thoughtful of him. Mayo, I know we've not seen each other for a very long time, but today is not a good day at all for me. You caught me at a very bad time and I'm so sorry, but I really need to lie down and rest."

"If you don't mind, I can come back another day when you're feeling better so we can talk properly?"

"Yes, that's a good plan."

"So you'll let me know when, right?"

When I nodded, my head felt like it belonged to someone else.

"Okay, I'll go, but I'll be back soon. I want to be sure you have truly forgiven me, and that we can be friends again."

I nodded again and stood up to walk him to the door, but he gestured for me to continue sitting where I was. I couldn't help smiling as he walked out. Mayo's caring nature had been the one thing that had endeared him to me throughout our relationship, and perhaps the reason we had lasted as long as we had, regardless of everything else that had happened in between. But I still could not say for sure what it was I'd felt for him. This inexplicable emotion I knew I felt for him was the reason I could not bring myself to tell him about Osas and me. I did not want to hurt him more than I'd already done. For some reason, what he thought of me was important to me.

But whatever I felt, the moment he had shown up at my door had made one thing clear: he was not the person I was carrying in my heart.

Twenty-nine

Sister Adaora and Mama had arrived in Lagos the day before but had decided to stay with Aunt Nene — "A very wise decision," I had muttered when Aunt Nene called to inform me. I knew it was more Sister Adaora's decision than Mama's because of the awkward situation we both found ourselves in and which we hadn't figured out a way to deal with yet. I'd not had the opportunity to be alone with her because I'd been deliberately avoiding her. What would we talk about now that we were no longer just sisters but mother and daughter too? Nneora had flown in from Enugu the next morning and decided to wait at the airport for Lincoln's arrival to avoid traffic.

When I got to the airport, I could see Sister Adaora, Nneora, and Mama waiting in a car a short distance from the airport entrance. As I made to cross over to their side of the road, Sister Adaora got out of the car and began to walk towards me with Nneora behind her. She reduced her pace when she got closer to me but I smiled to reassure her.

"Sister."

"Udom. How are you?"

"I'm fine ..." We stood awkwardly staring at each other, with neither of us making any attempt to move any closer. Nneora then approached me and I walked into her outstretched arms.

Ever since I'd overheard Mama and Sister Adaora that day in Awka, I had struggled to reconcile myself to the fact that Adaora was my birth mother. It did explain her relationship with me when I was a child, not to mention her and Mama's treatment of me. But I could not bring myself to see her as anything other than my sister.

I had returned home from work a few days after Mayo's visit to receive a letter from Akpan that one of the drivers from Chisco Transport on the Nnewisouth route had brought to the house while I was at work. I knew instantly where it had come from and who had sent it. I put the letter away unopened until the following week.

Papa, whom I hadn't seen nor heard from in four years, had written to say that he had been sick and wasn't getting any better. He said he was now too weak to travel, that he wanted to see me, and that as usual Mama had left him all alone and was now living permanently in Awka. He also wrote he had heard I had dropped out of medical school and therefore would not be a doctor, and he wanted to know why. He had finished the letter with these words:

*I know they've told you things about me and
that's why you've abandoned me, but I want
to let you know that they're all lies, Udonwa.
Come home and let's talk. Have I been anything else but a good father to you? Please come
home, my child. Come and visit your poor old
dying father before they poison your mind completely against me.*

I did the next best thing I could think of — called Aunt
Nene, who called everyone to come down to Lagos, including
Lincoln. We'd all agreed on one thing: it was time to confront
Papa.

As Nneora and I chatted, I noticed Sister Adaora looking at
me out of the corner of her eye. She had just opened her mouth
to say something to me when Nneora started screaming that
she had seen Lincoln, who came out of the airport with a heap
of luggage atop several trolleys. Zukiswa was following a short
distance behind him with their son on her hip — a very chubby
little fellow.

"Linc-Linc the handsome. I'm sure South African women
have suffered in your hands," Sister Adaora said in Igbo,
stretching out her arms towards Lincoln.

"Hell no, Sister. I know only one woman and that's my
Zuks," he replied in Igbo, laughing, before greeting the rest
of us.

"Welcome home, o. Nno nu," said Sister Adaora. "Hello,
my dear brother's wife, you're welcome to Nigeria." Sister
Adaora hugged Zukiswa.

"Hello, Sister Adaora," Zukiswa said. "And, everyone, this
is the famous Onyedikachi."

"The naughty Dikachi, you mean," Lincoln said, pulling him down from her hands, and the little boy started crying immediately.

Six months after I'd left South Africa, Onyedikachi was born, a name we all shortened to Dikachi. I had been shocked because I'd had no idea Zukiswa was even pregnant when I was there. Apparently they had only found out weeks after I left. Mama had insisted on naming the baby Onyedikachi, saying that it was a worthy question: Who is like God? The name, she said, should always remind us that there is indeed no one like God, for he never fails to come through for those who are patient enough to hold on to his promises.

As we all walked to the car park, Sister Adaora kept stealing glances at me. Dikachi was calmer now, and falling asleep to the Igbo lullaby Nneora was singing to him, while the rest of us chatted happily. This would've been one of the happiest moments of my life if not for the fact that standing next to me was someone who not too long ago had been my sister but now was undisputedly my mother.

• • •

"Such a delicious egusi soup, a bit peppery but very, *very* well done," said Mama to Zukiswa.

"Thank you, Ma. I learned how to make it from my friend."

"You have friends who cook our dishes?" Mama asked as she licked the rest of the soup trailing down her hand.

Zukiswa handed her a serviette before saying: "Yes, Ma. A Nigerian lady called Nkoli."

"Oh, are there many Nigerians there in your country?"

"Yes, Ma, there are quite many of them," she said, laughing.

"Ah, Mama, there's no Nigerian soup Zukiswa cannot make. You need to taste her nsala, ah, you'll bow," said Lincoln, puffed up with pride.

"Ehn ehn, no wonder you're so happy with her — everyone knows how important your stomach is to you," said Mama, making Zukiswa laugh.

"Besides that, Mama, she makes me happy in many other ways," Lincoln said and slid his hand into Zukiswa's.

Eno and Zukiswa took the dirty dishes to the kitchen while I wiped the dining table. As soon as Zukiswa was out of sight, Mama lowered her voice and began to fire away at Lincoln.

"Do her people know you are married to her? I hear they marry differently from us?"

"They don't, Mama, who told you that? Nneora and her big mouth! Of course her people know we're married. I met her uncles before we went to the Home Affairs office for legalization."

"It was Udonwa who told me, o," Nneora shouted from the living room, where she sat flipping through the channels on the cable television while Dikachi ran around the table threatening to break the ornaments on it.

"Someone should please hold this boy before he breaks all the nice things Udonwa suffered to buy, o," Lincoln screamed, watching his son drop another table decor plaque that spelled "love" in fancy letters.

"Her uncles? Doesn't she have a father?" Mama said, lowering her voice again as she pierced the last piece of meat on her plate with her fork.

"She has never met her father. He left her mother even before she was born."

"Hian! O Chim o, men! Poor child, it's a pity. But I guess it's better not to have a father than to grow up with one like yours."

"You can say that again, Mama ... When are we embarking on this trip? Nneora, when did you say Jefferson is arriving again? See eh, Mama, I'm so ready to see that man right away. I'm so ready to tell him what's been on my mind for years and years. How could he, eh?"

Mama sighed and looked in my direction; I caught her eyes and looked away immediately.

"And my wife and son are not coming with us. That man deserves to die without knowing the joy of laying eyes on his grandchild. I refuse to grant him that honour."

"Do as you please, my son. Can you believe that after everything with Udonwa finding out what he did, he still shamelessly wrote her a letter saying he's sick and she should visit him? But what really made me angry was that he said Udonwa should not believe anything we tell her — that we are all lying about him!"

"By the time I'm through with him —" Lincoln started, but Mama stopped him from saying more.

"My son, let's leave that talk for now. Let us talk about this beautiful home of yours instead."

"Mama, it's not my home; it's our home. I built it for all of us. It's one of the reasons I decided not to marry a woman from home, otherwise this place would've been filled with her own family and there wouldn't be any space for you people. When I return to Joburg with my wife and son, you can live here for as long as you wish. And I intend to start making plans for the new Iruama house. I'm very happy everyone moved in before we arrived. It looks lived in and very tastefully furnished. Udonwa did an outstanding job," said Lincoln, looking at me.

"But you sent the money to make it look so beautiful. Look at the chairs … Ah! So it's me, Obianuju, that's sitting in her own son's house! A house built with decent money. Let your father come and see this now. Not that warehouse of a house Ekene was building and could not complete."

"Nna eh, that is such a shame. So they say he is in jail over there in South Africa?" Nneora called from the living room.

"The dude is in for a *very* long time. Ekene is done for," Lincoln called back to her.

Mama's eyes widened at the news. "Eziokwu?"

"I don't know the exact years he was given, but usually, depending on the severity of the crime, like drug dealing, he could be in prison for ten to fifteen years."

"Eh! Akudo o. I still can't believe Ekene's wealth is ill-gotten. So, Ekene made his money through dubious means? Chai! Your father was shattered when he heard the news. All of a sudden, nobody was sending money to him. The uncomplet-ed house has been there for years now, collecting dust. Most of the intended furnishings were sold off for survival. The last time I spoke to Akudo, she said her anger was that Mazi sold off the expensive things for next to nothing. And there's noth-ing she could do about it. They needed the money. You won't believe that all those unopened products for the completion of the building were bought by another man building his own house. Ime ife ojo ajoka — to do bad is evil. Just look at how such a promising young man wasted his life. How could he be involved in such a dangerous business, eh?"

"That's no business, Mama. Drug dealing is not only criminal but immoral too. It's nothing but the destruction of human lives. Please, let's leave Ekene and his miserable life for now. Papa can go to South Africa and carry his special nephew. Let's enjoy this house I built with my sweat and hard-earned money. N'odiro easy, Mama. It's not easy at all."

"Yes, my son, it's not easy at all at all. What you've done here is quite commendable. But still, speaking of Ekene —"

"Mama," I interjected, "you know some of us need to go and rest if we must wake up early to travel to Iruama tomorrow."

"I know, my child, but you people should please hear me out ... Seriously speaking, our people need to change their ways. When our children who live very far away return home with unexplained wealth, we should not just wave it off as 'ona eme ofuma' ... Ehn — we should never wave off the unexplained sudden display of wealth as success. How can someone be said to be successful when the source of his wealth is questionable? To tell you people the truth, eh, I had my suspicions when Ekene started displaying excessive wealth and sending your father and Mazi so much money all those years ago, but I did not want to say anything for fear of being labelled as a jealous woman. Now look at a promising young man like Ekene wallowing away in a foreign prison. It's really a pitiable situation."

Mama fell silent and looked at her empty plate. In her silence, my mind returned to Iruama, where it had been on and off for most of the day, a spectre of Papa's frail body spread across it.

Thirty

"**D**id you have carnal knowledge of Adaora, Papa?"

"Carnal what? What the fuck is carnal knowledge, eh, Jefferson? Ask this man the right question or I'll do it myself ..." said Lincoln, pacing around the room.

If the question had been what Papa was expecting, he didn't show it.

Moving closer to the bed where Papa was lying facing the wall, Jefferson said: "Papa, I asked you a question. Did you rape Adaora? Did you sexually molest her as a child?"

"Answer him now, you sick old man!"

Jefferson looked sternly at Lincoln. "Easy, Linc, that's not why we are here."

"Then why are we here? Because, God help me, I will break this motherfucker's head …" said Lincoln. With every bark, his gold chain with the Z&O pendant swung back and forth.

Jefferson walked around to stand on the other side of the bed, where I was. "Papa we need an answer or else we'll not leave here today."

We had just arrived in Iruama after an unnecessarily gruelling ten-hour journey because Lincoln had insisted we stop to buy almost everything being sold on the roadside from Ore to Benin to Onitsha, with the last stop at Eke Iruama where we bought bush meat and some kegs of palm wine. This proved the saying that, as some things change, so do they remain the same. Lincoln might be living in a foreign land and embracing its lifestyle, but Iruama still ran in his bloodstream like a river.

Papa tried to sit up and that's when I got a good look at him. His frame was now reduced from gigantic to tiny. He lay back on the bed with such force that I thought he had broken his back. Finally, Papa replied, muffling his words as he spoke after taking a long breath: "It was a long time ago …"

"Jeez, Papa, so it's true. You fucked your own daughter?"

"Lincoln, will you keep quiet!" Jefferson barked.

"Why should I keep quiet? Tell me why the hell should I keep quiet? This … This … oh my God. I knew you were a monster, but not the devil himself! Oh, God … Papa, how could you?"

"What of Nneora? Did you try to sleep with Nneora too?" Jefferson asked Papa. He was hovering over Papa so close their faces were almost touching, but he held himself back from touching even the bedspread on the bed.

"Did she say I did anything to her?" said Papa, as saliva drooled from the sides of his mouth.

"She said you almost did."

"Even you should know there's a difference between almost and doing something," Papa said quietly and tried to turn his face to the other side. In all of this, his eyes carefully avoided mine.

"Look, the bugger is not even showing any remorse. What are we doing talking to this pedophile? Let's tie him up and beat the crap out of him," Lincoln yelled.

Jefferson walked to the far end of the room and rested his back against the wall. He was breathing slowly and rubbing his hand over the top of his head. Finally, after assessing the situation, he said: "Come, let's go."

I looked at Papa, all shrivelled and curved like a deflated ball. The wrapper around his waist was almost falling off, exposing his shrunken legs. I did not know what came over me, but I walked over to him and began stuffing a pillow behind his back. "Papa, let me help you up," I said.

"Help him up to do what?" Lincoln barked, yanking the pillow from my hand.

"Lincoln, leave her alone. She needs to do this," said Jefferson, holding on to Lincoln's arm.

I positioned two soft pillows behind Papa's head until I was sure he was comfortable. Just then, he looked me straight in the eyes. I wanted to look away but his gaze held mine and I could not resist his stare. He looked frail; his entire mass resembled a roll of something stuffed in a sack. His smallness was the kind of small that meant you were not sure if someone could be classified as an adult anymore. He was in a pitiful condition, but that was all I felt for him. It was the kind of pity you feel for a stranger you meet on the roadside begging for alms. And with Lincoln looming over him asking for his blood, it was impossible to feel anything else. The pain Papa had caused our entire family negated the fact that he had sired us.

I remembered him in his reverend's robe in the pulpit on Sunday mornings, giving his sermons. I remembered him after many of those services shouting at Mama on our way home from church, telling her to keep quiet, that she was a fool. I remembered him on one particular Sunday after church beating Lincoln because he had been blocking Papa's view of the television, and with the other hand slapping Nneora across the face because she was not bringing the glass of water that he'd asked her for quickly enough. And I remembered him pulling me to himself, hugging and patting my shoulders while hailing me "Dr. Udonwa."

"Bastard son of a bitch," Lincoln hurled yet again at Papa and spat on the bed.

"Lincoln, let's go …" Jefferson reached for his arm to lead him out of the room. But Lincoln continued as they both walked out into the corridor, his voice reverberating throughout the house.

"Destroyer of the human race! Why did you marry Mama if you knew you did not love her, going as far as alienating her from her family? Why did you keep making babies when you knew you would not love them? How can a normal man, a father, a reverend who should know better, someone who mounts the pulpit every Sunday to preach the so-called good news to hundreds of people, go home and put his penis into the vagina of his own daughter until he makes her pregnant? What kind of a father is that, eh? What kind of a fucking father is that?"

"Udonwa, come out now. Let's go," Jefferson called to me.

I got up from the bed with Papa's eyes fixed on me as though he wanted to say something. Through it all, he had not said why he had done it or that he was sorry. Not a word about Sister Adaora. Not a single word of apology.

Mama Ekene entered the bedroom. "You people can go. I'll stay with him until the bishop comes." She walked up to the bed and began to pull the wrapper up to Papa's shoulders to cover him. I stood and watched for a few minutes before she added: "Greet your mother for me. Tell her that when I come to Lagos, I will come and see her."

I knew she had been listening to everything that had been said. In fact, the entire neighbourhood must have heard Lincoln's barking. I nodded, and walked out of the house towards the car where Lincoln and Jefferson were already discussing how they would put up another structure after demolishing the house.

That night, after we left, Papa died.

Thirty-one

"Ewoo! Jefferson egbu o m, this boy has killed me. What do you mean by you are no longer a priest?"

"Mama, he wasn't supposed to be one in the first place. For goodness sake, we are not even Catholics," said Lincoln, downing the drink in his hand — a stiff combination of St. Remy and Hennessey.

"But I was ... I am."

"How can you say you're a Catholic, Mama? You were only born one. You were not even married in a Catholic church. Besides, Mama, the last time you stepped foot in a Catholic church was for your confirmation, donkey's years ago."

We were all sitting in Mama's room in Lincoln's house, except for Sister Adaora who was visiting Aunt Nene. The room was huge; Lincoln had made sure of that. After he had commissioned me to design the house, he had called one day and spent about half an hour explaining how he wanted Mama's room to be — that the windows should be north-facing to let in fresh air and for her to wake up to sunshine every day. When I had designed the room, I had imagined just this scene: how she would be perched right where she was sitting now, the window to her left, letting in enough air to clear her mind.

"Lincoln nwam, what I am saying is that a consecrated child of God, a consecrated *soul*, will not leave the fold. What will his parishioners do? It's like a shepherd deserting his flock. What will they do? They will scatter!"

"Let them scatter! O di.egwu. Brother Jefferson won't be the first, Mama. You should be happy for your son now that he's happy. Now that he's found himself. He was lost before, Mama — you know that. Lost," said Nneora.

"Jefferson nwam, o. I saw it in your eyes the moment you were born. I knew it the very second the midwife handed you to me. You were so peaceful. Even your cries were of peace and not trouble. You did not wake in the night like Lincoln here who nearly sucked me dry each night. And when you started growing, I noticed it too. You sought peace with everyone."

Mama was speaking to Jefferson, but her eyes were positioned somewhere to the north of where he was sitting. She couldn't even face him; she didn't want to acknowledge that he was at peace. How his eyes were so sparkling, it was as though the brightest of begonias were growing in them. His eyes were as I remembered them as a child. All Mama cared about was his priesthood, his so-called calling. Would it have mattered to her that he was having unholy dalliances as long as he remained a priest? The spirit of religion was indeed as arduous as it was treacherous.

"Mama, just because I was a quiet and thoughtful child does not mean I was born to be a priest."

Jefferson's remark had no effect on Mama. She continued staring above his head, believing what she wanted to believe.

Nneora got up and came to sit by me. "Udo, you don't want to say anything. Are you all right?"

I ignored her and kept my eyes on Mama. The only place I could think of to focus my anger. I wanted to hit her, to scream at her. I wanted to slap her face until she explained why she had stood by and watched her husband sleep with her first daughter. Their first child. I wanted to hurt her like Papa had hurt Sister Adaora. To scream at her until she confessed what her silence meant. I wanted to scream and scream until I lost my voice.

She chose that moment to look at me, and for the first time our eyes locked and I saw a different look on her face. I knew she could tell what I was thinking. And in that moment, I realized she had been shouting at herself — screaming herself hoarse, most likely — for years. I realized my shouting wouldn't have any more effect on her than hers. I saw the fire burning in her heart. The fire of anger for her weakness towards her husband during those early years.

Just then, I started remembering how Papa had hit her. I had been alone in the sitting room at the time and Papa had come to where I was sitting and placed me on his lap. The vision was clear to me now; like it was the day it had happened ...

I was sitting on Papa's lap, playing with his glasses. I remembered how I couldn't see one of his hands. I was holding one of his hands and wanted to place them both together to form a clap shape. I started to wiggle and twist my tiny waist, and I looked down and realized why I couldn't see his other hand. It was between my legs and he was fiddling with my clitoris. I remembered it clearly now.

I also remembered him making sounds of what I could now identify to be moans of passion. My face was against his chest, and I was there until Mama came in and I heard her scream at him: "Papa Adaora, give me that child. What do you think you are doing?" Mama pulled me off of him and screamed when she saw his zip was undone too. Papa got up in a frenzy and slapped Mama's cheek so hard, she fell backwards. She struggled to stand up, and he hit her on her back as she ran off with me. I was five at the time. I remembered it clearly now.

I also remembered him taking me to Afor Oheke the next day and buying me FanIce lollies. He also bought me Bazooka chewing gum and Okin biscuits. Special treats, he had called them. We came home and he fed me everything all by himself. I remembered Lincoln lamenting how he never got special treats like Nneora and I did. I remembered Nneora looking at me as though she knew what those gestures of treats meant. I also remembered purposefully blotting the incident out of my memory. Focusing on my gratitude that that was all he had done to me. That he didn't hit me at any opportunity he got, for any little misstep I took.

There was always a reason why a man hit his wife, many men like Papa would say. Papa would have said, if asked, that he hit Mama because she dared to challenge him. Same for Uncle Ikemefuna and Sister Adaora, I would presume. All those years ago in Awka, Sister Adaora was always stifling her sobs. I imagined that her sleeping on the sofa in the sitting room was because she couldn't bear to let Uncle Ikemefuna touch her, to fondle her, to do to her things that a husband would do to his wife. I imagined she couldn't bear to sleep with her husband, because each time he climbed on top of her she had pictured Papa's face, doing the same thing that Uncle Ikemefuna was doing to her. How could that ever be called lovemaking? I imagined her recoiling at every touch. I imagined her screaming out of pain rather than pleasure. And I could finally imagine all of this, because I now shared her anger at the man who had caused all this pain.

"So if you won't be a Catholic priest, will you join the Anglican Church and become a reverend? Maybe you can then find a woman and get married?" asked Mama, breaking into my thoughts.

I knew she meant for it to be a question but it sounded like a command. I felt sorry for her, sorry that sooner or later she would find out that her precious born-priest son was gay and wouldn't be getting married to a woman any time soon. Jefferson had told the rest of the family, but not her, insisting that he would do it at a more convenient time. I could only imagine what that day would be like. She was now wiping tears from her face and neck with the edge of her wrapper.

"I don't think it's that easy to make such a switch, Mama. To be sincere, I don't think I want to serve God anymore. Not in that sense, anyway. I just want to go to church like any normal person would, listen to the sermon and go home."

Nneora got up from my side, where she had been keeping vigil, and walked towards the window. "Who can blame you, Brother? It's the best decision, if you ask me."

From her tone of voice, it was easy to tell that she was also lost in her own world of pain-filled memories.

"But doesn't it surprise you guys that even though Papa did all he did, he never played with our education? I mean, he insisted Jefferson get a degree at the same time he was in the seminary, without which he wouldn't have had much choice of getting a good job, or venturing into business for that matter, now that he's left the priesthood. It's as if Papa knew one day he would leave the priesthood, and was preparing him for his future," Nneora said quietly.

"I don't know, Nneora," said Lincoln. "I think a simple reason is that Papa and Grandpa were also educated, so it should be expected that we were all educated too. Besides, the church mission paid for our school fees, otherwise Papa would have decided who should and shouldn't go to school."

"You are right, Linc. What still baffles me was how he allowed me to become a priest," said Jefferson, "even though we aren't Catholic and he was an Anglican reverend ..."

"Now that you mention it, Brother, that is so true. At the time, I didn't see anything to it, but after everything that I now know happened, it makes me wonder why he allowed it," said Lincoln.

"That's because I threatened him." Mama's eyes were shut when she spoke, her voice an almost inaudible whisper.

Suddenly the room was as silent as Amokwe cemetery, as Grandpa would have said. And for the first time, I heard Eno chasing Dikachi around the living room downstairs. I heard him saying "I don't want to bathe" over and over again. And from the sitting room on the first floor, I heard Zukiswa trying to cajole him into listening to the maid.

"What do you mean by you threatened him, Mama?" Lincoln asked the question on everyone's lips before the rest of us could voice it. "Wait, I'm not sure I want to hear this. Gosh, I sense a nasty headache coming on."

"Mama, please tell us. What did you threaten Papa with? We have a right to know — you do know that, Mama?" Jefferson was almost pleading.

"Udonwa, ask Eno to bring me some water. I need to wet my throat; it's getting dry."

"Mama ..." I said, and everyone turned to look at me, daring me with their eyes to get up. I looked from Jefferson to Lincoln to Nneora, their faces all saying the same thing. They knew Mama wanted to change the topic. We could see she was tired of talking about Papa. But Jefferson was right — we had a right to know. It felt as though the secrets in our family were a mountain with its peak leading straight to the skies, one that the physical body could never summit.

"Mama, I'll get you water after you've told us what Papa did that made you threaten him into allowing Jefferson to become a Catholic priest," I said as slowly as I could.

"I threatened your father that if he didn't allow Jefferson to go to a Catholic seminary to become a priest, I would tell the bishop he had committed adultery and fathered two children outside of our marriage."

"Bloody hell!" Lincoln leapt to his feet.

"Jesus Christ!" Nneora joined him, her hands cupped tightly over her mouth and nose.

"Okay, that's enough, Lincoln and Nneora. Mama, please go on. You said Papa fathered two children outside of marriage ... Who is their mother? Who are they?" Jefferson tried to sound calm, even though he was glaringly not. He moved his chair closer to Mama's, his eyes boring into hers.

"Who gives a fuck who they are? The bloody bastards and their slut of a mother."

"Lincoln! If this were not your house, I would have asked you to leave this minute. Calm down. Ogini di — what is it? Papa fathered a child outside marriage, is that the worst thing he did?"

"Bro Jefferson, I know this is not the worst thing Papa did, but Lincoln is right. This is too much. Chẹi, Papa!"

Mama started cracking her fingers. First her pinkie, then her ring finger, then her middle finger, then the index finger, and finally, her thumb, before beginning on her other hand. We all waited. She knew we wouldn't let go until she told us who these children Papa had fathered were. My heart started pounding at the thought. What if they were someone I or Nneora had slept with? What if I or Nneora had somehow slept with our own brothers without realizing it? I knew I wasn't making sense; I knew the possibility of that ever happening was small but I couldn't help thinking it.

Mama began to cry, sobbing so heavily her entire body vibrated.

"Mama, it's okay. Papa is gone now. He can't trouble you anymore. Please tell us what we need to know o." Jefferson's tone of voice had gone from calm to impatient.

Lincoln went to sit next to her. He had always been protective of Mama, perhaps because he had been the only boy at home left to care for Mama after Brother Jefferson had gone to the seminary. "It's okay, Mama," he said. "You heard what Jefferson said. Papa is gone forever." Then he turned to the rest of us, and said: "Maybe we should let her rest now. This has become more of an interrogation than a discussion. I can't bear to see her like this."

"Yes, you're right, Linc," said Jefferson, sighing. "Let's call it a day. Mama, when you feel like it, you can let us know. No one is judging you — it's not your fault that Papa did all he did …" Jefferson got up to stretch, raising his arms high in the air, when Mama dropped a bomb that threw him back on his bottom.

"It's Ekene and Ebube."

"Ekene and Ebube kwa? Which Ekene and Ebube? The only Ekene and Ebube I know, and I'm sure I speak for the rest of us, are Mazi Okoli's children. Mama Ekene's twins. There's no other Ebube and Ekene … Mama … are you saying …" Nneora dropped down to sit on the floor, weak, as the truth dawned on her.

Mama responded with a nod, her eyes focused on an empty shelf next to the bathroom door.

"Hei, Papa egbuo madu — this man has killed somebody, o! What am I saying … This is worse than murder! So our so-called cousins are actually our siblings?" said Jefferson.

"Yes, they are your father's children. Your father was having an affair with Akudo and she fell pregnant."

"Hei, Papa! God, what sort of man did you give me as a father? Tufia! God forbid! If this is a curse, may it not come to pass!" Jefferson said in Igbo.

"What is left? Ole si go nu — a curse that has already taken root and borne fruits! Papa was cursed, and the curse took effect, o ha!" said Lincoln.

"But that curse ended with him, in Jesus's name," said Jefferson.

"Amen," Mama, Lincoln, and Nneora echoed in agreement.

"Mama, how did you find out about the affair?" said Nneora. She was positioned with her right thigh on the arm of the chair where Mama sat, one arm wrapped around her. With her other hand, she carried on running her fingertips through Mama's hair, up and down.

Mama took a deep breath and sighed. "By accident, o, my children. I found out by accident. I came home early one day from the market. I cannot say I heard a sound or anything.

Okwa Chukwu, it must be God that spoke to me, because I don't know how else to explain why, when I got home that day, I peeped through the bedroom window. They must have finished whatever it was they were doing because Akudo was resting her head on your father's chest. She was saying how Ebube needed new shoes for church ... How Ekene desperately needed new clothes, that all his old ones were in tatters. Your father reassured her he would give her the money, that nothing was too big to do for his twins. When I heard this, I almost went crazy. For over a month I had been pleading with him to no avail to pay Adaora's and Jefferson's school fees and that Lincoln needed milk, that I couldn't breastfeed him anymore since I was nursing a new pregnancy. So I saw the situation as an opportunity and grabbed it with both hands."

"What of Mazi Okoli — does he know the twins are not his?" Jefferson said, his face still positioned before Mama's, as though from it the mysteries of his life would be solved.

"Not in the beginning, but he found out years later. He's the reason your father was asked to retire from the clergy. The bishop told your father it was the best thing to do under the circumstances."

"But Mazi Okoli and Papa remained close, or am I mistaken? They never appeared to me like they were nursing any grudge towards each other," Jefferson said.

"You were not around long enough to notice. At a point, they were always at each other's throat. But it died down after a while. Mazi Okoli must have realized that, even though your father was the biological father of the twins, traditionally they were his. Your father could not lay claim to them. Besides, Ekene is his only son. None of his wives was able to give him sons. But that didn't stop him from sending Akudo away. That's the reason she only returns home when there is an event in the family."

Mama continued: "Your father became a shadow of his former self after that. If you ask me, I would say he died years ago, when he was stripped of his robe. But he should have known he lived in a glass house."

"Where's Ebube now? We know Ekene is in prison in South Africa …" said Jefferson.

"Ebube used to live here in Lagos before she and her family moved to London," Mama said, before resting her head back against the chair with her eyes closed.

"She's married? How come we didn't know?" asked Lincoln.

"It was years ago," said Mama. "Apparently Ebube was living with a childless couple as a maid when the husband of the woman impregnated her. Akudo went there, threatening fire and brimstone that the couple must pay damages for defiling her young daughter. Luckily for Akudo, and for everyone involved — except the man's wife, of course — he chose to make Ebube a second wife. As a result, the man's childless wife left him and never returned."

"I'm not surprised at all; like mother like daughter," Nneora hissed.

"But Mazi was not happy about the whole debacle and opted to stay out of the arrangements. So, as usual, Akudo confided in your father. He not only played uncle but also father at Ebube's wedding. Everything about the wedding was rushed to avoid the news of the scandal spreading. That's the reason none of you heard about it. More than that, the wedding was on the same day as Adaora's." When Mama finished speaking, she began gently rubbing her forehead.

"You mean Papa went to Ebube's wedding in Lagos instead of attending Sister's?" Jefferson and Lincoln remarked in unison.

"But, Mama, why? You knew about all this and kept quiet. Why didn't you say something? Do you know what Papa's absence at the wedding cost Sister? What it did to her relationship with her husband's family?" said Nneora, wiping tears from her eyes.

"I was tired, very tired of your father's antics and everything else. Besides, I wasn't sure I wanted him at Adaora's wedding. He was never a father to her."

As Mama spoke, I imagined Sister Adaora saying the same thing. But she would have put it more plainly. No coating, no decoration. I imagined it would sound something like *I don't want the man who took my virginity to walk me down the aisle.*

"I'm sorry, Mama …" I almost didn't hear my own voice. The words came out as a whisper.

"You don't have to be sorry about anything, Udo. I'm the one who should be saying sorry to all of you — for failing you all, for not doing enough."

"Mama, please, you did more than enough. Don't say that. You stood up to Papa, and you fought for your children with the tools available to you," Lincoln said, sighing deeply.

"I'm sorry I called you weak, Mama. You're anything but," I said.

Everything I thought I had known about Papa had been a lie. Everything I thought he had done out of love had been done under duress, out of fear of his sins being found out. I didn't realize I was crying until Nneora pushed herself up from the floor and walked to me, wrapping her arms tightly around me.

"Udonwa is crying," she said.

"Good. That's the first time she's shown any emotion since Papa died," said Jefferson.

Thirty-two

A week later Sister Adaora arrived from Awka where she had filed for both divorce and adoption papers. Apparently, Aunt Nene had encouraged her to do so after she had sought her advice. She had left for Awka straight from Aunt Nene's, informing the rest of the family via telephone of her intentions. I understood it was the right thing to do in light of all that had happened. Since Uncle Ikemefuna had left and never returned, I had wondered how she had coped for years being alone.

Today was our first time together, just the two of us, after several years, as the rest of the family had gone out for the day.

"Udom, kedu?" she said to me when we'd made ourselves comfortable in the living room. I knew it was time to have the much-needed talk with her.

"I'm fine, Sister," I said, looking away.

"I know you're angry with me for not telling you, especially considering how close we were …"

"Yes, I am."

"I had my reasons."

I did not respond. After a few moments of silence, she continued: "You see, Udom, I was protecting you. You were so ignorant of who he was. I knew what he was capable of, and I knew you and Nneora were not safe. Do you know he tried the same thing with Nne?"

I sighed and shrugged. "I heard that too."

"Yes, he did, Udom, he did. But he was stopped before he could do anything. You must be greatly disappointed to hear this about Papa." She paused, then said: "Remember that dress he bought for you on your fourteenth birthday?"

I nodded.

"That was a replica of the dress I wore the night he … h—"

She choked up and I froze in my seat rather than moving to comfort her, the scene reminiscent of my early years in Awka. I remembered that one night when she had been curled up on the sofa in the sitting room, pretending to be asleep, and I had insisted she share my bed, and she had vehemently refused. That night she had opened her mouth to say something but had choked back the words. Today, no matter how hard she struggled to say what she needed to, I knew she would eventually get it out. It was time.

"That was the exact style of the dress I was wearing on my fourteenth birthday — the day I fell pregnant with you."

"Was that why you took me to Awka? You thought he'd repeat the same thing after giving me the same type of dress?"

"Yes. He had started raping me two years earlier. But I could not tell anyone after he warned me not to."

"How did he warn you? What did he say to you?" I couldn't imagine what would have stopped her from telling someone and getting the help she'd so desperately needed.

"He said he'd kill Mama."

Tears began to flow down my cheeks as her words unravelled.

"I did not know it was a pattern until he tried the same thing with Nneora, on her fourteenth birthday too. Early on that day, he had given her the same type of dress and when Nne had proudly showed it to me, I'd called her to the back of the house and warned her that if he planned on taking her to Afor Oheke, she must find a way of escaping. And she did exactly that."

It was as if Sister Adaora's words were a series of lights being switched on in the midst of darkness. All these years I had grown up with more questions than answers, but now everything made sense. Now I understood why she'd taken me with her to Awka. Now I understood why she had never spoken to Papa again.

"Thank you for what you did, Sister — for protecting me."

Sister Adaora faced me for the first time that day and said: "You thought he was the next best thing after Jesus, and so I knew he would succeed with you one way or another. I had to act fast, and taking you with me to Awka at the time was the best way I could think of to stop him." She dropped her eyes to the ground before saying in a whisper: "But then again, Awka brought on another form of abuse from Ikemefuna ..."

I let out a short staccato laugh in spite of myself. In comparison to Papa's crimes, everything Uncle Ikemefuna had done to me seemed like a joke.

"You know, he found out about you being my child."

"Was that why he hated me?"

"I suppose so, yes. We would fight every night because of it. He wanted you to go back home to Iruama but I told him I would rather die instead."

"Did he find out before or after you got married?"

"Before the traditional ceremony, Aunt Nene accidentally mentioned it in his hearing. She thought he already knew, since he knew about what Papa had done to me. In fact, it was when I met Ikemefuna that I began to heal from what that man did to me, to all of us. He helped me through it; he hated him too, regardless of everything else that happened afterwards."

"How did you and Mama hide it from the people of Iruama?"

"It was very easy, actually. Before I started to show, Mama told Aunty Nene about it and we both planned our trip down to Lagos. We took Nneora along, leaving only Jefferson and Lincoln alone with Papa. Three months after you were born, I returned with Nneora to allay everyone's suspicions. By then, Papa had told everyone who asked that his wife had gone to Lagos to give birth to their last child. A few weeks after Nneora and I returned, Mama returned with you. But, more than anything, I think we were able to pull it off because he was a man of the cloth. Nobody suspected such a thing was possible from a man of his calibre."

At forty, Sister Adaora looked older than most people her age, with several strands of grey lining the front of her hair. In the past I would have hugged her in an instant and she would have held me tighter but right now nothing felt necessary but our silence.

"I was hoping … We all hoped that by not mentioning how you were conceived to you, we could all erase how it had happened forever. We thought you'd never be able to live with yourself if you knew … In fact, we believed it wasn't necessary for you to know at all."

"And that would have been the case if I hadn't overheard you and Mama that day?"

"Yes." Sister Adaora looked away from me. "Although it had all gone downhill when Ikemefuna found out. He had begun visiting various so-called prophets after we got married, who advised him that I would never bear another child unless the secret was revealed. They convinced him that you would bring a curse to our marriage and home, that you were nwa aru — *an abominable child*. So I was torn between bringing forth another life into this world and protecting yours."

Now it was my turn to look away. "So did I? Did I bring a curse to your home?"

"Nonsense. I loved you the moment I set eyes on you. I thought you were the most beautiful thing ever. You were so tiny and innocent. I remember swearing I would protect you with my life."

"And you did, Sister, you did. At the expense of your own happiness."

I stretched out my hand to hers and held it. At the same time, I imagined our hearts locking together.

"I dreamt of Grandpa a while ago," I said. "Just before Papa died."

"And what was the dream about? Did Grandpa say anything to you?"

"He said quite a lot, but he also didn't. He mentioned something about Papa not being appreciative of what he had … That if he had as much as Papa had, his life would have been better off. It didn't feel like a dream. I only realized I had been dreaming when I woke up."

Sister Adaora nodded for me to continue.

"He also said something about Nwamgboli Afomma not being as good as her name suggested. He alluded to her starting everything that had happened in our family. Do you know anything about what he meant?"

"Ah … Ichie onyenkuzi … Grandpa was a noble man indeed. After all these years, his spirit is still active. And I'm not surprised that he chose you above everyone else to visit with. You were always so dear to him," she said, smiling at me. I responded by putting my head in my hands and exhaling.

"Mama told me once that Nwamgboli Afomma used to bring men home to sleep with in their matrimonial bed every time Grandpa went to work at the mission school. One day, Grandpa came home unexpectedly and caught her in the act."

"God forbid! Papa was truly the son of his mother."

"Exactly … But the worst part was that she did it in front of Papa. She slept with other men right in the presence of her young son. Papa was basically watching his mother commit adultery on a daily basis."

I realized my heart was racing while Sister Adaora revealed these terrible facts to me.

"I know what you're thinking," she said. "It makes sense why Papa became the way he was. How he became who he was."

I lifted my head and nodded, still too shocked to speak.

"That may have ignited his sins — that Papa was exposed to such a thing at a tender age was basically child abuse on the part of his mother. But it does not exonerate him. He chose his own path as an adult. He had all the tools at his disposal to make it right. He was a reverend, for goodness sake! I don't feel one ounce of pity for him and you shouldn't either.

Nothing, and I repeat, nothing, can ever justify a father sleeping with his daughter. No circumstances, no explanations, no reason whatsoever can ever justify it. I just thank God for Aunt Nene — without her, my life would have been a completely different story."

Every word she uttered unravelled something hitherto twisted up within me, something previously hidden. I was a bundle of turmoil and resentment, and yet also of renewed calm and healing.

Until that fateful day in Awka when I had overheard those sickening words coming from Sister Adaora's and Mama's mouths, Papa had been all I had thought about before and after I had done anything. I now realized that I had lived my life to please him, to receive his praise, and would have gladly become a doctor to perpetuate it.

PART V

PART V

Thirty-three

When I saw him walk into the store, I thought I had seen a ghost. He looked so different but there was no mistaking him. It was indeed Chinua, standing in the same supermarket where I bought my weekly supplies, a shopping basket in one hand, the other clutching a woman's hand. Her hair was a flowing weave that went past her shoulders. She turned to a shelf opposite where I was hiding to pick up some items and I got a good look at her face. She had big round eyes and when she smiled, her mouth revealed a gap in her teeth like Jefferson's. I hid deeper behind one of the shelves and watched as she walked to the till with Chinua at her side.

I should have been walking up to Chinua and greeting him, but something held me back, an inexplicable force I wished weren't so powerful. Nneora's words reverberated in my mind: *There's a new girl in the hospital where Nnamdi works who said she knows Chinua is definitely back in Nigeria. In fact, she was at a party just last week that Chinua organized.*

I had brushed it off as gossip, but here in all his glory was Chinua, holding hands and giggling with a woman like school children. I watched as they stood at the till, still hand in hand, while their items were rung up. Then Chinua reached for his wallet and paid the cashier, leaving a generous tip for her. As they left, Chinua, as if on cue, cast a look around the store one last time and his eyes almost met mine. I watched as they walked out of the store to the parking lot, where Chinua walked around to the front passenger side of his car and held the door open for her, while the porter loaded their purchases into the boot. I sighed at the sight. I had thought it was an act he had extended only to me.

This hadn't been anything like I'd imagined my reunion with Chinua to be. For the most part, I had assumed he would come looking for me if for nothing else but for old times' sake, then afterwards I would try to figure out a way to tell him about Ifenna. But, randomly bumping into him in the middle of town giggling and holding onto another woman's hand annoyed me more than I would have liked it to. With my emotions in a haze, I realized I might have lost that right — the right of expecting him to walk up to my front door to enquire how I was doing after years of separation and no contact. Perhaps he knew about Ifenna. Or perhaps he had heard about the Ilechukwu family secret and decided to stay away.

· · ·

A few days later, I saw Chinua again, but this time he was alone. Books et al, the newest bookshop in the neighbouring town of Ikoyi, was having a sale on magazines and non-fiction books, and an invite had been sent to my office. Usually, I would have sent one of the junior staff, but after they all gave one excuse after the other, I decided to go. For people who worked in a part-publication company, many of my colleagues did not like to read. They would always avoid going to book and magazine launches, or sales like this one. Growing up, Jefferson would often say that Nigerians' lacklustre reading habit was part of our culture. We would rather gather in beer parlours, eating and dancing, than attend any event that had to do with books and reading.

Walking into the store, I discovered that the sale had been postponed but there was an ingenious system in its place, and I imagined my colleagues beating themselves up for passing up this opportunity. Displayed in bold posters around the store were the words: *Buy one book and get any snack and drink free. The more books you buy, the more refreshments you get.* I smiled at the shop's marketing style as I browsed the aisles. Picking up a book and flipping through its pages, I heard a voice behind me say: "Hello."

A smile played at the corners of Chinua's mouth as he gazed into my eyes, his hands tucked into the pockets of his trousers. I gripped the book harder, my heart pounding. We stood mute before each other, with neither of us attempting to initiate an embrace. My pride made sure I resisted the urge to make the first move. He looked better than ever before, and appeared fresher than out-of-the-oven chocolate cake. His skin shone like always and he'd left his beard to grow. I wanted to reach out and run my hands across the sides of his face. I wanted to rub my hands over his head and watch him relax into my arms like I used to do in the past when he walked into my flat complaining about the heat outside. Then I realized it wasn't pride but fear that held me back. The fear of being rejected by him. The fear that he could tell with just one look that I was no longer his Udom.

Perhaps sensing my anxiety, he finally spoke, now smiling broadly: "How are you, Udonwa? It's been ... well, ages."

"Chinua ... I ... I don't know what to say. Yes, it's been so long. But, I'm fine and y—" I was cut off as the cashier beckoned to him to pick up his refreshment and books he'd purchased.

"Excuse me for a moment, please." He walked off to the cashier and soon returned with a tote bag containing the items. One of the purchases appeared to be a magazine. I tried unsuccessfully to see the title, hoping it was *Homez*.

He looked down at the tote bag. "Clever, huh?"

"What?"

"Everything — this place, their system. This cute tote. I think it's all very clever."

"I suppose it's a way of making people buy books — you know us and our reading culture, or lack thereof."

"You're right. Our bellies first before anything else. But this way it's a win-win for everyone, both for the customer and the store owner."

"Well, I'm not too sure about that. It may seem like a fantastic idea to get people to buy books but if they actually read them is another thing altogether."

His eyes sparkled at our banter and he said: "Hmm, I see your point. I did not even consider that possibility."

"So what are you doing here? Not that I'm surprised to see you in a bookstore. But this is new and I assumed only certain knew about it — people in the industry."

By adding the last part, I was hoping he would ask me what I meant by "people in the industry," but he just said: "I was in the neighbourhood and decided to get a book or two to unwind with when I get home."

Now I wanted to ask where home was, but he began to speak before I could organize my words.

"And you, what brings you here?"

"Well, I was here for a sale of some sort, but when I got here, they informed me the event has been postponed until further notice. I guess I came all the way here for nothing."

The moment the words came out of my mouth, I realized how they sounded and wished to take them back. I looked away, my mind racing, wondering whether he knew about Ifenna and me, about my family secret, about my career change … about everything. I wanted to ask him about his life while we'd been apart and why he had stopped contacting me … But I was crippled with the fear that he might reciprocate these questions, and I realized how terrified I was to tell him about anything I had done over the years we'd been apart.

"Can we go somewhere else? We have a lot to talk about …" he said, as if reading my thoughts.

"I'd like that very much," I said. "I'll drive ahead to lead the way."

"Oh, I didn't come with a car. I came by taxi. Could we ride together, or would you prefer I —"

"No, it's fine, you can ride with me," I said, wondering whose car I'd seen him get into with that woman … That woman, another thing I couldn't bring myself to ask him because it meant I would have to tell him about the whole supermarket encounter, which in hindsight felt too embarrassing to even think about.

"I was thinking we could go to Higgles Club? You still remember it, don't you?" he said as we walked to my car.

My jaw tightened at his suggestion. *Isn't it too early for clubbing, though?* I wanted to ask. It wasn't even 7:00 p.m. yet. But I knew I couldn't tell him my reasons for not wanting to go back to Higgles, and I ended up agreeing to his suggestion.

"Higgles — Club and Lounge" read the new sign in bright fancy letters above the building which had undergone some significant changes. This was the place that had started me on the path to men, so to speak. I sighed.

The brightness of the sign came into full view as we approached the building from the parking lot — bright dancing lights. The frontal exterior of the building was covered in reflective glass windows and the rest of the building gave off a rather shiny feel from black panel covering. Due to obvious soundproofing, the music blaring from the upper floor of the building could now only be heard from the entrance, unlike in the past, when it could be heard all the way from the parking lot. Two bouncers wearing body-hugging T-shirts stood on either side of the entrance. As we walked past them, one of them smiled and winked at me. I returned a blank stare at him and continued walking, annoyed at his audacity, wondering if Chinua had noticed. Chinua brought out his wallet and flashed his ID before he was let in. I was already waiting by the kiosk — another new addition in the lobby downstairs — when he got in and made straight for the stairs.

"Don't you want to have a drink first before going up?" I pointed to a set of seats in the corner of the hall and motioned for him to join me there.

Everything seemed to have changed in the club. There were new additions in almost every part of the building, including the cosy little corner with the imported furniture we were sitting on. I ran my hand across my chair, enjoying its smoothness. The centre table in front of me looked imported, like something picked out of a foreign catalogue. Two huge flower pots stood adjacent to the seats and a large standing air conditioning system filled the room with so much cold air, I saw a few patrons wrapping their arms around their upper bodies. This was so removed from the dingy place it used to be. It seemed to have a new owner who was on a mission to wipe away any semblance of what the club used to be. And the owner might have succeeded, except for the smell of cigarettes, Indian hemp, beer, and liquor, enhanced by the snowy air conditioner.

If Chinua was curious to know if I had visited here after he'd left, he didn't show it.

"You know what would be fun?" he said. "Dancing the night away. It's been ages since I had any kind of fun."

"Really?"

"Come, let's go upstairs," he said and got up before I could answer him.

I followed him like a lamb to the slaughter up the stairs to the dance floor. I had wanted us to talk. I had hoped that talking was part of the reason he'd wanted us to go someplace else from the bookstore. There were a million and one things I wanted to talk about, to ask him. But he wanted to dance because he had not had any kind of fun in a very long time. Which made me also want to ask him why he had not had any kind of fun in a very long time. Was it because of me, or was it because he had been too busy for fun?

"Yes, it'll be fun to dance," I heard myself say, smiling through my teeth. The kind of smile I knew I should not be smiling because it was not really a smile.

"It's been ages since I let myself move to a rhythm, any rhythm at all," he said as we got to the top of the stairs.

He downed the drink in his hand and a waiter appeared out of nowhere to take the glass away. I looked around the club, amazed at its transformation. Instead of its old clientele of students, it now seemed to be filled with young professionals, rich kids of politicians, and older Lagos businessmen.

The night was getting stranger by the second. But the refreshing thing was that he still drank his favourite brandy. Also refreshing was finding out he still maintained his composure by not getting drunk after several glasses, making me wonder if he still got horny and frisky after being in a club like he had in the past. I was shamelessly starting to wonder if he would jump on me like he used to when he cut into my thoughts.

"I love this song, Udonwa. C'mon, let's hit the dance floor."

Udonwa ... He had never called me Udonwa before, not even the first time we met. He had for some reason always felt that the name needed to be shortened, and had gone straight to Udom from the outset. To hear him say my full name now felt like a betrayal.

My eyes caught the barman's behind the bar next to the dance floor and we stared briefly at each other. One thing about the club hadn't changed — all the old staff I used to know still worked there, with only a few new workers I couldn't recognize. The barman carried on cleaning the glass in his hand with a napkin before pouring a drink into it. He looked swiftly away to the customer in front of him and did not look at me again.

I began shaking my hips in time with Chinua's moves on the dance floor, and soon the movement of both our bodies was all I could think about. The music blasting through unseen speakers was one of those record mixes of foreign American and British musicians that every single Nigerian was familiar with, from Michael Jackson and Kool & the Gang, to Bell Biv DeVoe, Lionel Richie, and Sting.

Compared to Lincoln, who had taught himself to do all the breakdance moves of Michael Jackson, Chinua's attempt at breakdancing always resembled a scenario of two dogs attacking each other. I stepped back slowly to give him space, gently ducking and missing almost being knocked over. When Whitney Houston's voice came through the speakers, Chinua moved closer to me, holding my waist as he ground against me. Before I could say anything, he pulled my face to his. I responded to his kiss with equal precision and only realized I wasn't breathing when he let go, cupped my face in his hands, and murmured: "Let's go." I could feel the barman's eyes on me as Chinua and I made our way out of the club.

A few minutes later he drove in front of Lincoln's compound and hooted while we waited for Adamu, the new gateman. Before he left, Lincoln had asked the tenants in the boys' quarters to move out and instead asked Akpan and Eno to bring their children to live there to keep me company. As we walked into the entryway of Lincoln's house, Chinua stopped to stare at the imposing chandelier like everyone did. I remembered my undergraduate days at UNILAG. How he would curl up on the sofa in front of the TV watching the Seattle Sonics battle it out with some other team on the basketball court while I fixed something for us in the kitchen. Or he would be lying down in the bedroom, or seated with me on the couch where we'd stare into each other's eyes for such a long time while holding hands that I would start to feel our eyes and hearts merge into one.

Tonight, though, Chinua sat quietly on the couch and began flipping through the pages of one of the magazines stacked on the centre table. And for the first time since I'd moved into Lincoln's house, I regretted not having a television set in my bedroom. I had wanted the bedroom to have a different feel from what I was used to, especially since my workstation was just across from the bed. But now I could see how my decision meant he was bound to be anywhere in the house but my bedroom — somewhere I wanted him to be as soon as he had stepped into the house.

Chinua dropped the magazine he'd been looking at and picked up a copy of *Homez*. I knew that if he looked at the first page, a conversation would start. It was a conversation I was desperate to have because it would involve speaking about how I'd ended up in the design and architectural industry, which surely would lead to why we'd left off things the way we had, and virtually every other thing I wanted to know about him. But he put the magazine down after looking at the front cover. And we were back to knowing nothing about each other.

"Do you want something to eat?"

The familiarity of the question hit us both the moment it left my mouth. We locked eyes, I from my standing position in the dining room, and he from where he sat on the couch. The expansive house and the smell of new items was the only thing distinguishing the past from the present.

"I need to use the restroom," Chinua said, cutting into the awkward silence. I led him down the hallway to the guest toilet, resisting the urge to take him to the one in my bedroom, and returned to the kitchen.

"I don't see any toilet here," he called to me as I began putting away the dishes in the drying rack, just to keep myself busy.

"It's the door on the left."

"That's where I am, but it appears to be a bedroom … There's a bed in it."

"That's not a bed. Go in, the bathroom is inside the door on the left," I said.

I imagined him rolling his eyes as I had when Lincoln had insisted that a chaise longue be put in the guest bathroom. For one, the bathroom was already the size of a bedroom and I had seen no reason to complicate it even further. Even worse, it distracted everyone who went in there, making them stay longer than required. In front of the chaise was a glass table that was stacked with copies of decor magazines, and the opposite sides of the room had gigantic flower pots with ceiling-high twigs sticking out from them. The entire space resembled the bathroom of a resort hotel, which was exactly what Lincoln had hoped to achieve, prompting him to blurt out "poverty is a bastard" when he'd stood in it for the first time.

Chinua emerged from the guest bathroom, his sleeves now rolled to his elbows from habit. All his buttons were undone, showing off bare skin with trickles of hair on his upper chest down to the lower part of his body where his belt began. His belt buckle was undone and hanging from the belt loops, another of his old habits. I took one look at his forearms and swallowed hard.

"You did not reply to my question earlier," I said after I realized I'd probably been staring for too long.

"No, thank you, I'm not hungry. I wouldn't mind some chilled water, though."

He took his former position on the couch in the TV room and still made no attempt to switch it on while I fetched him a bottle of water from the fridge in the kitchen. As I handed him the bottle, it dawned on me that we needed to talk — *really* talk. Apart from staring at the chandelier, like everyone else who had been to the house did, he hadn't said anything about the decor of the house. This surprised me; by now, anyone who visited the house would have commented on the finishings.

After all the dancing at the club, I had expected for my energy to be depleted, but instead since we'd arrived home I seemed to have been energized by an unknown force because all I wanted to do was to talk for hours on end until the sky was bright with sunshine. And judging from the clock on the wall on the living room, the sun would rise soon. I was still lost in thought when Chinua announced he was leaving, downing the water and handing me the empty bottle.

"What? What do you mean?" I stood in front of him, not sure I had heard him correctly.

"I said I was leaving. I'm travelling to Nnewisouth tomorrow and I have a few things to sort out before leaving."

The words hit me hard as they left his mouth. They reminded me of that day he'd told me he was going to the States. Words that brought on many moons of loneliness, uncertainties and mental torture that ultimately had led to powerlessness and helplessness, culminating in hearing that conversation between Mama and Sister Adaora. With Chinua's utterance now came the realization that I was not healed of all I knew I needed to heal from. And Chinua was inextricably linked to my problems.

I sat back down on the chair and folded my hands between my thighs, allowing a deep sigh to say the words that would not leave my mouth. I watched as he re-buckled his belt and buttoned his shirt, leaving the sleeves rolled up at the elbows, silence hanging between us like a third companion.

With just a glance at me, he walked to the front door and said: "I'll see you soon."

Thirty-four

Chinua left so fast, I wasn't able to ask him how he was planning to get home or even where home was exactly. By the time I moved from the chair in the living room, it was already past 4:00 a.m. which did not help me feel any better. I had thought going to Higgles and returning to my place afterwards had been his way of rekindling our friendship, and perhaps more ... Had I been so wrong to think this, especially after the way he'd kissed me?

I had had it all planned out in my head. When we'd arrived at the house, I had wanted us to talk about everything. I had been willing to be truly honest with him about my feelings for him and how I had felt after he had stopped communicating. I had wanted to see how he would handle my confessions, if he could handle them at all. I had wanted us to talk about the fact that I was now sexually active. That I had mastered the art of lovemaking, and that I could do one or two things that would blow his mind. I had wanted to talk to him about my job at Adeneye Architects — how I had left medical school to begin training at Xenox and was now fully employed in an arm of the institute made up of some of the best architects in the country. I had wanted to tell him how much I loved my job because architecture and interior design were what I was born to do. And during all the talking, I had imagined we would have those moments where we just stared into each other's eyes and knew exactly what the other one was thinking without saying a word, like we used to do in the past. I had just wanted us to talk.

But instead I'd spent most of our time together drifting in and out of thoughts of what Chinua had or hadn't found out about me. I had been terrified he was just waiting for a good time to tell me how disgusted he was by all the things I had done over the past few years. I had ended up acting like a nervous teenager. And afterwards, I was left moping, sleep eluding me. When I finally fell asleep, I dreamt about him, waking up wet between my legs, leaving me with a feeling of utter hopelessness.

. . .

Nneora called first thing after I arrived at the office later that morning, wanting to know every detail about the previous night. I knew it was a mistake informing her about Chinua's visit but in true Nneora style she had forced it out of me. When I told her I had just stepped into the office and needed time to settle in first, she hung up but ended up calling again less than an hour later. I asked the receptionist to tell her I would speak to her later and ignored her calls for the rest of the day. When I got home that evening, Nneora was waiting outside the front door, an overnight bag hanging from her arm and a mischievous smile playing on her lips.

"I'm staying for one night; I'm meeting Nnamdi's aunt tomorrow afternoon." She stepped aside for me to unlock the door.

Before I could put my handbag on the entrance table, she said: "Biko, tell me how Chinua is. How is he looking? Has he changed?"

"Chinua is fine."

"Just fine? Hian, Udonwa, tell me more now … How was it? You know, your first time doing it with him?"

"There's nothing to tell," I said, heading to the kitchen, where I took a bowl of chicken stew from the fridge and put it in the microwave. After I'd put the rice on the stove, I turned around to find Nneora staring intently at me, one hand resting on the curve of her waist.

"Han han, there must be a story to tell now, haba. Your first time with Chinua, ha, it's a big deal, o."

"What big deal? Did I tell you that Chinua and I had sex? Rapum, Nneora, leave me alone, biko. Besides, from the look of things last night —"

"Sorry, o, but please, after you've dished out your boring white rice, put a dash of curry and yellow pepper in mine. I learned a new way of eating rice from the last restaurant Nnamdi and I visited."

"Yes, Ma," I said, rolling my eyes.

"Anyway, you were saying …"

"Yes, I was saying that I don't think Chinua likes me like that anymore."

"How do you mean? Did he say anything to you?"

"More like what he didn't say to me. He left so abruptly, I don't know what to think. I was so nervous the whole time."

"Don't be too hard on yourself, Udo. It's only expected. You have not seen each other in years. Give yourselves time; everything will unravel soon. At least he came looking for you."

"Who said he did? We met at a bookstore by chance. Anyway, what does it matter? He did not even let me know when he'll be back. He only said he'll see me soon."

"Then he'll see you soon."

"Like he said he'll be back from America within two years and never returned?"

"And did you make it easy for him to do that? Were you even ready for him to return then? I think it's a blessing in disguise that he didn't return, if you ask me, Udo. You needed to go through this journey on your own and discover your own strength."

Nneora's reasoning made sense; for the first time it put a bit of the puzzle into perspective for me. But then again, only the future would determine if the past had been worth it because the present made it seem as though it had all been for nothing.

"Okay, enough about me … I want to know the real reason you're here because I can bet my life it isn't just because of Chinua and me."

"Take a very good guess. But don't rush, ehn, I have all day."

"Oohm, Nneora, biko, I have an early morning presentation tomorrow — I don't have the energy for your guessing games, abeg."

I dished up for us and we walked to the dining room with our plates of food. She rolled her eyes at me and carried on eating. She was now munching the second piece of chicken lap on her plate, sucking off the juicy stew while holding onto what I could already sense to be a juicy tale.

"Okay, I'll take a wild guess. You performed your first heart surgery today."

"Mtchewww."

"Ah ah, why the hissing? What's wrong with what I said? I told you it was a wild guess, didn't I?"

"Too wild. Try again."

"Okay, I'm officially tired of this silly game." I got up and picked up the used dishes, heading to the kitchen, but before I made it past the long dining table she dropped a bomb.

"I'm pregnant."

I stared at her for a moment.

"Who is the father?"

Her mouth formed a big O. "Is that all you have to say? *Who is the father?*"

"Nne eh, look —"

"It's Nnamdi, okay. Nnamdi is the father and he proposed too."

My face broke into a smile. "Well then, congratulations! I'm truly happy for you."

"That's what I've been calling nonstop to tell you. But, Udo, you should have seen your face. One would have thought I confessed to a murder or something like that."

"Well, you can't blame me. Considering where we're coming from …"

"Hey, hold it right there. What do you mean by where we are coming from?"

I sighed. "Have you forgotten who our father is? That we're daughters of an abusive and damaged man? A man who got aroused by the sight of his own daughters?"

"So? Is that all we are? Wait, is that even who we are? Who said it's okay to refer to us as that?"

"I don't know, Nne … Really … But … Will he always be a shadow over us, you know, like a real shadow?"

"Firstly, Udonwa, I don't know what you mean by that. Secondly, a shadow is just a shadow. Contrary to popular belief, your shadow does not follow you everywhere you go. There's a reason it does not appear at night." I frowned at her. "Look, all I'm saying is, if you want Papa's shadow to stop hanging over your head, you have to stop living in his light."

I took a long and hard stare at Nneora and saw a different person. This was a different person to the easily scared little girl who would scream and cry for days after Papa unleashed his fury. With admiration, I realized she had not only grown past her fear of Papa, but had shed all of these personas and blossomed into this person who was full of wisdom.

"So when is the traditional wedding? Or won't you have one?"

"Of course we'll have one. It's all Nnamdi and I talk about." She looked at me and said: "So will you be my maid of honour?"

"I'll do it on one condition, that you make me the god-mother of your child."

She grinned and took my hand, nodding.

"So, how does it feel being pregnant for the first time? Wait … that weird rice you just ate is all part of it, right?"

"Who says it's my first time?"

I stared at her, not fully understanding what she meant, and snatching my hand back from hers when the realization hit me. "Oh my God, Nneora Ilechukwu, you've had an abortion?"

"So?"

I continued to stare, my eyes looking her over and scream-ing the rest of the words my mouth was scared to say. What was it with young Nigerian women and their penchant for having abortions? And now my own sister was part of the statistics? Back at UNILAG, Nifemi and Amara would state emphatically that abortion was not rampant in Nigeria because it was a convenient option, but rather because it was a direct result of Nigerian society frowning on single mothers while exonerating the men who got them pregnant. Nifemi had opined that, if not for this, many young girls who made the mistake of falling pregnant out of marriage would face the consequences of their actions by birthing their children, but that, until then, Nigerian men would have to deal with the consequence of their hypocrisy by being with women who had possibly had many abortions. Hearing Nneora's confession took me back to our cousin Muna's experience, and the manner in which she had lost her womb — an incident that had remained a secret to the rest of the family, and I presumed also to her new husband. Abortion really was the one secret of nearly every young Nigerian woman.

"Look, Udo, I'm not proud of what I did, okay. It was one of those decisions that had to be taken."

"And I put it to you that abortion does not have to be the conclusive action for an unwanted pregnancy. There are other options," I said.

"What other options? I wasn't ready to be a mother."

"If you weren't ready to be a mother, maybe you shouldn't have been having unprotected sex."

She turned her face away. "You sound like you're judging me and I don't like it."

"Well, forgive me if I'm finding it hard to accept that you had an abortion when Sister Adaora has been hoping for a child for years now."

"Look, Udo, I'm not prepared to discuss this with you if you're going to be like this. I'm sure you've done some things in the past you are not proud of too, so please, enough with the judgements." She paused and took a deep breath before continuing: "Moreover, as a doctor, I know there are situations that warrant having an abortion. Under those conditions, medically, abortion is deemed necessary."

"Excuse me; did you just say 'necessary'? When is taking the life of another ever a necessary thing to do?"

"It is. And I said within the context of specific medical situations. Such as when the fetus is in danger, or the mother's life is threatened, or both. Or even for other social reasons ... like a pregnancy resulting from rape or incest."

"So you mean you can sit here, look me straight in the eye, and say I have no reason to exist? So you think that my existence is not valid? Nneora, you're one of those people who think I should have been aborted? You know that's what is implied by what you just said?"

She swallowed hard when her words dawned on her and reached for my hand again. "I'm sorry, Udo, that was harsh and stupid of me. I wasn't thinking ..."

"Of course you weren't," I said, wiping away sudden tears brought on by her words.

She reached forwards to wrap her arms around me. "Please, I'm sorry, okay, please stop crying."

I nodded into her shoulder as her perfume filled my nostrils. We held onto each other silently, our conversation replaying in my mind. I was that one living thing that everyone feared to have — nwa alu, an abominable child. That child of incestuous rape that must be got rid of because she would cause nothing but pain and ultimately bring shame to the family she was born into. As a result, my future had already been decided for me, with everyone who knew this secret carrying on as though I hadn't been conceived incestuously, for fear of what the news would do to me … and them. And they were right, because the pain I had caused myself had taken me back several times to that day in Awka, standing behind Sister Adaora's bedroom door, wishing I had knocked to announce my presence instead of eavesdropping like I had. Wishing I could erase all I had heard that day. By keeping the way I had been conceived a secret, the entire family had grown a rigid unwillingness to have an in-depth talk about it, even after the series of recent revelations. Their attitude made it seem as though they would have preferred for the secret not to have come out. And this was why Nneora could blurt out such an ignorant statement.

Finding out about my start in this world had led to my understanding of the war I always knew existed in our household. The one I thought they wanted me to bring peace about by naming me Udonwa. It clarified the war as the one I would face within myself, a war that would nearly consume me. This was why Grandpa had named me Udonwa. He had predicted how I would react to the news of my conception. He had seen clearly that I would never make my way through life without finding out the truth one way or another. And that, when I did, a war would erupt in me that would question my existence just like the rest of the world had questioned my right to live. I realized Grandpa had named me Child of Peace because he had wanted me to find the peace within me ahead of my inevitable future.

Loosening her grip around me, Nneora said: "Truly speaking, that part of my life is a time I do not want to go back to. It was a painful time for me and I had no one to speak to about it."

"You could have called me, Nne; abortion is a serious issue."

"I could have called you so that you'd do what? Act like you just did and ask me to keep the baby? Besides, Nnamdi said it wasn't such a big deal, and I knew what he meant. At least, at the time, I did … I still do … It was the best decision for me, for us, at the time."

I wasn't surprised that she had switched back to the topic of her abortion rather than speak about my incestuous conception. Increasingly, I was coming to terms with knowing that my family would never be comfortable talking about it. And perhaps they were right, for all our sakes. For our sanity's sake. Of all Papa's evil acts, it remained the most inconceivable.

"Oh, Nne, how did we get here? Our family, our lives, everything seems a mess. Especially Bro Jefferson's issue. The whole thing still makes me very sad. The shock of it all …"

"I'm still baffled that you are surprised about that. I tried to tell you years ago but, as usual, you chose not to see what was right in front of you. All the signs about Jefferson have always been there. You know it; I know it; we all know it. Let's face it, Udo — Bro Jefferson did not disappoint anyone; we disappointed him."

"How? It's not like our society can readily recognize these things, never mind accept them. My only worry is if he's going to be okay. Will he ever be truly happy living like this in Nigeria?"

"That, I can't guarantee, because you know our people and their judging ways. But I think what matters most to Jefferson is our acceptance and not that of society. No one else matters."

"I know that. But I think it may do him well to relocate; you know, leave Nigeria. Don't you think?"

"Yes, I think so too."

We both sighed, allowing a necessary silence to occupy the space with us. A thick noiseless atmosphere that nearly suffocated us with its heaviness.

"What a journey our lives have been ..." I finally whispered. "From little girls growing up in a home filled with cries of pain and hate and secrets ... to women who are pursuing their dreams ..."

Nneora placed her hands on her still-flat stomach and leaned back in her chair. "Life brought us here, Udo. These were lessons we had to learn."

I nodded, then said: "And I suppose Papa was our biggest lesson."

Thirty-five

Four weeks after Chinua abruptly left Lincoln's house, I walked into my office early one morning for an emergency board meeting. My receptionist, Biola, greeted me and said: "There's someone here to see you. I told him you'll be in a meeting for a while, but he said he'd wait." I thanked her, assuming it was a client, and began walking down the passageway to my office when I heard footsteps behind me. I turned around and she said, grinning broadly now: "Ma, the visitor, he speaks like an American."

And that was all I needed to know I was not about to meet with an early morning client but Chinua. Since the day Chinua had left, I had not heard a word from him. But my time alone had given me time to think about how to comport myself when next we met, determined to have him open up about our time apart. In the back of my mind, there had been the fear that Chinua had left for America without telling me, never to return. Hearing he was waiting for me now was like being thrown a lifeline, one I was determined to grab with both hands.

The chairman of the board, Mr. Sebanjo, was in his usual mood of throwing around silly jokes that meant the meeting took much longer than it should have. He was impressed with the back issues of *Homez*; he was also impressed with the new boardroom furniture and the other new decor in the building. "You know," he said, "in an addition to our commission clientele, we must continue to showcase ourselves as the country's leading home design and interior magazine, so that when our potential advertising clients walk through the doors to our building, they will be transfixed, knowing that this place is being run by people who know what they are doing." Everyone nodded, but I ticked off time on the jotter in front of me, presenting my ideas as quickly as I could when it was my turn. All I could think about was seeing Chinua in a few minutes, a smile playing on my face, which attracted a few inquisitive stares.

When the meeting was over, I found Chinua in the reading room opposite my office. Lying open in front of him on the table were several copies of *Homez*, as though he were carrying out a minor research project. I could see one edition in particular had been opened to the editor's column, alongside which was printed a bold portrait of me smiling. I motioned for Chinua to follow me into my office.

As he got up, he picked up that edition of the magazine before following me and said: "Impressive … The work you guys are doing here is really impressive."

"Thank you," I said as we walked to my office. "The magazine really developed after my trip to South Africa. They had beautiful magazines detailing some of the best interior designs on the continent. I took it as a challenge. This is my own way of ensuring we put an end to our egregious taste in interior design and decor."

"Good for you, and I suppose for us all. Who would have thought that you had this fire and passion for something other than medicine?"

"This is who I am, Chinua. I would've been a basic doctor at best, nothing more. But with this, I feel whole."

"I believe you. Everything here is impeccable. I knew you had an eye for decor and design, but not like this. What I'm seeing here is someone who is an expert."

I could feel a blush rising up my neck. "Please have a seat," I said, sitting down behind my desk.

He ignored my request and paced the floor of my office. Placing his hand on my desk, he whistled as he ran his hands across the surface. "Real mahogany …. So what do you do exactly, aside from designing? I know you edit the magazine but from this office it seems you are quite senior in the company?"

"Well, sort of. My boss is the principal architect and I'm the only qualified interior designer among us. As for the rest of the staff, they carry out sales and marketing duties. I'm also the managing editor of *Homez*. And I handle all our publication and media briefings."

Chinua was silent for a moment. Finally taking a seat on the other side of the table, he said: "It's like I'm looking at a completely different person."

Not knowing how to respond to him, I ran my hand across my face. So far our conversation had gone well, better than

I'd imagined. But I could not shake the feeling that all these questions masked what he really wanted to ask me.

"Do you have any free time this evening?" he said. "I was hoping we could go somewhere nice and relax ..."

I smiled and nodded. "Where do you have in mind?"

"I've been dying for some local delicacy."

"Didn't you just return from Nnewisouth? I thought you would have had enough of local dishes by now and be gunning for your oyibo food."

"Nothing beats our local dishes," he said, grinning.

"Well, I could make something for you."

"How about some edikaikong?"

"I can see you've not got over your love for Calabar food ..." I said.

"Blame it on Eka," he said and walked towards the door and held the handle.

"Eka? And are you leaving so soon? You only just got here."

"No, I didn't just get here. Besides, I'll see you this evening," he said. "I had to see you first, like I promised, and also to invite you personally for an outing tonight."

I nodded. "I'll see you later then," I said, forcing a smile.

"Yeah," he said and walked out of my office.

. . .

Deliberately avoiding my question about the name Eka like he had indicated in more ways that Chinua was not yet ready to go down the route leading to the past. This played on my mind as I drove home from work later in the evening. Chinua arrived exactly thirty minutes after I did, and I was thankful I did not have to come up with a lie to make him enter my bedroom because, as if reading my thoughts, he followed me there.

I noticed he still could not bring himself to call me Udom.

"So everyone has gone back to their respective bases?" he said.

"Yes. Lincoln and his family are back in Johannesburg, but now he has a home here he will be returning often. He and Jefferson will be starting the construction of the Iruama house soon. They are demolishing the old house."

"That was long overdue, if you ask me."

I nodded. "Ekene had promised Papa to do it after completing his house, but he never got around to it."

"Is he still in jail?"

My eyes widened in shock. "How did you hear about that?"

"It's no secret, Udonwa. Besides, I have my ways."

I tried to speak as normally as possible, wondering what else he knew. "He did not get to attend Papa's funeral."

He shrugged. "Life is full of twists and turns, Udo. So, what of the rest of the family — Nneora, Jefferson?"

"Nne is with Nnamdi's family as we speak; they are getting married soon, although Lincoln has asked them to wait until the house in Iruama is built. He wants no memories of Papa at the ceremony."

"I suppose that makes sense ..."

"It should, but I doubt Nne has the luxury of time. She's pregnant."

Chinua raised his eyebrows. "I guess congratulations are in order then. You're going to be an aunt."

"Yes, and maid of honour. My first official wedding duty."

"Wow, congrats, Udo," he said in mock admiration, making a soundless clap. He dodged the cushion I threw at him, chuckling.

"Jefferson is fine," I continued, "and has returned to his base in Oyegun."

"Still living with the chief's son?"

"Chinua, how on earth did you know about that too?"

He raised one corner of his mouth in a wry grin. "Like I said, Udo, I have my ways."

I stared briefly at him, before saying: "Anyway, I don't know what to make of the whole thing, seriously ..."

"Then don't."

I frowned at him.

"Look, it's no one's business what a grown man chooses to do with his life. You just concentrate on living yours."

"That does not make me feel any better ..." I said, looking away.

"I'm not trying to make you feel better, Udonwa. This is not about you or your feelings. This is about your brother and his life. Put yourself in his shoes for once and perhaps you'll begin to understand."

"I just miss what he would have been," I said quietly. "I miss what my family was supposed to be."

"Try having a brother like Ifenna, then. I promise you you'll grab yours back in a heartbeat."

I wasn't expecting to hear Ifenna's name and it shocked me that he would even mention him after so many years of us not talking about him. We usually avoided speaking about Ifenna because of the way he had behaved the first time we'd met in Nnewisouth. And now, of course, I consciously avoided mentioning Ifenna's name because of what had transpired between us.

"So can you please explain to me why there's a TV in all the rooms in this house," Chinua said, swiftly changing the subject. "I mean, there's one in the entryway, in the two living rooms, the dining room, and I can see another in the actual TV room. What's the logic behind that? Your bedroom seems to be the only room without one in it," he said, looking around the room.

I burst out laughing. "That's Lincoln for you. The definition of extravagant."

We ate silently on the bed across from each other and I almost exploded with sheer joy. I wanted to pinch myself to ascertain I wasn't dreaming the entire scene or imagining it, to be sure he was as real as the flesh on my body. After the meal I excused myself to put our dishes in the kitchen, and when I returned I noticed he had pulled his shirt out of his trousers and unbuttoned the two upper buttons like he always did when he was trying to relax.

I released a deep breath and my mouth formed a mini O when I saw his slightly exposed chest. He walked up to me and with his forefinger touched my lower lip, tapping it gently. I closed my eyes, expecting his lips on my mouth, but instead he placed another finger on my upper lip, shutting my lips together, and whispered to me to open my eyes.

"I can't do this," he said when my gaze connected with his. "You know that, right? I can't touch you, not while —"

"Why ... Why won't you make love to me? I want you so much," I said, strangled with desire.

"That's the problem; you never wanted me in the past. You were always the one pushing me off and not wanting me near you ... And now ... I need to get used to the new you first. I can't ... I'm sorry ..."

He was still holding me against his body, and I could feel his erection pushing against my hip. Cupping my face in his hands, he slid his tongue into my mouth. He tasted so sweet, his pace unhurried. I struggled to remember the last time we had kissed like that, if ever, and I was just beginning to moan when he stopped.

"Chinua, please don't stop ... Please."

"No, Udonwa. I can't do this. Not this way, not now."

"Please, I want you so much. I don't know if I can survive this if you stop ... I can't ..."

"You see, right there is the reason I can't go on. I don't want to make love to you like this. I don't want you to want me. *I* want to want you."

"Then want me, Chinua," I said, close to tears. "Please. I need you."

"No, you don't. Stop saying that. You don't need me; you don't need any man. And you certainly don't need sex."

Tears began streaming down my face.

He ran a finger over my cheek, and said: "Listen, Udonwa, we've both been through a lot; we need to discover who we are again before we move to the next stage. I would like to get to know you again before crossing that line."

I knew what he said was supposed to make sense. His words sounded so true, so real, but I hadn't done real or true with a man in such a long time ... I could feel the anger rising in my chest.

"But, Chinua. This is too much for me. You come to me and ... and —"

"You are addicted to sex, Udonwa, but it can't solve your problems."

He said this so bluntly, it felt as though he'd been wanting to say these words for some time. His words stung with accuracy. The same words Fortune couldn't bring himself to say but which I had heard anyway. Their truth wrapped itself around my entire being and brought a newfound meaning to shame. I walked out to the living room and sat down, my hands clasped between my closed thighs while echoes of silence threatened to smash the room to smithereens.

Chinua followed and came to sit beside me but made no attempt to touch me. I could feel his eyes searching my face, as though he were trying to locate the old Udonwa, his Udom. The one who was not addicted to sex.

"Hey, it's okay," he whispered. "I'm here for you. But we do have to talk."

My body began to shudder with shame. I had known this day would come; now I had to face the truth.

Thirty-six

"I know about you and Ifenna," he said.

I swallowed hard before a voice I couldn't recognize as mine filled the room.

"So everything you've been doing since you returned was planned? Taking me to Higgles Club, coming here ... You did all that on purpose? I suppose I should have known."

He sighed, and then said: "Yes, I first went there when I returned because Ifenna said that was where he met you. That you were some sort of club girl and almost everyone knew you there. I wanted to find out for myself if all he said was true."

I kept my head up, determined not to shed another tear.

"I couldn't understand what he was talking about — you, Udonwa, in a nightclub? You used to hate the sight of nightclubs and all they stood for. And of all places, Higgles?"

"So how did you confirm that Ifenna wasn't lying?"

"Do you really want to know?" I remained silent, so he said: "When we were there, I caught all the stares and stolen exchanges between you and some of the staff. But I also caught your reaction to some of the looks. I was relieved to know you'd not been there recently."

"So you've been spying on me all this time?"

"Not spying, keeping tabs. I needed to know certain things for sure. But everything I did, I did to help. I went there first with the intention of buying the club if I could confirm anything, anything at all, and I did. After our last visit, I fired all the staff who confessed to knowing who you were."

I turned to stare at him, incredulous. His audacity! But it had been my weakness with Ifenna that had prompted all of this in the first place. That moment of madness had caused Chinua to snoop behind my back.

"What else did Ifenna tell you?"

"He said you guys had sex. He said you were a pro."

"What? Those were his exact words?"

"Verbatim."

"Well, I'm sorry, but Ifenna is a bastard ..." I muttered, livid. "Ifenna was my first."

Silence took over the room as what I said reverberated. Chinua placed two fingers on his lips and shut his eyes, pain vibrating in the vein on his forehead. I wanted to cover my face and weep.

"I'm sorry, Chinua. I'm so sorry for hurting you. If only there was a way I could undo what we did, I would in a heartbeat."

"I'm sorry too, Udonwa. Jeez, I thought I had dealt with all of this," he said. "Hearing Ifenna say those words ... My heart broke into a million pieces. Although that wasn't his first time taking something of mine — he's been doing that our whole lives. But now it was you, Udonwa — you, of all people — that he'd taken. I couldn't believe it. I refused to believe him."

I dropped my head into my hands.

"You know what," he said, "I don't care about any of that anymore. Ifenna is ... Never mind. We weren't even an item then, technically."

I lifted my head to wipe away my tears. "I'm sorry for the pain it must have caused you. I can't imagine you hearing that from him."

"For me, back then, it was over after I heard him say those words. I couldn't even bring myself to call you and confront you about it. I could have returned and done just that, but I didn't. I suspected something more must have caused you to do what you did, to bring yourself that low. I could feel it because I knew you, Udom, but instead I allowed you to cause yourself so much pain — pain that you wouldn't have brought on yourself. I knew there was no way you could have slept with Ifenna in a clear state of mind."

I looked up at him, and in that moment I could see that he knew my biggest secret.

"When I heard what had happened with Ifenna, I swore never to have anything to do with you ever again, which was why I didn't return to Nigeria. I saw no use coming back. Not until I heard what your father did. Only then did I realize how it all made sense. It took me back to how I was never there for you when you needed me most. How I wasn't there for you when Jefferson was accused of rape. It dawned on me that all I really ever wanted back then was to sleep with you. Even though I know I loved you, I was selfish with the way I chose to express it. And so, when I heard what your father did, I realized how unfair my treatment of you was … I mean, how could I not have known that something more was behind your sudden change of character? I refused to give you the benefit of the doubt because I wanted to be angry that you had given my own brother what I'd stupidly believed was mine to have. But you know what, Udom, no one owns you but you. All I have of you is my love for you, which alone should have been all that mattered. I should have known that finding out about your father would have shattered you. You adored that man, Udom. You found yourself in that situation with Ifenna because you were made extremely vulnerable by hearing what your father did. I of all people should have known that …"

I wanted to ask him how he knew all he said, and I wanted to ask him how he figured it all out but settled for something else instead. "Literally. I let myself loose, Chinua. It wasn't just Ifenna," I said, determined to have no more secrets from him.

"And I don't care about any of that. I'm no saint either," he said. "I guess what I'm trying to say is that I should have been here to provide the support you so desperately needed when you found out about your father, and for that I'm sorry."

"I was so angry when you left for America, Chinua … So broken." I wiped away the stream of tears from my cheeks.

"I know, and when you stopped picking up my calls, I reached out to Adaora. I spoke to her on a number of occasions and she assured me you were doing fine under the circum-stances. Then, after Ifenna told me what you two got up to, I stopped calling her. She tried contacting me, but I ignored her calls. That was the biggest mistake I ever made. She was obviously calling to inform me of the new development and how you were not handling it. Ifenna was never your favourite person; you never even liked him. If that alone wasn't an indicator that you weren't in your right mind and that something drastic had led to you doing what you did, I don't know what is … It was bigger than you, Udom; the truth was too difficult for you to handle. You needed help, real help, and there was no one to render that."

I wanted to add that sought help at some point but nothing positive had come from it because I'd started fucking the pastor's brother instead. But that would be giving away too much too soon. I knew I'd loved Papa, but I had not realized how much space he had taken up in my heart. I knew I'd lived to please him but not how much I had been willing to give up for him. He had deserved none of my admiration. And until that truth hit home, I did not know what had been chasing me. I did not realize I had been running from something until the very moment I heard Papa had died. Only then had my life returned to some semblance of normality. Except for the puzzle of Chinua and how to face him.

Now Grandpa's words made sense to me; I knew who I was carrying in my heart.

Thirty-seven

Eke Iruama no longer smelled of dust but rather engine oil. A smell so unfamiliar I did not know how to inhale when I stepped out of the car. I wrinkled my nose and squinted, both at the bright sunshine and at the fumes. I had asked Chinua to drive on ahead to the house in order to walk through my beloved village.

The smell of engine oil hung in the air and followed me as I walked down the path leading to our house. On my way, I walked past the spot where Nwakaibeya the carpenter's workshop used to be. The small parcel of land had been converted into a yard littered with rusted shells of vehicles. There were stores lined up on both sides of the yard selling motorcycle spare parts. One, in particular, stood out: "Igweatu and Sons Motorcycle Workshop and Spare Parts Dealers" read the inscription on a board above its zinc roof, in the exact spot where Nwakaibeya's workshop used to be. I wanted to ask the proprietor where the rest of the people who used to trade in this area were, but fearing the worst, I continued walking.

Even Eke Iruama market across the road was wearing a new body in the form of several connected bungalows selling various goods. Iruama no longer resembled a village; it was swiftly turning into a busy town. This was the sort of development I knew the villagers would welcome, but which I wasn't certain they needed. Development should not only be about introducing new things. Developing the rural areas should be about the provision of basic amenities, thereby improving the quality of life. Electricity in every home, running water in the taps, good roads. I felt our leaders had confused development with urbanization. What was next — chopping down trees and levelling our rainforests to put up factories? We didn't need bridges that led to nowhere, and we certainly did not need a mechanic-slash-motorcycle spare parts yard that only polluted the clean air of Iruama — a distinct smell of rain-scented dust and fresh harmattan breeze that had followed me throughout my life.

Papa's grave was the first thing I saw when entering our compound. On top of it was a heap of rubbish and rubble. Ahead of me, the foundation of the new house had already been laid. It was all very symbolic, to say the least. Leaves rustled beneath my feet as I walked around the compound. I smiled on seeing the guava and udala trees, the only things that had remained the same. There was a newly built bungalow where Mama now lived and from where she supervised the construction of the new house. Lincoln had not been joking when he'd said he would wipe Papa's existence from the face of the earth.

Papa's funeral had been a day's event, unlike the three days required for a man of his social standing. Mazi Okoli had been so busy worrying about his family woes that he had not even attempted to argue with Lincoln and Jefferson when they'd informed him of their plans. The night before the funeral, we had all gathered in the sitting room.

"I think it would be in everyone's best interest if Papa is forgotten, you know, like he never existed. Let's just forget everything about him and everything he did," Lincoln had suggested.

"I concur," said Jefferson.

Everyone seemed to avoid the elephant in the room — me. It was as though they were scared to call a known word by its name. To them it did not matter that I had been born as a result of what they were asking to forget.

By nine o'clock the next morning, Papa was hastily buried and before noon everyone had dispersed. There was no fanfare or funeral party. We as a family had decided beforehand that we did not give a damn what people thought about it.

I was comforted by the knowledge that Papa had lived a miserable life in his later years leading up to his death. A wife who detested him and children who had abandoned him while he was still alive. No punishment could be worse. He'd thought he could run away from his past mistakes by pretending I was his last child from Mama rather than a child he had fathered with his own daughter. And that by ignoring that same daughter, it would somehow erase the memory of what he had done to her. By holding on to Ekene and his material largesse, Papa had believed he would get a new lease on life outside of his immediate family.

And now I knew a complete obliteration of the man I called my father was the only permanent requirement for total healing.

I sighed as Chinua put his arm around me; I hadn't realized he had walked up to me until I felt him standing next to me.

"There's no trace of him anywhere," he said, looking around the compound.

"No. There isn't."

"Let me know when you're ready to leave. I'll be in the car outside."

"There's no need for that. We can go now."

"Are you sure? I can wait a few more minutes."

"I'm certain." I smiled, feeling whole and complete.

We drove in silence to Nnewisouth, where we found an almost empty house except for the occupants of the bungalow in the backyard. Chief Aforjulu had gone for a prostate operation in Maryland with Chinua's mother, was recovering and still too weak to travel. But Chinua's mother was expected back in a week. Just in time for the return of Ifenna's body.

My heart sank as we stepped into the house, just like the moment Chinua had informed me: "Ifenna died in a car crash earlier today." Chinua said he had just arrived home from leaving my house the night we had had our much-needed talk when he got the call from Seattle informing him that Ifenna had been killed in a car accident. "He was dying while we were talking about what he did with you." His words hit me again like they had two weeks ago when he had called to inform me, but since then we hadn't spoken about it. Suddenly, Mama's words many years ago about the rumours surrounding Chief Aforjulu's diabolical escapades filled my head … And now Chinua was the only child in a house that should have had five grown children. Chinua's father and Papa, it seemed, had been cut from the same cloth. We were well suited to each other. His house was made of glass, just like mine.

Thirty-eight

Seattle smelled of rain, the fallen and the looming, refreshing and threatening at the same time. It was May and supposedly the beginning of summer, but it could easily pass for winter in this west coast American city. The night we'd arrived at Seattle-Tacoma Airport, we had headed straight to a hotel where Chinua said we'd be spending the night. The hotel was close to Ifenna's apartment where he said he had to be first thing in the morning. From Ifenna's apartment we had driven to Chinua's townhouse apartment located on the other side of the city. At Ifenna's apartment, the landlady, an elderly white woman, with a full head of blonde hair and a mole the size of a stud earring adorning her upper lip, met us at the top of the stairs with the keys and let us in.

Ifenna's apartment did not have his smell, for which I was grateful, but it was so sparse compared to what I'd thought it would look like. It had the usual plasma screen television on the wall and a couch in the sitting room. The master bedroom was in the same state as the sitting room; save for the bed, which was too large for the bedroom, it had no other furniture. The room was poorly lit and the rug had dark patches across its length and breadth. Ifenna had bought a new place, which he had been planning to move into before he'd suddenly died, Chinua later explained. As soon as Chinua had taken out a folder containing documents from the wardrobe, we left.

Since Ifenna's funeral, Chinua and I had not spoken much about him except once in connection with his personal belongings and how to dispose of them. But I made it my duty to speak with his mother almost on a daily basis. On one occasion, she told me I was the best thing that had happened to Chinua. I had choked up at her words, not only from joy but also fear of what she would say if she were ever to find out about Ifenna and me.

Chinua's mother had remained her usual warm self through most of the day of the burial. For someone who had just lost a grown-up son, she did not look too sad. It seemed as though she had got used to the painful act of burying her children, or perhaps hers was the disposition of someone still grateful for having a surviving child. It was only when Mama and Sister Adaora came to represent our family and pay their condolences that Chinua's mother broke down and wept on Mama's shoulders. Before they left that day, Sister Adaora called me aside and handed me a sealed envelope from Aunt Nene; in it was a letter that contained just one line:

*I know it's wrong to speak ill of the dead,
but in this case I'll make an exception.
Congratulations.*

Culturally, as a single man with no children, Ifenna's funeral
ceremony had been a day's event. It was quiet, without pomp,
but still in style. When I saw him lying in his casket, dressed
in a white shirt and black bowtie, I did not know what to
think. Trying to contain my thoughts and calm my mind, I
had looked up to the opposite side of the casket where Chinua
stood with some of his family members, and he had given me
the reassuring look that would keep me sane throughout the
ceremony.

Two days after the funeral, Chinua and I had been sitting
on the balcony on the first floor of their house in Nnewisouth
when he had asked me the question that had set us off on our
current journey.

"Come with me to Seattle for a few weeks. Can you take
more time off work?"

I had looked at him and nodded.

Today, the weather in Seattle was overcast, much like the
day we had arrived. The air was chilly and unwelcoming, and
rain had begun pouring since early morning. It had intermittent stops that gave way to showers, then drizzles, repeating the
cycle. The weather combined with the quiet neighbourhood
Chinua lived in had not helped to improve my mood.

I was standing in the window of the master bedroom overlooking the freshly mowed garden when I heard Chinua unlock
the front door and let himself in. He was soon standing in the
bedroom dressed in a suit like someone from a business meeting, and in his hands was the folder he had taken from Ifenna's

apartment two days earlier. Since the day we had arrived in Seattle, we had been nothing but civil to each other. Although we slept in the same house, he disappeared early each morning, only to come back very late at night when I was fast asleep. We had never met in the bedroom, except for today. It was as though he had retreated to the Chinua I had met at the bookstore, the one who had made me so uncomfortable being in his presence. I thought it was because of Ifenna, that he could not get out of his mind what we had done with each other. Or perhaps this was just what America did to him. Whatever the case, right now it felt as though we had taken two steps forwards and ten backwards.

"I've decided to put Ifenna's new place back on the market. It's really nice but I can't afford it at the moment; I have too much on my plate as it is," he said, taking off his tie and shoes.

I wanted to ask him what was on his plate that was too much. There was still so much about him that I did not know.

"Who's Eka?" I asked, surprising myself as much as him.

"What?"

"Eka, the lady you mentioned some time ago who cooks edikaikong for you?"

"Where's this question coming from, Udom?" said Chinua, staring at me. He was sitting on the edge of the bed now, his shirt unbuttoned, sleeves rolled to the elbows as usual. He lay back on the bed.

"I just want to know, but it's fine if you don't want to talk about it."

He started laughing and got up from the bed, coming over to where I was now sitting on the chair in front of the window, his hands deep in his pockets. The velvet fabric of the curtain felt smooth to my legs as I pulled them up to my chest. I wanted to ask him if Eka was his girlfriend, if they slept with each other, but I could not find the courage to do so. Besides, what did it matter if he'd slept with her, or anybody else? He had confessed he was no saint when I'd mentioned I had slept with other men apart from Ifenna, and he'd never asked me for specifics.

"Eka is no one, Udom. She was one of the engineers on a training program from our partner company in Calabar. Being the only two Nigerians in HT Tech here in Seattle then, it was only natural that we clicked. Don't you think so?"

"Sorry, I had no right to ask. It's just that sometimes I don't know where I stand with you."

"Quite a lot has happened, Udom, and there are still many adjustments to be made. We need to give ourselves more time."

I hugged my legs tighter to my body in response, realizing how much he sounded like Nneora. But I wasn't finished yet; I felt strongly that I needed to know about certain things, things that I hoped would give me some clarity and perhaps provide me with some peace to feel safe with him again. There was no doubt about his love for me but a missing link remained.

"Do you miss the old me, Chinua? You know, the old Udonwa. Do you miss her?"

He stared at me for a very long time, then said: "How about we go somewhere for some sightseeing and get some lunch afterwards?"

He made to leave but I held onto him. "Please, Chinua, I need to know this. It's very important that I know." Seeing the look on my face, he sat back down.

"Okay, Udom, since it's so important to you. Here's what I told myself after you stopped picking up my calls and before we eventually lost contact, and I hope it answers your question: I said to myself that if I came back and found out you were married to someone else, I would feel no iota of guilt chasing you to have sex with me."

I glanced up at him, his brown irises intoxicating me, his lips slightly curled at the corners. He gave me a straight and serious look. I carried on staring, trying to ascertain if he was hiding a wry smile, but there was nothing. He was serious about what he said and wanted it to sink in that he was. Then, when the words sunk in, my eyes, ears and nose started to twitch in sweet pain and every other part of my body ached to commit the hypothetical adultery with him right away — before the hypothetical marriage, before everything else that was yet to happen. But then again reality set in: this was before he had found out about Ifenna; this was before everything got messed up with me finding out about Papa. So no, it did not answer my question but it provided an insight into his thoughts back then.

"I don't know what you want me to say to that," I said, frowning. "It may seem like a compliment but at the same time an insult. What if I had refused to have anything to do with you then? What if I was committed to my marriage with this other person?" I said, wiping an unshed tear from my eye.

"That'd be my loss then, wouldn't it? My love for you has always been a forever thing; it has always been forward looking, always been hopeful. That's why I was prepared, albeit painfully, to wait till you were ready in spite of your monumental prudishness. To be sincere, in hindsight, from the look of things, I thought you'd never be ready, but it was a chance I was willing to take. But right now, all that matters is the present. On my side, a lot happened since the day I got that heart-wrenching piece of info from Ifenna. So, Udom, the past plus the hypothetical future … None of that matters now. What's there to miss or wish for when you are right here with me and the future promises to be brighter than it can ever be? I do not regret my love for you, Udom — not back then and certainly not now. The past is there for a purpose: for reflection and correction, but never for regret." He paused, carefully measuring his next words. "Regret helps no one, Udom — it never has and never will. Everything that happened when we were separated, everything we did, brought us to this very moment. I've come to terms with all of it and so should you. So, no, Udom, I don't miss the old you — quite the contrary, actually. I love the new you, flaws and all. Come, I have a surprise for you." He reached for my hand and pulled me up gently from the chair.

I nodded and stood up slowly, heavy with the love soaring in my heart for him as I watched him change into something more casual. Grandpa's words echoed in my head: *The person you're carrying in your heart holds the key.* Now I knew what those words meant. At the time I had thought he meant someone would come to rescue me, but now I knew it was not about that at all, because I didn't need rescuing. All I needed was to be shown what it meant to truly love; I needed for it to be put into perspective, as Chinua had just done. True love is neither selfish nor conditional; it does not stem from a place of power, like Papa's love. True love is not the kind of love that looks over you, threatening to stop if you don't do as it bids. I understood that now — true love is a love that loves in spite of. It is the kind of love that hopes and forgives and believes and endures.

Chinua brought out an overnight bag from the wardrobe and asked me to pack a few things, saying that we'd be spending the night out of town. Forty-five minutes later, we arrived in a town called Langley, an island on the other side of Seattle, on a ferry ride that took less time than I could register and ended just as I was about to relax. If towns could be said to be siblings, judging from my training and textbook knowledge of architecture, Langley had one in Hermanus, another small coastal town thousands of miles away in South Africa. Both towns had reportedly been built in the 1800s, and apparently both were whale-watching spots.

I hadn't been expecting the whale watching to be the surprise Chinua had planned; I was thoroughly disappointed, to say the least. Apart from the goats and chickens that roamed Iruama, I'd never particularly observed any animal in its natural habitat nor did I understand the quest for human pleasure from doing so. But Chinua seemed so excited.

Among the whale watchers on the observation deck in town, I could hear a little girl exclaim: "Look, Mom, I see one spraying!"

I stole a glance at Chinua, who was now clicking away with his camera. We waited for the whale to make a proper appearance, but nothing happened and the excited crowd began to disperse.

He turned to me, adjusting his camera around his neck like a newbie tourist. "Let's go get something to eat; the surprise is waiting for us afterwards."

I jumped into his arms in relief. "Oh, thank goodness!"

He laughed and held me tightly for a few seconds before we left the observation deck. With our hands firmly clasped together, we walked across the road to a restaurant with floor-to-ceiling glass windows.

Acknowledgements

To the best mother any girl could ever have, Mrs. Gladys Okonkwo — my first love, teacher, confidence instiller, and number one praise singer. Thank you for all you did. I miss you infinitely.

To my dearest family — my husband, Adolphus, and children, Kansy, CJ, Ezinne, and Chobachi, my nieces and nephews, cousins, and in-laws, scattered around the globe. And great friends too numerous to mention. And to everyone who genuinely loves and believes in me — I love you all right back.

To my publisher, Dundurn — Julia, Kwame, Erin, Laura, and everyone that continues to work tirelessly for this work to shine, I'm beyond grateful.

To my PRH Pty family — publisher and editors. My special appreciation will forever go to Catriona Ross for her overwhelming support, then and beyond.

To my Hedgebrook/Vortext family, 2017 session, you guys are the real deal. Thank you for the time spent with you, all my fellow literary sisters, as we push on with authoring change in the world one story at a time. And for being the space where I found the arc to the ending of this work. I'll forever wear my experience with you like a crown!

And finally, to the CAPS faculty and my Creative Writing and Crafting a Novel students at Sheridan College, HMC Campus, Mississauga — a special thank you to you all for the opportunity of a lifetime to impart my literary knowledge; it has been a wonderful journey.

With all my love,
Chinenye

About the Author

Chinenye Emezie studied creative writing at the University of the Witwatersrand, South Africa, and has a bachelor's degree in public administration. Her short stories and essays have appeared in anthologies and literary journals including Africa Book Club, Kalahari Review, and Book Lovers Hangout. Chinenye is a 2013 winner of the Africa Book Club Short Reads competition and an alumna of the Hedgebrook VorTEXT women writers' workshop on Whidbey Island in Washington. Her award-winning short story "Glass House" was picked as a recurring study material in the Theatre and Performance programme at her alma mater. *Born in a House of Glass* is Chinenye's debut novel and was first published as *Glass House* by Penguin Random House, SA, in October 2021. She currently teaches creative writing courses at Sheridan College's HMC campus in Ontario, Canada.